Praise for Lora Leigh's Novels of the Breeds

Navarro's Promise

"Highly charged and carnal . . . another powerful and highly erotic saga of the Breeds."　　　　　*—Fresh Fiction*

"Incredibly sexy and emotionally riveting . . . tons of action and seriously hot, erotic sex. It was a book that I could not put down."　　　　　*—Goodreads*

Styx's Storm

"Delivers with Ms. Leigh's trademark fast-paced, high-adrenaline ride into the intriguing world of this series and leaves readers ready for more."　　　　　*—Night Owl Reviews*

"Scorchingly intense."　　　　　*—RT Book Reviews*

Lion's Heat

"Powerful and sensual with enough fast-paced action to make your head spin."　　　　　*—Fresh Fiction*

"It is phenomenal."　　　　　*—Joyfully Reviewed*

continued . . .

BENGAL'S HEART

"Wickedly seductive with sizzling sex scenes that will leave you begging for more."   —*ParaNormal Romance*

COYOTE'S MATE

"A tantalizing read from start to finish . . . a rousingly fantastic read."   —*Night Owl Reviews*

MERCURY'S WAR

"Erotic and suspenseful."   —*Romance Junkies*

"I am completely addicted! A great read!" —*Fresh Fiction*

DAWN'S AWAKENING

"Held me captivated."   —*Romance Junkies*

"Heart-wrenching."   —*Fallen Angel Reviews*

TANNER'S SCHEME

"The incredible Leigh pushes the traditional envelope with her scorching sex scenes."   —*RT Book Reviews* (★★★★✓)

"Sinfully sensual . . . [This series] is well worth checking out."   —*Fresh Fiction*

HARMONY'S WAY

MEGAN'S MARK

Stygian's Honor

Lora Leigh

BERKLEY BOOKS, NEW YORK

THE BERKLEY PUBLISHING GROUP
Published by the Penguin Group
Penguin Group (USA) Inc.
375 Hudson Street, New York, New York 10014, USA

Penguin Group (Canada), 90 Eglinton Avenue East, Suite 700, Toronto, Ontario M4P 2Y3, Canada
(a division of Pearson Penguin Canada Inc.) • Penguin Books Ltd., 80 Strand, London WC2R 0RL,
England • Penguin Group Ireland, 25 St. Stephen's Green, Dublin 2, Ireland (a division of Penguin
Books Ltd.) • Penguin Group (Australia), 250 Camberwell Road, Camberwell, Victoria 3124, Australia
(a division of Pearson Australia Group Pty. Ltd.) • Penguin Books India Pvt. Ltd., 11 Community
Centre, Panchsheel Park, New Delhi—110 017, India • Penguin Group (NZ), 67 Apollo Drive,
Rosedale, Auckland 0632, New Zealand (a division of Pearson New Zealand Ltd.) • Penguin Books
(South Africa) (Pty.) Ltd., 24 Sturdee Avenue, Rosebank, Johannesburg 2196, South Africa

Penguin Books Ltd., Registered Offices: 80 Strand, London WC2R 0RL, England

STYGIAN'S HONOR

A Berkley Book / published by arrangement with the author

PUBLISHING HISTORY
Berkley mass-market edition / August 2012

Copyright © 2012 by Lora Leigh.
Cover art: "Gray Wolf" by Art Wolfe/Stone/Getty. "Young Man Portrait"
by Anna Bryukhanova/Vetta/Getty.
Cover design by Rita Frangie.

ISBN: 978-0-425-24607-8

BERKLEY®
Berkley Books are published by The Berkley Publishing Group,
a division of Penguin Group (USA) Inc.,
375 Hudson Street, New York, New York 10014.
BERKLEY® is a registered trademark of Penguin Group (USA) Inc.
The "B" design is a trademark of Penguin Group (USA) Inc.

PRINTED IN THE UNITED STATES OF AMERICA

10 9 8 7 6 5 4 3

ALWAYS LEARNING   PEARSON

For Bret, Holly, and Maddy.

Sometimes what you believe is the answer is in reality the shackles that will bind the heart and the adventures that have always filled your soul.

Sometimes, what you see isn't what you can believe, and what you hear isn't always what was said.

As you travel through life, reaching out for all the adventures you've dreamed of, braving the storms of life, of love and, sadly, heartache, always remember that each scar your heart takes, each tear your soul sheds or refuses to release, and each lonely moment spent searching for answers, is what leads you to the person you will become. Strength, truth, and courage are values you should go to bed with each night and awaken to each morning.

Listen to your heart, but also remember you have a brain for a reason.

Common sense should always guide you, but compassion and mercy, tempered with strength of will and trust in yourself should walk hand in hand with it.

Have your adventures.

Sing from your heart, play from your soul, take the pictures that will last a lifetime and will inspire generations.

Live every moment as though it's the most important moment in your life, and always know that your heart, your love, and the strength you will bring to the ones who will eventually hold it all are gifts that you should never allow to be taken for granted.

Love isn't always kind. It isn't always gentle. It's rarely soft, and it never makes allowances for those who are weak.

Be strong. Keep your head high, your shoulders straight. Be honest. Be just. Be courageous. And once disillusionment, pain, and tears have honed you into the adults you will become, then the greatest of adventures will find you.

The adventure of love.

This was the last thing she needed this year, Liza Johnson thought as she moved along the deserted jogging path that cut through the Window Rock Navajo Nation Park.

This was supposed to be her year.

It was supposed to be the year her life truly began, or so her best friend's grandfather had promised her.

Orrin Martinez, one of the secretive spiritual advisors of the Six Tribes, had sought *her* out. She hadn't gone looking for his advice, now had she? He'd had no earthly reason to lie to her and yet he had done just that.

Or at least, that was how it seemed.

Because this wasn't her year.

It was the year of the Breeds.

The arrival of the Breeds and the director of the Bureau of Breed Affairs demanding access to one of the Navajo's most sacred possessions, a database of DNA profiles the Navajo Nation Council kept under the strictest security, had set in motion events that unsettled Liza in ways she couldn't explain.

The calling together of the chiefs of the Six Tribes, whose sole mission was the acquisition and protection of the profiles, had thrown her entire family, as well as her friends' families, in upheaval.

Such a sacred part of the Navajo wasn't left to politics to protect.

And the protection of it was becoming dangerous not just to her friends, but also to herself.

One of Liza's best friends had nearly been abducted by the man who had attempted to rape her weeks before. Another friend had been shot trying to defend her. And now here she was, risking not just herself but also her undercover status to draw out soldiers who were stalking her for unknown reason.

She'd been working, training, and honing her abilities to work with the Navajo Covert Law Enforcement Division.

"They're moving in," the voice stated softly over the tiny—all but invisible—electronic link tucked in her ear. "Just bounce those pretty ta-tas, sugar girl, and look pretty. We'll take care of the rest—Oh shit, Cullen."

Liza managed not to laugh but she could see exactly what had happened. Their communications and electronic guru, Reever Jacobs, had obviously taken a blow from their commander, Cullen Maverick.

Flirtatious, sensual, teasing as hell and a complete killer, Reever absolutely loved a good fight, and—as he more often claimed—corrupting a good woman.

Their commander, Cullen, rarely agreed with his various philosophies, but Reever was a hell of a communications expert and a warrior comparable to those who lived during the golden years of the Apache Nation.

The large circular design cutout in the hill, the aptly named Window Rock, rose behind her. The first rays of warming sunlight were barely caressing the earth and had yet to peak into the small valley of cottonwoods and pinon trees that the path wove through.

"Heads up, you have Diane Broen coming up on you. Behind her, moving in fast, are your shadows. Get ready for a party, Munchkin."

Liza almost smiled at the nickname Cullen and Reever had given her when they had first met, nine years before.

She was still short, but now, he only called her Munchkin

when they were on a mission or assignment together—
thankfully.

"Here we go," Reever announced softly. "Bad-ass Broen
is coming to visit."

Liza felt the presence behind her the second it moved into
place. The hairs at the back of her neck rose in anticipation
of danger and a certainty that she was pushing her luck far
past its limit this morning.

She twisted, throwing her body to the side before coming
to a crouch and staring back at Diane Broen with narrowed
eyes.

The other woman came to a stop, her brow arching in
mocking surprise as Liza faced her suspiciously. "What do
you want?" Tense and prepared, she stared back at Diane.

This woman was a highly trained mercenary and lover to
one of the Bureau's most trusted Breed enforcers. What the
hell was she doing here?

"A nice jog?" Diane queried with a small smile as she
crossed her arms over her breasts and stared back at Liza
curiously.

A nice jog, her ass.

"You're lying." Clipped and clearly distrusting, Liza
remained on guard as Diane faced her. "Now, what do you
want and why are you following me?"

"Who trained you?" Diane asked rather than answering
the question.

Never trust anyone who answered a question with a question, her father had always warned her.

"No one you know, I'm certain," Liza sneered back.
"Now, what the hell do you want?"

The other woman tilted her head to the side as Liza considered her options if this woman turned out to be the enemy.

Tensing, she prepared for attack.

"Easy, Liza," Cullen, obviously watching her closely,
murmured through the still-in-place link. "Let's see what
she wants."

Oh, she had every intention of at least giving the other
woman a chance to show her hand. Diane Broen was part of

the Breed community as well as the Bureau of Breed Affairs now that her sister, Rachel Broen, was married to the director of that Bureau, Jonas Wyatt.

Not that there was much of a chance of kicking Ms. Broen's ass if she had to, Liza knew. But she might be able to hold her off until help arrived.

Or until she could run.

"I'm no threat to you," the other woman said with a soft, friendly laugh as Liza straightened, her gaze moving around them quickly as she searched for signs of the Council soldiers she knew would be moving in.

She didn't have time to stand around and chitchat all morning.

"Then you'll kindly leave the way you came," Liza said, desperate to get rid of her. How the hell was she supposed to get the information she needed when there wasn't a chance the Council soldiers would move in as long as Diane was here.

Diane grinned back at her ruefully. "Sorry, Liza, but we really need to talk. Just for a bit, you understand. We could return to the hotel for the discussion if you like?" She glanced toward the direction of the Navajo Suites. "I promise it won't take long."

Liza's gaze jerked over Diane's shoulder.

For precious seconds she had to fight the panic threatening to tear through her and overtake her at the sight of figures moving in behind the other woman.

She'd been a part of the Navajo's Breed Underground Network for over a year now, and she had never been as frightened as she was now.

A moment of static at her ear confirmed for her that Cullen and Reever were still there. "Bureau Breeds are moving in fast behind them. We have you covered," Cullen assured her, but she heard the concern in his tone. "See if you can get the bastards talking. If you can't, just be sure to hit the ground when I give the order."

"He's harmless," Diane stated as Cullen's soft voice faded away.

He?

Oh, what was coming in behind the other woman was far from harmless.

Swallowing tightly, Liza stared back at the other woman. "We have to get out of here."

"Thor's not going to hurt you." Exasperation and impatience filled Diane's voice as well as her expression, as though she were dealing with a nervous debutante or nearly hysterical woman.

"Honey, I've seen that hot-assed Thor of yours, and he makes one. Not four," Liza assured her.

Diane swung around, her hand whipping to her back, where her weapon was holstered. She merely gripped it as though needing the reassurance that it was there.

Adrenaline flowed like a river racing through Liza's bloodstream as she and Diane now faced four Coyote Breeds, their gazes amused, weapons held at the ready.

And if Liza wasn't mistaken, she and the Bureau of Breed Affairs agent were now in a hell of a lot of trouble, because they didn't look like the good guys.

Neither did what appeared to be a human male who stepped from the shadows of a heavy oak several feet from the other woman. He didn't seem the least bit friendly either.

Liza recognized him. She'd seen him jogging past the house several times. Hell, he'd even stopped to talk to her when Cullen had accompanied her to the grocery store in the past few weeks.

John Malcolm, he'd called himself, yet she and Cullen both had been certain it wasn't his real name, despite the fact that the background check Reever had run on him—and the tags of his vehicle—had checked out.

Now she knew why she hadn't been comfortable during those brief meetings. It hadn't been his flirting or his blatant sexual interest in her. It was because he was the enemy.

"Malcolm." Diane Broen whispered the name with an edge of pain.

She obviously knew him, and it was more than apparent he'd somehow betrayed her.

Liza swore she could feel the pain pouring from the other

woman. It was in her voice and in her expression as she stared at the man as he stepped forward.

"I thought it was Brick," Diane whispered when he smirked back at her.

Brick was another member of the four-man team Diane commanded since her uncle's death, Liza knew. Cullen had managed to uncover the identities of most of the men on her team; unfortunately, he'd still had one to go.

This one, she guessed.

Malcolm chuckled, a cruel, vicious sound. "Good ole Gideon would have gotten me if I hadn't managed to find a way to trip that dumb bastard Brick and throw him in the way. Son of a bitch never figured it out either."

Interesting.

He had to be talking about the attack Gideon Cross had made on the team in D.C.

"Where's Thor?" The rasp of fear in Diane's voice warned Liza that the hulking Viking should have been close by.

The fact that he wasn't obviously didn't bode well.

The sudden disconnected feeling of watching rather than participating in life overwhelmed Liza at that moment. All of her senses seemed centered on taking in each iota of information, every expression, every feature.

The unique qualities of her photographic memory would take care of the rest.

"He's a bit under the weather, boss." Malcolm mocked Diane. "It might have something to do with the knife I shoved in his chest. I do believe I even managed to pierce that bastard's icy little heart."

"The Bureau's moving in." Cullen's voice was barely a whisper as he alerted her to the cavalry's arrival. "Thorsson is wounded but breathing. But these aren't the soldiers we were targeting. We have another group moving in."

As Cullen spoke, Liza watched as Diane pulled the laser pistol from her back and pointed it at Malcolm's heart while activating it.

"Liza, run," she ordered, her voice heavy, resigned.

Diane was going to kill him; Liza could sense it. Unfortunately, Malcolm wasn't the only one there and that laser pistol would only get perhaps one shot off before those Coyote soldiers descended on her like rabid dogs.

The link in her ear activated again with a soft, electronic hiss.

"Stay in place." Cullen spoke softly, warningly. "Keep her there."

"Run where?" Liza forced disbelief to fill her voice as she protested Diane's order. "Have you noticed there are four Coyotes here, lady? Does it look like I have a chance?"

One of those Coyotes grinned.

A tilt of his lips, which covered the curved canines, had her gaze sharpening on him.

There was something in his gaze as it met hers. Amusement, definitely, but perhaps also a hint of a wink? Was he flirting?

Or was there something more there?

"The first one who moves will die," Diane snapped as she spared a glance back at Liza. "Now get the hell out of here."

"If she runs, one of us will chase," the lead Coyote murmured with an irrepressible grin. "We can't resist. It's like a dog with a ball. We just have to fetch." He wagged his brows playfully.

He was definitely flirting. But there was also a slight edge of reassurance.

What the hell was going on here?

For a moment, Liza could only stare at the flirtatious Breed, aware that the woman standing in front of her was doing the same. It was obvious she was just as astonished as Liza, if the expression Liza glimpsed on her profile was anything to go by. Of course, all Breeds had the ability to make most women consider escaping in the opposite direction from them more often than not.

"Malcolm, where did you find your Coyotes?" Diane asked with insulting disbelief. "They're fucking crazy."

"They're fucking effective," Malcolm snapped back. "They caught your ass, didn't they?"

Liza wondered just how true that was.

"Where is your mate, little warrior?" the Coyote murmured silkily as his dark gray eyes danced with laughter as he glanced at Malcolm then back to her. "I can smell his mark on you and it's fresh. You know when he gets his hands on you he's gonna show you exactly how a Breed punishes disobedient little mates, right?"

The mating mark?

Liza had seen it on her friend Isabelle's lower neck. So the information Cullen had that Diane Broen was Lawe Justice's mate was evidently true.

"Go to hell!" Diane rasped furiously.

The Coyote grimaced back at her. "Aw, come on, it's just hot as hell there and my AC doesn't even make a dent. Let's try for something cooler."

Liza stared back at him in complete disbelief as she realized Diane's expression mirrored her own.

"Great, a comedian," Liza murmured as she restrained the urge to roll her eyes.

"Yeah, and all before breakfast." Diane sighed. "I think I might be nauseous."

"I warned you not to bring him, Malcolm." Another Coyote spoke up from behind the one standing carefully between the rest of the Coyotes and her and Diane. "He's going to start playing his incessant games again."

"Loki, stop playing the fucking horndog," Malcolm snapped at the flirting Coyote. "We're here to kidnap a Breed mate, not see if we can seduce her."

Breed mate? Were they not here for Liza then?

"I'm still maturing." The Coyote shrugged with a cold, far too experienced, far too cruel expression of displeasure as the one behind him almost smiled in response.

"He has about as much common sense as his brother, Farce, had," another drawled. "Remember what happened to him, Loki? The wrong end of a Feline weapon, I believe."

Loki shrugged with a careless smile. "Yeah, but he wasn't as charming as me, either. I just charm those Felines to death."

Liza had a feeling there was nothing playful or flirtatious about the four Breeds, but there was definitely something going on that they weren't revealing to the lone human with them.

"Liza, go!" Diane hissed again.

"We'll just chase her." The taller, broader Coyote behind Loki stepped forward to remind them before reaching into his shirt pocket and pulling free a slim cigar.

With lazy amusement, he holstered his weapon before lighting the tip, filling the early morning air with the scent of tobacco.

Diane turned to Malcolm, leaving Liza to try and decipher the expression on her face from her tone of voice. "I'll kill you first."

Malcolm smiled complacently. "No, Diane, you won't," he assured her. "Because if you do, we're going to take your little friend behind you as well. And I think you know what will happen to her then. You have only one shot. That'll leave three Coyotes for her to deal with. Do you think she'll survive?"

For the briefest second, a memory surfaced. It wasn't a flashback or a remembered nightmare. It was a memory out of place; one she knew couldn't possibly be hers.

Clenching her fists and breathing in slow, deep breaths, it was gone as though it had never been.

But it had been; just as several others had been in the past weeks.

The heaviness that settled in her chest was like a crushing weight.

"Keep them talking," Cullen ordered. "Help is almost there."

They'd better damned well hurry. Things weren't looking real good here, in her opinion.

"I'd rather fight," Liza whispered to Diane, hoping to distract the other woman from doing anything that would hinder their chances of survival before that help arrived.

Diane nodded slowly. "Do you have a weapon?"

Not ones she was ready to reveal at the moment. At least, no more than one.

"A knife, that's all I have." Liza forced regret to fill her voice.

Diane drew in a hard, deep breath. "Don't let them take you. It would be far better to use that knife on yourself than to be captured by them. Once they come for me, run for the hotel. Breeds will be looking for me. They'll take care of you."

"I'm surprised, Ms. Broen," the sandy-haired Coyote drawled as he moved ahead of the flirtatious one. Smoke curled lazily from the cigar clenched between his teeth as his gray eyes gleamed wickedly. "I've heard of your mate. I'm shocked he's not at your side facing us with that prick-assed attitude of his. Or did he do as he always swore he would and run the other way the minute he realized he was mated?"

"He was only delayed a bit," Diane assured him.

"More like expecting her to be the good girl and stay in their bed rather than heading out to save this little bitch." Malcolm waved his gun in Liza's direction. "How did you know we were coming for her, Diane?"

That was something Liza would like to know herself.

She just hoped Cullen was able to do what he was so good at and read between the lines of this little conversation for the information he was searching for.

Liza remained carefully still as Diane stepped back protectively to cover her, the weapon in her hand never moving from Malcolm.

"Poor Malcolm," Diane drawled in an amused tone. "You just couldn't face me alone, could you? You had to bring the bullies to protect you."

Malcolm's gaze narrowed hatefully as the sibilant hiss of the communications link sounded in Liza's ear.

"Get ready," Cullen murmured. "Reinforcements are easing in. They're there, just being careful."

His updates were all that was keeping her sane at the moment. Her heart was pounding against her chest, racing at a terrified pace and tightening her throat with panic.

Malcolm scowled as the Coyote with the cigar chuckled wickedly. "Sounds like a challenge to me, little man." Geez, could this crew get any more ridiculous?

She was beginning to doubt it.

"Shut the fuck up," Malcolm snapped, his face flushing a brick red as his eyes glittered with fury. "No one asked you."

"No one had to ask me." The Coyote gave a low, amused laugh once again. "She's cute as hell, Malcolm."

"And she can kick Malcolm's ass to hell and back," Diane assured them all. "He knew he would have to face me." She nodded to Malcolm. "He didn't come for the girl. He came for me."

The Coyote turned his head to Malcolm. "That true, Malcolm?"

Malcolm's lips thinned angrily. "Two birds with one stone, right? She got her uncle and his second-in-command killed so she and that bastard Thor could take over the team. I told you I wanted blood."

"That wasn't the mission," he was reminded as the Coyote briefly gripped his cigar between two fingers and lowered it from his lips. He didn't look happy.

Diane chuckled. It was a forced sound of amusement, but it was amused nonetheless.

"Four Coyotes." She sighed. "For little ole me? That scared of me, Malcolm?"

His jaw tightened, his hands clenched on the weapon.

"If you want me, come fight me," she suggested with a laugh. "I dare you."

Every Coyote there seemed to perk up.

Liza stared at the back of Diane's head in disbelief. Everyone knew you didn't make a dare in front of Coyotes. Good or bad, there wasn't a Coyote living, it was said, who wouldn't take a reasonable dare.

Or was that the point? This woman would know more about Coyote Breeds than most. She was more than just an agent for the Bureau; she was the director's sister-in-law. No doubt, she knew all their strengths, their weaknesses, and exactly how to get to them.

"A thousand on the girl," the leader murmured, proving the supposition.

"Shut the fuck up, Dog," Malcolm raged, his body shaking with fury as he wiped his hands through his short dark hair.

"I got your thousand on the prick there. He has muscle

where she doesn't." Loki took the bet before turning to the other two. "Mutt, Mongrel? You two in?"

"Thousand on the girl," another Coyote drawled.

"Thousand on the prick." Black-haired and intense, the last nodded his assent.

Malcolm was about to explode with the anger surging through him. A wave of brick red swept over his face as his brown eyes glared back at Diane in pure disdain.

Diane smiled in anticipation.

"Knives or fists?" she asked, evidently knowing his strengths as well as his weaknesses, just as she did the Coyote Breeds.

"You fucking whore," he snarled, his teeth clenched, as a muscle throbbed in rapid reaction to the tightening of his teeth.

"I win, we walk away," she demanded as she kept her eyes on Malcolm.

"I'll kill you first," Malcolm charged, his face reddening further as the flames of fury burned beneath his flesh.

"Take the challenge or walk away," Dog snapped. "We won't take her without the fight."

Liza couldn't believe this. "They're betting my safety on a fucking fight?" she muttered incredulously, knowing Cullen was there, and praying he would have an explanation that would make sense.

"We got this," Cullen promised as Liza fought to breathe. "Bureau Breeds have all of you covered. Just be ready to roll when they pull you out. We'll capture one of the Coyotes coming in behind this mess when this is over and interrogate him."

The mess being the less-than-bloodthirsty Coyotes ranged around her. They looked mean enough, heartless enough, yet Liza detected the flash of laughter in Dog's gaze once again as she met his eyes.

Liza stared at the tableau around her, wondering just how often Breeds turned danger into a joke.

She didn't particularly like it.

Dog's smiled was clearly anticipatory, but he nodded easily. "Whip his ass and you walk. He whips yours—you run. How's that?"

Diane gave a sharp, firm nod as she smiled at Malcolm. "It's a bet."

As Diane accepted the terms, the enforcers for the Bureau of Breed Affairs stepped from the cover of the trees and surrounded them.

Liza was still trying to get a head count when one of the few couples she knew, Megan Fields Arness and her husband, Braden Arness, stepped up to her and gripped her arm.

Megan muttered, "Let's go," at her ear.

She didn't want to leave.

Liza had to force herself to hold back the involuntary protest. She wanted to stay. She needed to stay. The fight that was about to commence would no doubt display a variety of skillful moves she had yet to learn by attempting to watch the agents from the Bureau spar from a distance.

Grimacing, she followed Megan, knowing that convincing the other woman and her mate to allow her to stay wasn't going to happen.

The link in her ear was silent, which was standard operating procedure whenever Control knew another Breed was within hearing distance.

The acute hearing and exceptional sense of smell were only two of the extraordinary senses they possessed. So much as a sizzle of static and any Breed within feet of her would sense it.

"Well, look who's joining the party, boys," Dog drawled as Megan and Braden hurried her away. "Looks like the bet's off."

"The hell it is." The last thing she heard was Diane's lover stepping into the fray, his voice a hard, animalistic growl.

That growl, its raw fury, brought on a flash of another memory threatening to intrude, to overcome reality as Liza was hustled quickly to safety.

They were occurring more frequently since the Breeds had arrived in Window Rock, bringing with them a disconcerting fear that Liza hurriedly pushed back.

Show no weakness.
Show no fear.
Show no mercy.
Show no remorse.

Those were the first things they were taught when they were accepted into the Navajo's Breed Underground Network.

A Breed's ability to sense those specific emotions was too well honed to allow any of those working with the network to go out without first being trained—rigorously—to hide them.

And now, that training was coming in damned handy.

Hell, it had been coming in handy for nearly two months now.

And now, Liza was nearly accosted by Breeds on a morning run designed to learn exactly why the Genetics Council had arrived on the tail of the Bureau of Breed Affairs.

The Bureau wasn't telling the truth about what they were after; the deception had been detected and confirmed by its own sources. Unfortunately, those sources had no idea exactly what the Breeds were after either.

Watching Diane Broen entering into a fight while the Breeds around her were taking bets on who would win, who would lose and how many blows it would take to do them in seemed fascinating. Still, Megan and Braden were forcing her away from the fray.

Actually, it was insanity.

The very Breeds who at first appeared intent on abducting her and the human enforcer, Diane Broen, now seemed to be working on the Bureau Breeds' side. They had even encouraged the betting with the promise that if Diane won, they would walk away without the prize they had been paid to collect.

Namely, Liza herself.

She watched until she was pushed into a Dragoon and couldn't see anything more. Damn them, she wasn't a child anymore, yet that was exactly how she was being treated.

As the scene vanished from view, she turned and faced forward, her arms crossed beneath her breasts as she remained silent.

The earbud, all but hidden in her ear canal, was silent, deactivated at Cullen's end. It wouldn't be activated again until they arrived wherever she was being taken, or until the network's agents following her lost sight of her.

Until then, she was on her own.

Swallowing tightly, she tried to put another inch of distance between herself and the big Breed sitting next to her.

Stygian Black. He was a bit of a lone Wolf according to the information Cullen had managed to acquire. A Wolf Breed who worked exclusively on missing cases that involved hidden Breed labs and/or missing Breeds or their mates.

He wasn't a Breed who worked well with others, the report said. And he was one that would just as soon kill a man, or a Breed, who got in his way as he was to look at him. Yet, he'd been working with the Bureau of Breed Affairs for years, and he did so without killing anyone.

Was it a testament to Jonas Wyatt's skill as a commander or simply his control over the animal genetics that were so much a part of the Breeds he commanded? Whichever it was, she could do nothing but admire his ability to work with a man whose animal was as close to the surface as this one's was.

His gaze turned on her every few seconds as though to be certain she was still sitting there. Black eyes gleamed with amusement each time she caught him watching her. Each time she caught him, he would deliberately allow his eyes to flick to the upper mounds of her breasts where they rose above the exercise bra.

As she felt his gaze pin her once again, she turned her head and glared up at him through the veil of her lashes. The fact that she could tell when he was staring down at her, and all that had moved were his eyes, was distinctly disconcerting. Bothering her even more was the fact that her nipples were hardening further with each look. Having such a response to a man, any man, wasn't a situation she wanted to deal with, especially with a Breed.

"Are you comfortable?" his voice rumbled with a primal, erotic rasp that sent a shiver of sensation racing up her spine.

"Not really," she muttered.

She was distinctly uncomfortable with the warmth traveling across her nerve endings as the sensitive flesh of her clit tingled in interest.

As far as she was concerned, this was the wrong man, or Breed, and the wrong time for such an attraction.

"You could sit on my lap," he suggested with a slow smile as he patted a hard, well-muscled thigh. "There's plenty of room."

Oh, hell—

The real problem where that question was concerned was that she was way, way too tempted.

"No, thank you." Jerking her head forward, she stared between the front seats to the road beyond.

"I'd be more than happy to accommodate you." Leaning closer, he all but whispered the words in her ear.

Oh, she just bet he would.

"No." She didn't have the breath to put that "thank you" in there a second time.

Chills were racing over her skin, tearing up her spine and, she swore, sizzling in her lower stomach. Her flesh was warming, her nipples sensitive and the need for touch was like an ache just under her flesh. An ache she had no idea how to assuage because she was damned if she thought it was completely advisable to sleep with him.

But, yes, she did want to sleep with him. She wanted him to touch her, to hold her, to give her what she had so far managed to deny herself. To share a bed with a man, or with a Breed, and to learn all the things sexually that she hadn't really had an interest in until now.

And why now?

Never had she ever had a reaction like this to any man, let alone a Breed.

As he sat back in his seat, she peeked up at him, swallowing deeply at the impression of pure raw power that surrounded him like an invisible mantle.

Dark-skinned, more so than any other Breed she had seen before, he was rumored to have the DNA of a rogue black Wolf and a voodoo priestess, and the dark bronze tone of his skin reflected both.

His eyes were as black as midnight with what appeared at

times to be small pinpoints of blue. His jaw was so hard, so arrogant and savagely hewn she knew he would be as stubborn as hell.

High cheekbones, strong, arched brows, and such long thick black lashes, they simply made her jealous.

His skin fascinated her. Darker than the strongest tan, but it wasn't black. It was simply such a dark, dark earth tone that she wondered if it held the warmth and vibrancy of the earth it so reminded her of.

The name, *Stygian Black*; the name suited him.

The black eyes, the nut brown flesh, the air of power and strength.

Damn, she could feel him watching her again. Her shoulders were tingling.

Narrowing her eyes, she glanced up, glared—

She could do without another once-over, if he didn't mind. If she became much more interested in the fact that he was glancing at the upper curves of her breasts—

The sound of Braden clearing his throat from the driver's seat as he slid the driver's-side window down an inch or so had a flush of raging embarrassment staining her face. It was probably staining her entire body, damn it.

Flattening her lips, she considered kicking him, but he was wearing those damned black boots Breeds wore with their mission uniforms. She'd read they were so tough that a snakebite couldn't even penetrate them. She doubted he'd even feel her foot slamming into his shin.

He smiled.

The bastard.

"Leave me alone." Pushing the words through clenched teeth as she clenched her thighs against those stirrings of arousal, she wondered if there wasn't some way to get the door open and just push him out of the moving vehicle.

"How am I bothering you?" he murmured with such false innocence that the Breed on the other side of her actually chuckled.

If only she had a few more years' training on her. That vehicle-tossing thing was something Cullen was really good at; perhaps she could have convinced him to teach it to her.

As it was, in a physical confrontation with a man like Stygian, her only hope was in simply running.

And she had a feeling she couldn't run far enough or fast enough to get away from this Breed.

If the look in his eyes was any indication, running wouldn't be an option.

No, a Breed would expect her to mildly stand in place until he gave her the order to do otherwise.

She didn't think so.

Turning back to stare out the front window, Liza tightened her arms beneath her breasts and gave him something to look at. Or to slobber over, she thought. He was definitely acting like a dog.

Yeah, she knew the sports bra plumped her breasts and left her belly bare. She knew her running pants were a little snug and she wasn't wearing panties beneath them.

But did he have to act as though he knew it as well?

Because each time his gaze flicked over her, the warmth that suffused her flesh was just irritating. She didn't need this. This was the last thing she needed. An attraction to a Breed would completely foul up her plans, and she really didn't need that at the moment.

A hard turn to the right threw her against him before she could brace herself. Instantly, his arm went around her, the powerful, bare flesh of his forearm heating her skin where it touched her lower arm, while his hand quickly gripped her hip.

She had to swallow tight as she held on to the edge of her seat, refusing to look at him.

Breeds had no true body hair, she'd heard. What they had were tiny, almost invisible hairs more closely resembling a fine pelt.

She believed it now.

She could feel it.

Each invisible, silken hair caressed her overly sensitive flesh everywhere they touched.

The Desert Dragoon bounced across the rough terrain until it hit the smoother road leading to the hotel and, thankfully, stopped jostling her against him every other second.

Unfortunately, it did nothing to force him to remove his arm.

If it hadn't been for that strength wrapped around her and the fingers gripping her hip, however, she would have been thrown into the driver's seat when the vehicle came to a screeching stop at the back entrance of the hotel.

Breeds piled out. Stygian Black lifted Liza from the vehicle.

Then, surrounded by big, burly bodies, she was pushed through the entrance to an elevator. Within seconds, she stepped out onto the secure fifth floor, which was reserved for Breeds alone.

Would explanations now be forthcoming?

They damned well better be. The last she'd heard, Breeds were not exempt from the legal repercussions of kidnapping. Jonas Wyatt, the goons' boss, better have some damned answers.

And didn't it just figure that he wasn't there?

Instead, a team of Breeds were in place with their electronic bug detectors.

Each member of the team that had brought her in was scanned thoroughly before Stygian took the device from one of the team members and turned to her with a grin.

"Just get it over with," she ordered, frustration running rampant through her body as she lifted her arms and waited.

And prayed the earbud and skin tags were as undetectable as Cullen was certain they were.

"Testy today, aren't you?" Stygian grinned before moving the paddle-shaped device over her body.

"You'd think with all the technology you guys have going for you, you wouldn't be working with such antiquated electronics." She eyed the twenty-year-old device skeptically.

"Don't let looks fool you," he murmured as he ran the wand over her head.

Her heart nearly tripped from her chest as he paused at

her ear. A second later the device was moving again, then pausing on the other side as well.

Thank God Cullen had instituted shutting the earbuds down completely when in the presence of Breeds.

Giving her a small, flirtatious little wink, he turned and handed the device over to the Breed next to him before, surprisingly, striding to the door and leaving the suite entirely.

Liza turned to Megan questioningly. "Where's he going?"

"He's part of the independent security force," Megan answered, her dark brown gaze amused. "Trust me, he'll be back."

Trust her? At one time, years ago, she had trusted Megan Fields with her life. Now, trust wasn't so easy. She was a Breed mate, and because she was a Breed mate, her first thought was for the Breed community, rather than friends, and in many areas, even family.

Trust her? Trust any of them?

Liza looked around the room, taking in the hard gazes and ready stances of each person in the room.

She really didn't think so.

Stepping into the connecting room, Stygian glanced at the monitors on the wall, watching as Ms. Liza Johnson shifted uncomfortably and gazed around with a resigned expression.

Turning to Jonas, he was at first taken aback. He always was, whenever he saw the hard-assed, merciless, manipulating director of the Bureau of Breed Affairs cradling the too-delicate toddler he'd taken as his own.

Amber was curled against his chest, delicate and frail, her normally bright blue eyes closed, her breathing gentle and easy for a change.

It was one of the rare times he hadn't sensed the baby's pain when in her presence. For now, despite the hell she'd been through in the past two years, she was at peace.

"Just keep your voice low and you won't disturb her," Jonas assured him.

Wiping his hand over the back of his neck, he pushed back his frustration before grimacing. "They attacked, as we knew they would."

Jonas nodded, thoughtful for a moment before replying.

"Malcolm's team moved in the minute they thought she was unprotected," he murmured as Stygian watched him closely. "I was listening to the reports as they came in. Lawe and Diane are fine, by the way. They're heading back to the hotel now and should show up in the next five minutes."

"She kicked his ass then?" Stygian asked with a grin as he thought of the cocky, traitorous Malcolm.

"Was there any doubt?" Jonas grinned. "She's a hell of an addition to the Bureau, though Lawe has definitely bowed out of the assistant director position."

That wasn't really a surprise.

"Lawe prefers the field and now he has a mate to share that with," he agreed as Jonas's lips tightened.

The director had been certain Lawe Justice would take the position of assistant director.

Those who knew Lawe had known better.

Jonas glanced at the monitor then, watching Liza thoughtfully, before murmuring, "Ms. Johnson wasn't alone either, was she?"

Stygian grunted at the comment. "That girl is never alone. She had two shadows on her ass and two lying farther back from the minute she left her house, just as she's had every morning. And they're damned good. They're always damned good. And she knew they were there."

Jonas turned his head, his brows lifting curiously at the information. "Really?"

"Damned straight," he growled. "To add to it, she has a deactivated earbud tucked completely out of sight in that dainty little ear of hers and three skin tags. One on each hip and one on her left shoulder."

"Then her shadows are friendly?" Jonas leaned back in his chair carefully, propping one expensively shod foot on the coffee table as he ensured not so much as a shift of movement disturbed his toddler.

She didn't budge. One little hand lay at his neck, the other beneath her cheek. The soft pink-and-white frilly dress she wore looked at odds against the black shirt and shoulder holster it lay against on Jonas's chest.

"The shadows are friendly." Stygian nodded. "Between her and them is the enemy." He sighed. "The ones I glimpsed the other morning as she went to work are not part of Dog's team. But we already knew that."

Jonas nodded slowly as he gently, rhythmically, rubbed his daughter's back.

She was the reason Jonas was there; the reason he was searching desperately for ghosts.

"What do we have, Stygian?" he asked as he stared out over the tiny head tucked beneath his chin.

The girl's once-brown locks, still thick with a slight curl, were now tricolored. Golden blond and sunset red streaked the once dark brown strands as though nature hadn't yet made up her mind what color the child's hair would be.

"Hell if know." Stygian breathed out roughly. "She's important to someone though—damned important. She and her housemates, Claire and Chelsea Martinez."

"Cousins," Jonas said softly.

Stygian nodded. "Before the attack on Malachi's mate, only Liza Johnson and Claire Martinez had these shadows, though. Chelsea picked up hers after her sister's attack."

"Liza was bait this morning then," Jonas suggested.

Stygian nodded. "The earbud was active until Braden and Megan rushed her to the Dragoon. It disconnected before she entered the vehicle and hasn't reactivated since."

"You have the frequency locked yet?"

Stygian nodded again. "We managed that before we took the Jammer over it. Their connection should be interrupted for the next few hours."

"Let's let her wait for a while then," Jonas suggested. "See if her shadows come out of the woodwork again. I want an ID on them."

"You think if we hold her here long enough they'll make a move?"

That was Jonas, manipulating and calculating as hell when he was after something.

Or someone.

In this case, he was after two women and two Bengal

Breeds. The two girls had disappeared twelve years before, and many believed they were dead.

Of the two Breeds, they knew one was alive and killing his way through the lab techs and scientists who had run the secret experimental labs of the pharmaceutical company Brandenmore Research.

"I don't think they'll make a move." Jonas smiled. "Unjam the transmission, let's track it back to her friends when it reactivates and see what they know."

Stygian's brows arched. "They could have abandoned the link once it was jammed. That seems to be normal procedure."

"But we also blocked the locator tags," Jonas pointed out. "If she were important to you, what would you do?"

Clenching his jaw, Stygian knew exactly what he would have done, whether she was important or not. She was a woman and part of a mission. There wasn't a true Breed alive who would have walked away.

A true Breed was one whose sense of loyalty and honor was greater than those of the Council Breeds, whose honor was closer to those of human criminals.

Which was exactly where most of the genetics of those particular Breeds—Honor Roberts, Fawn Corrigan and the Bengals Judd and Gideon—had come from. "I'm a Breed," Stygian finally stated after considering Jonas's question of the choice he would make. "Her shadows are human. They're wild cards."

Council Coyotes were more human than Breed, more mercenary and merciless than loyal.

Council-loyal Breeds weren't known as the most fastidious or the most reliable. They were a boil on the ass of the Breed communities and avoided at all costs.

Or until the Council sent them out. In that case, any and every Breed associated with the Breed communities jumped between them and their goal.

This time, Stygian was certain the Council's goal was the same as the Breeds': the search for the four victims once held by the pharmaceutical giant Phillip Brandenmore in a secret genetic and medical experimental lab.

"Wild cards or not, they're protecting someone," Jonas disagreed. "They're not imprisoning or attempting to apprehend or control. They're shadowing, and they're protective. That's the difference."

Crossing his arms over his chest, Stygian glared down at the director. There were times when Jonas seemed amazingly naïve when it came to humans, which was surprising considering the Breed's stone-cold manipulation tactics.

Jonas smiled back at him. "Review the vids the enforcers have made of her shadows," he suggested. "That's what they are, literally, and she knows they're there. She communicates with them often through that damned ear link and she has affection for whoever's on the other side of that transmission."

"I've watched the vids," Stygian growled.

He hated to admit it, but Jonas just might be right.

"You're a hell of a commander, Stygian," Jonas stated then. "But the lone Wolf thing you like to do hasn't helped you to understand humans."

"Who wants to?" Humans weren't exactly his preferred type of company.

Coming into the Bureau hadn't been easy for him, but once his team had begun mating and settling down, Stygian had found himself at a crossroads. The paths he had been offered weren't exactly ones he would have preferred.

Train a new team, or take the position Jonas offered and command a team already trained and needing only a commander willing to guide them? They were Breeds he had known, Breeds he'd fought with on at least one occasion, and Breeds he trusted. But nothing was the same as the team you'd fought with, gotten to know and could count on no matter the situation.

"You need to understand them," Jonas warned him as Amber moved, a childish little mumble of displeasure sounding from her pouty lips.

Stygian's gaze jerked to the little girl. She wasn't emanating any pain, but something was distressing her.

Jonas continued to rub her fragile back, his gaze locked on the little face that came into view when she shifted position and stretched out against his chest. Her head lay in the crook of his arm before she finished maneuvering for the position she was after.

The smile that quirked the director's lips was damned surprising.

Pure tenderness.

"This meeting is over," Jonas stated firmly though softly. "Go back to her, keep her occupied. Once the link reactivates, I'll meet with her. Let's see what happens when her friends learn what we're really searching for."

"Is that a good idea?" Stygian had never been one to give the suspected enemy any information at all.

"She's going to tell them anyway," Jonas reminded him. "This way, we can track the transmission to the source and identify her shadows. That could help us figure out why they're tailing her and why she's working with them."

"Have you considered they could simply be friends who are worried about her? Friends with the same paranoia and resources that you have?" Jonas's mate and wife, Rachel Broen-Wyatt, stepped across the open door frame that led to the suite's bedroom.

Leaning against the wood frame, one hand tucked into the pocket of her jeans, the other propped on a slender hip, love suffused her expression as her gaze settled on the man and child across the room.

No Breed could ever doubt the pure, soul-deep love that existed between the couple. The room was suddenly scented with the power of it. Sensual, yet pure, innocent and yet erotic, the emotions that swept between the two were almost too intimate for Stygian's comfort.

"Hello, Stygian." Rachel straightened from her position and moved slowly into the room. "I see you're once again enmeshed in one of Jonas's schemes." Pure pride enveloped her despite the teasing tone of her voice.

"So it would seem," he agreed, suddenly uncertain what to do with himself.

Shoving his hands into the pockets of his mission pants, he waited impatiently as she crossed the room to her husband, then bent to him.

Her hair cascaded over her face, hiding the greeting kiss as Jonas's hand lifted, his fingers spreading to cup her cheek and neck.

That scent; Stygian had learned to associate it with the deepest emotions shared between mates. What Jonas and Rachel shared was as deep as that of couples mated for a decade, though.

It was rare to sense such depths of emotion after only a few years.

The kiss lasted only seconds. A true greeting kiss, but the impact of the dedication between the two sent a chill racing up Stygian's spine.

Without one, the other would cease to exist, he thought, and such realization would be terrifying for the babe cradled between the two, should it ever happen.

Then, as the mother drew back and her attention joined Jonas's on the child, he felt a chill of foreboding tearing through him.

Amber had awakened, and suddenly what had been shared love between two became a circle of pure emotion.

There was nothing sensual or erotic in this. It went beyond soul deep though, and for the first time Stygian could sense the enormity of what Jonas was facing if he lost the battle for the little girl's life.

"Momma, Da sings." Amber lay back in Jonas's arms and clearly told a secret Jonas would have preferred she kept to herself. "Da sings purty, Momma."

Rachel's laughter was filled with love as she straightened and stared down at her mate. "Da sings, does he?" she asked the little girl. "What does Da sing, Amber?"

"Uh, Rachel—" There was a definite thread of amusement in Jonas's tone.

"Da sing bad cotie go bye-bye." Amber laughed, obviously aware she was telling a great secret. "Ba' cotie go bye-bye, boom boom," she suddenly sang as Jonas fought to hold back his laughter and Rachel turned a look of mock anger on him.

"Jonas, shame on you," she chastised him, though her tone lacked anger. "I thought we were teaching Amber to be compassionate and kind?"

"To be fair, it's called putting them out of their misery."
Jonas laughed, handing the little girl over to her petite
mother. "Snitch," he accused the little girl, but his smile and
tone of voice was anything but chastising.

"Da called me 'itch, Momma," Amber gave a mock little
pout, though her blue eyes were gleaming with childish
laughter as her arms wrapped around her mother's neck as
she turned back to her da. "Don' call me 'itch, Da." She
wagged a little finger at him, obviously mimicking his
actions.

Jonas chuckled at the childish order before moving to his
feet and stealing a kiss from the girl's cheek. "Then don't
snitch on Da," he warned her, the laughter in his voice
another surprise.

Stygian would be damned if he could ever remember seeing laughter in Jonas's gaze, let alone hearing it in his voice.

"Come on, snitch, let's get you bathed and dressed for
dinner. Do you think you and your da could refrain from the
food fight tonight? Those carrots were not easy for Erin to
clean . . ."

She continued into the other room as her voice trailed off
and Amber's laughter became indistinct, leaving Stygian to
miss it more than he was willing to admit.

That moment of tenderness, of family intimacy was
nearly more than Stygian could bear. And in that moment,
the young woman waiting in the other room jumped into his
mind.

Skin like the softest silk; eyes the sweetest, softest gray;
and a body that would tempt a monk. Full breasts confined
beneath the sports bra, gently rounded hips and toned thighs.
Lips with the slightest sensual pout and a temper that would
test even the most patient Breed.

Being next to her in the Dragoon had tested not just his
patience, but also his self-control. He had wanted nothing
more than to taste those sweet lips before moving on to certain other body parts.

"Control your lust, Wolf, or I'll start thinking she's your
mate," Jonas murmured, amused.

Stygian frowned back at him. "Hell, a Breed can't even get horny anymore without being accused of mating."

Jonas's lips quirked in a hint of a smile. "True, Wolf. Very true." Then he nodded to the monitors. "Go on out there, distract her a bit. Once the link reactivates, I'll join the rest of you. Have the others keep their distance from her in case the skin tags she's wearing are programmed to shut everything down once Breed body heat has been detected."

Breeds had a body temperature that ran a degree or two higher than humans and made some electronics much easier to shut down if they were programmed correctly.

Stygian nodded, turned and headed back to the sitting room where the young woman waited.

And he started praying—

Praying she wasn't his mate. Praying she was his mate.

And praying he could keep her alive.

∙ C H A P T E R 2 ∙

Waiting wasn't high on her list of things she enjoyed, Liza admitted as she was forced to wait for Jonas Wyatt.

And waiting nearly an hour before coming face-to-face with none other than the big bad director of Breed Affairs himself didn't help.

Not that she hadn't met him before.

She had.

Just never quite like this.

And definitely not with what appeared to be the Alphas of the Wolf and Coyote packs as well as Callan Lyons, leader of the Feline Prides and acknowledged spokesperson of the Breed communities, entering behind him along with more than a half dozen other Breeds.

The room suddenly seemed way too small; the air around her too thick and heavy with male testosterone and dominant power.

"Miss Johnson," Jonas greeted her cordially as she rose from her seat and Jonas stepped in front of her. "We need your help."

Liza's jaw tightened furiously as she came to her feet. "You need more than my help and you're sure as hell going to need a few good lawyers."

She really wasn't happy over this. And if Cullen and

Reever's comments were any indication, then they were furious. The team of Coyote soldiers that had actually been following Liza had managed to completely disappear.

Reever had already threatened to have several of the men in the room neutered. Jonas was threatening to castrate them himself.

"We just saved your life," Jonas stated, as though that were a boon she owed him.

She didn't think so.

"Your people just endangered it," she snapped. "Let me tell you now—" She was suddenly distracted by Jonas's hand slicing quickly into the air as Diane Broen, Lawe Justice and Rule Breaker each made a quick, silencing move themselves.

They had been searching the room as she and Jonas squared off, and were now lifting what appeared to be small electronic devices from several points in the luxurious sitting room.

Listening devices.

The room had been bugged.

Jonas stared at the device Diane handed him, his expression slowly tightening into sharp, icy lines.

Someone had managed to bug his suite. They had invaded his mate and child's safety and security.

The signal had piggybacked on their own wireless devices and betrayed them.

And Jonas had no idea how long it had been in his rooms.

Or if there were more, let alone how Gideon Cross had actually managed to get them in there.

Fucking Bengal bastard! He was like a ghost haunting every area of Jonas's life now.

Turning to Lawe, he lifted his hand and gave a slow circle with his index finger, indicating a full-suite electronic blackout, white noise as well as jamming technology.

It would unfortunately block the transmission between Ms. Johnson and her protectors, but his family's security outweighed any possible manipulation of the Bengal Breed.

Gideon Cross had just upped the ante.

Jonas turned then and stared back at Liza Johnson and in the scent of her fear, learned something more.

His sense of smell was rated off the charts. He was believed to be one of the strongest sensory Breeds to have been created.

If there was a stronger Breed, then they weren't revealing it.

And what he scented in this woman's very DNA had him smiling slowly.

The game was just beginning.

It wouldn't be easy, and it would skirt damned close to breaking his own personal rules, but he had to do what had to be done.

Not just for the two young women and two Bengal Breeds affected by the serum that monster Brandenmore had created, but for Jonas's daughter as well.

For that sweet bit of innocence his mate had given birth to and had given into his keeping as his own.

For Amber, he had to make this work.

Liza watched a smile cross the Breed's lips and the way those liquid mercury eyes seemed to brighten with anticipation.

He looked like a predator that had finally found its prey.

A shiver of dread raced up her spine and clenched her stomach with impending panic.

"As I said, we need your help," he repeated, the icy, merciless smile snapping at the panic rising inside her. "And in return, we'll ensure you're protected from the men determined to abduct you."

If they'd left her alone to begin with, she might have known who the hell those men were.

She crossed her arms over her breasts and glared back at the room filled with Breeds. She didn't miss the fact that Stygian had moved closer to her, his stance protective.

Evidently Jonas was noticing it as well if the slash of his eyes in Stygian's direction was any indication.

Turning back to the arrogant director, determined to hide her interest in a Breed she wanted nothing to do with, Liza directed her attention to Jonas.

"From what I've seen, Director Wyatt, it's all you can do

to protect yourselves," she suggested coolly. "What would make me believe you could do anything to protect me?"

His lips quirked with a hint of amusement, though his gaze flashed dangerously.

"We've done quite well, I believe," he drawled. "We didn't lose any of our men and managed to capture all that weren't killed of those attacking us as well as you. Those are rather good odds, if you ask me."

Great. That meant there was no one left for Cullen and Reever to question.

"But they keep attacking the Breeds," she pointed out. "And the odds aren't always so great, Director. I do listen to the news fairly often."

"If you listen to the news, then you should be aware of the fact that not only Breeds are at risk from the Genetics Council and their loyalists," he told her. "They do target others on occasion."

"Unfairly so," she agreed. "But they wouldn't have attacked me if it hadn't been for her."

She nodded to Diane Broen, the human enforcer who worked for the Bureau of Breed Affairs. "She was the one they came for, not me."

She knew better. He knew better. But she was supposed to be unaware of the fact that she had been targeted? Keeping that impression would be preferable.

"And there is where you're wrong." He smirked back at her, and Liza found herself gritting her teeth in return. So much for hoping she could appear to remain in the dark. "Diane just happened to have been there to distract their attention for a moment, nothing more. It was you they were after."

He seemed entirely too satisfied to relay that information.

Once again, Liza let her attention stray to Stygian as he stood several feet to her side. With his arms crossed over his broad chest, the black enforcer uniform and heavy boots, his long black hair tied back at his nape, he could have been a warrior from more than two centuries before.

There was something about his stance, the straight shoulders, the ready preparedness in his muscular body. He wasn't a Breed who would be easy to catch unaware.

"They have no reason to be after me," she retorted as she forced herself to face the director once again.

Jonas was known as a master manipulator. Even his own enforcers were known to curse him to the pits of hell for his machinations.

"You wouldn't think so," he agreed. "I have to admit I can see no reason why they would target you. But the fact is, they have."

Narrowing her eyes, Liza kept her arms crossed over her breasts as she wished she had worn a light jacket. Something, anything she could have pushed her hands into, could have found a way to hide some part of herself.

"Then we're in agreement that I'm not their target." She shrugged as she fought the need to disappear. "Does that mean I can leave now?"

She was suddenly all too aware of the scantiness of her running pants and top. Her midriff was left bare, her legs growing cold in the air-conditioned chill of the room. As Stygian's gaze flickered to the exposed flesh of her midriff, it suddenly heated, warming as though it were his hands touching her rather than just his gaze.

She did flush then.

Damn it.

Because her face and neck weren't the only parts of her body flushing and heating.

Her nipples were hardening, her clit becoming sensitive, moisture gathering between her thighs.

Her response to him wasn't just shocking, it was frightening.

And she wanted no part of it.

"I said I couldn't see the reason why, not that you weren't being targeted," he pointed out as though speaking to a child and patronizing her for her stupidity.

"I'm certain I don't know why they would target me either," she assured the director. "What I do know is that I'm not in the mood for the third-degree here. You guys have done nothing but cause trouble since you arrived. First Isabelle was kidnapped and nearly turned over to those deranged Coyotes Holden was trying to take her to, a friend is nearly murdered in front of her and now I'm being accosted during my morning run no more than weeks later. What's next with the lot of you?"

With each accusation, Jonas's expression turned stonier while Stygian eyed her with greater intensity.

"Your abduction could be next."

Liza followed Jonas with her gaze as he moved to the long table against the wall.

"Let me show you something," he suggested. Turning, he indicated that she should follow him.

Liza's gaze shifted to Stygian before she turned and moved carefully to the table.

She had a feeling she didn't want to see what the director was pulling from the files stacked there.

Stepping to his side, she stared down at the photos he was setting out on the table.

The eight-by-ten glossy photos were of a very ill child, her little head bare of hair, blue eyes filled with sorrow.

She was pale, obviously in pain, and stared into the camera with a sense of resignation.

Her heart beat faster, her throat felt tight with dread. She tried to tell herself, to convince herself it was because of a child's pain seen so clearly in those frightened, worn blue eyes.

But that didn't explain the flash of some long-forgotten sensation attacking her arm. The feel of phantom needles inserted into an arm so thin, already so bruised and abused, sent a shock wave of horror traveling through her so quickly that before she could react, it was gone.

What was that? It couldn't be a memory, because Liza knew she hadn't ever been so ill as a child.

The next photo was one of another young girl, though her illness wasn't as apparent. Dark brown eyes and hair lay around her pale face. Her lips were cracked and dry, her gaze distant as though she were forcing herself to see beyond the camera.

She was living, but she wasn't really with them. They

were desperate to pull her back. What if she never came
back? What if she went away inside herself and never
returned to them? All the planning, all the deception and
the lies would have been for nothing?

Liza felt her breath catch as she fought to hide the shock
and fear that nearly overcame her. Clenching her fingers into
fists and tucking them beneath the fold of her arms, she kept
her gaze centered on the corner of the photos until the wave
of disorientation receded.

But she couldn't keep her eyes from them for long.

There were pictures of the two girls together; then, there
were pictures of the hairless girl with two adults Liza
assumed were her parents.

The tall, broad male had a haunted look in his gaze,
while the mother's face was filled with pain and love. They
weren't staring at the camera; rather they were standing next
to the hospital bed where their child lay sleeping.

Sleeping?

Or dead?

There were other pictures.

The two girls with two Breeds. It was obvious because
they were displaying their incisors in the pictures. In their
eyes though, Liza could glimpse the hell all four were
clearly enduring.

Compassion filled her, as well as a sense of sorrow.

"Who are they?" Looking up at the director, she had to
refrain from rubbing at the chill that suddenly raced over
her arms. "Will they be okay?"

Jonas gathered the photos together before replacing them
in the file.

"They grew up," he stated. "The one with her parents is
Honor Roberts. The leukemia she had was diagnosed as a
particularly fast-growing and fatal illness. There is no
known cure or procedure for remission, even now.

"The other girl was Fawn Corrigan. At two months of
age she was near death, diagnosed with infant AIDS and
given only weeks to live. As you saw in the photo, at age ten,
she was still alive."

"But still ill," she stated.

"Not necessarily," he said. "Did you recognize any of them?"

"Why would I?" Her gaze jerked back to his with a hard frown. "The two girls were with two immature Breed males. There are no Breed males of that age in Window Rock that I'm aware of."

Tightening her stomach, she refused to allow herself to think about them—or her reaction to the photos.

"Those pictures were taken more than a decade ago." The obvious impatience in his voice was reflected in the darkening swirls of gray in his eyes.

"Then why would I know them?" She glanced around the room at the Breeds gathered there before turning her gaze back to the director. "Why don't you just tell me what the hell is going on here, Director Wyatt? That would be a hell of a lot easier than the games you seem to so enjoy."

If she wasn't mistaken, he didn't particularly care for the fact that she called him on his habit of deliberately manipulating anyone and everyone he came in contact with.

Megan Fields Arness stepped forward. "Liza, the point is that we're searching for the two girls. Finding them is of the highest importance to the Breeds, to ensure the Genetics Council doesn't acquire them for whatever research purposes they have in mind. There's nothing nefarious in the least in the Breeds' wish to find them."

The knowledge that Megan would lie to her—probably was lying to her—had her fighting back the sting of tears.

She had known Megan most of her life.

Megan's grandfather and Isabelle, Chelsea, and Claire's were both part of the chiefs of the Six Tribes. Besides that, the Martinez family was a very close unit and socialized together often.

They were friends—or so she had thought. Friends weren't supposed to lie to each other to this extent.

"Well, there's nothing nefarious in the least about the fact that I haven't seen or heard of them. But I would like to know what the hell they have to do with me?" Liza stared

back at Megan, meeting her gaze and wishing she could find
that sense of calm that Megan seemed to hold in her dark
brown eyes.

"Those girls are currently the focus of a search by the
Genetics Council as well as the Breeds," Megan told her.
"They were part of an experiment that lasted for more than
a decade. The two girls and the two Breeds all survived but
disappeared about ten years ago. We have to find them
before the Genetics Council does."

And if the four had disappeared and never come forward,
then it was apparent they didn't want to be found.

"Why?" Liza questioned her. "Why would you believe
you have the right either to find them or to acquire them?"

Damn, she felt sorry for the former kids now being
hunted by two such powerful, merciless forces.

"If we don't," Stygian said, stepping forward, his voice
dark and rough, rasping over her senses like velvet, "then trust
me, Ms. Johnson, the Genetics Council will make damned
sure they regret the fact that the Council found them rather
than the Breeds."

She had to physically restrain the shiver that wanted to
race across her flesh at the sound of his voice caressing her
senses. It reminded her of dark, wicked sex.

Of sinning in the most pleasurable of ways.

Every cell in her body tingled at the sound. Her breasts
became swollen and heavy, her nipples taut and eager for
touch. And between her thighs, her clit throbbed in heightened alert as she suddenly became aware of the emptiness in
her vagina.

Damn.

No man had the right to make a woman so aware of the
fact that a male wasn't possessing her.

"Well, if I could help you, I would," she assured, stepping
back carefully as he moved just behind Jonas Wyatt. "The
fact is, though, that I can't. As I stated, I don't know them,
nor do I know who they are."

Jonas pulled another file free.

Opening it, he drew two photos free. The first was of one

of the Breed boys in the former pictures. The second was obviously an "after" version.

Nothing could hold back the shudder that rushed up her spine at the changes in the boy to the man.

Stone-cold eyes the color of living amber stared out from the photo paper with a brilliance that was almost terrifying when added to the Bengal stripes that crossed his face from his forehead, across his right eye, over the bridge of his nose and across his left cheek, over his jaw then around to the nape of his neck.

Where it went from there she wasn't certain.

The savagery of the mark, the primal quality of his gaze and the inherent predatory intent would have been terrifying if it were in person rather than in a photo.

"What does he have to do with this now?"

"Gideon Cross is searching for those women the two girls became. His intent isn't to stop by and say hello, Ms. Johnson," Jonas warned her. "If you've followed the stories of Breed creation and their weaknesses, then I'm certain you've heard of psychotic emergent feral fever."

Liza nodded slowly.

"Gideon is suspected of having been thrown into level-five feral fever by the Genetics Council's experiments. And he's searching for those two women because he believes one of them is responsible for it. He won't bother questioning them. He'll strike out at both. He will kill them. And he won't care that they had nothing to do with his illness."

"Does one of them have anything to do with it?" she asked, her gaze lifting—not to Jonas but to the Breed behind him.

"Stygian?" Jonas spoke softly.

"Director?"

"Do you want to answer Ms. Johnson's question?"

"She had nothing to do with it, Ms. Johnson," Stygian answered. "Once feral fever has gone that far, nothing has any logic to it. She was there at the wrong place, at the wrong time, so he blames her for it. It's that simple."

She wanted him to keep talking. The sound of his voice was a caress to her senses, and she didn't want it to stop.

Still, she shook her head, forcing her gaze back to Wyatt's. "It doesn't change the fact that I don't know the girls, who they grew up to be or where they are. Neither do I have any information on the Breeds in those pictures. And even if I did, I doubt I would tell you, Mr. Wyatt."

She made certain the smile she gave him was just as mocking and confident as she could possibly make it.

She didn't trust him. She had no intention of attempting to trust him. She'd heard far too many stories of Wyatt's games and attempts to interfere in the lives of those who came in contact with him.

"I can see your popularity precedes you, Jonas." Megan gave a light, easy laugh as Jonas pinned her with that odd, silvery gaze.

"So it would seem," Jonas drawled before turning back to Liza.

She stared up at him, refusing to back down despite the trepidation she could feel tightening her stomach.

"Can I leave now?" she asked.

"Stygian." Jonas's voice was low as Liza looked over his shoulder once again only to have her gaze caught and held by the Breed watching her from behind the director.

"Director," he answered Wyatt.

"Would you please escort Ms. Johnson home?"

"With pleasure."

"Thank you." Jonas was smirking now, and the sight of it had an edge of panic tightening her throat rather than generating trepidation in her stomach.

Her gaze narrowed on him. He was up to something. She could just feel it.

"Ms. Johnson." Stygian stepped around Jonas, his powerful arm reaching out to indicate the door. "This way."

With pleasure.

With one last wary glance at the supremely confident, satisfied look on the director's face, Liza turned and made her way to the door.

She could feel the big Breed behind her as she walked. Another Breed—this one she knew by the name of Rule Breaker—opened the door and stepped back.

Nodding to him, she left quickly, eager to put this particular experience behind her, get home and figure out what the hell was going on.

She couldn't help but think of those pictures: the images of the two girls, so obviously in pain and filled with fear.

Especially the girl with her parents.

What kind of parents could turn their child over to monsters like the Genetics Council and just leave her with them? Alone? In pain?

Surely, those parents had to be just as cruel.

Just as monstrous.

Except, it wasn't cruelty she had seen in the eyes of the mother and father in the picture with their child.

It had been agony.

◆   ◆   ◆

Megan stared at the door, her senses penetrating it, following the young woman as she made her way to the elevator with Stygian.

She closed her eyes slowly, let her senses ease gently into Liza Johnson's emotions and searched for any hint of Honor Roberts, Fawn Corrigan, a Bengal named Judd or one named Gideon.

The only hint she found of them was a deep compassion and a sense of unease and disbelief that Honor Roberts's parents had left their child with monsters.

There was no sense of the girl, Honor, though, nor of Fawn.

As Liza entered the elevator with Stygian, Megan quickly retreated from the girl's senses, a flush stealing up her face as the sudden images that flashed through Liza's mind began to enflame her senses.

Some things were just invasive, and remaining with the girl's mind at that moment was just that.

Opening her eyes to find everyone watching her only increased the color in her cheeks. Clearing her throat, she glanced at her mate with a suggestive look. "Perhaps we do have things to learn." She laughed, thinking of the mental images that had raced through Liza's mind the second she and Stygian were alone.

And Stygian's reaction was so strong Megan had sensed it as well.

Braden gave her one of those slow, drowsy-eyed looks that never failed to make her body heat and her pussy tingle.

He just had that way about him.

"You two can get a bedroom after this meeting is over," Jonas growled, crossing his arms over his chest and glaring back at them.

He had a right to glower.

Megan sobered instantly, the knowledge that time was running out for his mate's child was at the top of his mind.

"She doesn't know anything about them." She sighed, shaking her head. "She doesn't know of them, or have any of their memories. It's another dead end."

"That's impossible." Diane Broen stepped forward.

Diane was an enforcer, a lethal weapon, just as her mate was. And just as Megan and her mate were, Diane was an enforcer desperate to save the child they all loved.

"There's no way she could have hidden it from me, Diane," Megan told the other woman gently. "Her mind and emotions weren't closed at all. She was an open book all the way to her lust for Stygian, who is her mate by the way. You can't hide only certain parts of yourself psychically like that. An empath can either read all of you, or none of you."

"An empath can only read what is a part of you," Jonas stated cryptically, immediately sending warning flares through her empathic senses. "Not what has perhaps been misplaced."

· CHAPTER 3 ·

The elevator door slid closed with a soft *swish* of air, leaving Liza enclosed in a space that seemed far too small with Stygian beside her.

"These women you're looking for have nothing to do with me," she stated as a wave of heated arousal swept through her.

No sooner had she experienced that sensation of flooding warmth, than Liza found herself lifted, pressed against the elevator wall and the iron-hot length of Stygian's erection lodged between her thighs, tormenting her through the layers of their clothing.

The tight running pants and thin exercise bra were little protection against the burning heat of his body—and his hunger.

"What—?" Lips parting, for breath or for his kiss?

Liza wasn't certain, but she knew she needed both— ached for both to the point that it took several heartbeats to realize she was holding her breath.

And that her hands were gripping the hard width of his shoulders.

"What?" he growled. "What are you questioning, Liza? My hunger—or yours?"

Her stomach tightened, rippling in response to the hunger in his voice as a growl rumbled beneath the word.

"Let me go." The demand was undermined by the whimpering need in her body.

Hell, she may as well be begging him to continue for all the denial that wasn't in her voice.

"Let you go?" He pressed tighter into the cradle of her thighs as his hands parted them further. "Are you sure that's what you want?"

The black in his eyes flickered with blue, fascinating her with the sparkle of color.

Her breasts trembled against the hard width of his chest as her breathing accelerated. Heat flushed her face, spreading through her body as she fought to keep her lashes from drifting closed.

As she stared up at him, she felt one hand move from her hips a second before his palm slapped against the elevator control panel. The cubicle came to a stop, lights flashing before they dimmed and remained steady. The electronic voice warned: "Please be patient, we are working to reset operation."

Liza's eyes widened.

"Don't leave the hotel." He lowered his head and the rasp of the day-old beard against the sensitive shell of her ear had her eyes closing in desperate need.

"I can't stay here. Why would I want to?"

"To stay with me?" he suggested, his lips touching just beneath her ear, sending tingles of incredible sensation rushing along her nerve endings.

To stay with him?

God, she wanted to stay with him.

She didn't know him, she only knew of him. She'd watched him for weeks as he moved about the periphery of her life, always surprised when she saw him though always expecting his presence.

"This won't work."

"Won't it?" As he nuzzled against her ear, heat and searing need flashed through her senses. "Then why are you holding on to me as though you'll never let go?"

Her nails were biting into the fabric of his shirt as though desperate to reach his flesh.

The sensual side of her *was* desperate to get to bare skin, to feel him against her, the warmth of him, the pleasure of him stroking her.

"Why did you manhandle me against the wall?" she accused back, but once again there was no anger to her tone, nothing to really impress him with the fact that she meant it.

If she did mean it.

"I want you, Liza," he rasped at her ear then. "From the moment I saw you the night your friend approached Malachi, I've wanted you. I've wanted you bad."

The words affected her more for the sheer simplicity of the statement than the roughness of his tone.

"You want to draw me in." That was her fear, her certainty. "Whatever Wyatt thinks he can use me for, you want to convince me to allow."

The knowledge of that hurt.

It ached deep inside her but did nothing to change the power of the arousal building between her thighs.

"Is that what you really think?" Anger colored his tone as his head lifted, the blue in his eyes brighter, nearly overtaking the black as he glared down at her.

The anger couldn't overshadow the hunger in his gaze. It was there: clear, bright and unapologetic.

"Don't do this to me, Stygian," she whispered rather than answering the question. "Don't destroy my life."

"I could complete it."

But something warned her that completing it could also destroy it, and that destruction terrified a dark, hidden core of her that she rarely allowed herself to dwell upon.

She was certain she would have had an argument, that she could have come up with one if the elevator hadn't given a small jerk and resumed its journey downward.

Her feet were settling on the floor and Stygian stepping back from her as the doors slid open to the hotel lobby. A half dozen Breeds were waiting to step inside.

They moved back, their expressions inscrutable, gazes shuttered as they flicked between her and Stygian.

"Excuse me." Ducking her head, Liza rushed from the elevator and headed for the exit.

"Slow down," Stygian murmured as he came to her side, keeping pace with her as he placed his palm at the middle of her bare back.

"Why?" Pushing through the doors and striding to the side of the entrance patio, she turned in frustration as she planted her hands on her hips and confronted him. "Why should I? They all knew," she bit out between clenched teeth. "They all knew we were—" Her lips clamped shut.

Stygian's lips quirked into a half smile of pure male appreciation as he stared down at her.

"That we wanted each other? Honey, it wouldn't take Breed senses to figure that out when those doors opened. Anyone with a knowledge of lust would have known it in a microsecond."

Just what she needed. A reaction to a man that anyone could see in a microsecond.

"Take me home, now." She had to get away from him.

Oh God, had the link been active?

She hadn't heard it disconnect after it had reactivated in the suite, seconds after the mass of Breeds had moved away from her.

She didn't need this.

Raking the fringes of hair that had fallen forward across her face, she turned and stared around the entrance to the hotel.

"Do you have a ride here, or am I walking?" Turning back to him, she swore she could feel the caress of his gaze as it touched her breasts before sliding slowly back to her face.

"We have a ride." He shrugged before lifting his hand, never taking his eyes off her, and giving a quick backward wave of his fingers.

She couldn't tear her gaze from his.

She didn't want to.

As his hand lowered, Liza realized there was something unsettling, yet something so secure in the depths of those black-and-blue eyes.

She was all too aware of the vehicle moving up beside them though and coming to a slow stop.

"Our ride." Opening the back passenger door, he watched her expectantly.

The SUV was all luxury: black, pure leather seats and a gentle rush of cool air.

Taking the hand he extended her, Liza stepped into the vehicle, settled into the seat and gave a small flinch as the door closed gently.

A second later Stygian was sliding into the front passenger seat and giving the dark Breed behind the wheel the order to drive.

There was something almost surreal about the ride.

Sitting in the leather comfort of the luxurious vehicle, Liza closed her eyes and tried to tell herself this was going to work out. Everything was going to be okay.

Her assurances were quickly wiped away by another flash of an image.

A limo, the seats luxurious and soft, the couple sitting across from her grief-stricken.

The older woman held her hand: her incredibly small, pale, childlike hand.

Liza jerked her eyes open, her head turning to stare through the dark window as the vehicle made its way toward her home.

What was she seeing, and where were those images, those memories, coming from? Why were they suddenly flashing through her head?

What was happening to her?

✦   ✦   ✦

Gideon watched.

He was an excellent watcher.

It was one of the things he had been trained to do as a child, but it was also an inherent part of his genetics.

Concealed in the upper thickly needled branches of a towering fir tree, he watched the suite Jonas and his family resided in.

They'd found most of the bugs he'd had put in place. Getting them into the room to begin with had been a pure bitch.

There were two left.

One was concealed in the electronics of the video and television screen—thank goodness, he could still see and hear most of what went on—and one in the connecting living suite.

That one, he refused to engage just yet. The babe was there. The babe and her mother, and during this phase of the serum's effect on her little body . . . his lips tightened.

He couldn't bear to hear her pain.

There were too many memories there.

Too many dark images of another child who stared up at him, tears in her eyes as she valiantly fought to be brave.

He didn't blink.

His eyes didn't fill with tears.

But his throat tightened with an emotion that came only when those dark memories intruded once again. Emotions he refused to let in again, regrets he refused to revisit.

"Her shadows have evaporated. Their location was deserted by the time our teams arrived."

Gideon wasn't certain of the face that went with the voice. He didn't dare risk activating the video portion of the bug at the moment.

"Then we have no idea who they are, or what she's a part of," Jonas growled.

"Not yet," the Breed answered. "We're working on it."

"Let me know the minute you have news," Jonas ordered.

A second later, the sound of a door closing was heard then silence filled the room.

Gideon risked checking the vid-device strapped on his wrist then.

The picture came through: the image of Jonas standing at the glass sliding doors, his back to the vid-screen, hands propped arrogantly on his hips.

He was a worthy if challenging adversary.

There were days Gideon wondered . . .

Jonas turned, his gaze centering on the screen as his lips quirked.

"Fucking Peeping Tom," he said, his tone icy. "Come out, Gideon, I dare you."

Deactivating the monitor, Gideon grimaced.

Hell, he hadn't expected that.

Somehow, Jonas had known that bug was there.

Gideon couldn't trust any of the information he'd gained in the past few hours now. Not that much had really come through.

Liza Johnson knew nothing, and the Alphas of the Breed communities were all in one location.

Not a fucking sliver of information was worth using now.

It was almost amusing.

He had been butting heads with Jonas Wyatt in one way or another for two years now. They were pretty even actually, when it came to wins and losses against each other.

He thought Jonas might see it another way.

Gideon had information Jonas wanted, information he thought he needed.

Gideon could tell him there was nothing anyone knew—even Honor and Fawn and Judd—that could help him.

Brandenmore had injected the child, there was no doubt about that. The little girl Jonas had taken as his own had become an experiment and had never stepped into a lab.

"Come on, Gideon." The audio link was still activated. "I know you still have a link in here. Face me. Face me with what you have and I'll help you with what you need."

Gideon deactivated the link.

He didn't want to hear the dares, the challenges or the child's whimpering cries.

Jonas Wyatt had nothing he wanted—

Yet.

Maneuvering the classic Harley through the crowded parking lot of the Desert Rose, Stygian let a grimace twist his lips at the thought of entering the building.

He was a solitary sort of Breed. He had rarely worked with more than a four-man team until joining the Bureau of Breed Affairs.

He didn't like crowds and he didn't like the press of dozens or more human bodies bearing down on him, as they seemed to do in nightclubs and bars.

But tonight, Liza was in there.

His mate.

Son of a bitch, he hadn't expected to find his mate in this sunbaked land.

Hell, he hadn't expected to find his mate at all, actually.

Parking the Harley and engaging the anti-theft security, he stepped from the motorcycle, all too aware of the gazes locked on him.

Customers had spilled from the bar, some to socialize, a few to make their way to their vehicles, while two couples in the shadows had been making out with heated lust. Hell, if he had Liza stretched out in the back of a pickup, the last thing he'd have on his mind was some mangy Breed who had just pulled in.

Pushing back the long strands of hair that had fallen over his forehead, he made his way to the entrance and stepped inside. Narrowing his gaze, he searched the interior until he found her.

A growl rumbled in his throat at the sight of the four men she was sitting with.

Deputy Cullen Maverick, a former Special Forces demolitions expert; Steven Jacobs and his brother, a communications expert on the same team, Reever Jacobs. Next to them was a man even the Breeds hadn't managed to pull information up on yet. The one they had all agreed had to be the Bengal Judd, Klah Hunter.

He'd shown up nine years before in Window Rock and survived doing odd jobs. He never stayed at one job long, and he had never made many friends outside the Jacobs brothers and the deputy.

Claire and Chelsea Martinez each sat on one side of Liza, and all seven of the group were leaning in close and talking low.

Stygian had noticed, though, that Klah Hunter's gaze had locked on him the minute he stepped into the bar.

Moving across the room, Stygian watched as they all straightened and Liza's head slowly turned toward him.

Long strands of what he knew had to be living silk, dark blond, highlighted and streaked, her hair flowed over her shoulder and fell across the thin navy blue silk material covering her breasts.

She'd come to the bar straight from the office. The slim white skirt and dark blue silk blouse looked as damned sexy now as it had when he'd watched her leave the house that morning.

As he neared their table, the four men watched him warily.

Stygian grabbed a chair, flipped it around and angled it in beside Liza.

Pure dislike entered several of the men's gazes.

Straddling the chair, he leaned against the back and met each of their gazes firmly.

"What are you doing here?" Liza hissed as the silence around the table became distinctly uncomfortable.

"Even Breeds enjoy a cold beer every now and then." He let a grin touch his lips as the perfect arch of her brows lowered in a fierce frown.

"I bet they do." Chelsea's grin was filled with teasing enjoyment as she sat back and glanced between him and Liza. "According to Malachi, they enjoy messing with our heads even more."

Stygian had to chuckle. Chelsea Martinez wasn't one to keep her smart-ass thoughts to herself, or to sugarcoat much.

"That's always an enjoyable exercise," he agreed with a quick grin as he caught Liza's frown turning to a glare in his periphery. "Though, to be honest, I much prefer a more straightforward approach."

"Oh, really?" Liza muttered. "And how do you manage that? I thought Breeds were allergic to honesty."

He could see how she might feel that way after her meeting with Jonas two days before.

"Not so much allergic as merely wary." Leaning his arms against the top rail of the seatback, he turned his head to her, ensuring she glimpsed the arousal raging inside him.

Two days.

He'd managed to keep his distance for two miserably long days, and he'd had enough.

She was his.

His mate.

She would be his woman.

His world and his life.

If he could convince her to take that chance.

Well, if he could manage to steal a kiss from those sweet lips.

It might have been easier if he wasn't aware of the fact that Isabelle Martinez, mate to Malachi Morgan, had already warned her friends of the mating phenomena.

"You're not wanted here, Breed." Klah Hunter kept his voice low, but his tone was nothing if not dominant and filled with warning.

Stygian didn't bother to even glance his way.

"Dance with me." Staring into Liza's eyes, he knew if he

didn't have her against him soon, he was likely to end up in a fight instead.

"If she wanted to dance with you, then she would have invited you," Klah snapped. "This is a get-together for friends only, Breed. You're in no position to apply for the title."

"I'm not applying for the position of friend," he assured the other man—Breed?

He didn't bother to explain the position he was after. Hell, he wasn't picky at this point. He'd take missionary if that was all she was offering.

Though, he was partial to doggie style.

He was certain that wasn't exactly the sort of position any of them had in mind, though.

"What exactly do you have in mind then?" Cullen Maverick spoke up as he leaned back in his chair and lifted the frosted bottle of beer to his lips. "Or should I just go ahead and kill you for thinking you can have more than Liza might want to give?"

"Whoa, enough." Liza turned on them all then. "I don't need bodyguards nor do I need anyone to defend my honor."

The four men turned as one to frown back at her.

The air of sudden male dominance had a snarl threatening to pull at Stygian's lips.

His woman.

His mate.

He'd never allow another male to order her to do anything. Especially anything in direct opposition to what *he* wanted.

"They're not telling us the truth in regards to why they're here, Liza, you know that as well as the rest of us do," Klah argued. "He has no business around you."

"Maybe he has other things in mind." Chelsea grinned then. "Things that are none of your business, Klah."

Liza's chair scraped back from the table, a hint of fear and nervousness suddenly scenting the air around her.

"Let's dance then," she muttered as he rose to his feet beside her. "Instead of starting the fight you seem intent on."

"Me?" He almost laughed as she grabbed his wrist. He

allowed her to give the impression that she was pulling him to the dance floor. "That was your friends, baby, not me."

The fast, hard beat of the country-western music faded away and as they stepped to the dance floor, the band eased into a slow, sensual tune instead.

He caught the little muttered curse as it slipped free of her glossy lips and couldn't hold back a low chuckle as he took her into his arms.

"How did you know I was here?" she asked. Her small hands pressed against his chest almost defensively.

The fact that she felt she would have to protect herself against him, her mate, had him tensing in regret.

Her fingertips were rubbing against the fine cotton of his shirt though, making him wonder if she was searching for the warmth of his chest. That gesture, small though it was, gave him hope that perhaps a part of her knew she could trust him.

"I make it my business to know where you are. And who you're with."

Tightening his arm around her back, he brought her closer, luxuriating in the sweet response of her body, the heavy throb of life in the vein at her throat and the hunger he could scent building in her slight body.

The need to cover her, to push inside the liquid heat of her pussy was going to make him crazy.

"Why do you make it your business?" Confusion filled her now. "I'm nothing to you, Mr. Black."

Oh, how wrong she was.

Stygian stared into the gray of her eyes and sensed something more than the bravado she was fighting so hard to bolster as he held her against him.

"Perhaps I'd like for that to change."

Liza stared up at the Breed, feeling their bodies swaying in perfect accord, before she was even aware that she was moving in time to his much larger body.

She couldn't believe he'd just said that. That he'd made his intentions so clear, so quickly.

"And if that's not what I want?"

"I would find that very hard to believe," he retorted. "As

you said as we left the hotel, it would be impossible to miss the fact that you are very interested."

"Oh God, I hate Breeds and their sense of smell." She had to tear her eyes from his, but she couldn't force her body away from him.

"Come out with me tonight." It was more a demand than a request. "We could just ride around awhile. Maybe find a nice place to stop and talk."

Her lips parted to refuse. She couldn't afford to become involved with him.

Not with him or any other man.

"I brought the motorcycle." His head lowered, his lips at her ear, the warmth of his breath teasing the sensitive flesh. "The wind in your hair. The night surrounding us."

"Danger stalking us? A Breed who's obviously searching for a ghost and believes I could lead him to her?" she asked, incredulous. "How intelligent does that sound?"

"Do you think I wouldn't protect you? That where I took you I would allow you to be in any danger?"

"Control the world that easily, do you?" She snorted. "Besides, I'm not exactly dressed for a motorcycle ride."

But he could feel the desire inside her to go with him. To take that chance.

"Talk to Chelsea, have her exchange clothing with you," he suggested. "Come on, Liza, be brave," he dared her.

He sensed her need to do just that, to step outside of herself. The animal inside him could feel that need.

That dark, inner core of a woman so locked down, so hidden inside her subconscious that he wondered if even she was aware of it.

"Why me?" The question was whispered against his ear as he bent closer to her, nuzzling her hair from her neck as he moved her around the dance floor.

"Why you?" The rumble of the growl was involuntary at the slender column of her neck as he spoke. "Because I've been so hard for you, and only you, for the past two days, that I swear my dick is going to permanently have the imprint of my jeans zipper."

Her breath caught.

Liza felt the overwhelming need to push her own boundaries, to ask Chelsea to change clothes with her, to slip onto the back of his motorcycle and escape into the night with him.

"I want you, Liza," he said. "My lips on yours, slow and easy, then deeper. Harder. I want to lick your lips, taste them. Then, I want to taste the rest of you. Every inch of your sweet body."

Every inch?

Her thighs clenched, her clit swelling, moisture gathering between the folds of her pussy at the thought of him touching her—tasting her—there.

"I can't do this." She didn't know if she could allow herself to take what he was offering. The implications of the cost could well be more than she could bear.

She could sense it. Deep, deep inside herself she could sense the knowledge that by allowing Stygian to take her, she would be destroying herself in ways she never wanted to face.

"No." The music eased away as she suddenly pulled from his arms, forcing herself away from him as she gave her head a hard shake. "I can't do this. I just can't—"

Catching her arm as she turned away from him, Liza found herself facing a full-grown, dominant, lust-driven Breed intent on having the woman who dared arouse him in such a way.

"This isn't good-bye," he assured her. "We're not finished. I came here to spend the evening with you, Liza. And I mean to do just that."

As a fast tune began blaring from the band, Stygian shot the singer a hard glare before leading Liza from the dance floor. The fact that he wasn't pleased with the music was more than apparent.

The fact that he wanted her was even more apparent.

Malachi had warned her that a Breed, once certain that the woman he wanted was as drawn to him, could only be turned away if he knew the object of his lust, his affection, or whatever they called it, if her objections were stronger than her need.

Breeds didn't force the sexual aspects, they didn't stalk, nor did they harass. They charmed, cajoled and teased. They built the hunger and the need until their potential lovers fell willingly into their arms.

He'd been a fount of information after he and Isabelle had become lovers.

Or mates.

A tremble of trepidation skated across her nerve endings as he led her back to the table where her friends waited.

The plans she and the team were discussing before his arrival would have to wait. Stygian was on the prowl and he'd found his prey. He wouldn't be walking away anytime soon.

The problems inherent in such a decision on his part had her stomach tightening with dread. The team had already lost Isabelle due to her relationship with Malachi and her vow to never reveal what she had been a part of to anyone, especially a lover or husband outside the network.

The fact that Malachi was outside the network and not approved to be privy to that information had hurt them all. It was a decision no one on the team could make though, and permission had yet to be offered.

As they reached the table, Liza made her next decision quickly without taking the time to consider the repercussions of it.

"I'm going home," she told them, feeling Stygian stiffen beside her.

Cullen, Steven, Reever and Klah all turned accusing stares on Stygian.

"Yeah, I think I'll head back too." Chelsea rose to her feet and pulled her purse from the floor. "Are you riding with me?" She looked up at Stygian with a grin. "Or with him?"

"You." Jerking her light blazer from the back of her chair, she thanked God Chelsea had made her own quick decision.

"Then I guess I'm heading back too, because I came with them." Claire joined them, moving from her chair and collecting her purse and light jacket. She too was dressed in the

clothes she'd worn to work that morning: a light cotton
blouse and slim, sedate skirt.

God was smiling on Liza.

"We'll follow you home." Steven nodded and the four
men rose as well.

Beside her, she swore Stygian chuckled.

She was certain of it as his head lowered. "Very, very
good," he murmured at her ear. "You surprised me."

It sounded as though he was rarely surprised.

"Good night, Mr. Black," she said.

"Good night, Ms. Johnson." Nodding, he stepped back
and seconds later disappeared into the press of bodies as he
made his way to the exit.

"This isn't good," Klah stated softly.

Liza glanced at the dark Navajo, seeing the nearly black
eyes and the anger burning within.

Klah was their logistics and planning guru. There were
times when his instincts were so strong that the other members of the team swore he was psychic.

"But perhaps not bad." She shrugged. "He can't know
anything either way. He's just—" She trailed off, shaking
her head.

"Just horny?" Chelsea suggested teasingly. "Honey, that
Breed is damned interested and damned certain you're just
as hot for him."

"She's not," Klah snapped as he and the other men surrounded them as they began moving for the exit themselves.

"Reever, take first watch on the girls' house," Cullen
ordered, ignoring Klah's exclamation. "Steven, you have
second, and Klah will take third. I have duty the next three
days, but I can pull members of the other teams in the area
to cover them until this situation is resolved."

"That could be why someone seems to be stalking us,"
Liza suggested as they left the club. "Someone could be
using the Breeds' presence here to draw out as many members as possible and get information on the network rather
than anything else."

"That's always possible," Cullen agreed. "But I'd rather ensure your, Claire's and Chelsea's safety."

"Don't pull from the network," Liza suggested. "We have enough friends who are members of the military or law enforcement who could fill in. I'd rather not risk the identities of the teams involved in relocation. We're the only team not involved in that phase."

And team members rarely had the identities of other team members. It was a safeguard, a precaution in case one was caught. Or in case a member became greedy and decided to sell information to the Genetics Council.

It had happened only once in all the decades of the Navajo Underground Network. But if it had happened once, it could happen again.

"We'll see what we can do," Cullen answered without giving an indication of whether he agreed or not.

It wasn't that he didn't trust her opinion, she told herself. She, Claire and Chelsea were junior members of the group, and in ways, still in training.

As they reached the car, Liza gave in to curiosity and glanced around the parking lot. She couldn't see Stygian, but she was certain he was there. He wasn't a man—a Breed—who would give up easily.

"All these hot and handsome Breeds are going to make me start wishing one would go nuts on me now." Chelsea was laughing despite the declaration as she pulled her small sedan out onto the highway and headed back to Window Rock.

The night closed around them, and as Liza opened the passenger-side window, she couldn't help but wish the wind was whipping around her as she rode behind Stygian on that motorcycle he had claimed to be riding.

And no doubt he had. He was big enough, strong enough, bold enough to risk life and limb on a hot desert night and a highway that could hold any number of surprises.

"Thank God it's Friday." Claire sighed wearily. "This hasn't been a week I'd want to repeat."

The planning and implementation of several assignments

designed to draw in at least one of the shadows watching them had been an exercise in futility.

Until the morning Liza had taken her run, they had been certain they wouldn't have to deal with the Bureau of Breed Affairs's enforcers. Liza, along with the others, had been certain that capturing one of the forces tracking her would be a piece of cake.

Only they had watched that prized cake squashed into nothingness as Liza became immersed in a sensual battle with one of the most powerful Breeds. And he didn't appear to be the sort to give up easily.

Or to do anything easily.

He would take her as he lived, she thought. Confidently, powerfully. He would hold her with those strong, broad hands, kiss her into senseless submission with lips that mesmerized her, and invade not just her body, but her heart as well.

"Did you hear me, Liza?" Chelsea complained as Liza fought to bring herself back from that place where Stygian's arms enfolded her and his kiss heated her.

After all, she had been pretty cold lately, she thought wearily.

"No, I'm sorry, Chelsea, I was thinking of something else," she answered her friend as she pushed back the images of her and Stygian together.

"Or someone else," Chelsea smirked from the seat beside her. "That Breed, no doubt."

"He's arrogant," Liza accused.

"He's fucking hot." Chelsea laughed.

"He's too dominant," Liza tried again.

"Yeah well, he could tie me to the bed and spank my ass any day he wants," Chelsea proclaimed. "Damn, Liza, I know you're not going to turn down that chance to have the most incredible sexual adventure of a lifetime. You know, Wolf Breeds' cocks are supposed to be twice as thick as any human man's. And you know what we've heard they do."

"And Isabelle won't say either way if her Coyote does that Coyote Breed thing when he comes," Claire piped in.

"Do you think their cocks really swell larger when they ejaculate, locking them inside a woman?"

"The fact that Isabelle refuses to say is a pretty good indication." Chelsea sighed as though in anticipation. "No wonder they have such female groupies. I think I want to join the club."

"Chelsea, you ignore the Breeds who do offer," Claire pointed out as Liza felt her mouth go dry at the thought of being so exquisitely stretched and pleasured at the height of release.

"So do you," Chelsea pointed out. "It's not as though I'm the only one."

"Then why are we telling Liza to take her Breed up on it?" Claire asked, clearly becoming more amused by the moment.

"Well, just because it beats me having to deal with those bossy creatures." Chelsea laughed.

Grimacing, Liza watched the darkened scenery as they made their way to the outskirts of Window Rock, following Cullen's Super Cab pickup as he rode with Reever. Klah and Steven rode behind them in Klah's Land Rover.

Pulling into the driveway of the house, Liza restrained her sigh of relief before she and her housemates slid from the car. After Isabelle moved out to be with Malachi, their cousin Claire had decided to move in with them.

Of course, the men had to come in and check the house from one end to the other.

Liza wondered if they would do that for each other? She rather doubted it.

Actually, she knew they wouldn't. Hell, someone had broken into Klah's house the week the Breeds arrived and he hadn't even called anyone until after he'd checked everything out himself.

But there was no telling them that she, Claire and Chelsea could take care of themselves. They refused to hear it.

Did they actually believe she would lie?

When the search was completed and their good-byes were said, the four men finally left.

As the door closed behind them, Liza locked it with a snap then turned, crossed her arms beneath her breasts once again and faced her still-silent friends.

"Well?" she demanded when they said nothing.

Claire moved into the living room and turned on the television. She increased the volume enough that once they moved into the kitchen, nothing they said could be heard over the din of the television.

"I didn't say anything about this in the car, but don't you remember what Isabelle said about mating while she was in the hospital?" Claire warned her somberly. "Did you let him kiss you while you two were on the dance floor?"

Liza's gaze widened at the memory of what Isabelle had claimed a Breed's kisses could do to a woman. "It had to be the drugs they had her on. Remember, she had a reaction to them?"

Isabelle had been half out of her mind from the pain after her near abduction by Holden Mayhew. Surely her warning that a Breed's kiss was addictive and to watch out for mating had to be some far-fetched dementia caused by the drugs and amplified by her affection for her own Breed.

"Liza, she wasn't joking," Claire assured her, her gaze searching as she moved nearer.

Chelsea moved in just as close, listening in rapt attention.

"You can't be sure of that, Claire." Liza shook her head decisively. "There's no proof."

Claire swallowed tightly and spoke before Chelsea could. "Not proof, exactly. But remember when those Breed doctors arrived and took over her care?"

Liza nodded, as did Chelsea.

"I heard them talking when I slipped outside for some air. One of the doctors told the other that they didn't like her reaction to the drugs while she was in mating heat and that the mating hormone was reacting strangely."

Liza stared back at the other woman in disbelief.

"And you're just now telling us this?" Chelsea hissed in disbelief. "Claire, how could you keep this from us? It's been nearly a month. We could have kissed dozens of Breeds by now."

Liza swung her head to the other girl, staring at her in surprise. "Dozens?" She blinked back at Chelsea uncertainly. "Sorry, girlfriend, I'm not exactly a teenager any longer. I don't think I kissed that many boys even when I *was* a teenager. Hell, I haven't kissed that many in my entire life."

"I was being facetious." Chelsea sighed. "You know what I meant."

Claire bit her lip indecisively before drawing in a deep breath. "I thought I had to have misunderstood something, and I knew Malachi would never hurt her." She lifted her hands in indecision. "But tonight, I knew I had to tell both of you when I saw how Liza was reacting to Mr. Black." Her eyes widened a bit, the hazel depths filled with concern. "I'm still not certain I didn't misunderstand something. I mean really, we were all in shock. And terrified. I could have misunderstood the entire conversation."

Liza blew out a hard breath. "Wow," she said in disbelief. "Those tabloid stories are true then."

It was inconceivable. Yet no matter how much she wished she could brush away Claire's information, she knew she couldn't.

Isabelle's reaction to Malachi Morgan had been much too intense to be considered normal, and Liza as well as Chelsea and Claire had known it.

But that was Claire. She kept to herself, and she kept others' secrets very well. Her friends had always worried about that deep well of reserve she possessed and the quiet nature that often allowed others to run roughshod over her unless her friends put a stop to it.

"Damn, if those tabloid stories are true," Chelsea hissed, "then it makes them like, fuck machines hyped on natural steroids." She swallowed tightly, her expression almost glazed with wonder. "It would be like—"

"That's enough, Chel." Liza held her hand up quickly. "Enough with the adjectives, okay?"

The "fuck machine on steroids" was enough to make Liza's body hum with amplified interest. She didn't even need to hear anything more to assure her that allowing

Stygian Black in her bed would definitely ruin her for any other man or Breed. For life. Period.

"But it's only when they do that mating thing," Claire reminded them. "That's what the tabloids said, and from what those two doctors were saying, that's true. Wolves only have one mate for life in the wild, right? It makes sense that Wolf Breeds would follow that course. Lions as well—"

"But Tigers, Coyotes and all those other wonderful species do not," Chelsea assured her.

"Then it's a quirk of nature or their creation." Chelsea shrugged. "Whatever it is, it's something they're obviously desperate to hide, otherwise the Breed scientists would have leaked it to the world themselves long ago."

"Maybe." Liza sighed.

She was going to overheat for sure. Liza could feel her body burning like an inferno at the thought of having a man, hell, a Breed, who belonged to her and her alone.

"Talk about having a license to be an asshole." Chelsea gave a low whistle as she stared back at Liza. "Hell, normal men are a pain in the ass. But one who knew you couldn't ever allow another man to touch you? A relationship where there's no threat of divorce? An addiction to their kiss that you can't get rid of, no matter how pissed you are, how bloated you feel or how bad your head really doesn't hurt?"

Whoa, talk about a splash of cold water.

"I don't think so," Liza informed them both. "Not in this lifetime."

"How much is true and how much is made up?" Chelsea questioned in disbelief. "How much can you believe? Surely it can't be so bad or Isabelle would have shot Malachi by now. She's no wimpy little miss when it comes to defending herself."

"Fifty-fifty maybe?" Claire suggested.

"No way," Chelsea retorted, shaking her head as she unclipped the rich black strands of her hair from tortoiseshell clips. "I'm going to say at least seventy-five percent has to be pure fiction. That leaves twenty-five percent in their favor. The fuck machines with a kiss that's like an aphrodisiac. I draw a line at addictive. Sorry, girls." She shrugged carelessly. "It's not going to happen for any man in this life-time. It would be far too easy for them to simply rule us. God wouldn't allow it. He does have a sense of humor, you know."

Liza nodded slowly.

Chelsea had to be right.

There were always checks and balances.

No way would nature give Breed males such a one-up on either the Breed or human females they encountered.

"So do we mention any of this to Ashley and the others when they get here tomorrow?" Chelsea asked.

"God, no! They're Breeds!" Liza stared back at her friend, wondering if she had somehow lost her mind. "I love them like crazy, Chelsea, but we don't mention this to any-one. We keep it to ourselves."

The four Breed females Ashley Truing, Emma Truing, Chimera Broussard and Shiloh Gage had been training the girls to be a part of the Navajo-based Breed Underground Network for the past six months.

The underground network was a group of Navajos that aided the Breeds who required complete anonymity and a secure refuge from the Genetics Council. The network aided them in hiding once they managed to escape their labs, shel-tered them, provided medical aid and ensured they found a place to bury who and what they had once been.

"We could find a way to question them, perhaps," Claire suggested. "See if they'll just give us a little hint. All based on the tabloid stories, of course."

Liza shook her head fiercely. "We can't chance they would lie to us, or worse yet, have more loyalty to their own than they do to friendship. We keep this to ourselves and see what happens."

"Does that mean you get to be the first guinea pig?" Chelsea wagged her brows suggestively. "You'll give deets, right? Surely you wouldn't torture us like Isabelle does? She doesn't tell us anything."

"Yeah, I look all furry and stupid." Liza snorted. "It means we watch our asses and forget about kissing one of them. At least for the time being," she amended. She couldn't

deny herself at least the possibility of being able to kiss
Stygian.

At least at a later date.

The other two nodded.

"Malachi is supposed to be in meetings with Wyatt and
the other Alphas in the next few days. We'll be able to talk
to Isabelle without Malachi around then," Chelsea decided.

"Maybe." Liza nibbled on her fingernail nervously. "We'll
have to see."

To which Chelsea straightened her shoulders and stared
back at them with a look that was totally her: pure determined stubbornness. "Oh, trust me, he will. I promise you."
She smiled wickedly. "I'll simply shed a few tears for my
big sister. Bet me she won't run him off to find out what
baby sister's problem is."

"Wicked." Liza breathed out in anticipation.

"Dangerous," Claire warned, despite her awe at Chelsea's
daring.

But they were in agreement.

For the moment, it was wait and see.

And definitely, keep each other in the loop. What one
learned, they had to tell the other two.

It would be the only way to be certain.

◆　◆　◆

Stepping beneath the water, she closed her eyes and, just as
during that meeting with Jonas Wyatt, she was assaulted
with the images from the pictures the director had shown
her.

She saw their eyes, felt their pain, their fear. It would be
hard not to. Those photos had been graphic in their detailed
imagery of the children's suffering.

Stepping back from the spray, she opened her eyes
quickly, unwilling to see more.

Her parents had always told her she felt things too deeply,
that she let things bother her too much. That vulnerability
had caused her to get hurt more than once.

She'd never fallen in love though.

She was a virgin, and she had no idea what it felt like to

want a man so totally and so completely that she was willing to give up her independence as well as her sense of self for him.

She wasn't certain she could do it either. She'd spent far too many years holding herself aloof. She wasn't certain if she could let go now and give herself to any man. And unfortunately, she wasn't certain if she could give him her body without giving him her heart.

Even for a Breed who stared at her with black-blue eyes and an expression that assured her he held all the secrets of pleasure, and he was more than willing to share.

He was more than willing to show her all the sensual, dominant secrets she dreamed of, and all the fiery pleasure she ached for.

For a price.

Always for a price.

Nothing came for free, her mother had warned her.

There was always a price.

A price for laughing, for loving.

A price for living.

Now she wondered, exactly what was Stygian Black's price?

CHAPTER 5

Liza hadn't imagined the situation with Stygian could worsen. Surely she would have had a few days to settle her nerves.

Instead, the next morning he was on her doorstep, dressed in snug jeans and a dark T-shirt, that wicked black Harley parked in her driveway.

She guessed he hadn't been lying the night before about having one. Not that she had really believed he was.

"Why are you here?" Gripping the door with desperate fingers, she stared back at him with a frown.

A grin curved his lips. "I hoped I could convince you to come out with me this morning." He glanced at the white shorts that barely covered her thighs before his gaze drifted to the light peach cotton camisole top she wore. "Come on, Liza. Slide some jeans on and live dangerously for a few minutes. You know you want to."

Oh, she wanted to, more than he could know.

"Not today." Shaking her head, she backed up and prepared to close the door.

The slight smile on his lips shot a surge of sensation straight to her womb. It clenched with a heavy punch of need and sent that weakening spill of moisture between her thighs once again.

"I'm not dealing with you this morning."

Releasing the door, she stalked back into the kitchen, searching desperately for a way to fight her reaction to him.

Turning to face him as she reached the sink, Liza's lips parted breathlessly to find him so close her nose was nearly buried in the cotton of his shirt.

Lifting her eyes, she watched as his arms extended around her, his hands bracing on the cabinet behind her as he blocked her in.

Yeah, there was that dominance that both turned her on and warned her she was walking into the path of more danger than she could have ever imagined.

Her eyes jerked upward, becoming locked with his as his arms remained braced at each side of her, his gaze intent as he watched her closely.

"The scent of your arousal is about to get us both in a hell of a lot of trouble."

Her eyes widened, because he was close enough that she could feel his erection pressing against her stomach. As her gaze dropped, she watched the blood pound in the vein at the side of his neck as a trickle of perspiration eased along the strong column.

She had to lick her lips.

God, she wanted to taste him.

She wanted to bite his neck. Just sink her teeth into that tough hide and hold on tight as he rode her—

A shudder tore up her spine as aching need surged through her core. Her juices spilled, coating the suddenly sensitive folds and heating her clit further.

"Do you know what I can smell, Liza?" The sound of his voice was definitely a growl.

She shook her head slowly.

His head lowered until his lips were caressing her ear. "If the scent of summer heat was addictive, I'd be worshipping at your pussy for life."

She jerked away from him, breaking from his hold with an ease that assured her he had simply let her go.

Staring up at him, Liza told herself she was certainly

insulted at the crude language, though she couldn't make such an asinine statement pass her lips.

"I refuse to become a summer fuck for you," she informed him, wondering exactly how much trouble that particular falsehood would get her into if she ever had to face her sins. "So you may as well leave now and stop harassing me. I assure you, I'm not enjoying it."

He chuckled at the so-obvious lie. And she knew he could sense it as easily as he could sense the building arousal coursing through her body.

"You're as beautiful lying as you are telling the truth," he told her, amused. "But, in this case, I could definitely satisfy the truth if you were of a mind to face it."

Liza tugged at the hem of her blouse before crossing her arms beneath her breasts and attempting to glare at him.

"This is not a complication that I need in my life," she finally told him as she tried to inject some semblance of determination into her tone. "*You* are not a complication I need in my life."

"Thankfully, life enjoys throwing us a few curveballs then," he stated, a hint of laughter urging her to meet his gaze once again. "Because I think I'm definitely enjoying the complication I know you're going to be. Come on, Liza, give me a try. You might enjoy me. It's just a ride on the back of my motorcycle. Nothing more."

At least he hadn't come right out and asked her to ride *him*.

She didn't dare allow herself to consider that. She was too weak in the face of his flirting, in the certainty that he would rock her little world.

There was nothing more certain to undermine her determination than allowing herself to admit any weakness at all to him. He was a Breed, and she was certain all that Breed-driven testosterone and dominance would be sure to test her will.

From what she'd seen between her friend Isabelle and her new lover, Malachi, Breeds enjoyed nothing better than pushing the women they called their "mates" into fits of anger or arousal.

As though it were some prerogative they had invented themselves.

"I don't need this particular curveball either," she assured him as she moved to leave the kitchen.

Instead, she found her arm gripped by his big hand as she was swung around and once again pressed against the cabinet.

Held there, captured between his hard body and the wood cabinet behind her, there was really no true escape.

No escape from him, or from the arousal burning through her vagina and clenching her womb.

"This curveball is going to be unavoidable," he assured her as she stared up at him, feeling the blood rushing to her nipples, her clitoris, and then surging in excitement back to her overworked heart.

"Few things are unavoidable, Stygian," she assured him, thought it was all she could do to keep her tone even and confident.

The even part, she was a little weak on. Come to think of it, she might have been a little lax in the confidence department as well. She was getting really good at the resigned part, though.

Resigned to the fact that the need was growing.

Resigned to the fact that there was no avoiding it.

Hell, resigned to the fact that soon, very soon, she would be begging him to fuck her.

Watching, her heart racing, her breathing uneven, Liza parted her lips as his head lowered, his lips almost touching hers, so close she swore she could feel the warmth of them caressing her softer curves.

"I don't want your kiss until I'm certain the sheer anticipation of it will make me crazy."

"Breeds are already crazy," she promised him, her voice weak enough now that she was mentally cursing herself for it. "So don't try to blame that one on me. And you can just keep anticipating, because I'm rather inclined to keep my kisses to myself."

Yet she was tilting her head to the side to give him greater access to the lobe of her ear as she felt his lips brush against it.

"You don't know what you're tempting." The rough, primal sound of his voice had her heart skipping a beat before racing double time.

"Let me go and it won't be a problem," she promised him, even though she knew from the bottom of her soul that the last thing she wanted was for him to release her.

The last thing she should do was remain there in his arms—not when she wanted his touch like she had wanted nothing in her life.

And that thought, so shocking, so terrifying, had her forcing her hands to push at him rather than simply absorbing the heat through his shirt, into her flesh.

"Letting you go isn't so easy, Liza." His lips moved lower, brushing against her neck, intensifying that arc of sizzling sensation from her neck straight to her nipples, then to her clit.

Liza forced herself to drag in a deep breath, only to find her senses infused with the scent of midnight and forests. And there wasn't a single damned forest anywhere close. Which meant it was the scent of the Breed holding her that was tempting her with the lush, sensual scent.

"Make it easy." Forcing the words to her lips was harder than she had ever imagined it would be. "Let me go, Stygian, because this isn't what I want."

He stiffened against her.

Oh God, if he didn't listen to her soon, she was going to be begging him to kiss her, to touch her, to fuck her right there against the kitchen cabinet where her friends could walk in at any moment.

"Liza, there's a strange cycle in the driveway. Do you think it's—Oh—" Chelsea's voice dwindled to nothing as Liza jumped in guilt and tried, once again unsuccessfully, to push Stygian's broad form away from her.

Her head turned, catching her friend's shocked expression as she stood frozen in the patio doorway. It was as though she was unable to tear her gaze from the sight of Liza held so close to Stygian's much larger body.

"Close your mouth, Chelsea," Liza ordered irritably as she pushed at Stygian again. "He'll let me go or I'm going to see how much damage I can do when I start driving my knee into certain parts of his body." She shot him a decidedly threatening look with a tight smile as she tensed her knee in preparation.

His lashes lowered again, that wicked "fuck you" look spearing straight to her core and clenching her womb in an exquisite need that nearly stole her breath.

She was going to leave with him. Liza knew she was.

She was simply too weak, and she wanted to be close to him, wanted to tempt her own destruction too desperately.

Emotional suicide.

That was what it was, emotional suicide, and she was helpless against the voice whispering inside herself to just go for it. To take it. To tempt fate. To tempt destruction.

To tempt a Breed.

"I'm going out for the morning, Chel," she told her friend as her gaze locked with Stygian's once again. "I'll have my phone on me if you need me."

If Cullen called and plans changed or if Ashley, Emma, Chimera and Shiloh decided to arrive earlier than normal.

But would either of those things really matter?

Because it was the job of the Navajo Breed Underground Network to find her first, and to offer her asylum.

That was her job, and if this Breed had information about how to find the two women and the Bengal Breed they were searching for, then perhaps it would help her to find them first.

"You're going with him?" Wide-eyed and a little too amused to suit her, Chelsea asked the question with artful innocence. "On the back of a motorcycle?"

Yeah, Liza could clearly understand her friend's confusion. Liza had always refused to ride in even a convertible because of the accident she'd been in as a teenager.

She'd almost been a wild child, she and Claire both. The first time they had slipped out and taken Joe Martinez's car for a joy ride had been their last, though. Being a wild child was stopped short when Claire lost control of the car and went careening over a desert cliff, nearly killing both of them.

A motorcycle had always been out of the question.

Until Stygian.

"I'll change clothes." Giving him one last look, Liza turned and left the room, wondering rather desperately if she had somehow lost her mind.

Stygian watched her go, a smile wanting to tug at his lips as Chelsea eyed him warily.

He could sense the questions she wanted to ask, and he sensed her hesitation.

"Liza doesn't ride motorcycles." Propping her hand on her hip, she frowned up at him.

"It appears she's in an adventurous mood today then." He could sense that about her, her need to reach out and do more, to live dangerously.

There was a courage inside her that she didn't allow the world to see. The only ones who saw it were the team she worked with in the Navajo Underground.

He knew of the Underground. Jonas knew of the Underground.

The organization had, and on occasion still did, rescue Breeds from high-level Genetics Council labs and advanced security experimental facilities for more than a century now.

That was about the extent of the information they had. Despite the Breeds the Bureau had in place to investigate the organization and identify its members, so far the only suspected member was Liza. And only because it had been painfully obvious that she was doing more than taking a nice little run when John Malcolm had moved in on her.

"She's not in an adventurous mood," Chelsea shrugged as she leaned against the door frame. "You're bewitching her, just like Malachi Morgan did with my sister. Breeds should be shot for stealing a woman's will and common sense as you do."

That was pretty much why the Alphas refused to verify the tabloid rumors of mating heat.

That was exactly how it would be seen—as a form of rape or mesmerism.

"And does your sister believe she's been bewitched?" Arching his brow, he kept his tone tinged with amusement.

"Her sister believes in happily-ever-after and the man she's in love with." It was Liza who answered his question as she stepped from her bedroom.

She was dressed in jeans that cupped and loved her delectable ass while giving her a leggy, exotic look. The white cotton top was sleeveless, tiny straps holding it in place, and he was betting the bra she wore beneath was strapless.

She was wearing one, as much as he hated the thought of it. He could see just the faintest outline of it beneath the material of her blouse.

"Then there you go," he commented to the answer she gave to the question he had asked Chelsea. "All's well, because I know for a fact Malachi is dedicated to Isabelle."

"And isn't that so unusual as to be unbelievable." Chelsea snorted. "Breeds are the ultimate bad boys, and we all know the ultimate bad boys really can't be tamed."

Arching his brow, Stygian turned back to Liza. "Are you ready?"

"Where exactly are you taking her?" Chelsea demanded then. "That way, I know where to send the search party to find her dead body when she doesn't return home."

Scratching at the side of his jaw, he momentarily debated assuring her that Liza was in zero danger. Chelsea though, was in definite danger of being gagged.

"Come on, Chelsea," Liza chastised her gently. "I don't think Mr. Black's going to allow anything to happen to me." Smiling back at him, he almost winced at the look in her eyes. "After all, his boss is far too interested in all that lovely information he refuses to accept that I don't have."

Yep, he knew it was coming, he just wasn't certain which form the smart-ass remark would be in.

Now he knew.

"Exactly." Shooting Liza, then Chelsea, a tight smile, he agreed with her mockingly. "If it wasn't for that, I'd have nothing but murderous intentions."

His intentions might not be pure, but the last thing she had to worry about was coming to harm in his bed.

"I'd like to know where we're going, though," Liza

informed him as she shoved a few bills and her ID in the back pocket of her jeans.

He could have sworn they were snug enough that even a breath of air wouldn't have fit.

"I thought we'd take a ride out by the lake," he told her. "I go out there every few days to feed the ducks." That, and to investigate the area several miles to the west where Liza and Claire had gone over a barren cliff and nearly died in the resulting accident.

Even twelve years later, Stygian had found evidence of the accident, but he'd also found evidence that something more had gone on during that time.

A sweat lodge had been set up not far from the wreck in the canyon below, though great effort had gone into ensuring all evidence of it was wiped away.

Certain things couldn't be wiped away, though.

The large rocks used in the fire pit had been scattered about the canyon, but even more than a decade later the scars and discoloration of certain herbs used in ritual sweats held to the rock.

Those particular herbs and medicinal roots were such an odd combination, their scent so powerful, even after such time had passed, it had sent a chill racing down Stygian's spine. Confused by it, he'd had Braden bring his empath Megan to the canyon, to help sort it out. The moment she'd picked up the first stone she'd dropped it as though it still held the heat of the fire and refused to advance any farther into the canyon.

"Fine then, you know where we'll be," Liza stated as she turned back to Chelsea.

"Yeah, thankfully, the lake isn't really that hard to drag. When old man Dunkirk fell out of his boat and drowned himself last summer, they even found that bag of bones secured to the bottom. Remember that?" she asked Liza.

And Liza did remember it. The discovery of that bag of bones had literally preceded the nightmares and odd flashes of someone else's memories.

A year's worth of tortured dreams, of waking, screaming, certain she was dying in the flames of the crash, only to have the dream twist, to morph into something far more sinister. It hadn't been a crash she was burning within. She had been burning from the inside out, restrained to a metal table, screaming for mercy—

"If you're ready, we can leave then," he offered, those blue-black eyes seeming to see straight into her soul as he met her gaze.

The urge to wipe her palms along the sides of her jeans was nearly overwhelming.

"Be careful, for God's sake," Chelsea called out as Liza stepped from the house. "The last thing I need to do, Liza, is watch you die again."

Liza flinched, the reaction nearly strong enough to steal her breath at the memory.

The overwhelming darkness, the sound of voices, singing—or was it chanting?—and then the feeling of her soul being ripped from the security of her body.

"Liza." Stygian was there, one hand gripping her arm, the other going around her waist as she felt her knees threatening to buckle.

Concern filled his voice as she realized she was gripping the door frame desperately, dragging in hard breaths, her chest tightening in something akin to panic.

"I'm fine." Giving her head a hard shake, she forced herself to ignore the fact that he was the only reason she was still on her feet, despite her hold on the heavy wood encasing the door.

Releasing it, she took each step with deliberate caution, forcing herself to move to the cycle.

"Are you sure?" Dark, dangerous, his expression appeared more savage than ever before, the planes and angles tightened into sharp relief.

"Bad memories." Yet she still couldn't seem to drag in enough oxygen. "Sorry."

"What was she talking about?" The growl in his voice should have been more frightening than sensual.

Yet, sensual was exactly the reaction it caused.

"She meant I died for a few minutes," she admitted. "Claire and I were in a wreck when we were fifteen. The EMTs lost me several times before we reached the hospital."

"Chelsea was in the wreck with you, too?" he asked as he led her to the Harley.

"No, she wasn't with us," she said, swallowing tightly. "She was with her father when he received word that we were in the bottom of the canyon. She arrived with him, from what I understand."

Chelsea never seemed to remember much of it except the three times she swore she had felt a part of Liza fighting to die.

She allowed Stygian to hold on to her as he swung a powerful leg over the cycle's seat before bracing herself on the foot rest and swinging on behind him.

She had never been on a motorcycle—had she?

"Helmet." Lifting one of the two helmets from the handlebars, he handed it to her.

Fitting it over her head, she then sat silently as he secured the strap before strapping his own in place.

"We're linked through com sets in the helmets." His voice came through the padded helmet, roughened, a male rasp of concern and dangerous interest.

"Just ignore the screams of terror." She tried to laugh off her racing heart as she placed her hands tentatively at his hard waist.

"Here." Gripping her wrists, he pulled her forward.

Her breasts pressed against his back in less than a second, the heat of his body sinking through her clothes straight to her nipples and sensitizing them instantly.

"Hold on tight, sweetheart," he growled through the link. "Losing you off the back of this bike wouldn't be the highlight of my day."

"It's not exactly penciled into my bucket list either," she assured him ruefully as the terror from minutes before began to ease away.

"We're in agreement then."

As his words trailed off, the beast of a machine turned over and began throbbing with leashed power between her thighs.

The heavy vibration was shockingly sensual.

With her arms wrapped tight around Stygian's waist, her

knees pressing against his thighs, Liza found herself grow-ing more aroused by the second.

God, what he did to her.

Mating heat.

The gossip rags had listed the signs of it over and over again, and the overwhelming need, almost impossible to control, headed the list.

But number one was the kiss.

They all agreed, the kiss came first—somewhere.

To the lips, the neck—her heart beat heavier at the thought—the nipples or the clitoris.

The thought of his lips touching her in any of those areas was enough to cause her thighs to clench in an involuntary reaction.

A reaction she couldn't control, and one she was begin-ning to fear was more her hunger, and even less some ani-malistic phenomenon impossible to control.

But she didn't have to admit that to Stygian.

CHAPTER 6

Window Lake shimmered iridescent blue and green beneath the cloudless sky, its calming waters lapping gently at the bank beneath the pristine cottonwood and pinon trees that shaded the picnic shelter Stygian had pulled the Harley up to.

He quickly dismounted before placing his hand at the small of her back and urging her up the slight incline. The six-table shelter had been built to catch the soft breeze that rippled out over the lake.

The water was fed by a vast, previously unknown lake far beneath the ground. It had been tapped into when the oil company had received permission to drill in the area.

The oil had camouflaged the lake below, but once the drill had burrowed past the oil it was seeking and broke through the thin layer of bedrock separating them, all hell had broken loose and Window Lake had been born.

Stepping up to the tabletop, Liza sat down slowly, elbows braced on her knees, facing the water. Stygian sat likewise on the table in front of her, facing her, watching her intently.

"Now, why was it so imperative that I take this ride with you?" Tilting her head, she watched him curiously. "You've been determined to get me alone since the meeting with Jonas."

"I can't simply want to spend time with a beautiful woman?" he asked, his expression thoughtful now. "You're intelligent, beautiful, interesting. What other reason could I have?"

"Information?" She was certain it was far more than simple male interest. Breeds never did anything for such a paltry reason.

"According to you, you have no information."

No man should be able to pull off such mockery and confidence with such a simple statement.

Pursing her lips and staring back at him ruefully, she admitted she was biting off far more than she could chew with this man.

"So we're just here to get to know each other better?" Crossing one leg over the other, she propped her elbow on her knee and rested her chin in the palm of her hand as she contemplated him.

"Is that so wrong?" Amusement filled the black and navy gaze.

"It depends on why you're so interested." And why she was so interested, when the thought of a lover had never been high on her list of priorities?

Men tended to believe their women had to be protected, controlled.

Liza had no intention of being controlled.

"You sound as though you've come to your own conclusions as to my interest." Bracing his palms on the table behind him, he leaned back and watched her with wicked male amusement.

Shrugging, Liza arched her brows at his comment. "There are a lot of rumors where a Breed's interest in a woman is concerned. Rumors of addictive kisses, a Breed's ability to control their lovers through some hormonal reaction to those kisses. All those stories could make a girl nervous."

She was nervous.

She'd watched Isabelle in the weeks since she'd become Malachi's lover, and the signs that the rumors could be true were all there.

"You're listening to rumors?" The chuckle that left his

lips matched the laughter in his gaze. "I would have thought you'd know better, considering your friend is a Breed's lover. They're considering marriage, you know."

Liza couldn't control her own mockery at that point. "They've been together less than two months and they're already discussing marriage. Isabelle is so wrapped up in that Breed, nothing else matters any longer."

Even the position Isabelle had attained on the team she'd trained with since she was a teenager was no longer important.

For some reason, Isabelle now considered herself a danger to the team, and none of them could figure out why.

Unless the rumor that lovers who were "mated" to a Breed carried a scent other Breeds could detect. Especially Coyote Breeds who worked for the Genetics Council. Add that to the fact that the reported attacks against Breeds and their lovers in the past few years by suspected Genetics Council Breeds were all against Breeds in committed relationships with their lovers. So committed there was no time, no room and no interest in anything else.

"What are you getting at, Liza?" Leaning forward, his booted feet planted squarely on the bench as he planted his broad forearms on his knees, he watched her thoughtfully. "I swear, I can feel that suspicious little mind of yours beating around something here."

"The rumors of 'mating heat'?" she questioned. "If that's why you're sniffing around me, then I'd just like to say right now I'd prefer not to be so chained to a man that I can't get five minutes out of his sight."

A smile curved his lips, but the amusement had dissipated just marginally from his gaze for the slightest second. If she hadn't been watching his expression closely, she would have missed it.

"Come on, Liza," he chastised her gently. "If it existed, don't you think someone would have come forward already?"

She shrugged at the question. "The *National Rumor* says there's a kill order against anyone who verifies information concerning Breed mating heat."

Stygian had to laugh at that. Not because it wasn't true.

Because she'd gotten straight to the point and didn't hesitate to inform him she wasn't interested.

He would have let it go if he didn't know for a damned fact she was more than interested. She could lie with her lips, but her body hadn't yet learned how to play along.

"That rag? Sweetheart, you should try reading the *National Press*. It's more fact than fantasy." He evaded the implied question carefully.

Not that she was willing to back down. He doubted she backed down from much at all.

"The *National Press* is owned by the Tyler family," Liza snorted. "Their baby sister is married to Callan Lyons, leader of the Feline Prides. I wouldn't exactly suspect the paper of being impartial, would you?"

She had him there. But for the moment, he stuck to his evasion rather than the truth and prayed she didn't push him any closer to lying.

Lying to his mate just somehow seemed wrong.

"Yeah, it is," he agreed with a nod. "That doesn't mean John Tyler reports fiction. He's a damned stickler for truth in the articles he publishes as well."

"And he just recently married a Feline Breed." She smiled smugly.

Well, hell, that information was so carefully buried that even the Alphas of the other Breed communities were unaware of it.

"I think we should discuss this later," he suggested— later, after he showed her, rather than telling her, the full truth involving mating heat.

"Why later, Stygian? When? After you've kissed me and tied me so irrevocably to you that I have no other choice but to keep your secrets?"

Pretty much.

The mocking thought had a rush of guilt pricking at his senses.

"Come on, Liza." Sighing, he scratched at his jaw and watched her thoughtfully. "Do you need an excuse for wanting me so desperately that you'll believe any trash story you find to explain it?"

"Why not?" Her brow arched suggestively. "It beats believing I'm suddenly so tired of living that I've chosen suicide by Breed."

"Suicide by Breed?" Incredulity filled his expression then. "How do you figure that one? Baby, we might kill ourselves fucking, but I'd never physically harm you."

Her face flushed, but the sudden darkening of her gray eyes and the scent of her pussy heating further assured him it wasn't from anger or embarrassment.

"*Emotional* suicide by Breed." She shrugged, though the subtle scent of her wariness wrapped around him like an invisible cloud.

"Emotional suicide?" he questioned her. "Do you think you're in danger of losing your heart to me, Liza?"

"Only if you're in danger of being honest with me." She snorted. "I detest liars."

"Honesty goes both ways, baby," he retorted. "If you want it, then you have to give it as well."

How could one woman look and smell so fucking innocent no matter the provocation?

"Your boss has no doubt had me so thoroughly investigated that the lot of you know the last time I masturbated."

She didn't even flush as she made the statement.

Innocence, sensuality and pure bravado.

Damn, she should have been born a Breed.

"The masturbating part we're actually uncertain of," he stated with a grin. "But next time you go there I wouldn't mind an invitation to join you."

The grin that edged her lips had his dick swelling impossibly harder and his balls drawing so tight they felt tortured.

Hell, no woman should have the ability to destroy a man's senses so easily.

"I'll keep that in mind." The look she threw him was less than reassuring.

He wasn't going to hold his breath waiting on that invitation.

And wasn't that too bad.

Damn, he was killing himself here, aching for her as he'd never ached for anything in his life.

He was here on a mission. A mission he'd been working for over a decade: Find Honor Roberts. This woman didn't appear to be the one he was searching for, but he was damned if he could pull himself away from her.

Watching as she shifted her head, her eyes moving to the lake again as her expression turned thoughtful, he realized there was nothing about this woman he didn't like.

Her strength. Her will. Her pride and determination.

She would make him crazy, but every instinct he possessed assured him this woman was one he'd gladly spend his days—and his nights—with.

"My family and I used to picnic here nearly every Sunday for years when I was a kid," she said softly, nostalgia and wariness mixing with a near-undetectable scent of deception.

What could she possibly be hiding from him here? Now?

Or was she trying to distract him?

He didn't doubt that in the least. Fortunately for her, he was already pretty distracted and really had only wanted to spend a few hours with her.

She was his mate, after all.

The need to get to know her, to understand the woman behind the secrets was nearly as fierce as his need to possess her. To cover her—to mark her. Hell, to wrap her in so much pleasure she couldn't even consider living a single day without him or his touch.

"I don't believe I've ever been on a picnic," he said with a faint smile. "That wasn't exactly part of our training."

A faint frown touched her brow, though she didn't glance back at him. "Every kid should know how great a picnic is. I remember when the first Breed came here to Window Rock after Callan Lyons made his incredible announcement that Breeds existed. He called himself Gabriel. He was there searching for his family. He told Dad what training versus raising truly meant."

Stygian nodded. "More than half the Breeds created died in the first three months from lack of touch and care. The nurses didn't hold or cuddle us. They fed us. They removed the pads beneath us when they were soiled and bathed us when they had to."

Stygian didn't remember that, though some Breeds claimed to remember their own infant years.

Being a Breed had been hell until the rescues. But life wasn't bad now.

Actually, sometimes, it was pretty damned good.

"Did Gabriel find his family?" Stygian finally asked when Liza said nothing more.

She breathed out heavily. "A half sister. His mother was one of the lucky ones. She was released, rather than killed, after giving birth to her second child. She later had a daughter but died in childbirth. Gabriel disappeared with her just after finding her."

Stygian watched her closely, knowing there was more to the story than the brief moment in Gabriel's life that she had mentioned. Like many Breeds, Gabriel, whoever he may be, had gone searching for roots that were often destroyed long before a Breed ever escaped.

"So, you tell me something now," she demanded, her look thoughtful.

"Ask." He would answer if he could.

"Why were you named Stygian?"

He chuckled at the question. "Breeds developed a habit in the labs, long before release, of naming themselves. Many, like Gabriel, took biblical names. They believed if we took the names of those God had found favor in, from the Bible, then He would find favor in us as well and gift us with a chance to see Heaven, as our human cousins took for granted."

"You didn't take a biblical name," she pointed out.

"True." Inclining his head in agreement, he allowed a smile to curve his lips. "I had a trainer who didn't always follow the Council's directives. From the time I was ten until my rescue at twenty, he convinced me that my chances at an afterlife were just as good as those of any human ever born."

"Man or woman cannot take that first breath of life without first the gift of the soul that only God can bequeath." She recited the declaration President Andrews had made when he had accepted and signed into law the mandates of Breed Law.

"Exactly," he agreed.

"So why did you choose the name Stygian Black?" She looked at him, her dove gray eyes somber.

She had no idea the temptation she was at that moment.

There was no pity coming from her, merely regret and sadness for the hell the Breeds had known as children.

"Actually, my birth mother chose it," he told her. "The trainer I was paired with had grown close to her before she died in the labs. She asked that he find a way to ensure I carried the name she chose for me."

"So why Stygian?" she asked again. "Especially Stygian Black?"

"She wanted me to carry the name of her ancestor. One known for his merciless vengeance decades before her birth. When his wife and child were taken by his enemies, he began spilling the blood of their abductors' families, beginning with cousins and working his way up until they were returned to him. They were dead, though. By the time he finished, every member of three family lines was wiped off the face of the earth. My trainer believed she wanted that same vengeance, and she wanted me to be the instrument of it."

"And were you?"

Stygian shook his head at the question. "I don't kill children or innocents no matter the provocation. And that's what it would have entailed."

There had been more than once that he swore his mother had reached out from beyond the grave in anger at his choice.

"What about you?" he asked, pausing until she gave him a questioning look. "Who created Liza Johnson? A woman willing to face a team of Coyote soldiers with no more than a knife in her sneaker, three skin tags on her body and a communications link to God only knows who tucked in her pretty little ear? What made you think you could face four men you believed were soldiers sent by the Genetics Council and survive without help?"

He hoped the bastard who had allowed her to do it had to made his peace with his maker. Because Stygian intended to kill him for daring to send his mate into such danger.

Not that she seemed inclined to answer him.

Oh hell no, it couldn't be that easy.

Her eyes narrowed. "Why don't you tell me why a Breed's kiss is so addictive? Or did you intend to wait until I couldn't walk away before telling me the truth?"

Bingo.

His expression never changed, but Liza assured herself she wasn't stupid. It had taken her a few minutes to figure it out—but once she had, she'd been certain of her conclusions.

"I asked first," Stygian growled.

His expression might not have changed, but his tone sure had.

She'd turned the tables on him, and he didn't like it.

As a matter of fact, he seemed completely surprised by the fact that she had done so.

A second later, she narrowed her eyes on the smug smile that tugged at his well-molded, sensual lips.

"I'll take it that the rumors of a Navajo-based Breed Underground Network that helps Breeds and humans running from the Genetics Council is true. I'll also assume you're part of that network."

A soft laugh left her lips. "You know what 'assume' does," she reminded him. "It makes an ass of you."

"Touché," he congratulated her. "But the statement stands."

Her arms crossed over her breasts defensively, but Stygian sensed her amusement.

Damn, she was enjoying every minute of the dangerous byplay.

Stygian knew well the consequences of allowing Liza more information on mating heat that could contradict the Breeds' stance that it was all rumor and false accusations.

Breed Law—the Breed mandates rather than those President Andrews had signed into law—expressly forbid the sharing of the information before mating occurred.

If Liza were to betray the information—before or after mating—then Breed Law could see them both dead. Unless

Liza were pregnant, then it would merely see them imprisoned for life.

"We're at a stalemate then?" she asked when he said nothing more.

"Not exactly." He grinned and considered her bravado. "You could always let me kiss you. That would settle the issue once and for all."

Only then would the risks of discovery, and the laws forbidding exposing it, be revealed to her. Perhaps then it would mean something to her as well.

"And the risk of being at your beck and call night and day because I'm so addicted to your kiss that I can't walk away?" She snorted at the thought. "That's okay, Mr. Black."

So much for the subtle dare. Not that he had really expected her to fall for it.

"At least there's a way to prove or disprove the theory." He shrugged. "What do you have to offer to disprove my suspicion that you're part of the Navajo Breed Underground Network that relocates and rescues Breeds that the Council has targeted?"

"The same as you have." She shrugged as one little brow cocked a little higher than the other and laughter gleamed in her eyes. "Yep, sounds like a stalemate to me."

Oh, he could show her a stalemate.

Stygian stood slowly, straightening before moving toward her.

"Just because you're not lying doesn't mean I can't smell the deception beneath your words."

He faced her as the primal hunger tearing through him fought for dominance. Keeping his hands off her was possibly the hardest battle of his life.

"Just because I'm human doesn't mean I can't sense your deception," she informed him defiantly as she stared back at him with narrowed eyes. "And don't think you can intimidate me so easily."

She straightened, anger flaring to meet the irritation she could see brewing inside him.

"It's a damned dangerous game you and your friends are

playing, Liza." Raking his fingers through his hair, Stygian clenched his jaw and fought to deny the animal instinct that he bind her to him immediately. That he turn her need to fight against the Genetics Council and their soldiers to a hunger so hot it would blister both their senses.

"Me and my friends?" She propped slender fingers over the curve of her hips, facing him with innate feminine defiance. "Excuse me, Mr. Black, but the Navajo did not come on your land demanding your most precious treasures, nor did we lie to you to search for ghosts that may or may not exist. You and yours came to us." Her stubborn chin lifted stubbornly. "You've all but taken over our capital. You attempt to force *our* president to bend to *your* will and you take advantage of an agreement the Navajo made in good faith to aid the Breeds in their battle for freedom. You"— one delicate finger was suddenly pushed with feminine arrogance into the center of his chest—"have done all that and more. If a foreign country attempted this with the U.S. president, then war would have been declared."

Her finger retreated.

The delicate hand returned to her hip, fingers spread, legs braced slightly apart in an unconscious fighting stance.

"And you think withholding information to punish Jonas is somehow justified because we didn't come to you begging?" he bit out between clenched teeth.

"And you believe because we do not know where three tortured victims of the Genetics Council are hiding that you can attempt to poke and prod and demand access to every part of our lives?" she questioned incredulously. "We owe you nothing, Mr. Black. But for more than a century, each time a Breed has come to the Navajo for help, we've given it. If we could help that poor little baby, then have no doubt every Breed in the Navajo Nation would be on Jonas Wyatt's doorstep attempting to do just that."

"Until now, the Navajo have always extended the information Breeds have needed." Until the information they needed possibly imposed on a promise to another.

"Listen to you," she snapped. "What promise was made and to whom? Do you think I lied to Jonas when he all but kidnapped me to question me about people I've never seen in my entire life?"

"You came into that hotel with a live link, possibly to an enemy, and didn't even attempt to inform us," he growled back at her. "You and your underground organization deliberately deceived us for your own agenda."

Disbelief filled her expression and turned the soft scent of summer to one infused with flashes of heat as she glared back at him.

"I am an undercover agent for the Navajo Law Enforcement Agency," she gritted out. "The op I was a part of to draw in the Coyote Breeds watching me for the past weeks had nothing to do with the Bureau of Breed Affairs, Jonas Wyatt or any Breed outside those currently stalking me. That was none of your business, nor was it any of Wyatt's or anyone else's, thank you very much."

It wasn't a lie. She was an agent for the covert division of the Navajo Law Enforcement Office. The operation was conducted by several of the agents of that office, and the Breeds would have been turned over to the proper authorities if caught, Liza knew.

If Stygian, Jonas or anyone from the Breed communities did as she and Cullen expected them to do and hacked the Law Enforcement Offices computers, then they would find that same information.

Stygian stared back at her, his lips pressed tightly together as he held back the curse that would have slipped past his lips.

An undercover agent? His mate was an investigator attempting to draw out Coyote soldiers so merciless that even their own Breed refused to claim them?

"There is no record of you working with the Law Enforcement Agency." One more second, one more confrontational remark and he was going to kiss her.

The need was pounding through him. It was racing through his blood veins and pounding hard and heavy through his dick.

"Well, now, if that information was so easy to find, then the undercover part would be rather useless, wouldn't it?"

The question was heavily laced with sarcasm. "What was I supposed to do, Stygian? Take out an ad in the paper first, just for you?"

If she didn't stop, the tenuous grip he had on his control would be shot. The defiance and sheer stubborn will was awakening a part of him he had no idea how to force back.

Before Stygian realized he was moving, before he could stop himself, he had his hands on her.

Gripping a hip with one hand, he pulled her to him. The fingers of the other threading through her hair, he drew her head back for his kiss as his lowered.

"Mate me, bind me to you without my knowledge of what you're doing or how it will affect my life, and I promise you, I'll make your life a hell you will never forget."

His lips were almost on hers.

The glands beneath his tongue were swollen and throbbing, aching for the heat of her kiss.

She knew, damn her. She knew what she was doing to him. She knew the agonizing need tearing through him and still, she was defying him, attempting to force from him what she had to know he had vowed not to give up.

"This time," he growled furiously, his hips pressing into her, his cock pounding at her lower stomach. "This time you win. But be prepared." His lips were all but touching hers. "Be prepared, Liza, because you are mine. Mine. And I promise you, I will claim you soon."

And it would be a claiming he swore she would never escape.

Her lips parted, he could see that mocking, sarcastic little tongue of hers getting ready to push him further, to shred the final threads holding back the animal inside him that was snarling for release.

And he could feel fate getting ready to completely kick his ass, because he knew, *knew* he was going to kiss her. It was just such an accepted, forgone conclusion that the explosion of splinters suddenly tearing from the wood post behind her took nearly a heartbeat to register.

A heartbeat that could have cost his mate her life.

· CHAPTER 7 ·

Liza knew the instant splinters of wood began raining around them exactly what had happened.

The report of a weapon couldn't be heard, but with the cover a sniper would have in the woods surrounding them, a silencer would have been sufficient.

"Down!"

The word exploded from both of them as they went to the side, rolling over the small incline that led to the bank and the water lapping below as another projectile slammed into the picnic table.

"Oh yeah, the safest ride I'd ever take." Liza snorted as she threw the Breed a hard glare. "Tell me you at least have a radio on you."

Flattening against the incline, she had to resist the urge to peek over it and attempt to get a bearing on the shooter.

"We're covered."

Oh, he sounded far too complacent as he kept a tight hold around her waist and kept her from checking above to see if anyone was moving in on them.

Turning her head, she looked over at him instead. "Was this Jonas's idea to draw someone or something out?" she asked, fighting back the urge to kick him, since Jonas wasn't there to take the blow himself.

"If it is, then I'll kill him myself," Stygian grated as he removed one arm from around her and flipped his wrist over to stare at the face of his watch. Maneuvering the arm still holding her to him, he depressed the small cylindrical post at the side. "Rule, do you have eyes on the bastard?"

"Eyes on. We're moving in. Stay where you are," a voice came through the link as the watch face slowly disappeared to reveal the image of the Lion Breed Rule Breaker.

The urge to growl was beginning to tighten her throat.

"Bastards," she muttered.

"Only technically," Rule drawled without a change of expression. "Hold tight. We have a team moving in on your position."

Hold tight her ass.

"We're too exposed here," she warned Stygian. "If they don't have a bead on the son of a bitch firing at us, then we're going to be screwed here."

"Tell her to hold on to her panties," Rule stated as though she weren't even there. "We may not have a bead on the shooter, but we have thermal imaging all around you. He won't get close enough to do any damage."

"And did he have thermal imaging before we were shot at?" she questioned. "If he did, then he's falling far short on the job, Stygian."

Stygian didn't say a word.

Glancing at him, she nearly rolled her eyes at the black and brilliant blue fury gleaming in his gaze.

"Are we going to sit here like paper targets waiting on some Breed-hating bastard to take us out?" she asked.

His eyes narrowed.

"Keep her there, Wolf," Rule warned him. "We're moving in. Dog's team will have sights on him within seconds."

Liza snorted again.

Narrowing her eyes, she stared around, taking in the peaceful setting and lack of tourists on that particular end of the lake.

"Seduction," she muttered. "You just had to go the seduction routine, didn't you?"

"I hope she's talking to you, Wolf." Rule chuckled.

"Move it, Rule," Stygian growled, the rasp in his voice a dangerous, primal sound.

"Got it—"

Dirt exploded above their heads, the projectile that had managed to bury itself in the ground obviously coming from behind them.

Liza noticed neither of them bothered making a sound.

Following him, she threw herself to the right, scrambling for the dubious cover of the boulders stacked along the bank several feet away.

"Which way?" Back flat against the cool stone as she crouched behind the stone protection, she glanced at Stygian.

He'd found a small crack between the two boulders that he was peering through before easing back, still crouched and prepared to move.

"Whoever's out there has to be the worst shot in the world," he mused with animalistic fury. "Just enough to fucking piss me off."

"Go out without a weapon again." Liza rolled her eyes despite the concern she could feel edging into the adrenaline-laced excitement pounding through her.

"Yeah, why don't you just do that?" he retorted back.

"Alas, the trusty knife is tucked in my boot." She sighed as she reached up and activated the earbud at her ear. She knew she'd picked it up for a reason. "I left the trusty sidearm at home though. You promised to protect me, remember?"

"Yeah, I remember." He sighed. But it was becoming clearer by the moment that his mate could do a fine job of protecting herself.

"We're on our way, Munchkin." Cullen stated. "We're heading from the east dock. ETA is two minutes or less. Reever has an eye on your location and taking bead."

She watched as Stygian's head turned slowly, his acute Breed hearing no doubt catching the sound of Cullen's voice at her ear.

"Watch out for the Breeds," she stated softly as she turned her head to speak, hoping to keep Rule from hearing her. "I don't have a good feeling about this, Cullen."

They were being drawn out. Reever was in the trees somewhere, his handy-dandy sniper rifle poised and ready while Cullen raced toward them. Steven would be somewhere close by, and Claire and Chelsea each would have been alerted to Liza's situation while God only knew what position Klah was taking.

There were times Klah scared even her.

"They take out a Bureau Breed and we're going to have problems, sweetheart," Stygian warned her.

"If Cullen finds out the Bureau was behind this little show-and-tell, then there will be even more problems," she warned him in turn. "What the hell is going on here, Stygian?"

Was it a calculated move designed by Jonas Wyatt to draw members of the Breed Underground Network out into the open? Or was it Council soldiers determined to find the research projects the underground had hidden over the years?

"When I find out, I promise you, whoever's behind this will pay hell for it," he swore.

Whatever it was, he wasn't involved.

"They have him," Rule announced quietly. "Sights are on your shooter. He's searching for your location. Mother—" She had a feeling the curse that cut off was due to the shot that was likely heard around the lake.

At least, they heard it.

The explosive retort was muted, coming from the East as the sound of the Navajo Lake Patrol water cruiser could be heard racing for the bank.

"The cavalry is here," she murmured.

"Cleanup in aisle five," Rule stated with quiet disgust as Liza and Stygian rose slowly to their feet as the lake cruiser eased up to the bank. "Jacobs just took our shooter's head off."

"Better his head than yours." Jumping from the cruiser, Cullen's glare was dark enough to shred any man's confidence as he suddenly gripped Liza's arm and turned her to the cruiser. "Get—"

The words broke as Liza felt his grip jerk before she was released.

Swinging around, she watched, her lips parting in shock at the sight of the normally unconquerable Cullen suddenly thrown against the largest of the boulders, his back nearly bouncing against the stone as an enraged, primal snarl tore from Stygian's throat. His lips were peeled from his teeth, his incisors flashing in the brilliance of the sunlight as one hand closed brutally around Cullen's throat.

Cullen stared back at the aberration calmly, as though this were an everyday occurrence.

"When you've finished—" Cullen began.

"Touch her again and you'll lose your fucking throat." It was like hearing a Wolf attempting to speak, his voice was so savage, so animalistic.

Liza could only watch in shock, seeing the slow flex of Stygian's fingers around the strong column of Cullen's throat as the other man simply stared up at him unconcerned, his arms relaxed at his side, his gaze mocking.

The battle of wills was fought silently, neither man dropping his gaze nor blinking as they seemed locked in some weird moment of time as violence thrummed in the air.

"Let him go!" Liza snapped as she watched Stygian's fingers tighten again.

Cullen wasn't moving. He wasn't taking his eyes from Stygian's, nor was he attempting to defend himself when Liza knew he could. She had seen him do so before.

Stygian's fingers flexed at the sound of her voice.

"I said let him go!" Jumping forward, her fingers locked around his wrist, jerking back and nearly losing her balance as his arm followed the forceful pull she exerted on it.

Stygian caught her, his arm going around her waist as he caught her against him, ignoring her struggles as he and Cullen continued to stare each other down.

Stygian could sense the power, the promise of violence and the ability to fight as it pulsed beneath the other man's flesh, but Cullen Maverick hadn't used that power. He'd instead stood still and silent despite the hold that had tightened around his neck.

"What are you hiding?" Stygian growled at him. "Why would you allow a Breed to all but rip your throat out?"

Cullen's gaze moved slowly to Liza. "For her."

Liza stilled.

Stygian could feel her now: watchful, silent, her body tense at the answer the other man gave.

"For me?" Liza snapped. "Why the hell would you do it for me? You should have kicked his fucking ass."

Rage was spilling from her, the scent of it fiery as she jerked out of his hold.

"Let it go, Liza," Cullen said then, his voice soft as Stygian allowed him to continue to keep his gaze.

He was damned if he could decipher what the other man was trying to silently tell him though.

He hadn't quite learned that whole male-to-male silent-messaging bullshit humans seemed to practice.

"Oh, I'll let it go," she snapped.

Stygian turned his head, watching as she stalked to the cruiser and in a graceful move gripped the side of the low vessel and vaulted into it. "I'll let it go, forget it, ignore it, and I'll even fucking pretend it didn't happen."

Stygian knew that one was a lie. She'd be throwing this up to him for years to come, he could feel it.

"Fuck," Cullen muttered. "She's going to be bitching at me for years."

The comment matched his thoughts so completely that Stygian couldn't help but throw the man another snarl. It was the animal pacing just beneath his skin, it refused to return still and silent to that place within his psyche where it normally watched, silent and content.

It wasn't content any longer.

"Snarl all you like." Cullen snorted. "You're the one that backed off when she ordered you to, not me. So which of us do you think she has the most whipped."

Stygian's nostrils flared. He would have loved to go after the man's throat again, but before he could move to do so, Cullen had managed to vault into the water cruiser and jump behind the wheel of the craft.

A flick of his wrist and it was expertly shooting backward before giving a hard turn on the water, digging in deep and cleaving through the lake before Stygian could more than step toward it.

Instead, he stood on the bank watching his mate until the cruiser disappeared around the small bend of the bank toward the east dock.

"I think he needs his ass kicked." Rule jumped silently to the bank, followed by the four Breeds following.

"No doubt," Stygian growled as he turned on the other Breed slowly. "Was this a Bureau strike and watch?" he asked, referencing Jonas Wyatt's habit of making an attempt to draw enemies and friends alike out of the woodwork by staging an attack.

"Not with your mate in the line of fire." Rule gave his head a hard shake, his black hair fanning against the side of his face as his deep blue eyes narrowed against the brilliance of the sunlight. "And he wouldn't have put one of his enforcers where anyone could take him out. One of Cullen's men just sniped that bastard shooting at the two of you like it was no more than spitting distance." He nodded toward the cliff rising above the lake from the other side. "He took a next shot up there on the cliff and took the shooter's head off, and that's no shit."

And no easy feat.

Stygian felt the muscles at his jaw flex. "Have you ID'ed him?"

"We had to use fingerprint ID." Rule shrugged. "Report came back as a former trainer for the Genetics Council. What he was doing here, though, I'm not certain. Who was he shooting at? You or your mate?"

"Both," Stygian bit out before moving to the edge of the incline and quickly making his way back to where he and Liza had been sitting. "How did he manage to follow us with you watching?"

"There's no way." A hard shake of Rule's head was decisive. "He had to have already been here."

"He couldn't have known where I was taking her, or that we'd be here," Stygian growled as he moved quickly to the cycle. "I want a background report ASAP and I want to know every fucking second of his life since the day he stepped into the Genetics Council and I want it yesterday."

"Yeah, you Wolves are an impatient lot." Rule sighed, though he was far enough away from him to evade any strike Stygian could make for the smart-assed remark. "Why don't you take it up with Jonas?"

"He's next." Flipping the key to start the motor, Stygian was burning rubber a second later as he tore from the parking lot and headed back toward the hotel.

Jonas had better have some fucking answers.

CHAPTER 8

"He did what?" It was Ashley Truing's shocked exclamation that drew Liza's attention from the fighting stance Emma was trying to teach her.

Oh hell. Oh hell.

She should have never, never told Chelsea and Claire what had happened before the shooting earlier that afternoon, Liza thought as her attention was pulled from her opponent to the three women on the other side of the room.

She found herself flat on her ass and staring up at Emma Truing in surprise a second later.

"Keep your mind on the bastard trying to kill your ass, not the pretty girl with the bottled-sex voice as she tosses her hair." Emma snorted.

Liza sat up and hung her head, breathing heavily as she felt the perspiration rolling down her back and the ache just beneath her skin at each point where Emma had touched her.

She rubbed at her arm irritably where the Breed female had gripped it to—oh so casually—steady the hold she had when she threw Liza off balance.

"You're getting stronger," Liza muttered as she glanced over at Ashley, Chelsea and Claire where they were whispering and giggling in amusement, while Shiloh and Chimera stared back at Liza in amusement. "Your hands feel like hammers tonight."

Emma arched her brow. "Really? Ashley swears I baby everyone."

"She babies me." Ashley threw her sister a hard look. "Every Coyote in town has been babying me too. It's damned humiliating."

Ashley was delicate, impossibly pretty and as spoiled as any debutante, and every time she bitched about getting kicked out of a fight, Liza wanted to laugh. She didn't look capable of swatting a fly, let alone committing some of the bloody mayhem she'd heard of the other woman doing.

"And they'll keep babying you or answer to my knife at their throat one night," Emma stated, the cold hard tone an indication of her complete dedication to the threat.

"Stop interrupting the conversation over here if you two don't mind." Ashley displayed her incisors aggressively at her attempt to ignore her sister's threats. "Em, did you hear about Liza and Stygian's little ride out to the lake earlier today?"

"You mean the one where Stygian had her pinned against that post beneath the shelter a second before that shooter tried to rearrange her head?" Emma grinned. "Hell yeah, the Breeds on protective detail were ribbing Stygian over that one before we left the hotel tonight."

Liza glanced at the girls gathered at the side of the room. "Just what I need, a bunch of Breeds gossiping about me when they should have been watching for the bastards using me as target practice."

"Honey, you should have expected that the minute you hopped on that Harley with him," the Jaguar Breed Shiloh Gage spoke up with effortless sarcasm. "Breeds are nosier than any woman created. They're bigger gossips too. The fact that you managed to evade a professional assassin's bullet is just fodder for the rumor mill. What I can't believe is that he actually comes home instead of rushing you straight to his bed."

Emma and Ashley snickered at the declaration.

"I still can't believe he didn't just kiss you." Ashley

giggled, her gray eyes twinkling in a merriment they hadn't seen since she'd been shot by Holden Mayhew.

And though Liza was damned happy that the other girl seemed to be recovering so well, she still wasn't pleased that Chelsea had placed her head on the chopping block to amuse Ashley.

At least Chelsea and Claire hadn't told the other girls how he refused to deny mating heat existed. That part, they had sworn to never tell. She should have made them swear on the rest of it as well. At least, until they knew for certain about the whole punishment-by-death thing.

Yet there they were, all watching her after her friend had been so kind as to inform them of what may have transpired before the shooting.

"How much did you tell them, anyway?" Liza questioned her with suspicion.

She should have told them not to mention that almost kiss. She'd remember next time not to.

Chelsea gave a light shrug and a smirk. "Probably more than you would be comfortable with, but come on, Liza, it was so interesting."

Liza felt heat wash through her face as she remembered the sensuality that had tightened Stygian's expression.

"Great," she muttered, resting her face against her upraised her knees.

"Hell, I just can't believe Stygian got so fresh," Shiloh drawled. "He doesn't even get sexy-nasty with the Breed females he takes to his bed. He hasn't even been known to flirt."

Oh, he knew how to flirt—just as he knew how to make a woman insane with anger.

"Why don't you guys find something else to talk about?" Liza demanded.

"Because, this is just so interesting," Shiloh assured her with practiced mockery. "Come on, Liza, it's simply uncalled for to hear of Stygian actually going on a date."

"Well, you can at least take a break and let us finish here," Emma declared as she moved back to the center of the mat where Liza sat, finally breathing regularly. "Come on, bad girl, get off your lazy ass and see if you can't find a way to at least tip me here." Turning her palm, she gave Liza a backward wave. "Up and at 'em."

Liza rolled her eyes as she came to her feet and gave her arms a loose shake to relax her stiffening muscles.

"Take it easy with those paws of yours," she ordered the other girl. "Hell, my arms still ache."

"Sissy. Stop wussing out on me."

Wussing out on her?

Liza glared back at her.

She had yet to wuss out on anything.

Watching Emma carefully, she was able to dodge the first set of jabs as well as Emma's attempt to trip her.

Liza focused her memory on the fight she'd managed to glimpse between Diane Broen and one of her former mercenaries. She concentrated on coordinating her movements to match the practiced symmetry the Bureau enforcer had used.

Why hadn't she tried that before? she wondered distantly.

She'd watched enough Breeds sparring over the years that she should have already been incorporating what she'd watched them do.

She blocked Emma's next attempt to grab and throw her to the mat. As though she had slipped into someone else's skin, she began moving automatically. Blocking, jabbing, moving offensively instead of defensively until she had Emma actually breaking a sweat.

She had watched the Breeds—Cullen, Reever, and Klah—sparring for most of her life, and had resisted the urge to attempt to use the maneuvers she'd seen. Her body always felt ready, prepared to execute the moves, but her confidence in putting into practice what she had seen without training, had held her back.

Until tonight.

Until the urge to do so overcame her lack of confidence and she learned she had a talent she'd never recognized before. It was a talent she realized she'd had since her and Claire's accident. The fiery car crash had nearly taken both of their lives, and had left each with subtle talents that for some reason they were terrified to reveal. Talents they had only shared the secrets of with each other.

"Geez," Emma muttered as Liza blocked another move and came back at her quickly with an offensive jab to her jaw, then followed with one to the midriff.

Emma barely had time to block before awareness of another move slid into Liza's consciousness and went straight to the instinctive impulses snapping through her brain then to her body.

Emma sent a jab to her jaw. Sweeping back and going to the floor, Liza caught herself on her shoulders and arms, legs swinging out as she rolled and swept Emma off balance.

As the Breed went down, Liza was there, her fist coming in and stopping short of Emma's throat in what would have been a killing blow for a human. For a Breed, at the very least, it would cause a lengthy incapacitation, giving Liza a chance to escape.

As Liza blinked down at the shock in Emma's face, she quickly jumped back, stared down at her hands, then to the Breeds and two friends watching her in wide-eyed disbelief.

In Claire's eyes though, Liza saw fear—and a desperate warning.

Fear that the minute changes they had experienced after their recovery would be detected and alter them in the eyes of their loved ones.

The warning that she was skirting the line and placing them both in danger.

"Who the fuck are you and where did Liza go?" Emma sat up slowly, her gaze narrowed.

"I told you she was holding back," Shiloh crowed in triumph as her mocking laughter filled the basement. "What have I been telling you for months and you couldn't see it? Every damned time she could have shown she was picking up these damned moves she would back off like a scared little baby."

"I never showed her that move." Emma watched Liza as though she were a particularly complicated puzzle.

"Neither did I," Ashley stated.

"No, we didn't. But have you forgotten what Liza does for fun? She buys fighting videos and practices without us. I told you all along she was going to kick your asses one day when you least expected it."

The suspicion, thank God. Oh, thank God. It eased from Ashley's and Emma's gaze as Shiloh's explanation sank in.

Chelsea shook her head in amazement as Claire slowly began to relax.

"I watch Breeds fight too," she reminded them all. "Their sparring sessions can get real interesting."

"It can't be easy sparring alone though," Emma pointed out, a frown beginning to mar her brow.

"Tell me about it," Liza breathed out roughly as she collapsed on the mat and took a deep breath. "Do you have any idea how many bruises I've gotten down here?"

It wasn't a lie. There was no deceit in the statement. That part was easy to cover, especially when she was able to hide her face against her knees and simply concentrate on breathing.

One breath in, one out. One in, one out.

"Well, hell, I can actually tell Link now you're just about ready." Emma gave a short nod. "Claire will take a little longer, but she's getting there."

"I'll so obviously not be on the front lines," Claire said in amusement. "I prefer driving anyway."

And there, Claire was excelling.

"Yeah, she has like fucking mad driving skills," Ashley exclaimed in sudden excitement. "She'll never lose control of a vehicle again."

The sudden reminder had Liza taking in a hard breath. Her head jerked up, eyes opening wide.

She didn't want to see that memory flashing through her mind again, or feel what she had felt when she had seen the darkness of death opening up around her.

She could swear she'd heard the wails of the dead. And it wasn't a white light she'd seen. It had been darkness. Nothingness. Such a void of complete nothing that it had rocked her soul.

The same sight Claire had faced as the car exploded

around them, the force of the blast blowing the doors open and throwing them from the vehicle seconds before flames had engulfed it.

"Okay, shower." Liza jumped to her feet, feeling the sticky residue of perspiration drying on her flesh. "How about pizza?" she asked the others. "We could phone in the order before we shower and eat it hot."

The others called out their agreement in unison as Chelsea, Claire and Liza headed upstairs to shower.

The four Breed females made their way to the gym-style shower that had been built into the house by the owners before they'd moved, who had left the three-bedroom rancher with a finished basement intended to serve as a fully functional gym.

Liza called in the pizza order before heading into her bedroom and quickly stripping.

Stepping into the shower, she let the hot water wash away not just the memories she didn't want resurfacing again, but also that irritating sensation just beneath the flesh in each area Emma's hands had gripped her during their sparring.

She felt bruised to the bone in several areas; in others, it felt as though the Breed's touch had somehow become allergic.

It wasn't until she'd showered, dried and dressed in loose cotton pants and a T-shirt that she began to feel human once again.

She was quickly twisting an elastic band into the damp strands of her braided hair when a horrified scream pierced the silence of the house.

"Claire!" A breath of fear rushed from her lungs as Liza felt the sweeping autopilot sensation rush through her once again.

She didn't rush.

Claire screamed again, but as though she were watching someone else, Liza quickly slid open her dresser drawer to retrieve the laser-guided, laser-powered, ammo-loaded side arm her father had given her after Isabelle had been attacked by Holden Mayhew.

The distance between her and her actions slowly receded

until she was moving, blessedly no longer watching herself, to her bedroom door. Flipping out the lights, Liza jerked open the door and went out in a roll, her gaze sweeping over the room.

Claire's cry was weaker this time, the sound of a struggle in a room indicating the danger her friend was in.

Council-controlled Breeds.

In the next breath, the sound of gunfire rocked the house.

Liza shuddered with each blast, counting four even as she rushed for Claire's room.

"Chelsea! Emma!" She was screaming out for the others as she gripped Claire's doorknob and tried to jerk it open.

Locked.

Claire never locked her door.

The sound of glass breaking and Breed snarls filled the night as Chelsea burst from her room on the other side of the house, her voice rising in fear as she screamed out Claire's name.

At the same time, she could hear Ashley, Emma and Shiloh tearing up the stairs from the basement, shouting orders and calling out something to Chelsea as they reached the kitchen.

Liza didn't hesitate. Lifting the gun, she fired on the doorknob, watching the metal knob shatter and fly from its secured position as the door released.

Kicking it in, Liza threw herself into the room, her weapon lifting, instantly finding her first target as she brought herself up with her back to the wall and froze.

Blood splattered along the wall on the far side of the room where a Coyote Breed was slumped, staring sightlessly, lifelessly out at the scene before him.

Claire's scream pierced the night again, but she was backed into a corner, a weapon similar to the one Liza held in her hands, shaking, trained on Stygian, then to Rule Breaker, then the Coyote and finally at Dog. Her finger tightened on the trigger.

"Claire. Please help me," Liza cried out, keeping the plea just weak enough to pierce the haze Claire was in with the appearance of another's pain.

"Liza?" Claire didn't sound dazed or uncertain, but the weapon was still shaking as Stygian and the others watched her now, clearly uncertain of what to do next.

"Claire." It was Dog who spoke up, his voice holding a soothing, tranquil tone Liza hadn't really expected he could possess. "Do you remember me, sweetheart?"

Claire stared at him, wide-eyed, terror whitening her face, though only a cold, hard look filled her gaze.

Claire licked her lips and gave a jerky nod. "Why are you here? Are you with them?" She gestured to the dead Breed.

"Them?" Dog glanced around. "Are there more, Claire?"

"There were two." A sob broke in her voice. "They were waiting when I came from the shower." Tears spilled from her eyes as she steadied the weapon. "Were you with them too?"

"Claire, Stygian wouldn't hurt us." Liza laid her own weapon aside, reality setting in as she began shaking as hard as Claire had been.

Her friend's gaze jerked to her, then back to the Breeds. At the door to the room Ashley, Emma and Shiloh were holding Chelsea back and keeping her quiet.

"Liza." Claire's lips trembled violently. "They were going to take us," she suddenly whispered. "They were going to take both of us, and they were going to hurt us—"

"I know," Liza assured her quickly. She had to get Claire calm and settled. She couldn't say more. "Claire, Dog, Stygian and Rule are here to help us, honey. Let me have the gun."

Liza took a step toward her.

A low, barely perceptible rumble of a growl feathered through the room, causing Liza's head to jerk around and Claire's weapon to jerk back up, her finger tightening on that trigger again.

It was aimed directly at Stygian's chest.

"Claire, please, don't hurt Stygian." The sudden terrified tremble in her voice must have pierced Claire's terror long enough for her friend to finally realize who she was training the weapon on, and who was thrown back against the wall, dead.

They knew that Coyote.

The weapon suddenly fell from Claire's hand.

In a movement so fast Liza swore he was a blur, Rule caught the weapon a second before he caught Claire in his arms.

She slumped against his chest, unconscious, lying limply against him as Stygian and Dog, Emma, Ashley and Shiloh suddenly started moving.

Rule lifted Claire into his arms and rushed through the empty shell of a frame where the large bedroom window had once been. Outside, lights were swirling, flashing as the sound of a heli-jet landed in the yard outside.

Stygian was snapping orders into the comm-link at his ear while Dog was quickly going over the dead Coyote's body.

Then, and only then did Liza see the other body stretched out on the other side of the bed.

Only the boots at first were visible.

Stepping closer, Liza lifted a trembling hand to her lips as she suddenly turned to Stygian.

He was directing the female Coyotes, giving orders in a hard, commanding tone when he turned quickly to her as though he knew exactly where she stood.

His gaze dropped to her feet.

"We have another!" Stygian suddenly called out. "Apprise cleanup we have two assailants. I repeat, we have another body."

Stepping over to her, he stared down at the human, stretched out on his back, his dark gaze staring lifelessly up at the ceiling.

Lank, dark brown hair fell back from his face while the pale, hard-angled planes of his face seemed twisted into an expression of bemusement.

"Holden Mayhew's brother," she whispered. "His name is Harlen."

Holden Mayhew had been, Liza had hoped, the only psychotic in the family.

Evidently she was wrong.

The month before, his brother had died attempting to first rape, then weeks later, kidnap Isabelle Martinez.

Holden's fury at his inability to have the niece of the

president of the Nation had so infuriated him that once he'd learned she was a Breed's lover, he'd attempted to abduct her and sell her to the Genetics Council–loyal Coyotes who had made the bargain to give him a fortune for her.

It had been his brother, Harlen, who had first warned Holden of Isabelle's interest in Malachi. Liza hadn't really believed such insanity could be hereditary.

"She killed them both," Liza whispered as she turned her gaze to the Coyote still sitting motionlessly against the far wall, his blood sprayed around him from the chest wound he'd sustained.

"Good for her." Stygian's tone was savage. "Her father's been notified and she's being flown to a secured section of the hospital now. She's just in shock, unconscious, but we want to be certain she's okay otherwise."

Liza nodded. Joe would be at the hospital. He would ensure only the Nation's healers oversaw her care rather than the Breeds, who would most certainly use this to their own advantage if given the chance.

"This was my room," Liza suddenly realized.

Stygian's gaze jerked back to her as two Breeds moved past them and began preparing the bodies for transport.

"What did you say?" he growled.

Liza turned her gaze up to him. "Until a week ago," she said faintly, "this was my bedroom. I wanted to paint the walls in Isabelle's former room before I moved in, and we weren't able to get it done quickly. Claire was sleeping on the couch until we finished it. I just finished moving in days ago." She had to swallow before she could go on. "They were coming after me again, weren't they, Stygian?"

She could feel it. Her stomach was tight with dread, her chest clenched with panic.

"They've been after you since before the morning Diane Broen found you on that jogging trail," he agreed. "We warned you of that, Liza. That morning, we warned you that you were a target."

"But it doesn't make sense," she whispered. "Stygian, I can't help them get whatever they want. I don't even know what they want. Why come after me?"

Gripping her arm, Stygian moved her carefully into the living room, where Chelsea, Ashley, Emma and Shiloh were waiting.

Chelsea moved to join them, though after a quick, whispered comment from Ashley, hesitated before she stepped back to the other three girls.

"Stygian, what the hell is going on?" she demanded again, keeping her voice low, quiet.

"I'm not certain yet, Liza." A quick shake of his head had her realizing how his hair flowed, like a warrior's, around his face.

Falling to his broad shoulders, the raven black strands looked like living threads of coarse silk.

Even now, amidst a danger she hadn't expected and had no idea how to deal with, all she wanted to do was touch him. Have him touch her.

She wanted his arms around her, because suddenly, she felt so damned alone and so adrift in a world she had no idea how to understand.

Nothing made sense any longer.

"Come here." As though he had read her mind, sensed her need, as though somehow those incredible primal senses he possessed were able to see into the heart of the woman and the fear clogging her mind, his arms were around her and he was wrapping her close to the warmth of his body.

She hadn't realized how chilled she had become, how cold she was. She hadn't realized how much she needed his body heat to still the ice slowly moving through her system.

"Oh God, Stygian." Holding her arms between their bodies, her fingers clenching onto the fabric of his shirt, over the reassuring beat of his heart, she let that shudder of terror have its way.

It tore through her, shaking her until she felt weak, pulling several tears from her eyes despite her attempt to hold them back.

"What's happening to me?" she whispered, almost terrified to let the words free. "Please, tell me what's happening."

She felt as though she were tearing apart inside, twisting into so many directions that nothing made sense anymore.

The sparring match and the sudden release of the abilities she had been fighting so hard to hide.

Claire's screams and her reaction, so outside the realm of what she had been trained for so far.

None of it made sense. None of it meshed with the world she knew and understood.

"We'll figure it out, baby." His head bent over hers, the endearment whispered against her ear as he all but rocked her, easing the terrible fears tearing through her. "I don't know what's going on yet, but I promise, we're going to figure it out."

Stygian held her as close to his own body as he could, trying to share his body heat, to warm the icy chill of her flesh as she shivered and shuddered in his arms.

Glancing over her head to Ashley, he mouthed the word *blanket*, concerned with the unusual cold attacking her.

No doubt it was her reaction to the shock tearing through her, but the severity was concerning him. And it was concerning Chelsea as well.

The other girl was on the phone; if he wasn't mistaken, she was talking, if not to her uncle, the president of the Navajo Nation, then to her father, Terran Martinez. There would be no time to have the blood and saliva samples taken from Claire Martinez that Jonas wanted, in the hospital by certified technicians who could testify to having collected it, before the Navajo healers reached her.

It wouldn't surprise Stygian to learn the healers were waiting at the hospital. There were forces definitely determined to stand between the Breeds, and Liza and Claire.

Fortunately, Rule had raced her straight to the heli-jet and would take the samples himself before arriving at the hospital, just to ensure they were collected.

It wouldn't be exactly what was needed, as the supplies needed wouldn't be in the heli-jet. But what was there might be enough for Jonas to collect those samples needed for the deep-level DNA testing.

As Ashley stepped forward with the blanket and helped Stygian wrap it around Liza, she quickly drew his attention.

"Unable to heli-jet," Ashley whispered, her voice low enough that he doubted Liza heard her. "Navajo intercepted Rule. Transport is by Navajo Nation law enforcement with Rule and Dog following to ensure arrival."

Stygian's brows lifted.

Now that was damned unusual. So much for getting samples in the heli-jet.

But it wasn't the first time it had happened.

Getting Breed doctors in to take care of Isabelle Martinez after her attempted abduction by Holden Mayhew had been nearly impossible.

Like Liza, he was beginning to wonder just what the fuck was going on.

Tightening his arms around the woman he knew in his soul was his mate, and swallowing the taste of the hormone easing from the glands beneath his tongue, Stygian lifted her gently into his arms and moved to the bedroom Chelsea had informed Emma was Liza's.

He wanted her away from the commotion and the knowledge of the dead bodies being removed from Claire's room. He wanted her calm and warm and able to talk.

He wanted to know why his mate was suddenly attracting Genetics Council Coyotes and soldiers when he knew beyond a shadow of a doubt that for the first time in his life, someone was exactly as she seemed.

Faults.

A dark past.

Mistakes made that he knew caused her pain now.

It was all there.

And she would be all his.

Soon.

CHAPTER 9

She had to be dreaming.

Liza pinched the tender flesh on the inside of her arm.

Fuck, that hurt.

Looking down at the mark, she glared at the reddened area of skin the small wound had left.

Okay, so a pinch could actually hurt in a dream. She would go with that.

What else could prove it was a dream?

When she was younger, she had tricks she had used, just to assure herself that she was actually alive and not just a figment of someone's imagination.

Or one of her parents' nightmares.

She'd picked at her cuticles until they were raw.

That had always assured her she was actually a real person.

She looked at her nails.

Damn, her cuticles looked good too. Nice and healthy in ways they hadn't been when she was a teenager.

What else could she do?

There wasn't a lot left. After all, there came a point when she had to admit she was either asleep or awake. Surely she would reach that point soon.

If it hurt, it was supposed to be real.

Right?

She could kiss Stygian, some demonic imp suggested silently. Just kiss him hard and deep and see if that mating stuff was true.

If it was, then that would assure her she was alive.

"Liza?" Looking up from where she sat on the comfortable couch in the suite of the hotel the Breeds were pretty much staking claim to, she stared at the cup of coffee Rachel Broen-Wyatt, Jonas Wyatt's wife, was setting on the table in front of her. "Here's some coffee. It will help with the shock."

Shock? They thought she was in shock?

Well, God bless their hearts.

Actually, they had no idea how little things had ever shocked her.

It wasn't the shock, it was that sense that this simply could not be happening. She couldn't be a target.

She was an anonymous person.

She was a nobody.

There was no reason in the world that the infamous Genetics Council should want to target her. Not even for information on the underground network she was a part of. Until the day before, the Breeds hadn't been certain she was part of it.

Liza accepted the coffee. It was creamy and sweet. Strangely enough, just the way she liked it.

"Are you okay?" Rachel knelt beside her, dark eyes filled with abject concern.

"Fine." She swallowed tightly before lifting the cup to sip at the hot, sweet liquid again.

It was warming her insides.

A little, anyway.

But it wasn't easing that sense of unreality, and she really wasn't in the mood to pinch herself again.

Besides, the director's wife was watching, and that probably wouldn't look rational in her eyes.

"I'm very sorry about this, Liza," Rachel said softly, her gaze heavy with guilt. "I hate the danger you're in now."

"What do you have to do with it?" It made very little

sense that this woman would feel guilt for something she hadn't orchestrated.

Her husband perhaps, but not her.

"Amber is my child," Rachel whispered. "She's the reason we're so desperate to find Gideon."

Ah yes, the baby.

Liza breathed out roughly. "I just wish I could have helped. If it would ease whatever your baby is going through, Mrs. Wyatt, then maybe this would make a little more sense to me."

"Please, call me Rachel." Easing to the couch, Rachel turned to face her.

Liza sipped at the coffee again, hoping to buy herself some time and a bit more of her equilibrium before she was forced to actually converse and make sense.

"Unfortunately, no one but the four involved in the experiments that created the drug Amber was given can help." Rachel grimaced as a young Breed female set another cup of coffee on the table for the director's wife.

The petite Breed was smaller than most Breed females. She was dainty, almost fragile, with shoulder-length dark brown hair and soft green eyes.

"Thank you, Erin." Rachel's smile was tired as she looked up at the younger woman. "Is Amber still sleeping?"

"Yes, ma'am," Erin answered with a nod. "And the fever seems to have eased a bit."

Rachel's lashes lowered in relief for long moments before they opened once again.

"I'll be in the kitchen if you need me," Erin told her before turning and heading to the other end of the room.

"Everyone is here to find more than just Gideon then?" Because that wasn't the story the president of the Navajo Nation had been given.

Rachel shook her head. "Gideon is the only one of the group the Breeds have been able to track down. The other boy and two girls have simply vanished." Her voice thickened. "The two girls are truly the ones we need information on, but if Gideon is all we can find, then perhaps he can remember something from his time with the girls and the treatments they were given. Anything, Liza, that he could remember is better than the nothing we have now." Emotion filled her voice, and tears gathered in her eyes.

Liza reached out and took the coffee cup and saucer that was shaking dangerously in Rachel's hands and placed it on the table.

Rachel's distress wasn't forced. Her love and her concern for her daughter went to her soul. For a moment, as strange as it seemed, Liza swore she could sense that pain, the desperation and fear the other woman was feeling.

Her heart was really breaking for the mother forced to watch her daughter suffer.

How horrible it must be, a nightmare beyond compare to have to watch, day by day, as your child grew sicker, weaker, more pale—

"I'm sorry." Rachel's smile was shaky as she quickly wiped her eyes and looked around the room. "Thank God Jonas isn't in the room yet. We try to be strong for each other—"

She broke off as the door to the suite opened and Jonas entered, along with Stygian, Malachi, Isabelle, Isabelle's father, Terran, and the president of the Nation, Ray Martinez. There was Lawe Justice and his new wife, Diane Broen-Justice. Behind them trailed Rule Breaker—hell of a name—and a small, dark-haired woman. Liza actually recognized her.

Elyiana Morrey was the Feline Breeds' genetic and physiological specialist and their main medical expert. Behind her was another woman, her long black hair hanging in thin braids nearly to her waist, her café au lait skin tone only a shade lighter than Stygian's.

It took a moment, but she'd seen her picture in an article on the Wolf Breed community of Haven. Dr. Nikki Armani, the Wolf Breed genetic and medical expert.

It was a Breed convention, and she had no idea how the hell she had managed a personal invitation.

"Ms. Johnson." Jonas stepped forward. "I've been in contact with your father. He's in New York on Navajo business."

Liza let her eyes close briefly.

Was she suddenly ten again?

They were calling her parents?

Opening her eyes, she shot Stygian a fulminating look before glaring at Jonas.

"Why would you call my parents? I wasn't harmed."

"It's a basic courtesy," he answered coolly. "We've extended our offer to provide the protection needed to ensure that today's and tonight's occurrences don't become a repeat. If the offer is acceptable to you, then he's in agreement with the Bureau of Breed Affairs providing security until his return in a week's time."

Liza leaned back against the couch, crossed her arms over her breasts and turned her glare on Stygian once again.

She wasn't having fun yet.

He was rather cute, though, as he grimaced before turning a much harsher glare back to Jonas.

But Jonas being who he was, the bastard he could be, simply ignored it.

And wasn't it interesting that her father had agreed to the Breeds' offer to protect her? He knew the cover story in place if anyone came in too close. Her status as an undercover agent for the Navajo Law Enforcement Agency gave her an excuse for many of the assignments she took with the Navajo Underground.

Hell, her father was the reason she was part of the underground—her and Claire both. He had actually convinced Claire's father, Ray, that it would be in Claire's best interests to know how to protect herself should an attempt be made to abduct her because of her father's position.

"And who will my guard dog be?" she asked curiously. "Am I allowed to approve or veto your choice?"

"Well, the Bureau does provide such services for quite a high fee," he stated coolly. "And this *is* pro bono, of sorts."

"So the answer is no." She gave a brief, amazed shake of her head before glancing at his mate.

Rachel would be of no help, Liza realized.

She was staring at him as though he was the sun, the moon and the stars all rolled into one too-arrogant male. As far as she was concerned, her husband could do no wrong. It was evident in her expression and in her adoring gaze that convincing her that her husband was being an asshole would be a waste of time.

"The answer is no," Jonas agreed. "But I don't think you'll disagree with the options we've come up with."

"And all without me having to worry my pretty little head over the discussion involving it." Oh, yeah, this was really going over well with her.

It was going over so well that she was nearly shaking with the force of the anger it was sparking inside her.

Damn them! Everyone one of them.

She didn't need the Breeds to take over her life and protect her.

She was a part of Cullen's group for a reason.

She knew she should have excused herself to the ladies' room before Jonas and his asshole enforcers arrived. All she needed was the earbud—

"I think I should inform you that from now on, whenever you're in this room, the communications link you have with your friends will not be active. No other discussions involving Breed business will be overheard by Cullen Maverick, Reever and Steven Jacobs, or Klah Hunter," Jonas informed her with his characteristic iciness.

She jerked her gaze back to Stygian. "Shall I assume you're involved with this?"

A slow, confused frown creased his dark brow. "I assumed it would meet with your approval."

Okay, this was simply enough. Moving instantly to her feet, she didn't bother to hide the anger or her opinion of each and every one of them as well as their so-called plans.

"Arrogant asses," she snapped furiously, her gaze encompassing the entire room full of men and the few women who had trailed in with them. "You had to make this decision behind closed doors without so much as my say-so? You called my father without so much as allowing me, his daughter, the victim in all this, the chance to even speak to him?"

She didn't give them an opportunity to answer. She didn't even want to hear it.

"I am so out of here." Stepping around the small coffee table, she moved purposefully for the door.

"Liza," Stygian growled as she quickly stalked across the room. "You can't just walk out of here."

Oh yeah?

"Just watch me, big boy." Her lip curled in disgust. "I'll show you just how quickly I can and will just walk right out of here."

She was walking right the hell out of there and he could kiss her ass as she made her way right the hell out of the hotel along with it.

"Liza, come on, hear them out." Isabelle, traitor that she was, lent her voice to the protest.

She couldn't believe—

As a matter of fact—

She turned on her heel and glared at her friend. "I simply cannot believe, Isabelle, that you would be party to such a meeting and not demand they include me. What the hell was in your mind?" She slid a sneer toward the Breed at her side. "Or is that a question I even have to ask? Does he have you on such a short fucking leash with that mating bullshit that even friendship no longer matters?"

She wanted to cry. She wanted to scream and rage at the betrayal that was eating her alive.

It burned clear to her soul, making her sick to her stomach with the evidence that nothing or no one mattered to her friend but that damned Breed who held her hostage with his kiss.

"I warned them you were going to be pissed." Isabelle sighed, her gaze concerned if not exactly sympathetic to Liza and Claire's dilemma.

"Damn it, Isabelle, you know better than this," she cried out, her fists clenching at her side as the need to strike out began to override every other impulse slamming through her system.

Isabelle, above all others, knew exactly what Liza was involved in.

"Liza, I know you're upset, but honestly, this was all

done very hastily by conference call as we made our way here. There was no secret meeting and no deliberate decision made without you." Isabelle's dark eyes glittered with pain as Malachi moved to her, his arm sliding around her as though he knew, as though he felt, her pain. As though whatever there was to the matings she'd read about, the Breed's first impulse was still the welfare of his lover.

It was really too damned bad Stygian couldn't feel the same.

"Well, that's exactly how it sounds to me," she snapped, furious with herself for even considering that she could want such support from such a corrupt concept. "It doesn't matter if it was done in the lobby, on the elevator or in a fucking boardroom, it was still done and it was still done without my consent." She turned on Stygian, hurting, aching to such a depth that she felt as though a ragged gash had been sliced into her soul. "As though I were a damned child without the ability to garner help if I need it."

"The help you had was a bit ineffective," Stygian snarled, the pinpoints of blue that filled his gaze glittering with rage. "They were unarmed and completely unaware of the danger until Claire cried out for help. The two of you would have been abducted or dead by the time they arrived."

"Still not your choice." Stabbing a shaking finger in Jonas's direction, she barely restrained the need to scream out her rage.

"And as I said, the decision is the same that would have been made had we waited until we arrived in this room to discuss it," Jonas growled. "Something along the lines of Stygian snarling rather heatedly that his team and no one else would be providing your protection. Should you disagree with the decision, then you have my leave to take it up with him."

"And you were on the phone with my father while all this was going on?" She waved her arm toward Jonas furiously. "That's a lot of talking, demanding and snarling in the space of the time it took to meet in the lobby, get on the elevator and make your way to this to room, Mr. Wyatt." Glaring back at Isabelle and her family, Liza's lips curled in disgust.

"And you still managed to call in the president, his attorney, and the only member of Claire's family that you knew would side with her. The cousin that your Breed managed to hypnotize."

"Oh, Liza." Isabelle sighed painfully. "It wasn't like that."

"The call was made to your father seconds after Claire's father was informed of the attack and her arrival at the hospital," Stygian stated, his tone grating. "If you would throttle your independence for the amount of time it would take to make explanations, perhaps you could save that adrenaline you have tearing you apart for when you might actually need it."

She was shaking, trembling with the knowledge that her life was slowly being taken over and there wasn't a damned thing she could do about it.

"And maybe you might stop trying to take my life over entirely. You and your friends," she demanded angrily as she flicked a look to Jonas and the other Alphas. "You're making me feel like a shrew, Stygian, when I know damned good and well you could have consulted me before making any such decision about my life, my protection or who would be protecting me."

That was exactly what she felt like. A shrew who had no idea how to be grateful for the fact that they were trying to protect her.

It felt more like they were attempting to use her. That somehow, they had brought that danger to her.

She knew, *knew* in her soul that it was time to step back and let Cullen and his team, as well as the Breeds take over the search for whoever or whatever was stalking her. She wasn't experienced enough, not yet, to handle the danger surrounding her and Claire both.

But God, they could have at least allowed her to have a say in her own life.

"And perhaps that's true, Ms. Johnson," Jonas spoke, his tone calm, smooth and pleasant as he just patronized the hell right out of her. "We were merely attempting to expedite an order to lay in as many safeguards as possible for not just yourself, but also your friends Claire and Chelsea."

As though she needed to be reminded that her friends were in danger as well. Hadn't she been there with them? Hadn't she seen Claire, unconscious, the bodies of those Coyotes—

She had to swallow tightly.

"Is Claire okay? Was she hurt?" she whispered. Her friend wasn't a fighter, but she had learned how to handle a weapon like it was no one's business.

Her training had paid off, but it had paid off with a price, and Liza wasn't certain of the price Claire had finally paid.

Jonas nodded. "She did. Both shots were kill shots and both were meant to do damage. She knew what she was doing."

"That's the interesting part, Liza." Terran stepped forward, his bronze face lined with not just the grief of the past, but also the concern that shimmered in his gaze. "My niece took out two highly trained killer Coyotes with a weapon that's been outlawed for more than a decade. I'd like to know where she acquired it, considering the fact that neither you, nor Claire, should even have the contacts to acquire such dangerous weapons."

Her lips parted before she quickly shut them.

Oh boy. Claire had used the Glock. And hadn't she just forgotten they weren't still fucking ten and answerable to guardians who had no idea who they were any longer?

Liza breathed in deeply, fighting to force back a fury that Terran really didn't deserve. He was sincerely concerned and truly unaware of the life his niece had chosen to live. "I'd prefer she have an illegal Glock to kill them with than the alternative," she snapped defensively, knowing there was no way in hell to cover the fact that Claire had had that weapon.

"We're not debating that, Liza," Stygian growled.

"No, we're debating whether or not you're going to be allowed to step in and take over my life," she retorted combatively. "That seems to be the matter up for debate." She flicked a look at Terran as he crossed his arms over his chest and watched her suspiciously.

He and Joe Martinez were her father's best friends.

She also suspected that Terran had once been commander of a team of underground agents as well. He would suspect what she was doing, who she was working with, but he could never question it unless he went to her father. And if he did, then her father would never lie to him. But, knowing the truth could perhaps do more damage, considering Terran had lost his sister more than thirty years before to the Genetics Council.

No doubt, for what it was worth, Stygian and his Breed buddies were going to run right over her objections. Because if she didn't follow their plan, her parents would return from New York. Her father's eyes would be filled with concern. Her mother would stare at her with fear and worry.

Neither were looks that she wanted to see. Just because her father knew she was part of the Breed Underground Network didn't mean he wouldn't have nightmares where her safety was concerned. There was a reason she had been placed with a support team rather than rescue or relocation.

"What are you going to do, Liza?" Stygian asked, thinking fast and hard, trying to keep her from actually doing or saying something she would regret.

Trying to keep her safe.

The Breeds around them inhaled again, obviously detecting the scent that Stygian had only caught the slightest hint of moments before.

A scent he hadn't expected, not without a kiss. A touch. Something more than the contact they'd had to this point.

She glared at them before turning to Stygian, furious. "Tell them to stop that."

Stygian's jaw bunched as his lashes lowered over his blue-black eyes and he stared back at her. "I can't make them stop."

"Why?" Deliberately, her lips tight, she asked the one question he truly didn't want to answer.

Hell.

His scent was already on her.

Shit! How did that happen?

Mating heat. It was impossible to hide from a Breed's

senses. Every Breed who came in contact with her would scent it and be warned by it.

Even he hadn't detected it before he entered the room, but as Alpha Wolfe Gunnar, the Wolf Breed Alpha who had silently been awaiting their arrival, glanced between the two of them, his nostrils flaring, Stygian knew exactly what they were scenting.

"I hate Breeds!" she snarled.

God, just what he needed. The fury burning inside her was like throwing coal on a fire. It made the heat hotter, made it burn brighter, longer. And added to that now, was a resentment he couldn't really blame her for.

Wolfe turned to Stygian, a quirk tugging at his lips.

"I have a feeling she doesn't really hate Breeds," he murmured in amusement.

And did his mate take to that comment easily?

"I used to like you." She crossed her arms beneath her breasts, cocked her hip and glared at the Alpha. "Where's your wife, anyway? And why the hell did she let you out alone?"

Wolfe chuckled at the insult and gave his head a little shake.

"Liza?" Stygian drew her attention back to him before she could actually offend his Alpha. Which was exactly what she was considering. "What are you going to do once you walk out of here? Many of the Council's Coyotes are indistinguishable from humans except by other Breeds. You'll never know who they are. You'll never know when they'll strike. When they take you, they'll use you to drain your father dry. He'll lie. He'll cheat. He'll steal. He'll do whatever it takes—give them whatever information they ask for, whatever he might think they want—to make them stop hurting you. And they *will* hurt you."

Seeing the terror that flashed in her eyes was almost more than he could bear.

Dragging in a hard, deep breath, his gaze locked with hers, forcing himself to see and to feel the pain clenching at her.

She was his mate. From this moment on, his acceptance

of who and what she was to him would determine the love that would continue to grow between them.

He could damage her fragile female pride now, and watch the embers of love he had glimpsed heating between them wither to nothing; or he could slowly build those flames into the inferno that would see them through the decades to come. But now this moment, and how he handled it, would either stoke the embers or damage the fire forever.

Near immortality could be hell, he imagined, tied to a woman whose hatred stemmed from her mate's refusal to respect and to honor her.

"Why?" There were no tears, only stoicism and a sense of reluctant resignation. "Tell me why they want me."

She knew she couldn't fight the protection, but as far as that was concerned, she didn't have to accept it gracefully.

Or gratefully.

"It's not you they want," he promised her, his gaze sliding to Terran before returning to his mate's. "As we told you, they want Honor Roberts, Fawn Corrigan and the two Bengal Breeds who were part of one of the most immoral experiments known to have been conducted in the history of Breed genetics. Like us, they followed Gideon, one of those Bengals. Here to Window Rock. They won't leave until they've captured them, or we have them under Breed protection, as there is no evidence to be found that they're dead." He glanced at Terran Martinez.

The Navajo's legal representative working to block the Breeds' request to access the Navajo Genetic Database never outright lied to the Breeds, but the hint of deception was always there.

"This has nothing to do with me." Liza clenched her teeth over the words, the anger and hurt clearly sensed by all the Breeds there.

Especially by Stygian.

"You, Claire and Chelsea now have everything to do with this, Liza." Terran breathed out roughly, accepting the truth himself when before, he had fought it. "I'm sorry. If there was something I could do to stop this—"

She gave a hard shake of her head, obviously refusing to argue with Terran for some reason. "I understand."

But did she?

Stygian could see her face, her eyes.

Understanding wasn't there.

But neither was resentment. At least, not toward Terran.

"If we had the information we needed, if we had the genetic profiles in the database that matched Gideon's, then we could find him. Find him, and we'll find the others," Stygian informed her. "Find them all, Liza, and this all goes away."

The scent of Terran's anger was unmistakable, just as the scent of Liza's rejection of the solution swirled through the room. The energy tightened his chest.

She agreed with Terran's decision.

Son of a bitch. She was agreeing to give in, to end this fight for her independence rather than see the Navajo open that Genetic Database to the Breeds. What the hell did those records hold that caused the Navajo to be so frightened?

He hadn't met a single member of the Navajo Council or citizen of Window Rock who didn't feel the same way. Every member in a position to aid the Breeds' cause would die before giving up the information. Even for a cause as worthy as Amber's.

"We have a message out to every member who has donated to the Genetic Database," Terran stated roughly, "requesting any member willing to release their genetic information come forward. None have. Until the Breed in question makes that request, the database cannot be opened to match the profile."

And only the requesting Breed could receive the information.

They could have made the idea work if they had known of a single Breed born of Gideon's dam. Unfortunately, to their knowledge, those littermates had all been destroyed long ago.

The suspicion that Gideon would take refuge with blood relations was high. He would know the Breeds would encounter a roadblock in tracking him through bloodlines, just as Gideon would know Jonas would use every means possible to do just that.

Liza's lips parted in an irate, feminine grimace that was uniquely charming and yet filled with such emotional distress that it was all Stygian could do to hold back a snarl of fury.

Now he knew exactly why Breeds were so damned irritable when their mates were.

"I want to go home." She inhaled wearily, and suddenly, Stygian could feel the exhaustion pulling at her.

Weariness and uncertainty and a sense of defeat.

Because she knew she couldn't go home. She knew the place she had called home would be denied to her until Honor, Fawn, Judd and Gideon were together.

The weariness and uncertainty he could understand. He could even allow it. The defeat was another thing entirely.

"Not tonight. The damage to the house hasn't been repaired yet, and we're still trying to track down a few leads concerning the two Breeds Claire killed. A room has been reserved here for you. You can return to the house when it's safe again," Stygian assured her, his fists clenching at his sides with the need to go to her.

That need was a hunger that raged and tore at his guts, yet he could sense the knowledge that doing so right now would do more harm than good. Liza didn't want his strength at the moment, she needed her own. And she would never be certain she had done all she could to escape the obstacles fate had placed in her path at the moment.

"He's right, Liza." Terran turned to her as Stygian watched her lips part and the gleam of battle enter her gaze. "Let us get the windows repaired and get some additional security to the house. Then we'll rethink the matter."

Once again, she bowed down to Terran's request when she was ready and eager to fight Stygian's.

His back teeth clenched to the point that he was amazed his teeth didn't shatter with the pressure.

"What will it really matter, Terran?" Liza asked then, the bitter disillusionment in her gaze beginning to bother Stygian in ways he couldn't explain, even to himself. "The only difference between the Genetics Council and the Breeds is the manner in which they manage to extract the information from their victims." She turned back to Jonas then. "It doesn't matter how they hurt me, how they torture me or how much of it they make my father watch. There's no way he can access that information, Mr. Wyatt. There's no way *I* can access it."

"Any information can be accessed, Ms. Johnson." It was Rachel who stepped forward.

Somber. Her face pale from lack of sleep, the dark circles beneath her eyes attesting to her worry and concern for her daughter, she spoke with the heavy knowledge of certainty.

Liza shook her head. "Such information is too important to leave to chance, Rachel. The Navajo Genetic Database is the only one of its kind in the world. The only one that will allow the majority of the Breeds to find their place in the world. Just as their mothers, their grandmothers, their aunts and their cousins were taken from their home, their lands, their worlds." The scent of her tears reached Stygian, as subtle as the first breeze of spring, as heated as summer's kiss. "It's the only way some families who lost relatives will ever learn what happened to them. Do you think the safeguards we have in place aren't the best that could have been imagined or provided?"

Rachel clasped her hands in front of her as she hunched her shoulders defensively. An unconscious gesture toward the possibility that the plans her mate had put in place to find the answers to save her daughter could fail.

"It's information," Rachel said then. "Any time information is gathered, no matter where or by whom, when another knows of it, suspects it, then it's in danger of discovery. The Navajo Genetic Database has been secure only because none knew of it outside a very small group and because those supplying their genetic information had a reason to remain quiet. But now, others who have no such loyalty to what you've gathered know of it, Liza. And unless it's disbanded and all information destroyed, then it is at risk."

It *was* at risk.

Liza stared back at the other woman and saw the tears

shimmering in her eyes, the agony that resonated in her soul as she faced her daughter's possible fate.

Liza would give anything to help her save that perfect, sweet little girl.

The database wasn't going to save her, though.

Finding Gideon wouldn't save Amber.

And Honor Roberts and Fawn Corrigan did not exist within the database.

They did not exist within the Nation.

"My father wouldn't betray what he's pledged himself to, even for me." She turned to Stygian, that knowledge wrapping around in a certainty that raked across her already scarred soul. "He can't betray what he himself has no access to. If you don't believe me, ask Terran."

She turned to Isabelle's father with an arched brow.

Staring back at her for a long, silent moment, he finally nodded with a sharp motion of his head.

"That's true enough," he agreed—then he had to spoil it. "But I agree with the Breeds, Liza. The Genetics Council would believe otherwise and they wouldn't flinch at the thought of torture to get the answers they believe could be attained."

She felt betrayed. Betrayed and angry.

She needed to get home. If she were stuck here in this hotel, how was she supposed to do her job?

"Not to worry, Ms. Johnson, I'm certain your friends will find a way to stop by and say hello." Jonas's smile was tight and hard. "At least you left your comm-link home tonight."

"If I had known the lovely meeting we would have, I would have made certain to pick it up before I left."

"Cullen has no business pulling you into this," Terran bit out. "I'm sure your father will have something to say about it."

Lips tightening, she turned to Jonas. "And just what fairy tales have you been carrying to Terran, Mr. Wyatt?"

"I don't deal in fairy tales, Ms. Johnson," he assured her coolly. "I deal in facts and nothing more." There wasn't an ounce of apology in his gaze or in his voice.

Which left her only one alternative.

"Father has known about it since it began, Terran." She sighed wearily. "He's always stood behind my decision to do what I felt was needed. He won't back down from that decision."

God, she was tired.

Too damned tired to put up with this crap much longer.

Shoving her hands into the pockets of her cotton pants, she slowly turned back to Stygian, forcing herself to meet his gaze. "I'm tired. Either take me home or show me my room. I think I've had enough for the day."

"I can do that," he agreed.

There was something about that agreement that just didn't sit right with her.

Something that just smacked of a man with an agenda.

The arousal that burned between them was another warning.

She'd warned him not to mate her without her knowledge.

He hadn't kissed her. He hadn't taken her.

But still, she swore she could smell the subtle intensity of the hunger burning between them.

She shouldn't be able to smell any such thing. But the delicate, barely there scent of a man and a woman merging still seemed to pique her sense of smell.

And that knowledge terrified her in ways she didn't want to face at the moment.

"Where is my room then?" she asked.

His hand lifted, rubbing at the back of his neck before his expression turned pure, predatory male.

"With me," he answered.

The breath stilled in her chest, her heart constricting, the shame and rage burning inside her like a trail of lava seeping from her soul.

His room.

She so wasn't surprised.

"I don't think so." If she sounded belligerent, it might be because she was.

"You're going to hurt my feelings if you keep rejecting me, Liza." His lashes lowered, the heat in the glitter of his gaze seared her senses.

"You would have to have feelings first," she snapped, certain that wasn't at this moment.

No man, or Breed, with any clue to what emotions were, could possibly stand and do what he had done to her tonight.

Steal her independence.

Take everything she was and not even allow her the chance to fight for it.

"So where exactly would that be?" It was all she could do to force the word past her lips.

She wasn't going to bother to argue or to refuse to stay. They weren't going to let her out of there tonight, and she was smart enough to know it.

"Come on." He held his hand out to her.

Liza couldn't force herself to take it. She couldn't allow herself to touch him.

Because she wanted him.

She wanted him in spite of the fact that she felt manipulated as hell. She wanted him in spite of the knowledge that she was being used.

Used to catch a killer.

Used to save a child.

But she was being used all the same.

Slowly, his hand lowered.

"This way." Turning, he led her from Jonas's suite as she ignored Isabelle's whisper of her name.

Once the door closed behind them, he moved up the hall, glancing back only once to see if she followed.

While she was breaking apart inside and didn't know why.

While her own screams echoed inside her head and she didn't know where those screams came from, or why.

While she ached for him as she had never ached for anything in her life.

Liza followed.

❖　❖　❖

"Are you returning?"

The harsh tone pierced at Audi Johnson's heart.

He sat in the back of the SUV as it raced for the airport so torn inside that his soul felt ragged and raw.

He held the phone with one hand, his wife's hand with the other and stared out the window at the city lights while the driver battled traffic, pedestrians and time.

"I'm heading for the airport now," he answered.

"Claire is being guarded," he was told. "Liza is under the protection of the Breeds."

Audi's eyes closed briefly before he opened them once again.

"Have the Six come together yet?" he asked.

"Only two have received the vision to return," he was told. "That time is nearing, but it isn't here yet."

He had to fight back his tears and fight back the knowledge that when it happened, he would lose more than he had ever imagined possible.

He had never believed he would be unable to save his child from this. That once again, he would lose her. God knew he had fought, he had manipulated and used every string he could pull to save her from this day, always believing it was possible. Always believing he could keep her from ever hurting again.

Beside him, his wife fought back a sob that escaped despite the battle.

"We'll be there as soon as possible," he told the other man.

"We'll be awaiting you."

The call disconnected.

The feel of Jane's shoulders trembling had him releasing her hand to wrap his arms around her, pulling her close to his chest.

"I can't do this," she whispered tearfully, her fingers clenching the light jacket he wore as her tears dampened the cloth. "Please, Audi, don't let me lose her again. Please."

He had to fight back his own tears, his sense of failure.

"We have no choice." The sound of his own voice, rough with the tears trapped inside him, scraped against his senses. "We agreed, Jane. For their lives, we agreed. And she's our daughter. She needs us."

Ah, God, it hurt.

His guts were shredding, his chest felt as though jagged nails were tearing across it with demonic satisfaction.

"She's my baby," Jane sobbed painfully, her pain another jagged tear into her heart. "This wasn't supposed to happen, Audi. She wasn't supposed to be taken from us again."

"No one will take her. I'll keep her safe," he swore, yet he knew what he was facing. It was an empty promise at best, and Jane knew it.

"Why do they want her?" Her fists clenched against his chest as she trembled with her anger. "Why, Audi? Why would they come for her? Liza is nothing to them. There's no way she can be of use to them. There's no way anyone could know—" The last was barely a breath of sound.

Audi knew why, just as he knew the danger his daughter faced because of it.

"I'll fix it, Jane," he promised, closing his eyes and praying that he wasn't lying to his wife for the second time in their marriage.

Just as he prayed this daughter didn't pay for his failure to protect her as the first had. God help him, Liza was the child he and Jane had always dreamed of. She was a fighter, intelligent and adept, compassionate and loving. There wasn't a manipulative bone in her body or a single death wish to torture her family.

She had given their lives purpose at a time when he had wondered if they would drift forever in a haze of guilt that never seemed to find relief.

Yet, from the moment she had opened her eyes and called him "Dad," he had felt a healing begin. Just as Jane had.

She was a true mother to Liza.

Their daughter had learned to cook, to clean, to laugh and to tease. She had talked him into teaching her how to skate, how to rock climb, and finally, she had allowed him to teach her how to drive.

If he lost her—

God help them both if they lost her.

Liza had learned years before exactly how to avoid the facts of life.

Stepping into the hotel room and seeing the two beds separated by a small table, she sighed heavily.

"Really?" She turned back to him in disbelief. "They didn't have a larger room? A suite, perhaps?"

His shoulders lifted, a rakish smile curling his lips despite the somberness in his dark eyes. "Hotel's all booked up, sweetheart."

Of course it was.

"You have a few of your sleep shirts in the wardrobe." He indicated the tall entertainment center with its four drawers beneath the screen. "Isabelle had one of the officers who followed us to the hotel go back for them. There are clothes in there as well."

"Great, some guy pawing through my clothes." It was all she could do to hold back a shudder at the thought.

"It wasn't like that, Liza." The frustration in his voice only seemed to infuriate her further.

Turning on him, she crossed her arms beneath her breasts and confronted him with all the anger she couldn't seem to bury. "It wasn't like what, Stygian? Like some asshole pawing through my silk panties and bras? Do you think they didn't snicker as they chose the gowns? That they didn't imagine me naked or wearing one of the silk camisoles I sleep in? Since when are Breeds any better than any other man when it comes to lust?"

Dropping her arms, she turned to stalk to the bathroom, to get away from him. To strangle the fury tearing through her before she choked them both with it.

Before she was entirely certain what was happening, Liza found herself being pulled around and hauled against Stygian's chest, his large hand still holding the arm he had gripped to pull her to him.

"Do you really believe I would allow another man to do something so damned intimate?" he growled, shocking her.

That was possessiveness in his voice. That low, primal growl held a vein of pure, determined ownership that at once pricked her independence and pulled at the woman who longed to belong—

To something. To someone.

"I don't really know what you would do, do I, Stygian?" Her breathing was suddenly rough, heavy.

The need to know if Isabelle had been right about a Breed's kiss being addictive was suddenly overwhelming. If not addictive, then what about the aphrodisiac it was supposed to contain?

She licked her lips, suddenly desperate for the answer.

"No male Breed pawed through your clothing, your silk, or your gowns," he snarled down at her. "Ashley chose each piece and she alone packed it before the Breed who drove her back to the house returned her to the hotel. Never, ever, Liza"—his lips were so close to hers now that she swore she could almost feel them against hers—"would I allow another man to touch what you would wear so intimately against your flesh."

Breathing was a chore. Her chest was so tight with the need to hold back the moan rising inside it that she felt light-headed from the battle. Every second that she felt the heat of his chest sinking past their clothing to the sensitive, peaked hardness of her nipples, she could feel the flesh between her thighs growing wetter.

She wanted him.

She had never wanted a man in her life. She had thought that part of herself must have surely died in the wreck when she was fifteen. Before then, there had been very little interest in the opposite sex. Afterward, there had been none.

Until Stygian.

"I hate this," she suddenly whispered as her fingers curled against the powerful muscles of his chest, desperate to keep herself from ripping at his body.

"Hate what?" His free hand cupped her face, his thumb brushing against the plump curve of her lower lip then.

Oh, he knew what. She could see it in the sudden intensity of his gaze, feel it whipping through the air between them and torturing them both with the hungry need for it.

As her tongue swiped over the painful dryness of her lips, it licked over the tip of his thumb. The sudden, explosive taste of salty male flesh rushed through her senses, overtaking them for one destructive second.

"I've never wanted—" Her breathing hitched painfully. "I never wanted this, Stygian. I didn't want to be torn apart like this. To be destroyed by something I couldn't control or teased by a man who's far too aware of my weaknesses."

She couldn't bear it. To be played with. To ache and to want, to hunger for something and have no name to give to what she hungered for.

To her, it was the worst possible tease.

"Tease you?" His voice was suddenly rougher, grating as he wrapped one arm around her back and pulled her closer. "I'd never tease you, Liza. I promise, I'm entirely, wholeheartedly serious about this. About you."

His head lowered and his lips touched hers.

She was shaking. Like a leaf in the storm and any other cliché that slipped through her suddenly too-alert brain.

Shudders of reaction began tearing through her as her lips parted and his settled more firmly against them, opening them, owning them.

His tongue swiped over her lips, flicked past them and licked over her tongue.

Suddenly, she knew what Isabelle had meant. His kiss

was like a summer rainstorm, lightning and thunder chaos
clamoring through her system as the taste of summer heat
rushed through her senses.

His lips slanted over hers, his hands pulling her closer as
the feel of his erection pressing against her stomach had her
tilting her hips and arching to meet him.

Blood thundered through her veins, the fiery need spreading through her body, clamoring for more, burning away any
objections she could have made.

Desire burned through her in ways she couldn't have
anticipated. It sizzled across her flesh, sensitizing it, creating a receptive base for each touch he should deign to stroke
across it.

And she wanted each touch.

His tongue flicked across her lips, teasing and heating
them. She licked against it, loving that wild, stormy taste.
Then it sank between her lips once again, giving her only
seconds to close her lips over it, to contain the taste filling
her system before it retreated once again.

Oh God, the pleasure was exquisite.

Her nipples hardened furiously. The pressure of her bra
against the sensitive tips was almost agony, so she took it off.

It wasn't the fabric she wanted touching her. It was his
hands, his fingers. She wanted the feel of his flesh against
hers creating that roughened, electric pulse of sensations
that raced across her skin.

She ached for it.

She had to get closer.

Twining her arms around his neck, she arched to him,
and still it wasn't enough.

"I can't touch you like this," she whimpered, pulling at
his shirt as he released her lips for only a second. "I need to
touch you more, Stygian."

So much for not being that kind of girl.

At least she only wanted to be a sex slave for this man.

And oh yes, she could handle sex slave.

For a night or two, anyway.

For a lifetime or two, definitely.

"Oh." Her eyes flew open as she felt his hand push

beneath her shirt, the calloused, roughened flesh stroking up her back. "I like that."

No, she loved it.

She arched into his touch, her lashes drifting closed as his hand stroked back down, curved around her hip then moved up her midriff, her rib cage—

Opening her eyes, a ragged breath of air tore from her lungs as his palm cupped the swollen mound of her breast.

Why her hand was suddenly gripping his wrist, she wasn't certain.

She looked down to where her fingers curled over his powerful wrist, her flesh much paler than his, the feel of those invisible hairs beneath softening its toughness.

Breathing hard, barely able to draw in enough oxygen, she lifted her gaze to his once again. Liza pressed his hand more firmly against the curve of her breast. Still watching him, she let her own thumb stroke over the tight, hardened point of her nipple.

Oh, that was good.

Letting her lashes drift closed once more, feeling the caress of his gaze where her hand lay over his, she let her thumb rub against the sensitized peak as he watched.

His breathing grew heavier, the heat against her flesh seemed searing. The hunger rising inside her was suddenly clamoring to take more sensation, to amplify it and torture them both with a need she was finding impossible to deny.

Drawing her thumb back, a moan drifting past her lips, Liza was prepared to stroke the needy little nubbin again when suddenly, Stygian took control of the caress.

With thumb and forefinger, he gripped the tip and rolled it between them, then let his lips brush against her jaw.

"Get rid of this shirt."

Staring up at him as he used his free hand to tug at her shirt, Liza loosened her hold on his neck to grip the hem and pull it over her head.

Oh, sweet Heaven.

A brutal, ecstatic heat surrounded her nipple before the shirt fell to the floor.

The pressure of his thumb and forefinger around the tip

increased, milking the sensitive flesh and torturing nerve endings that suddenly burned in an ecstatic quest for more.

Oh God, oh God, wasn't that just like a Breed, taking advantage—

With her body arched back, her breasts pushed forward and high, Stygian lowered his head and immediately sucked the painfully sensitive tip into his mouth.

The cry that tore from her lips shocked her.

The speed at which her hands buried in his hair, clenched in the strands and tried to pull him closer astounded her.

As his tongue lashed at the pebbled hardness, Liza flinched with pleasure, shuddering in his arms as tremulous cries left her lips.

Her nipple felt brutally hot. Too sensitive. The pleasure flaying the tip with merciless strokes tore through her senses and jerked her into a realm of such pleasure she felt tortured by it.

"Oh yes, Stygian, please. Yes," she moaned, her head tipping back, her aching pussy rubbing against the hard muscle of his thigh as her hips tilted to him.

As he lifted her closer, his hard thigh pushed further between hers as he pulled her hips down to it and moved rhythmically against the sensitive, wet flesh. Even through the soft cotton of her pants she could feel the rasp of his jeans, the fiery warmth of his flesh and she wanted more. So very much more.

She felt so empty.

She swore she had never actually felt the inner flesh of her sex and the loneliness it felt. But she felt it now. It clenched and tightened and the slick layer of juices eased from it, creating a teasing friction that only amplified the need for more.

Plumping the firm flesh of her breast with his fingers, Stygian worked the agonizingly tight peak of her nipple with his tongue. Rolling it over the sensitive flesh, flicking the tip of his tongue against it, laving it, rubbing the side of his tongue over the pebbled hardness as it grew increasingly tender. It ached, the hard flesh demanded—

"Please." Her fingers buried in his hair. "Oh God, what are you doing to me?"

His head lifted.

"Don't stop." Eyes flaring open in shock, she stared up at him as she watched him jerk his shirt off.

Tight, hard abs flexed. The muscles of his chest rippled as his hair flowed around his shoulders.

His blue-black gaze was piercing, filled with a demand that her body was responding to with incredible force.

"Do we stop this now, or do we finish it, Liza?" His voice sounded tormented.

"Stop?" Shock filled her. "Do I act like I want to stop, Stygian?"

What the hell was wrong with him?

What happened to a man taking what was offered and just running off the next morning rather than asking questions before he ever managed to get a woman into his bed?

"I don't want your regrets in the morning," he stated, his tone rough.

She had to curl her hands into fists to keep from touching him.

All that tough-looking, prime, muscular male flesh did nothing but tempt her fingers and her lips to explore, to kiss.

A sharp shake of her head was a mistake. Allowing him to pause, to speak, to be the man he was, was definitely a mistake.

Because now, all she could think was, what the hell was she doing?

She could taste him on her tongue, even now, as the feel of his kiss should have been easing from her lips. Yet it wasn't. It was still there, the sensitive curves still swollen and aching for more.

"Don't," she whispered, suddenly overwhelmed by an emotion she didn't recognize or understand. "Don't do that, Stygian. Don't make me choose like this."

"Our tomorrows mean too much to me, Liza."

"Bullshit!" Anger shot through her as she jerked out of his arms, confronting him furiously. "Do you think I don't know a play for control when I see one? God, just take it and stop talking."

She could barely breathe now for the emotions surging

through her, for the hunger and the aching need for the return of his touch.

Oh, she wasn't having this.

She wanted him. She wanted him until it was all she could do not to throw herself back into his arms. But as he stood there staring at her, his expression dominant, full of arrogance, she just wanted to kick him instead.

Jerking her shirt from the bed, she pulled it over her head furiously.

"'Our tomorrows mean too much to me,'" she mocked him, her hands moving to her hips as she cocked one hip and faced him with such a surge of antagonism that she could barely breathe for it. "For God's sake, Stygian, if tomorrow meant so damned much to you, then you would have kept your mouth shut and just fucked me while you had the chance."

"Like any other man would have done?" His arms crossed over his chest, and for just a second, she hated him for the fact that he wasn't holding her. That he was blocking the heat she swore she was going to freeze without.

"Well, yeah, pretty much," she snapped back at him. "What do you want from me? Do I have to make you a few promises first? I thought that was your job? Come, Stygian, give me the empty promises, get me off, then leave me the hell alone."

Her father had always warned her that her smart mouth was going to end up costing her something she didn't want to lose.

It was her temper, she'd reminded him. A temper she'd gotten from him, so he really couldn't blame her.

But at the moment, she had a feeling it was going to end up costing her the night she'd really wanted to spend in this Breed's bed. Just one night to go crazy in his arms, maybe sleep there for a bit, go crazy with him again, then face the reality she wanted only to hide from tonight.

"Do you believe that's all this means to me?" he asked, his expression savage as he watched her, his gaze beginning to glitter with anger. "A one-night stand with a woman that means nothing? Is that all it is to you, Liza? A few hours you can forget when reality returns and a man that will be content to just disappear from your life?"

"Can I get that lucky?" God no, that wasn't what she wanted, but still, the words burst from her lips before she could control them.

"After that kiss?" The hard, triumphant smile that curled his lips had her heart stopping in her chest.

It was a reminder. She'd wanted the truth of mating before he kissed her, right? So what had she been doing accosting him?

Breathing rough, the need for oxygen suddenly slamming inside her, Liza stared up at him, the temper that had always been her downfall exploding at the satisfaction she glimpsed in his eyes.

"After that kiss?" she exclaimed furiously. "Sorry, Breed, but maybe it's not as damned powerful as you were hoping it was. I guess I have my answer. Those tabloids are full of shit."

Swinging around, she made for the bathroom with the intent of locking herself in and taking the coldest shower possible.

She had taken maybe two steps—counting them wasn't high on her list of priorities—when in the next breath, she was back flat against the wall and staring up at him as the first tear slid slowly from the corner of one eye.

Oh God, she hated crying. She never cried in front of anyone, and crying in front of him was just humiliating.

He was so strong, so dominant and determined. She wanted to be strong in his eyes as well.

Tears were not a sign of strength, thank you very much.

"Just let me go." Rough, those damnable tears rasping at her throat, Liza tried to look away and hold back that pain.

Meeting his gaze was the hardest thing she had done in recent memory, but she forced herself to anyway. She met his gaze and swore if she saw pity there, she was going to slam her knee straight into his balls.

His lips quirked. "The scent of your sweet pussy weeping for me only just slightly overshadows your hunger to do me harm, Liza."

Forcing the sneer to curl her lip and fight back her tears took everything she had. "Why not just call me 'mate.' That's what Malachi calls Isabelle. And we both know that's why my mouth is watering for your kiss almost as bad as my pussy is creaming for your dick."

Vulgar, meant to be insulting. It might have been just that if it weren't for the husky, phone-sex tone of her voice. And she might have felt just a smidgen of shame if his eyes hadn't suddenly dilated in pure, undiluted lust as a primitive, animalistic growl rumbled in his chest.

If they had been close before, a second later it wouldn't be possible for a breath of air to slide between their hips as his hands clamped on her rear, lifted her, and in one smooth move had her thighs spread, her knees clamping on his hips as he ground his erection, hard, into the vee of her thighs.

Suddenly, there wasn't enough air in the room again.

Breathing had never been so difficult. Her nipples pressed hard into his chest with each breath she took, and her clit was so swollen, so sensitive that the feel of her silk panties grinding into it was torturous.

"When I bury my dick up that tight pussy, Liza, you're going to wish you'd given more heed to whatever it is you think you know," he warned her, his voice harsh. "Mate." He nipped her lips, then licked the little wound.

Liza gasped, her lips parting, and as they opened, Stygian was there.

His kiss was incredibly hot. So hungry she could only give in to it as pleasure tore through her in a wave of sensation so intense she swore she nearly orgasmed from it. She could feel it building, pulsing, riding the edge of release with such sharp intensity that she shuddered with its need.

Just as quickly, he released her.

Liza swayed as she found herself alone, the wall the only thing between her and losing her balance completely.

Staring back at Stygian as he paced away from her, his hands tunneling through his hair in frustration, she wondered exactly how he managed it.

She couldn't have walked away from him if her life had

depended on it. Evidently the hunger was affecting her far more deeply than it was him.

Turning back to her, the blue glints in his eyes seemed to glow while his expression tightened with such savagery it sent an involuntary shudder up her spine.

"Mate." His lips pulled back from his teeth in a grimace of pure lust. "My mate."

Confidence and power filled him. Where was the fairness in that when she suddenly felt so . . . female. So much weaker than he, and for some unfathomable reason, ready to beg to submit to him.

Instead, she forced herself to lift her chin willfully.

"Yours?" Pushing herself away from the wall, she breathed in roughly. "Not hardly, Stygian. Some damned chemical reaction does not make me yours. Nor does it make me even want to be yours. So maybe you should consider revising your bedside manner, stud, because this one is only pissing me off."

With that, she stalked to the bathroom, slammed the door closed and locked it.

She sure as hell didn't want him smelling that particular lie.

Liza had learned over the years the fine art of the delicate lie as she worked, first with her father in the security division of the headquarters of the Navajo Nation, then as she began training to work with the Breed Underground Network.

Breeds could smell a lie or even the intent to deceive. Learning how to lie just in case it was a Breed one was conversing with had become second nature. But she had never had to learn how to lie about her attraction to a Breed, or her need. And lying about it was suddenly imperative. Otherwise, Stygian would end up with enough power over her to ensure that she was willing to do whatever he asked her to do. Just as she suspected Isabelle was willing to do whatever Malachi asked of her. Now, she understood, sort of, why her friend would stand so solidly with the man that called her "mate." Especially if he gave her the illusion of respect and a choice.

Not that she discussed her suspicions with Stygian. He would of course deny all of it. After all, what man, or Breed for that matter, would want to admit that his woman didn't have a choice.

Or did she?

As she showered, dressed and applied her makeup for work the next morning, she had to admit that she didn't feel

inclined to give Stygian anything other than sex. And honestly, the need for his touch was becoming so strong, so desperate she really wasn't certain how long she would last
before begging for it.

Crying for it.

Screaming for it.

It was really rather amusing if one looked at it from the
right perspective. That was, if the person wasn't the one suffering, then it would have been amusing, she told herself as
they rode to the Nation's headquarters that morning.

Yes, she would have been very amused, if it wasn't her
burning alive from the inside with the need to feel his touch.
His possession.

She was certain she should be traumatized from it, after
all, as a virgin, she should have been terrified of so much
hunger for something she'd never experienced before.

"I think you should put in a request for a leave of absence
as long as this situation in progress," Stygian finally spoke
as the black, unmarked Bureau of Breed Affairs SUV pulled
up to the front entrance of the Navajo Nation Headquarters.

"I think you should do your job and let me do mine." She
clenched her teeth and cursed herself for the quick, uncen-
sored response.

Damn, she hadn't wanted to be quite so confrontational.

She hadn't wanted to be, but her body felt miserable. She
was too sensitive, her flesh too warm, her breasts too swollen and her clit far too tender.

She was too aroused and too upset and too many other
things to even consider dealing with him on a less hostile
basis.

Because, of course, it was all his damned fault.

"What did you want me to do, Liza?" He caught her arm
before she could open the door. "Take advantage of the situation without giving you a chance to consider where it's
going?"

And, of course, he just had to step forward and throw
himself full force into that confrontation didn't he?

"Because I'm so damned stupid I couldn't possibly have
known it was headed straight to one of those nice big beds,"

she agreed mockingly. "Why, you did the right thing, of course, Stygian. Far be it for you to allow yourself to just be male for a change. To let the situation go and have a little fun. I agree, that would be so very uncalled for."

Damn it.

Pressing her lips together tightly, she promised herself she was going to keep the smart remarks to thought only.

What the hell was wrong with her? She couldn't hold back her need for him, her anger with him, or her verbal responses that she'd never had a problem keeping to herself before. For the first time in her life, she really wanted a man. Wanted him so badly that even before he shared that tasty hormone and this burning lust with her, she'd ached for him. She had wanted him like nothing she had wanted in her life before him.

The knowledge of that was simply terrifying, because the reaction to him was so strong, so overwhelming that it felt as though it were coming from someone entirely different than the person she knew herself to be.

More than once she had felt the power of it, a surge of possessiveness and lust that she could barely contain, mixing with a response so primal as to be more animal than human. As though the need for him, the "mating" as they called it, made her more Breed than human.

"You're pushing your limit."

"Oh, I have a limit?" Eyes wide in false innocence, she stared back at him as though she had never imagined such a thing. "Why, Stygian, you should have let me know before now."

"What I should have done was bend you over that fucking bed and paddled your ass before fucking you into a better frame of mind," he growled as he released her.

Before she could let loose with a scathing comeback, he was out of the vehicle and striding around the vehicle to her door.

She would have unleashed the heated comments that flashed across her mind if they weren't wiped completely away by the sight of him stalking, in a purely predatory way, his head high, shoulders back, chest as wide as hell, as he came along the passenger side of the vehicle. The sight of his erection bulging in his jeans as the wind whipped the loose cotton shirt close to his body threatened to take her breath.

Her mouth went dry, then began to moisten just as quickly as her pussy began creaming in need of him.

Oh hell, oh hell, oh hell.

Her door was jerked open.

Stygian's lips parted as though to say something more before his nostrils flared and his eyes seemed to glaze in lust for the barest moment.

A muttered curse left his lips as Liza stepped from the vehicle and tossed him a tight, satisfied smile. At least she wasn't the only one left aching with such misery.

She hoped it hurt him.

She hoped his balls actually ached with the need to come.

"We're definitely going to discuss this later," he warned her as he took her arm and led her through the wide glass doors of Council headquarters.

"Sure we will," she muttered. "I'm going home tonight. I refuse to be locked in a tiny hotel room with you ever again."

"We'll have a suite tonight," he assured her. "That room was only temporary."

"Not happening." Jerking her arm from his grip, she turned and flashed her badge at the security guard on duty before Stygian did the same.

"The hell it isn't. Haven't you seen yet that your home isn't secure, Liza?"

"I've seen that unless I lock myself in a box I'll never be safe again." She didn't like the surge of fear that raced through her at the knowledge.

"That's not necessarily true," he assured her as he led her to the bank of elevators.

"Isn't it?" Suddenly, a sense of weariness overshadowed the anger. "Come on, Stygian, you know it's true. Once the Genetics Council targets a victim, they disappear, one way or the other. That, or they've ended up married to a Breed and placed behind the walls of Sanctuary or Haven. They don't have little brick houses with white picket fences—"

"Not true." The elevator opened, empty for a change, and

they stepped inside. "There are several couples living in residential America. Adapting isn't always necessary, but possible."

She shot him a knowing look.

"Tarek and Lyra Jordan don't count." She sighed. "That residential street has become yet another Breed-designated area with more than three-quarters of the homes taken by Breed couples where one partner or the other is Breed."

His lips tightened.

"Tell me I can go home when all this is over and just adapt a little bit and be safe."

His jaw flexed as his expression darkened.

Liza didn't say more. There was nothing more to say, she had made her point. Her life would never be the same and they both knew it.

They arrived on the third and last floor of the Nation's headquarters with a soft *ping* of the elevator.

A second later, the doors slid open silently.

And Liza nearly punched the button to return to the lobby.

"Liza." Her mother jumped from the settee in the receiving lounge, her expressive blue eyes filled with fear and concern as Stygian led Liza from the elevator.

Almost as though he were aware of her inclination to run.

Jane Johnson rushed to her, her arms wrapping around her as Liza returned the embrace, her eyes closing for one thankful moment as her mother's warmth and love surrounded her.

"We came home as soon as possible." Her mother held her shoulders as she leaned back, her blue eyes filled with tears as she cupped Liza's cheek, her soft hand trembling as she tucked the side of Liza's hair back over her shoulder.

It was a habit her mother had. She would tuck Liza's hair back as though to be certain she could see her entire face. "Are you okay, baby? Daddy and I were terrified when Jonas Wyatt called last night."

"Mom, I'm fine." She hadn't realized how hurt she had been when Jonas Wyatt had told her that her parents had agreed to stay in New York if the Breeds provided her protection. A part of her had known her parents would come running no matter their trust in her, simply because they loved her. The idea that they weren't coming home had caused a hidden ache to begin building inside her, one she had refused to acknowledge until now.

She hadn't known until this moment how much she had needed her parents.

"That Jonas Wyatt just kept talking right over your father as though he wasn't even speaking," Jane told her irritably, a frown creasing her delicate face. "So he just shut up and let the director talk and agreed to the protection, and whatever else that arrogant man was promising. Then he hung up the phone and we left. Of course, you know I was packing as they spoke." She laughed in delight as she then slid her arm around her daughter's waist and pulled Liza to her affectionately. "As though we'd ever stay away at such a time."

"Thanks, Mom." Liza stopped and let her mother hug her again, feeling a security she'd always depended so heavily on.

Her parents were always there, and their love had always been assured. Liza realized that the past days' uncertainties had been worse simply because she had known her parents weren't close enough to touch, to run to.

"And here's your father." Jane released her, stopping long enough to give her a loving kiss on her cheek before Liza saw her father moving from Ray Martinez's office.

Tall and broad, at fifty-six her father was still a handsome, powerful man.

A full head of dark blond hair was cut to a short, almost military length, while the hard, chiseled features of his face softened at the sight of his daughter.

Liza didn't wait.

She moved quickly across the room to find herself enveloped in her father's strong arms as he bent to receive her.

"Daddy," she whispered, uncertain of what to say as his arms tightened around her.

"I have you, baby." She felt his kiss at her brow, the warmth of his love and concern.

"I'm sorry I wasn't stronger," she whispered against his

chest. "I'm sorry I couldn't figure this out before they called you."

She'd never wanted the life she chose to worry her parents, and had prayed she would have the training she needed if she ever came against a situation that would endanger her life.

"Sweetheart," he chastised her gently as he cupped the back of her head and held her to his heart. "It wouldn't matter if you were my daughter, or my son or how strong you were, I'd come running the minute I knew you were in trouble. Don't you know that?"

She had always known it, and that knowledge had always given her a confidence that had helped her make more than one decision in her life.

"You and Momma didn't have to come back so soon," she said, knowing that the quickly hidden feeling of loss she had felt when Jonas told her they weren't coming would have only built inside her.

"Didn't I?" He pulled back to stare down at her with one of those soft, approving smiles that always filled her with such a sense of accomplishment. "Sweetheart, a battalion of Coyotes couldn't have kept me away." He kissed her brow again before looking over her shoulder. "I understand I have this young man to thank for your safety?"

"Well, he's not so young," she muttered, flicking a glare over her shoulder. At the last second, her father saw the softening of that glare though, the warmth in her gaze and the way her gaze lingered on the Breed that had taken a protective stance just inside the door of the anteroom.

She was in love.

That realization pricked at his father's heart even as it filled him with pride but also a fury born of fear. Because he couldn't allow it. This man would destroy his daughter's life.

He had read the report on this Breed.

Stygian Black was a powerful enforcer, but he was also one who stood by his word and his own code. He was a man—a Breed—that Audi knew would follow his daughter into any battle she chose and always watch her back, protect her too-delicate body, and guard her too-compassionate heart.

He would also, Audi knew, instigate the revelation of secrets Audi had prayed would never need to be revealed.

And he hated the Breed for that. Hated him for the fact that he knew Stygian Black would take his daughter away from him. By time the Breeds finished in Window Rock, the child he loved, the child he would die for, would no longer even exist. And that knowledge made him wish he was the man he had been thirty years before. The man who could kill and not suffer a conscience born of the soul he had found when he'd met his Jane.

"To me, he's young." Her father chuckled as he pulled her close to his side and extended his hand to Stygian. "Mr. Black? It's good to finally meet you," he lied convincingly enough that his daughter relaxed in relief.

"You as well, sir." Stygian stepped forward and accepted her father's handshake, his expression as respectful as his demeanor. "I hope you were able to complete your business?"

"Everything's fine." Her father nodded.

Liza knew her father, though, and she knew he would be spending the better part of his time on the phone now that he was back, completing that business.

"You can go back now, Dad." She looked up at him, knowing she would be okay now.

He had come for her, he was here to protect her, to support her. Knowing he had made that sacrifice, as much as she regretted it, still soothed the little girl who would always need her father's guidance and offer of protection.

"The hell I can." He all but glared down at her as her mother gave her a firm look. "I think I'll be right here, Liza. There's no way in hell I'm going anywhere while this is going on. Ray filled me in on the attacks, and it sounds to me as though it's a little more dangerous than Mr. Wyatt let on." His glare shifted uncontrollably to Stygian and deepened. "He ignored my calls this morning by the way. It took forever to get ahold of him."

Stygian rubbed uncomfortably at the back of his neck. "Mr. Wyatt does have a tendency to do that," he agreed. "I'll contact his wife and make certain he gets in touch."

"No need." Her father grunted. "Mr. Wyatt and I have spoken. I've had to listen to his preaching about making the situation more dangerous by returning. I swear, Jane already had us packed and ready to leave before that man finished telling me all reasons why I wasn't needed here, and I just had to listen to it again. Last night, I just agreed with him, got off the phone and headed straight for the airport. It's more than obvious he has some growing to do as a father if he ever imagined I wouldn't be here as quickly as possible."

Stygian watched Audi and Jane Johnson with their daughter, but he paid more attention to Liza. To the scent of her relief and the easing of that tightly held fear inside her.

She had needed them here, he realized.

She had known she was safe, known Stygian would never allow her to be harmed, but her father had always been her protector, and she needed him as well. Stygian realized then he should never have agreed with Jonas's decision to assure the father it was fine to conclude his business before returning.

"I'd like to discuss the security you're using to ensure her protection," Mr. Johnson informed him as Liza moved from his hold and headed to her office doorway.

Stygian could sense the other man's tightly leashed anger, and his dislike. He was fooling no one but Liza, and possibly his wife. That knowledge had Stygian steeling himself for what he knew was to come later.

They followed her to the small sitting area across from her as she moved to her desk, her mother following close behind and chatting quietly about the trip to New York.

"I'd also like to know what you've learned about the assassin that shot at her." Audi's rage was so heavy now Stygian swore it would begin glowing red around him any moment. The fact that he was restraining it, hiding it so well from his daughter, was a testament to the control he'd honed as a younger man in Black Ops.

"Yes, sir." Stygian nodded, remaining polite, respectful.

An assassin with the Bureau of Breed Affairs, Mathias Slaughter, had once told him that should his mate's father ever decide he wasn't good enough for his daughter, Mathias would still treat the man with the utmost respect and consideration simply because his mate would always love that man as her father. The pain she would feel if her mate and father should ever dislike each other would be too great, the assassin had stated. The Wolf inside him had sensed the little girl that every woman was, who needed to always have the illusion that her father could do no wrong. It was a security, a safety net that even a Breed couldn't provide.

Stygian hadn't understood the reasoning at the time, but now, as he sensed Liza's father's disapproval of him, it made more sense. Never did he want his mate to hurt, to lose that innocent, vulnerable part of her inner self that her love for her father kept alive.

For just a second in the elevator he'd felt her reluctance to face her parents. That part of her had been terrified that her father would disapprove of her actions and her choices as an adult, and Stygian had sensed her need for that parental approval.

Now, it was as though part of that deepening pain she had felt was slowly easing away. The fear of her parents' disapproval had eased away, leaving her stronger, more confident in herself. The arousal was still burning through her senses, but that sense of desertion had eased away.

She was close to her parents, and they were dedicated to her. Taking his mate from her home and those she loved would be as Malachi had said of Isabelle: like stealing a part of her soul from her body.

"Mr. Black. The president and I would like to discuss with you the Breeds' security measures for our daughters." Audi Johnson turned to him then, his expression relaxed and friendly, though his eyes told another tale.

The Breeds' report that Audi Johnson had been in Army Intelligence with Ray Martinez years before hadn't been exaggerated.

Just what he needed, an outraged father. No doubt he had clearly sensed Stygian's interest in his daughter.

"Yes, sir." The inquisition.

Her father wasn't in the least pleased over how this situation had been handled or the attacks on his daughter, and it was clear the Breeds were being held responsible for the attention she had suddenly garnered from the Genetics Council.

Stygian almost allowed his lips to quirk into a grin at the latent anger and air of determined antagonism he could suddenly feel coming from Liza's father. Jonas had created a situation here, and as usual, one of his enforcers would be forced to face the flames he had lit.

"Daddy." Soft, a daughter's gentle tone with a hint of reprimand.

Audi turned to her. "I have to make certain they know what they're doing, sweetheart. That's my job."

And she didn't believe him for a moment.

"Trust me," she said softly, but even Stygian heard the edge of steel in her tone.

Slowly, her father's demeanor softened, but only slightly. Giving his daughter a quick nod, he glanced back at Stygian and indicated the Navajo president's office.

With a last glance to Liza's concerned expression, he gave her a reassuring smile before following her father.

With a brief knock on the president's office door, Audi Johnson opened it before leading the way inside.

The tension inside the room was thick enough to cut with a knife, as the saying went.

Nation president Ray Running Wolf Martinez wasn't alone. Sitting behind the heavy walnut desk, he was glaring at the man sitting before it.

Jonas Wyatt.

Standing to the side of the room, between two wide, tall windows, stood Rule Breaker and the Russian Breed known only as Cavalier. The Lion and Coyote Breeds didn't always get along, unless they were working with Jonas. And they only worked together with Jonas when the situation was likely to become explosive.

Stygian nodded to the two high-level enforcers before staring back at Jonas with silent demand.

"Your boss lied to us," Audi stated as he moved to stand behind Ray Martinez as he cast a short glare to Jonas. "He attempted to downplay the danger that our daughters are facing, as well as the reasons for it."

"You should have expected that." Stygian suspected that was exactly the reason they were all there now.

Jonas hadn't expected Johnson's return, Stygian knew. He'd clearly believed Liza's father would bow to his wisdom and stay put in New York where he couldn't interfere or begin calling in his own contacts or instigating his own investigation.

"I returned for a reason," Audi grunted.

Jonas, as arrogant as always, sat uncharacteristically silent, his expression curious as he watched the two men behind the desk.

"This is not a situation I appreciate," Audi Johnson stated, his gaze encompassing them all.

"Liza needed your return for the sake of her heart, not for her safety," Stygian inserted, wondering if the other man intended to try to pull his daughter from Breed protection. And he could, Stygian feared. Liza trusted her parents above anyone and everyone, and it would be a stupid man that doubted that. "My life stands before her and any danger that could stalk her, Mr. Johnson."

He wasn't certain what to say or how to say it. He was a Breed trained to kill in silence, not to seduce or to trick. He wasn't given to flowery statements nor was he given to reassuring anyone in any way. All he had was his strength and the truth. The pure determination to ensure his mate survived, no matter the obstacles.

Both Ray and Audi watched him carefully, though they said nothing.

In Liza's father's eyes, Stygian saw an easing, slight though it was, of the antagonism that had gleamed there.

"Very pretty," Jonas murmured, though his words lacked his customary mockery, before he turned to the other two men. "Are we finished now, gentlemen?"

The president glared back at him. "Director Wyatt, this

Nation is not your personal playground," he stated with icy disdain. "And I resent your attitude that it is."

Jonas rose slowly to his feet.

Tension increased tenfold as his expression tightened. Expressionless, his mercury gaze lacking emotion, he was the Breed he had been created to be: merciless, powerful, expertly engineered manipulator with a full agenda where the Navajo were concerned.

These two men had every right not only to distrust him, but also to be highly suspicious of any and all motives Jonas may present. He was a man fighting for more than his own life, or the survival of the Breeds now. And he had been dangerous enough with those agendas. Now, he was fighting for the life of his child, and that child was more precious to him than even his own soul.

Audi Johnson's gaze narrowed as the Navajo president slowly followed suit and rose to his feet as well.

"My daughter lies with a fever high enough to kill another child." His tone was so harsh, so grating, Johnson and Martinez flinched. Stygian stared back at him, surprised to see him laying his cards so clearly on the table. An unheard-of move for Jonas. "My child lies in pain and stares up at me, gentlemen, and asks, as only a two-year-old can, why it hurts so bad and why Daddy can't fix this." For a second unheard-of occurrence that Stygian knew would never be mentioned, Jonas's gaze gleamed with the dampness of an emotion that went far beyond tears. "So don't think for one moment that I won't be here, taking over where I can, testing your weaknesses and betraying whoever I have to betray to save my child. Just as you would. So let us not misunderstand each other now, nor in the future. That child is more important to me than your entire fucking Nation, and your lack of cooperation is something I find not only reprehensible but immoral."

Stygian felt his chest tighten. He'd seen it himself. Seen the pain and fear in the little girl's eyes when the feverish episodes descended on her. And he knew, if that child were his and Liza's—his by adoption or by blood would make no difference—he would do whatever it took, however he had to do it, to ensure that pain was never felt again.

"There's nothing we can do." Ray Martinez's voice rang with the truth as a sudden angry conflict seemed to battle inside him. Understanding gleamed in his gaze, was emphasized by the clench of his fists and the frustration in his voice. "We've made the request of the people and none have come back with an agreement. I don't have the access codes into the database, Director Wyatt. I cannot access it for you."

"I want Honor Roberts and Fawn Corrigan." The kid gloves were off as Jonas made the demand. "Fuck your database, Mr. President. I couldn't care less about it, any more than Gideon Cross could. He's here for the same thing, and by God, if I don't find those girls first, then he may kill them once he does find them." He leaned against the desk, palms flat, his expression savage. "Is that what you want?"

Both Johnson's and Martinez's gazes flashed with fear before they could hide it.

There was no way Jonas missed it. And Stygian had no doubt the director wasn't certain exactly what that fear was. What Stygian did know was that, somehow, the pair was hiding something.

Liza's father straightened his shoulders. "Twelve years ago," he stated heavily, "there was a crash in the desert several nights before our daughters crashed into a high ravine in the desert. Two girls died in that first crash."

Jonas's growl was rife with violence. "There was no report of it."

"A young Breed was traveling with them. He told us the girls were running from the Genetics Council and begged us not to report it. No one else knew of the crash or the deaths. We elected to follow the Breed's request to give him time to run. When no one came looking for them, we decided to keep it out of the reports. Until you arrived, Director Wyatt, no one seemed to care."

Stygian narrowed his gaze.

They weren't lying. There was the scent of truth and overwhelming sadness, almost of grief, as though they had known the girls. But there was no reason to believe they were lying.

Jonas stared between the two men; both Rule and Cavalier watched them closely as well.

"What did you do with the bodies?" Jonas's voice sounded strangled.

"They were incinerated in the desert, presumably to hide their existence there," Audi stated. "The young Breed walked away that night and stated that even his own past was gone. We assumed the two girls were Breeds as well, and from the same lab as he."

"And you are only now telling me this, why?" Jonas asked.

"Because you're only now telling us the truth of why you're here," President Martinez stated implacably. "Had you been honest to begin with, Director Wyatt, perhaps you would have been told sooner."

"I want to see the area where the bodies were burned," Jonas informed them, his tone implying he wouldn't be denied. "We'll leave at first light in the morning." He turned to Stygian. "I'll need you there, but to ensure Ms. Johnson's protection, perhaps you should bring her as well."

"There's no need for that," Audi Johnson rejected the idea instantly. "I'll take care of her while he's gone."

Jonas's smile was cold. "You'll be with us. And so will she."

With that, he turned, motioned to the two Breeds with him and stalked from the room.

As the door closed rather loudly behind him, both men turned to Stygian, their gazes accusing, as though it were his fault they had been forced to face the director.

He gave a quick shake of his head. "I rarely agree with him, but I wouldn't go head-to-head with him, so I rather doubt the two of you would have any luck with it."

Only Jonas's mate was known to have been able to outargue or outyell him when the situation warranted it.

"Then you should talk to him," Audi announced. "Number one, there's no reason for Liza to be in the desert at first light in the morning. And there's no reason for Director

Wyatt and his entourage to remain here in Window Rock. He has the information he needs, now he can leave. And I believe you should discuss this with him."

Stygian's brows lifted as a chuckle escaped him. "Why would I do that?"

The very idea was ludicrous. Judd and Gideon were still out there, and the information they held could still be of use to them.

He lifted his hand before the two men could say anything more. "Let me tell the two of you something," he growled. "It offends me on a level I can barely understand that the two of you, who nearly lost your daughters at one point, would even consider asking that man to give up the battle he's fighting." A snarl slipped free. "Get your fucking asses over to that hotel and see that child. See her laboring for breath, the damned fever burning her alive from the inside out, so painful she struggles to just breathe. Fuck you two. Get the fuck over there and see what you're asking him to turn his back on." The thought of Amber's pain, her tears, was enraging. "You're asking him to walk away before he knows in his soul there's nothing left to search for. You're asking him to give up on that child's life. And let me tell you something right now, gentlemen. He'd die and see your godforsaken asses in hell first."

"Why are you yelling over something Dad would never do?"

Stygian swung around.

The awareness that Audi Johnson and Ray Martinez wanted Liza in that room no more than he did almost slapped Stygian against the side of the head. The fact that it was his own damned fault didn't sit well with him.

Raking his fingers through his hair, he stared back at her, more irritated with himself than anyone, and just pure pissed off at the two men behind him.

Damn, and she loved her dad. Hell, he knew that look in her eyes. Daddy could do no wrong and he wasn't going to disabuse her of the idea. Because he *could* do wrong. He was doing it right now, standing there demanding that Jonas Wyatt leave Window Rock before he knew there was no way in hell he could save his daughter.

"You would go to see Amber, wouldn't you, Dad? If you knew anything that would save her, you would tell him." She stood in the doorway, and for the first time since Stygian had met her, he saw complete trust in her eyes.

Son of a bitch. Why couldn't she look at him like that?

She was his mate. His woman, and she stared at him with such suspicion that it ate into his soul.

Turning, he stared back at the bastard she put so much faith in and, before he could stop himself, he said, "I'm sure Director Wyatt would be more than happy to allow the visit, Mr. Johnson, should you and President Martinez have a mind to accept the invitation."

Both men stared back at him with dark, hostile gazes.

"We can set that appointment up on our own," the president said smoothly as he threw Liza a reassuring smile. "We'll let you know once it's been set, dear."

"Of course, Uncle Ray," she stated, her voice soft but with a glimmer of doubt that Stygian knew her father had to have heard.

Her gaze turned to his then, the soft gray filled with somber doubt.

"Can I go home now?"

She hadn't asked her father or her boss. She wasn't asking permission to leave, she was asking if it was okay to return to her home rather than the suite they had taken.

Stygian started to shake his head.

"I think it best you return to the house with your mother and me, Liza." Audi moved from behind the Nation president's desk, walking slowly to the door as Liza tensed.

"That wouldn't work, Dad." Her hands clasped in front of her as Stygian glimpsed the shaking in her fingers and the uncertainty in her gaze as she watched her father now.

Seeing it tore at his heart. For possibly the first time in her life, she was seeing the human her father was rather than the superhero he had always been to her.

"Liza, your life is in danger." He paused several feet from her, suddenly aware of the distance she had placed around herself.

Stygian hated sensing it. He hated how she suddenly

retreated within herself, watching, waiting, while another part of her seemed to be considering whatever it was that was suddenly so painful for her.

"Yes, I agree with you, Dad, it is." She breathed in deeply as Stygian tried and failed to restrain the urge to go to her. "But as much as I love you and Mom—and as much as I respect your strength—even I know the Breeds are more qualified and better able to protect me." And what he knew was left unsaid: that she would never be able to live with a reality where her father had died so she could live.

Going to her but not quite touching her, he could feel her fighting to maintain her distance even as she seemed to lean closer.

Stygian could feel the uncertainties in her, a determination slowly growing within her, and a fear and pain that she had buried so deep, buried so far within herself, that he wondered if she even knew the reason for it.

Johnson's gaze narrowed on both of them, no doubt taking in the appearance of solidarity that mating always seemed to bring.

"Then your Breed force can come to the house as well." Her father's smile was tight, the hostility in his gaze barely hidden as he glanced at Stygian then.

Audi still saw his daughter, despite her place in the Breed underground or with the Navajo Law Enforcement Agency, as a vulnerable child rather than the woman he knew she was. He was a man fighting to deny that his daughter was a woman, which made little sense to Stygian.

Certainly, Liza was inexperienced where men were concerned, he could sense that, just as he could smell the untainted sexuality that assured him it had been quite a long while since she had had a lover. But as far as her father was concerned, she was as pure and unspoiled as a young virgin.

"No, Dad." She shook her head again. "I know you'll worry, but if I go home, leaving again will be harder on all of us than it was before. I'm safe. And as long as I stay where I am, under Breed protection, you're safe as well."

Taking those few steps to her father, she let him embrace

her before reaching up and placing a kiss to his cheek. "I love you, Daddy, and I love Mom, but I have to do this the way I feel is best. I've been making my own decisions far too long to be able to give up that freedom now." As she stepped back from her father, she turned to Stygian. "Are you nearly finished?"

"Nearly," he agreed. "A few minutes longer."

"I'll be outside. Don't start yelling at them again. It upsets Ray's secretary, and I imagine she gets enough of that from Ray himself." She tried to smile at her father and the man she called an "uncle" before her expression became so femininely stubborn and commanding that he knew what was coming before it left her lips. "And I'll see you and Ray this evening at the hotel. We're all going to visit with Amber."

"Liza, if she's that ill—" Audi's nostrils flared, his gaze becoming shuttered as he began to protest while Ray Martinez stiffened and the sudden scent of deceit hit Stygian so hard it was all he could do not to react to it.

"Then we all need to see it." Her lips trembled for a brief second as Stygian sensed the slow, deepening fear inside her. "Please, Dad," her voice lowered, uncertainty filling her then. "This is something I need you to do." She looked to Ray then. "I need both of you to do it."

Audi glanced away from her a second as though shoring his strength to deny her request.

That was his intention, Stygian could see it in his shuttered gaze when his eyes met Liza's again. Then, within a heartbeat, what determination he'd been able to muster shattered. A grimace twisted his expression before he gave a slow, resigned nod. "We'll be there, sweetheart."

Stygian caught Ray's expression too. Audi may be unable to deny his daughter, but Stygian was certain Ray wouldn't have a problem with it. He had no intentions of showing up.

"Good." Liza drew in a long, almost weary breath. "I'll go to work then."

She moved toward her father rather than the door, though. Audi met her at the side of Ray's desk, his arms opening for her as he accepted his daughter's embrace. Her arms wrapped around his neck and for a second, she held on to him with a desperation born of a young woman's fears and a daughter's uncertainties.

Kissing her forehead, Audi released her a moment later, then watched silently as she turned and left the room. Quiet, thoughtful, Stygian could feel the woman and the daughter battling inside her and the need she was fighting to hide, the fears she refused to reveal.

She didn't speak as she neared him. Stepping to her enough to force her to pause, he gripped her shoulders and bent his head to her ear. "I'll let Jonas know they're coming."

She nodded shakily, and the scent of her tears almost did him in. "And I'm leaving early," she informed him. "Just after lunch, if that's possible."

"Whatever you want is possible." Releasing her, he let his hands linger against her shoulders for a moment before releasing her and watching her leave the room.

As the door closed behind her, he turned to the two men watching silently.

Her father didn't remain silent for long.

"I know what you're after," Audi Johnson rasped furiously, careful to keep his voice low. "Stay out of my daughter's bed, Breed. She deserves better than the likes of you."

"Better than a Breed?" He gave a short, mocking laugh as he was now forced to face the reason for the man's dislike. "Well, now, doesn't that just suck, because I'm exactly what she's going to get. And keep."

"Don't bet on it," Audi snapped. "She has better sense than to allow herself to be fooled by you for long."

Stygian stared at the two men then, sensing their determination to see him out of Liza's life, forever.

It wasn't going to happen.

"For Liza, I'll ensure she's unaware of the fact that you disapprove of the man she's chosen, because it would destroy her should she ever learn that you believe she's too inept not to allow herself to be fooled, or that you believe the man she's falling in love with is somehow inferior," he growled. "But never doubt, Mr. Johnson, should you ever attempt to destroy what I'm building with your daughter, I will make certain I take her so fucking far away that you'll never have the chance to hurt her again. Do I make myself clear?"

Audi's lips curled in disgust. "She would never go."

"Yeah, she would," Stygian assured him. "Her confidence as a woman and a warrior has stemmed from your belief in her. If she finds out you've lied to her, that your belief in her was an illusion, then you'll destroy her. When you destroy the young girl that still lives and breathes in her soul, then you'll destroy the ties that have held her to this area so firmly. And when you do that, I promise you, she will leave with me."

He didn't give them a chance to retaliate before he turned and pulled the door open. Stepping into the outer office, he faced the knowing sadness in Liza's gaze and the worry and fear in her mother's.

The animal inside him rose with predatory awareness.

She knew. A part of her was aware that more had been going on in the office than he or her father would want her to know.

Taking a seat in the outer office, close to the door, Stygian sat back, determined to bottle the anger and pretend it didn't exist.

He should have expected it, he realized. It was a common problem to those Breeds who had mated human women. Even those who professed a lack of prejudice suddenly found it in surfeit whenever their daughters, or close female relatives, found themselves mated to one. As she worked, her father came and went, moving about the offices and taking care of business as head of security for the Nations headquarters and the president of the Navajo Nation. Audi maintained the illusion of politeness, and Stygian followed suit. But hell, Liza was no fool, and she was so damned intuitive that he swore she would have made an excellent Breed.

It was just after lunch and her determination to work through it, that she closed down her computer and straightened the papers on her desk before lifting her gaze to him.

"I'm ready to go," she told him. "I e-mailed Ray and asked for half days for a while, and he's agreed."

"Besides, he and her father both know Liza needs

to concentrate on her safety now," Jane stated gently as she followed her daughter and rose to her feet from the couch across from Liza's desk.

Stygian had little doubt that the change of hours had been the mother's idea. She'd been nervous, antsy, each time the elevator pinged an arrival, and Stygian knew each time the doors slid open that Jane had braced herself for trouble.

She was terrified for her daughter's safety, even more so than her husband was.

"Very well." Stygian nodded, relieved at the decision. "I'll call down and have the car brought around."

"There's actually an elevator that goes directly to the underground parking area." Jane smiled back at him. "I've talked to Audi, and your driver can have his parking slot next to those elevators for the time being. That should eliminate any problems that could arise. The underground garage is used only for Ray, high-security visitors, and the tribal chiefs, and it's heavily secured. Everything's already been arranged and the guards on duty have been informed."

Stygian had been aware of the parking garage and had made a note to discuss parking arrangements before they left for the day. Having it taken care of by Liza's mother was a relief. The primal anger the other man had roused inside him earlier still had yet to settle.

Stygian held back his surprise. Her mother had remained in the room with them, chatting with Liza whenever her daughter had time and keeping coffee in full supply.

"Thank you, Mrs. Johnson." He nodded cordially.

"No, thank you, Stygian. And you call me Jane." Moving to him, she took his hand between hers and stared up at him, her eyes damp with emotion. "Just take care of my baby. Anything you need to ensure her protection, you have only to let me or her father know and it will be taken care of."

Stepping away, she turned back to her daughter, said her good-byes and returned Liza's hug fiercely. "I'll be here when you come in tomorrow," her mother promised.

"Mom, that's not necessary." Surprise filled her voice. And fear. She didn't want her mother there. In case there was danger, she didn't want her parents anywhere near her.

"It's very necessary, Liza," her mother assured her firmly. "You're my daughter, and I will be here. Now, rest, and we'll talk tomorrow."

He knew now where Liza had gotten her stubbornness, he thought in amusement as Liza gathered her purse and briefcase and moved to him.

She was more distant than she had been earlier, though, as they made the ride to the lobby and walked toward the SUV parked outside the doors. Opening the back door, he helped her in before following her. Nodding at Flint as he glanced in the rearview mirror, he gave him the go-ahead to leave before reaching over and covering Liza's hands as they clasped in her lap.

She was fighting something, fighting some fear or uncertainty that perhaps even she didn't understand. He could feel her confusion, though, and that dark pain brewing brighter and hotter deep inside her and, he suspected, causing the silent retreat.

He hated the lack of emotion and sense of warmth that was always a part of her.

How the hell did she do it? Was it voluntary or subconscious? And where the hell did she go?

Rubbing his thumb over the back of her hand, warming the cool flesh, he released the unusual, if quiet, sound of a primal question.

It was a sound he had never made before, one he'd never heard—somewhere between a half growl and a low questioning breath of a hum. As though the animal he carried inside him was calling out to her itself.

Her head whipped around as her heart gave a hard leap.

The animal he was raged inside him before that spark of her inner spirit showed itself in the surprise and eased his anger.

Just a spark. Just a hint of the woman she was.

And what he sensed coming from her all but froze his soul in terror.

For a second, he didn't sense the woman he knew, in any way.

For the briefest moment, it was a stranger he felt, a stranger he touched.

With his gaze locked with hers, her entire being open as Stygian gave the primal animal he was free rein to call to her, he realized he had opened a door inside her that he had never imagined existed, and for one heart-stopping second he swore he was going to receive an answer to he animalistic call.

And just that quickly, it was over.

Whoever, whatever, had nearly stepped forward, retreated just quickly.

"Is everything okay?" Liza asked, and he sensed her confusion, her uncertainty over what had just happened.

He didn't know what it was. He had no idea how to identify or describe what he had just felt, what he had just glimpsed inside her.

But he was determined to find out. One way or the other he would learn exactly who or what he had found hiding so deep inside the psyche of the woman he loved.

The woman he was determined to mark as his mate.

CHAPTER 12

Audi watched from the window as the SUV carrying the daughter Audi had traded his soul to protect twelve years before heading back to the hotel.

Fists clenched, his jaw aching from tension, he nearly flinched at the knowledge that she was sharing a room with that Breed.

Stygian Black.

If he wasn't Liza's lover yet, he would be soon.

"What are we going to do?" he asked the friend that stood beside him, knowing they hadn't expected this.

In all the years they had been protecting the girls they called their own, they had never anticipated this.

"They'll be protected." The same grief that twisted him filled Ray's voice as well.

"What are we going to do, Ray?" His question hadn't been answered. "Their protection at this moment in time isn't in doubt. Their protection, if our secrets are learned, is quite another thing."

Glaring at the man he had weathered a war, a prisoner of war camp and the politics of the Navajo Nation with, Audi realized they were finally facing the consequences of the choices they had made over the years.

Ray breathed out heavily. "Remember those articles we read on the Breeds and mating? And Father's suppositions that such rumors were true?" he finally asked.

Audi closed his eyes briefly.

God, no.

If those stories were true, then no doubt he had lost his daughter forever.

"Isabelle," Ray said his niece's name roughly. "She no longer uses her own doctor, but a Breed doctor exclusively. She exhibits all the signs of a Breed mating, and when Terran questions Malachi, the Breed merely stares back at him silently. What more proof would a man need?"

Would Liza tell him if such a phenomenon had occurred within her where the dark Breed Stygian was concerned? She was incredibly loyal to friends, he knew. If she mated with the Breed, then her emotions would be even more so involved.

Her loyalty would no longer be to her family first, but to the Breeds instead.

And if her loyalty was to her Breed first, then she could unknowingly end up betraying them all. And possibly destroying her.

Audi could handle the unintentional betrayal, after all, she had no idea of the secrets she harbored. After all, he and Ray had committed no crime, nor had they done anything that would betray their daughters. It was what it would do to her, it was the fact that the daughter he loved would no longer exist, that threatened to destroy him.

Hell, it would destroy him. He and Jane both. It would destroy them in ways that there was no way Ray and his wife could possibly understand. Unlike Audi and Jane, they hadn't developed the closeness and the bonds with their daughter, Claire, that existed between them and Liza.

Liza was his and Jane's life. They had worked tirelessly to protect her, to ensure her happiness, independence and well-being.

And now, it was all being threatened.

God help them if they lost her, because Audi knew, they would never survive it.

❖ ❖ ❖

It wasn't going away.

The involuntary separation of mind and body, of emotion and self. And she couldn't seem to find her way back.

As Stygian pulled into the driveway of her home, Liza stared as though she didn't recognize the place. As though it were someone else who had rented it. Someone else who had invited her best friends to share it. Someone else who had dreamed of freedom as she moved her belongings into it.

After returning to the hotel, he'd had Flint and Rule take another vehicle to follow them.

She'd demanded to return here. She didn't like the confinement of the hotel or the room they shared. She didn't like the feeling of imprisonment or of being watched every second.

Now, she was here, and she wondered where "here" was.

From the corner of her eye, Liza was aware of Stygian staring at her, his expression more savage than normal, the dark bronze skin of his face stretched tight over the sharp planes and angles that made up his face.

He was furious at her decision.

He could have been Navajo if not for the darker color of his flesh.

Of course, she had no doubt there were Navajo genes in his DNA. Almost all Breeds held the DNA of the Navajo, or one of the tribes that had joined with the Nation in the early part of the century.

"Where do you go when you disappear, Liza?"

The question threw her off guard but not enough to eliminate the mental and emotional distance between them.

A brief shrug was all the answer she could come up with.

To be honest, she didn't know herself where she was at the moment. Was she hiding? Or was she finding something she only found in her nightmares?

Strangely enough, though, she did feel something: the swollen sensitivity of her clit, the engorged readiness of her nipples, the ache just beneath her skin for his touch. The need for his kiss.

That was odd. She'd never felt such arousal for a man, especially not at a time when whatever emotions caused this distance pulled her back from reality.

Hell, she'd never ached like this for a man period.

"You won't do this." There was no anger in his tone.

That too was odd. Even her housemates were known to become angry when Liza let herself become lost, as Claire called it.

And what was it that he wasn't going to let her do?

She stared at the house. The pretty green, well-watered lawn. The blooms that sprang in abandon through the small flower beds and abundance of shrubs.

The single-story adobe ranch house looked bright, welcoming. The windows and curtains thrown open, the sheers giving her house a slightly hazy, serene look.

She'd worked hard to make the rental a home. Of course, the owner, a good friend of her father's, had already told her the house was hers whenever she was ready to buy.

She hadn't bought but perhaps she should have.

"Liza." He touched her.

The touch was as simple as the calloused pads of his fingers stroking down her arm.

A shudder rippled over her flesh, then, as she fought to steel herself against the consequences, it began to quake through her inner, hidden emotions.

"I don't want to talk." Maintaining the shield around her sensitive soul wasn't easy. "I just need to think for a while."

"You're not thinking, you're hiding," he accused her again. "You're hiding so well that even my animal senses can't seem to find you."

As though that was a bad thing. She was thankful for it.

The rough quality of his voice, slightly demanding and dominant, had the power to make her nervous though, to assure her he intended to drag her back from wherever she had gone to hide.

"I'm going in." She felt a hundred years old as she gripped the door handle and moved to release it.

"No." Just that easy, he stopped her as his fingers curled around her upper arm. "Let's take a ride instead."

"Where?" She didn't really care where. It didn't matter if she went inside. It didn't matter if she didn't.

"Where you and Claire were in that accident when you were fifteen."

Panic stole her breath as it slammed into her stomach with a punch of horror. No, she couldn't return there. She had never returned to the actual site where the accident occurred and she wasn't going to do it now.

"No." Shaking off the loose grip, she was out of the SUV and striding quickly to the house as she pulled her bag from her shoulder, opened it, and dug the house key from inside.

She never had a chance to use it.

The front door swung open and that damned cigar-smoking Coyote with the smug smile and knowing gray eyes leaned against her door frame with arrogant confidence.

"Hello, kids." He grinned around the cigar clamped between his teeth before reaching up to grip it in his fingers and lower it from his lips.

"What is he doing in my house?" Turning to Stygian, Liza found herself jerked back to reality with a suddenness that had her breath heaving.

The distance was gone. The inability to feel the panic, fear, but especially the overriding hunger and desperate need for something she had no idea how to describe, came crashing inside her as the abrupt appearance of the Coyote sent a rush of adrenaline crashing through her.

Dog straightened from the door frame, his expression morphing from the smug arrogance to complete business.

"He's merely helping his men complete the security system the Bureau ordered for backup in the house," he told them. "I apologize for the inconvenience, ma'am."

"Don't call me ma'am and please get the hell out of my way." Brushing past him, Liza entered the living room to find Chelsea, a suitcase sitting beside her as she stared around the house with a frown.

"You're leaving?" Liza came to a stop, her emotions, already thrown into chaos with too many sensations and suspicions, rife with confusion.

"I think you know we can't stay here, Liza." Chelsea sighed, her brown eyes somber. "Malachi and Isabelle have offered their spare room until this is over." Her lips tilted at the corner. "Besides, there are a few too many Breeds lounging around here." Her eyes slid to the Breed stretched back at the bottom of the stairs, propped on his elbows and watching them with mocking silence.

Loki. He pretended and played at charm and sensual abandon, but there was something tormented and angry that drove that Breed.

She barely held back the agonized cry trapped in her throat as fear slammed inside her. How did she know that? How could she sense those emotions churning inside the Breed? And why had she sensed her father's lies and deceits at the office? Sensed them with such strength that it was like staring inside him and seeing his hatred for Stygian and his fears for her.

"I understand." Forcing herself to nod as though she did understand, Liza admitted she didn't understand a damned thing anymore. "Hopefully this will all be over soon."

"That's what we hoped when Malachi's crew showed up. You know, I like Ashley and the girls who visit, but these male Breeds are pricks." Chelsea shrugged as she glanced around the room at the Coyote Breeds working there. "Oh well. I guess we have to take the good with the bad, right?"

"So we were taught," Liza agreed, aching with the loss tearing through her.

She hated this. She hated everything she was losing and everything she could feel threatening to come alive inside her. And for a moment, she hated herself for the weakness she could feel. Fear. Panic. It was all there.

The knowledge that there was something at the edge of her mind waiting to destroy her tormented her.

The aching arousal and burning need for Stygian's touch only seemed to make it worse. Whatever was awakening within her, it had begun with this hunger for a Breed.

"Come on, Liza, we knew this was coming when Isabelle was nearly taken." Chelsea sighed as Liza watched her painfully. "We've just been fighting it, hating the fact that we've had to give up our freedom for a while."

Perhaps all Chelsea was giving up was her freedom, Liza thought. Liza could sense losing so much more than her freedom though.

"Maybe." Liza shrugged. "Tell Isabelle and Malachi I said hi."

What more could she say? She couldn't beg Chelsea not to leave when she knew herself that even she couldn't stay. Not right now. Perhaps not ever.

Striding to her, Chelsea gave her a tight hug. "It won't be too long, Liza," she promised. "And you know we're going to invade that hotel they've stuck you in and have a total girls'-night-out shindig."

"I'll hold you to that." A tight, brief hug and Liza released her friend before stepping back.

"Well, come on, Loki." Chelsea gave the Breed one of those superior, you-are-my-servant looks that she was so well known for.

Loki eased from the stairs with a lazy smile and amusement gleaming in his dark gray eyes. " 'Please' not in your vocabulary, sweetheart?"

"Neither is 'sweetheart,'" she assured him. "So let's get moving. Isabelle promised me lunch."

"Lunch sounds good." Loki seemed a bit more energetic at the mention of food.

"You weren't invited," Chelsea informed him.

To that, the Breed only laughed as he picked up her suitcase and followed her to the front door as Dog, Mongrel and Mutt bid Stygian good-bye and left as well.

The house was empty but for her and Stygian now.

Turning to him, her gaze went instantly to his, the glints of blue in the night-black background more intense than before.

"You always know, don't you?" She had to draw in a hard, deep breath at that realization. "No matter what I'm feeling. No matter how aroused or how angry I am."

"Or how distant you are." He inclined his head in agreement.

"Can you sense it with everyone?" Wrapping her arms across her breasts, she considered how she would feel if he could sense every woman's arousal for him.

Because no doubt, there were quite a few women more than interested in taking him to their bed.

His lips pursed thoughtfully. "In some situations," he finally admitted. "But our senses in regard to our mates are incredibly heightened, Liza. That's how I know when you've retreated to the point that you're barely on the same plane with the rest of us mortals."

She flinched, jerking her gaze from his and looking away as he moved closer to her.

"It's how I knew the second that distance began easing and your need for me kicked in with a vengeance. The mating heat may ease when you do that, but it will also bring you back to me. You may have found a way to delay it at times, in ways no one else can, but you'll pay for it when you return."

"So you admit it exists?" Why wasn't she even surprised? Or angry? "So you have to wait until you kiss your mate before you can tell them about it?"

He shook his head. "No, I have to wait to be certain you won't reveal it to anyone, even friends or family. Because the news stories are partially true. Mating heat has the potential to destroy us, because we don't completely understand it ourselves. How do you assure others it's not something they should fear if you can't explain exactly what it is?"

"So why tell me now?"

He stared back at her, his gaze somber, intense. "Because we both know where it's going. You've known what was coming and you've still come to me. You know where it's going. Why fight it any longer?"

"Why me?" Turning back to him, she asked the question that had plagued her since the moment she realized something wasn't exactly right with the attraction she felt for him. That it was more intense, more primal.

"If I knew that, then I would have the single secret that could possibly save the Breeds from extinction should the world ever learn of the mating heat, Liza." His fingers curled around her upper arm as he pulled her closer.

The heat of his body met the chill in hers before it sank to that core of lava-hot arousal simmering and growing inside her.

A hard, involuntary breath pushed her breasts against his chest while he pulled her even closer with a hand at her hip. When she was flush against his body, the length of his erection imprinting itself against her lower stomach sent a wave of furious heat washing through her.

"See?" he murmured as he laid his lips against her temple. "It's like fire and gas. One touch is all it takes to make the arousal burn brighter, make it torment and ache until nothing helps but another, deeper touch."

His touch firmed, gripping the silk of her shirt and pulling it from the belted band of her skirt. Pressing his hand beneath the material, the calloused palm stroked up her spine, sending a shiver raging across her flesh as pleasure flared from each point of contact.

"And it doesn't stop?" Could that be possible? Could the tabloids have that much right? That the Breeds, like some of their animal cousins, mated for life?

"It doesn't stop." His breathing was heavier now, his tone rougher, rasping as his head lowered, his lips brushing down her neck, the wet heat of his tongue licking against her flesh.

Tilting her head to the side, Liza all but begged for more. Just that one careless caress against her neck was enough to send a spike of sensation racing through her nerve endings and peaking in her swollen clit and the clenched, saturated depths of her pussy.

Her hips moved involuntarily, rubbing the sensitive nub of her clit against the hard muscle of his thigh as his lips lingered at the base of her neck, his cheek rubbing against the sensitive flesh of her inner shoulder.

Each stroke of the wet heat of his tongue against her skin had her body tightening further. Pleasure and a violent need for more began to amass in her system.

"The night Isabelle met Malachi," she whispered, the words tearing from her as her fingers moved restlessly over his shoulders, "I watched you in that bar."

"I could smell your heat," he growled as his teeth raked

across tender nerve endings at the curve between neck and shoulder. "I waited for you, Liza. Until well after the bar had closed, still I lingered, certain you would return."

Liza felt a rush of regret and hunger as it tore through her. Lifting his head, he met her gaze with his, the blue in his eyes like dark stars on a midnight background.

"I won't wait any longer." He gripping the hem of her blouse and yanked it up.

Lifting her arms, Liza forced back a whimper as the erotic intensity began to build, the heat charging nerve endings she hadn't known her body possessed.

The blouse fluttered to the floor as his hand moved to the small button and zipper at the side of her skirt. Within seconds, it too slid to the floor, leaving her clad only in the lacy white bra, matching lace thong and nude stockings she'd worn beneath along with black, three-inch heels that she'd seen Stygian sneaking glances at earlier.

"God have mercy," he whispered as though tortured. He stripped his shirt, his gaze never leaving the sight of her.

As he jerked the shirt over his lean, well-muscled stomach, Liza's hands went to the belt of his jeans, fumbling, shaking as she released it and pushed it aside from the metal tab.

She felt like a schoolgirl. God, how she had longed for this feeling over the years: the excitement and fear, the anticipation and the trepidation caused by the unknown.

As the metal tab and zipper gave way beneath her fingers, Liza breathed out in shock at the heavy width and weight of the erection. Lifting her gaze to Stygian's face, she slowly shook her head.

"There's no way." She had to swallow past the dryness that attacked her mouth, but her lips still twitched in a vein of amusement. "My God, Stygian, that's simply not going to fit." And that was not her virginity speaking.

"Oh, I don't think we're going to have a problem with the fit," he assured her. "The problem will be stopping once I get inside you." His expression was so tight, so intense that once more she felt that punch of reaction to her stomach. A tightening of her womb, the clench of her pussy and heated throb of her clit just before he swung her up into his arms.

"What are you doing?" Surprise had her locking her arms around his neck.

"You're killing me here," he growled as he strode to the bedroom. "If I don't get you to the bedroom, I'm going to end up fucking you on the living room floor."

Oh God.

She held her breath, forcing herself to hold on to her control.

But God, how she wanted him.

She could feel the inner muscles of her pussy clenching, tightening, a sense of emptiness attacking the sensitive inner core.

She could feel her juices easing along the inner walls to the swollen labia below.

Reaching the bedroom, rather than placing her on the bed, he returned her to her feet next to it, one hand cupping her cheek as his head lowered, his lips taking hers once again.

One hand slid around her hip to the curve of her rear.

She rubbed against his thigh, grinding the swollen bud of her clit against the hard muscle.

It was so good. She wanted to cry with the pleasure of it tearing through her.

The blood thundered through her body, pounding torturously at her clit, her juices gathering along the folds of her pussy, sensitizing it further. Small, mewling little cries left her lips, her arms tightened around his neck, her fingers spearing into his hair.

Suddenly each touch, each hint of a spicy taste that stroked against her tongue was hotter, the sensation amplified and so strong it would have brought her to her knees if Stygian hadn't had one hand clamped to the curve of her rear to help her ride his thigh.

She had never known a hunger like this.

Hell, she had never known hunger for a man, period, until now.

And it was so much more than she expected.

Moving his hand from her cheek, it smoothed along her neck, her shoulder, between her breasts.

Her bra loosened, the delicate lace cups separating before he pushed one back from her swollen breast. He cupped his palm around the under curve and lifted his lips from hers.

Tipping her head back, she forced her lashes open, staring up at him with dazed pleasure as his thumb raked over a nipple and his lips moved steadily closer to the rigid peak.

"Stygian." The whimper of his name had him pausing.

It was only a pause. It only lasted long enough to find herself flat on her back across the bed, staring up at him in surprise.

In one second flat he'd shed his jeans and moved over her. Bracing himself with one hand, he hooked the fingers of the other in the band of her panties. With a quick jerk, he ripped the delicate lace from her hips.

Her gasp of shock was followed by a tumultuous cry as in the next breath Stygian had her thighs spread and his tongue raked through the swollen folds of her pussy, sliding around the tortured ache of her clit.

Her hands went to his head, sliding through his hair before clenching a handful of strands with a desperate grip. His lips capped over her clit, he sucked it inside the heat of his mouth and laid his tongue to it like a wicked whip.

"What are you doing to me?" The strangled cry was filled with an agonizing need for release. Liza's hips lifted, grinding against his lips as her orgasm remained just out of reach.

Each fiery brush of his tongue against the oversensitized bundle of nerves had her screaming breathlessly, her hips jerking, driving the overheated flesh harder against his lips as she begged for release.

Licking, stroking, his fingers caressing from her inner thighs to the clenched entrance of her pussy, Stygian gave no quarter. Primal hunger and male dominance filled each touch, each primitive growl that rumbled in his chest.

Stroking over the narrow opening to her vagina, his fin-

gers paused, pressed, working two of the calloused fingertips past the fluttering flesh to the inner tissue beyond.

"Please." She tightened her fingers in his hair and lifted
her hips as a strangled cry of aroused fury left her lips when
his hands clamped on her thighs, holding them open, holding her still. "Damn you, Stygian, damn you. Fuck me. Oh
God, please make me come, Stygian."

What she released at that point, she wasn't certain if she
should be terrified of, or if she should revel in the primitive
hunger of the animal that came over her.

His lips were drawn back, those wicked incisors were gleaming in demand. His eyes, once black with blue highlights,
were now a startling, sapphire blue and gleaming with a
raging hunger.

Hard hands caught her beneath her knees, bending them,
pushing them back as he knelt before her.

She lifted her hips and glanced down at the dark width of
the heavy erection tucking between the folds of her pussy.
Slowly, her gaze lifted to his again, and she swore in his face
she could see a hint of the Wolf part his genetics were taken
from.

"Mate." His gaze narrowed as the snarl lifted his lips.

At the same time, her gaze widened at the pulse of his
cock against the entrance of her pussy, the feel of a heated
fluid spurting against the clenched tissue inside bringing a
shocked gasp from her lips.

"Stygian?" She trembled beneath him, her hands clamping to his powerful forearms as an electric tingle began to
emanate through the inner flesh.

"It's okay, baby." The sound of his voice was a rough,
sensual rasp.

Then he pressed forward.

The burn of the erotic stretch had her breath catching,
because the pleasure of it was incredible. Sensual.

As the pleasure began to give way to a hint of discomfort,
Stygian paused again. The width of the wide crest was
barely inside her, throbbing, heated.

The inner tissue fluttered around the iron-hard flesh as
she struggled to accept, to adjust to the invasion.

A heavy throb of the crest preceded another spurt of the silky fluid, as though he were already finding his release, though she knew it wasn't possible. His body was hard and tense above her, his cock iron-hard and throbbing. And whatever release it was, like the one before it, it seemed to sink inside the inner muscles of her pussy, easing it, heating it.

"Oh God." The involuntary clenching of her pussy around the head of his cock was followed by the most incredibly arrowing sensation as it shot straight to her clit.

Shuddering, she stared up at him, gasping, fighting to breathe as another spurt filled her again and the head of his cock sank deeper inside her.

Heat began to bloom through her body. The stretching of her inner flesh, the slow pleasure/pain of each bold inch of his cock filling her, had her body humming with such nearing ecstasy that she was crying out with the intensity of it.

Then he stopped.

Her eyes flared open.

"Why didn't you tell me?" he growled.

"I thought you would have known." She breathed out roughly. "God, you know everything else, right?"

His cock was barely buried in past the throbbing crest, and what the hell did he want? Did she have to apologize for being a virgin?

"You're a virgin." It sounded like an accusation.

Liza blinked up at him, half tempted to laugh.

"What do you want, apologies?" She groaned. "I told you, you were too big."

"It's not too big," he gritted out, just as another heavy spurt erupted from his cock, further sensitizing the tender depths of her pussy. "Damn it, Liza, you're not ready for this."

Her eyes narrowed on him. "Not ready? You have your dick halfway inside me and you think I'm not ready?"

"You're a fucking virgin—"

"I promise it's not contagious!" Her knees lifted, gripping his hips. "Stop making excuses, Stygian. Now finish this or I swear I'm going—"

He surged forward.

Stygian felt each pulse of the pre-seminal fluid as it

spurted heavily from the head of his cock. The sensation was ecstatic, a pleasure he'd never experienced and one he knew he would never experience with another woman.

He had known she was inexperienced, but God help him, he hadn't expected her to be a virgin.

He felt the tearing of her innocence, felt the helpless male pride rising inside him, and had a moment to feel a glimmer of amusement at it. This was his mate. His woman. She was beneath him, the grip of her pussy tightening to the point that he swore he couldn't hold back his release another second longer. And she had waited for him.

Sensitive tissue rippled along the head of his cock, caressed the shaft then tightened again. Her legs wrapped around his hips, her short little nails pierced his back.

And she was killing him.

"Stygian," she cried as though he were the only anchor in her world.

And she was his anchor.

She was more than his mate.

The moment he realized who she was, what she was to him, she had begun stealing his heart.

This perfect woman, and she was more than even he had imagined he could deserve.

"Oh God. Oh God, yes." Liza felt flames licking over her body.

The brush of his chest against her nipples as he lowered himself against her, the feel of his erection pounding inside her, creating a friction that sent sparks of never-ending sensation racing through every erogenous point of her body was destroying her.

Moving against him, her hips lifting, grinding into his, feeling every inch of the heavy, thick spear penetrating her was like agony and ecstasy.

Each stroke inside her seemed to tighten her further. Her vagina rippled in steady pulses over his cock, her clit became more swollen, more sensitive with each stroke of his pelvis against it.

Each hot spurt of fluid she felt seemed to sensitize her further.

Sensation was like a kaleidoscope of color blazing through her senses until the world seemed to rupture around her.

Ecstasy poured through her in an orgasm she knew she would die if she didn't have again. It exploded with a force that stole her breath, lifted her against him and sent a keening cry spilling from her lips.

His teeth bit into her shoulder where it bent to meet her neck, the feel of the sharp incisors piercing her skin, barely felt, as her own teeth bit into the hard muscle of his chest.

He rode her harder, pounding into her, driving her higher even as she shook and shuddered through her release. Only to find that ecstasy could come again.

Swiftly.

With one last powerful thrust inside her, she felt the first blast of his release jetting inside her. With that first fiery spurt, came a sensation she couldn't attribute, though she knew what it was.

His cock began to fill her further. Midway up the already too-thick shaft, it seemed to be swelling further, stretching her, revealing nerve endings she hadn't expected, the throb of the hardened knot against such oversensitive tissue sent her hurtling higher, throwing her harder into a maelstrom of sensation that wiped all reality from her senses.

She was pure sensation, pure pleasure. A second orgasm ripped through her, detonating with a force that would have left her screaming if she'd had the breath to do so.

All she could do was hold on. Her bite against his chest tightened, her nails dug into his forearms, her body shook, shuddering with such force that tears began to ease from her eyes.

In the midst of it, hurtling through a wonderland of ecstasy, she swore she felt herself looking down, so deep inside herself that she was shocked. Shocked to see the core of her woman's spirit flaring outward, opening and accepting.

And assuring her she belonged to him.

Belonged to him with such a terrifying singularity that she wondered if she would ever recover.

Belonged to him as she hadn't even ever belonged to herself.

As the violence of her release began to ease, the shudders turning to ripples of sensation, she lost the strength to bite him. Releasing him, she fell back to the pillow, hands sliding down his arms as she collapsed, exhausted, both mentally and emotionally complete in a way she had never dreamed possible.

"Mine," he growled at her ear again.

And it was all she could do to keep herself from agreeing with him.

The only thing that stopped her was the sudden fear that in this moment, she wasn't even herself.

The fear that after this moment, she would simply live for this. For his touch. His kiss. For his possession.

For the certainty that this man, that this moment in time, had changed her in ways she would never be free of.

CHAPTER 13

Stygian was silent as he rose from the bed, moved to the bathroom and soaked a cloth in heated water before moving back to the bed to clean the proof of his release from Liza's thighs.

She lay exhausted, nearly asleep, and only a mumbled protest left her lips as he parted her thighs and wiped the slick essence mixed with her virgin's blood from the soft folds of her sex and her inner thighs.

His virgin mate. She had met him with a hunger and a need he could never have expected from such innocence. She had taken him, held him in a grip that had rippled over his cock and tightened around the mating knot as though she had been made for him and him alone.

Now, as she lay more asleep than awake, he could feel something more as well. The part of her that hid so deep, refusing to completely emerge, but awakening.

The animal inside him was pacing restlessly now at the hint of suspicion rising inside him.

No, it had been there all along, he realized. Just waiting for this moment, for the proof that somewhere, someone had been deceiving not just the Breeds, but also Liza.

Finishing, he returned to the bathroom, proceeded to clean himself then returned to the bed and his mate, where it seemed she had struggled to make her way beneath the heavy quilt.

His lips quirked into an amused smile. She'd managed to pull the blanket over her shoulders, but nothing more.

"Come on, sugar." Lifting her into his arms, he pulled the blanket, quilt and sheet back from the bed before laying her in the middle of the mattress.

Moving in beside her, he felt his chest clench as she curled herself into a little ball, and her sudden sense of uncertainty reached him.

He pulled the sheet over them both before pulling her against him.

"Do you think I'll allow you to sleep in isolation now?" he asked as she lay stiffly beside him. "Come on, Liza, I know you need warmth. Come to me and I'll warm you."

She turned slowly. "So I lie against you or I can stay cold?" A hint of gray eyes showed between narrowed lashes.

"Would you prefer the quilts?" he asked as he ran his hand caressingly along her spine. "I'll keep you much warmer."

"I have an electric quilt, Stygian," she told him, but she didn't move away from him.

"You'll need it no longer," he promised, relishing the feel of her silken back against the palm of his hand.

At the same time, he felt her hand, so soft he was amazed at the living warmth of it, in a fleeting caress against his chest before it stilled.

"Did I hurt you?" she asked then, her fingertips glancing across the vicious bite she'd bestowed to his chest.

It wasn't even throbbing. The bite was deep, yet there was no blood, no ache of muscle, as though the mating heat had been transferred to her saliva as well and bestowed on the wound to ensure it caused no true pain, just that slight, "it was there" ache.

The feel of that sensation was one he wouldn't change.

"It would take a much harder bite to cause me to complain," he assured her as he brushed his cheek against her forehead. "And the feel of it will remind me of the pleasure I gave you."

She was silent then, but he could feel her thinking, feel the frown that creased her forehead before she tilted her head back once again to stare up at him in the dim light.

It wasn't dark yet, though it was close. The heavy curtains were pulled over the windows, and the darkening feature on the newly installed security windows had been activated.

"English isn't your first language, is it?" She surprised him with the question.

"I have no first language, actually," he told her. "My training involved three language studies—English, Spanish and Russian—which began at birth and continued through my training."

"Why Russian?" The curiosity in her tone was a far cry from the nosiness of most who questioned him whenever they had a chance.

"They believed it would be the one I picked up easiest, as my paternal and animal DNA came from Russia."

"Really?" Drowsy interest filled her voice. "Where did your paternal genetics actually come from?"

Stygian grinned. "Attila the Hun. Straight from the source. When his burial site was found, they recovered enough DNA to actually track his descendents. They used some of that DNA to create my genetics."

"Attila the Hun?" Surprise filled her voice now. "Damn. I think I'm impressed now." She was actually laughing at him, and he couldn't help but grin.

"And your maternal genetics?" she queried then, her tone suggestive, teasing. "This one has got to be good."

No doubt she already knew, or had at least read the partial history that could have been attained if certain records had been hacked.

Moving the pillows more comfortably behind him, he lifted her against his chest until she sat comfortably against him, the sheet and quilt pulled to her breasts now.

"Her name was Nera," he answered. "The Genetics Council chose her for her ties to one of the greatest voodoo priestesses to have been born in the Caribbean, and she was rumored to have been quite powerful herself. They kept her twenty years but only managed to impregnate her twice. Just after her daughter was born, she disappeared from her cells and was never seen again."

"She escaped then?" Surprise colored her voice.

Stygian glanced down at her, his lips lifting in a slight grin. "Who the hell knows. One minute she was showing up on their monitors and in the next breath she was nowhere to be found in her cell. Her infant daughter, barely six weeks old, disappeared as well. They spent years searching for them, but each time a team was sent to the area where she had originally been abducted from, every soldier and Breed sent after her disappeared."

Damn, he was proud of her. However she had managed to escape, she'd done a damned good job of it.

"Where was she abducted from?"

"She was born in Haiti, but raised in the Jamaican rain forests. She was seventeen when she was abducted because of her rumored genetic ties to both an ancient priest and priestess of the religion. But rumors at the labs say she was so powerful herself that she nearly walked out of the labs with me when I was an infant. After that, she was isolated with limited contact while they continued to attempt to impregnate her. It took twenty years before she conceived again. Each time she was impregnated with an embryo that wasn't from her eggs, her body immediately rejected it. Finally, they once again tried using her ova. She conceived a girl, gave birth and six weeks later just disappeared."

"Did you ever search for her?" Liza asked then, a hint of forlorn melancholy in her voice now.

"Once," he admitted. "I spent nearly two months in one of the darkest jungles I swear I ever entered. One night, I awoke to find myself surrounded by six of the biggest, baddest-looking jungle warriors I swear a man or Breed could encounter. The biggest moved to the fire I'd made before sleeping, sat down and proceeded to explain the threat I represented to Nera and her daughter. And despite her fondness for me, and her concern, she couldn't allow me to venture farther. Then, four dead Coyote soldiers were tossed into the camp from the darkness. Their throats were slit; I hadn't even known they were following me. I left the next morning and left her in peace."

"How sad." Regret for him filled her, and Stygian realized he'd never sensed sympathy or an understanding of his loss from anyone else in his life.

"Not so sad," he told her, realizing that himself. "I found my own peace. She and my sister are alive and protected. That was what mattered to me."

"You didn't feel that her daughter was more important than her son?" She lifted against him, the outrage suddenly pouring from her touching him in ways he had no idea how to express.

"I was a grown man," he pointed out. "I was twenty when she and my sister left the labs. The child would barely have been ten by then. Her safety was more important."

"To have to choose to let a child go must have been heartbreaking." There was the slightest edge of an emotion in her voice that he couldn't quite put his finger on.

"I was a grown man," he repeated. "I understood her choice."

"And she never contacted you after that?"

He let his gaze rove over her, taking in the sheet that barely covered her breasts, the long, dark blond hair that fell around her face and shoulders, a few heavy strands falling over her breasts, before he answered with a small smile. "No. And I didn't expect her to."

He could feel her sadness reaching him. It wasn't pity, something he wouldn't have tolerated; rather, it was a sincere sorrow that such a choice had been demanded.

"I've watched all the documentaries on the Breeds," she said softly. "The scientists and soldiers were monsters in their treatment. To take something so essential as parents and family and make a crime of wanting or needing them was inhumane."

"That was the point," he reminded her. "We were led to believe we weren't human, Liza. That emotions, family, love, they were all things we had no capacity to feel, let alone ache for or hunger for. As though they could force us to be as unemotional and uncaring as the robots they wanted us to be."

It was no longer enraging.

At one time, talk of those dark, horrifying years would have led him quickly down a path of rage that would inevitably lead to snarling fury.

To allow such emotions to rip through him now would mean releasing the hold he had on the gentle warmth that filled his arms at the moment. It simply wasn't worth it. They were now days long gone, and if the Breeds were diligent, if Stygian was extremely careful, then they were days he would never be forced to repeat.

"I remember watching the video cast when Callan Lyons revealed the existence of the Breeds," Liza said then. "It was as though the world was holding its breath, certain it had to be some horrible farce. That there was no way humans could be so *in*human. That such monsters could exist. Only to learn it was much worse than we had ever imagined."

"Worse, yes," he agreed as he let his fingers thread into the heavy length of her hair. "But freedom was much sweeter, the realizations of the gifts that were actually given became more cherished. I would not trade who and what I am, because in doing so, I would have missed this night, and I would have missed loving you."

She was retreating.

Stygian felt it with a sense of shock.

Her reaction was so swift, so instantaneous he nearly missed that critical point in pulling her back.

A snarl pulled at his lips as his hand wrapped around her neck, jerking her to him with a swiftness that had that internal attempt to disappear from him emotionally pausing.

"You will not," he snarled, his lips nearly touching hers, his gaze holding hers, shock filling it as her lips parted on a gasp. "You will not go away from me in such a way, Liza. Never again. Do you understand me?"

"Don't." Her fingers curled against his chest, as though she could force him to release her with such a paltry resistance. "Let me go."

"Little coward," he bit out, feeling the strike of her anger as it began to burn inside her mind. "You run and hide like a child, terrified of the responsibility of being an adult. Have I mated a woman or a child in a woman's body?"

"You didn't even warn me of what was coming," she accused him roughly. "I didn't accept this."

"The hell you didn't." His laughter was rough, bitter. "You knew, Liza. Deny it all you wish. You watched Isabelle and Malachi for weeks, you knew there was more than just the love you could see in their expressions for each other. Such a deep, fierce emotion is more than humans experience without something paranormal fueling it. Admit it: You knew. And I told you before I brought you to this bed that you were my mate. That mating heat bound us."

She tried to shake her head, to jerk from the grip of his fingers around the back of her neck.

"Lie to my face," he growled. "Go ahead, mate. Say the fucking words, I dare you."

"Stop pushing me!" The cry was torn from her heart. "You didn't tell me you loved me."

Stygian felt her pain, felt something tearing at her, some knowledge rising inside her that terrified her. That terrified him. God above knew what he suspected it was. Such fear was more than simply a woman's fear of the unknown, of a broken heart, or a male whose dominance was unlike any she had known before.

No, this fear was pure self-defense.

"I won't let you go." Nipping at her lips, he lifted her to him, one hand jerking the sheet from her body, leaving her lying against his chest, naked and warm and filled with such emotion that he swore his heart would break from her pain. "You knew where this was going. Did you think nature and God would have bound us so tightly together, without love being at the core of those bonds?"

"Stop this, Stygian," she tried to demand, but he had heard enough.

Lowering his head, he caught her lips in a kiss that he feared would steal the soul from his body.

The glands beneath his tongue were pounding with a

sudden infusion of hormones. The spicy taste that filled his mouth was richer, more heated than before, the hormone strengthening in response to her denial of him, her denial of the mating that had already been established.

The animal genetics that drove him would never allow him to walk away, nor would it allow her to retreat.

His tongue pushed past her lips, stroked against hers and gave her the taste of pure lust. An ambrosia created to bind the perfect heart to his Breed soul.

And she was his perfect heart. His mate.

Holding her to him with one hand wrapped around her neck, his free hand stroked the curve of her breasts, the backs of them stroking over the swollen mound as she suddenly moaned, spread her fingers against his chest and let her little nails bite into his flesh.

As his tongue retreated, hers followed. It licked over his, drew it back to the warmth of her mouth, then drew a savage groan from his chest as she gripped it with her lips and suckled at the taste with delicate greed.

His cock jerked to attention, thick and furiously hard. The feel of her sucking mouth about his tongue struck at the hunger rising inside him.

He wanted her lips around his cock. He wanted her sucking it into the wet heat of her mouth, caressing him, her wicked little tongue lashing at it sensually.

Pulling back from her kiss, Stygian had every intention of silently leading her to the furiously throbbing length of flesh between his thighs. Hell, he would have begged her for the touch. Instead, he stared down at her in shock as her lips went to his chest, her tongue licking over it, swiping at the hardened discs of his nipples before moving lower.

Silken hands stroked, blunt nails rasped across his tough flesh, moving down the clenched muscles of his abs to the painfully hard length of his dick.

"Mate," he snarled, wrapping the fingers of one hand around the base of the heavy erection to hold back the ejaculation of the pre-seminal fluid he knew would spurt to her mouth with the slightest provocation. "Such a sweet, hot mouth."

He watched, mesmerized, as her lips moved over his stomach, lower, her tongue dipping into the indention of his navel before swiping at the thick head of his cock as it rose a breath below it.

Sinking his fingers into her hair, his lashes lowered, he watched her pink, heated little tongue as it began curling around the heavily engorged crest of his dick.

Her lashes lifted, staring up at him, her face flushed, lips parted as she began to relish each lick and taste of his erection.

"That's my sweet love," he growled, his fingers clenching in her hair as her lips parted further, then with a snarl, his hips lifted with a jerk as her mouth suddenly surrounded the flared tip.

And she sucked down the engorged crest until her mouth was filled with the throbbing head.

Her tongue lashed at it, stroking over the ultrasensitive flesh as another primal growl tore past his throat. His jaw felt locked from the tension, the glands beneath his tongue throbbing, so filled with the mating hormone again that it was a near agony.

His cock pulsed, the shaft flexing as the pre-seminal fluid threatened to spurt past his control. The heated warmth of her mouth was the trigger, just as the slick heat of her pussy would have been.

With each draw of her mouth he could feel, scent her arousal building. It was as though his refusal to allow the retreat of her emotions had thrown her deeper, harder into her own hunger.

Was this what she fought to reject?

The physical hunger was more than the need for sex in a mating. It was a bonding. There was no hiding from a Breed mate, no faking pleasure or orgasm. There was a pleasure that sank clear to the soul and opened emotions that were often much feared.

Her mouth worked over his cock head, suckling, licking it, moaning as a small spurt of pre-cum escaped his control. The taste of it against her tongue did as she had heard, as rumor had suggested. The hormone in that fluid was more potent, richer, hotter than any his tongue could possess. It was an instant aphrodisiac.

Sensuality seemed to stretch through her body, turning her into a glistening, fiery temptress. Her gaze became more languorous, pleasure suffused her expression, and as he watched, he swore he sensed the woman she hid within her begin to emerge.

Hunger and heat, emotion and need. It began to clash and coalesce inside her. Her hands stroked down his thighs to his hips and back. She sucked at his dick as though it were a favorite treat, one she feared she'd be denied in the future.

And he was preparing to deny them both, because he didn't dare allow himself to come in her mouth. He had to be inside her, filling her.

"No more." He was within seconds of filling her mouth, a release that would do little to ease the fury of hunger beginning to rage through her after that small release of pre-cum.

"No." Of course she would have to protest as he drew her from him.

Moving to lay her back, surprise filled him as she instead straddled his hips, one small hand curving around the side of his cock.

"Let me have you now." She groaned. "Let me take you, Stygian."

The wet heat of her pussy caressed the tip of his cock, burning him with the pure, sweet fire of her hunger.

As she tucked the engorged head at the entrance, Stygian felt the first blast of the easing qualities of the fluid jetting inside her.

Without it, the thick width of his cock would have only hurt her, the knot that would extend inside her, locking him to her as his semen spurted to the heated depths of her womb, would have been pain rather than pleasure.

As it filled her, her head tilted back, her gray eyes dark-ened and as the heavy strands of her hair caressed his sensi-tive thighs, she bore down and with one shift of her hips, took the aching head of his dick inside her.

It was like watching the animal inside him come alive,

Liza thought hazily as she watched Stygian's gaze flare, the
black receding beneath the brilliant sapphire blue.

As the thick, throbbing crest filled her, another heated
ejaculation spurted from his cock, filling her, easing the tension in her pussy even as it amplified the pleasure.

Tingles of exquisite sensation exploded in her vagina.
Nerve endings became more sensitive, more demanding.
Each incredible stretch of the ultrasensitive tissue revealed
nerve endings that throbbed in greater need and sent electri-
cal flares of such lush sensation racing through her that it
forced her to lift her head, to lean into his broad chest for
support as it overcame the last barrier of her control.

She didn't want to control anything anymore.

She didn't want to fight anymore.

She had spent so many years fighting some unnamed
hunger, some need that she was finding the answer to here,
in his arms, and in finding it, she no longer needed to fight it.

Shifting her hips, lifting by increments, lowering herself
again, Liza couldn't hold back the moaning whimpers of
pleasure that fell from her lips. With each downward stroke
of her tightened vagina over the thick length of his cock, the
heated fluid spilled inside her again. With each spurt the taut
muscles eased, allowing her to take more of him, while the
tension and incredible need for release became more amplified.

Holding on to his shoulders, her nails biting into his
flesh, she forced her eyes open, staring into the gem-bright
brilliance of his as he stared back.

As his fingers tightened at her hips, his expression was
tight with a savage hunger, each plane and angle defined
with brutal clarity to hint at the primal male animal that
stalked beneath his flesh.

"I need this," she cried out desperately, moving harder,
faster, desperate to force every inch of his erection inside
her. "Please, Stygian. I need this."

She needed all of him.

Lifting, returning, feeling her juices spill to the throbbing shaft filling her, Liza could feel the pleasure spiraling
out of control inside her. Like a vicious wind whipping

through her senses, but this wind was filled with lashing sensations and the promise of ecstasy.

Desperation edged at each shift and downward stroke of her hips. Each throb of her swollen clit and clench of her tightening vagina was an agony of sensations she could hardly bear.

His hands tightened at her hips again before sliding to her rear. Holding her still, he allowed a growl to erupt from his throat a second before he surged upward, shafting inside her in one full stroke.

Liza tipped her head back, a keening cry escaping her throat as pleasure and pain combined to send her senses spinning in a winding spiral.

Once he was fully embedded inside her, she couldn't remain still. She needed those long, hard strokes. She needed the fiery, pleasure/pain of the heavy thrusts fucking inside her, driving her insane with an ecstasy she couldn't have anticipated.

She wanted all of him.

His hard possession.

His arms surrounding her.

And his kiss.

"Oh God, kiss me," she whispered, the need for his taste riding her as hard as he was with the heavy width of his cock.

His hand cupped the back of her neck, pulling her forward with a move so powerfully dominant it sent a surge of pure sensation tearing across her nerve endings.

Hungry and filled with lust, his tongue slipped past her lips, licked at her tongue and gave her the taste she was craving.

Flames licked at her insides. Perspiration dewed their skin, making their bodies slicker, hotter as Stygian's thrusts became more powerful.

Each driving stroke inside the tender depths of her sex dragged a near-startled cry from her lips, the sound vibrating into their kiss as Stygian gave a harsh, primal growl.

In the next second, he was no longer propped against the pillows but lying flat as his hips drove upward, burying his cock to the very heart of her.

Explosions began detonating inside her as that hard, fierce stroke seemed to connect with every live nerve ending brought to painful awareness.

She wanted to scream; instead, she lost her breath. The power, the sheer depth of sensation allowed for no other response, no other function. She was trembling, ecstatic, hurled from reality to a place so brilliant, so filled with light, sensation and ecstasy that even breathing couldn't be allowed to interfere.

Stygian's release felt just as powerful. The jetting spurts of his release, the strength of the swelling in his cock as it locked them together, the fierce growl that broke from his lips, assured her he was there with her. Spiraling into flames so brilliant, so white-hot that she knew a part of her—an important, intrinsic part—had just been lost to him.

And it would have been terrifying. It *should* have been terrifying. But even as she lost that part of herself, she could have sworn she felt a part of him slipping into her soul as well.

There would be no more distance, not from this man, from this Breed she had allowed to mate her.

What had she been thinking?

Lying against his chest, fighting to catch her breath, to still the tremors still racing through her, Liza couldn't explain, even to herself, why she had taken that step to test the tabloid rumors.

Ashley had warned them years ago to tread carefully when dealing with Breed males and their sexuality. She had told Chelsea, Liza, Claire and Isabelle there were hazards they could never imagine.

Well, she could imagine them now.

Now that he was lifting his lips from her neck, laying a gentle kiss to the tender flesh where he had bitten her once again.

Slowly, she could feel the easing of the iron-hard knot that had filled her,

They were both exhausted, and she was starving. Too hungry to sleep, and too damned tired to get up and cook.

"I could have Jonas send us some food from the hotel," he said as though reading her thoughts.

Her thoughts, or the growling of her belly.

"'Kay," she mumbled.

"You have to move, mate." He chuckled beneath her.

"Why? Phone's by the bed. Use it."

"Sorry, baby, that line's not near secure enough to suit me." A quick kiss to her lips and he was rolling with her.

Depositing her to her back, Stygian lifted himself from the bed and padded naked into the other room.

Liza stayed where she was. Her legs were still jelly. She swore she'd fall flat on her face if she had to actually walk.

"We have to return to the hotel."

It was the harshness in Stygian's voice that had her turning to her back and staring up at him with a frown.

"What?"

"Get dressed. Gideon Cross was sighted at a service station just outside Window Rock an hour ago and he was asking about you and Claire. There's no time left, Liza. We have to move."

"How do you know that?" Gripping the quilt to her breasts, she stared back at him, apprehension beginning to churn through her. "Why would he let himself be seen?"

"I don't know why," he growled. "Ashley and Emma sighted him and called in. By the time they turned around, he was speeding away on a trail bike and hit the desert. They lost him from there."

He was asking about her and Claire?

Liza could feel herself shaking from the inside out. Feel a sudden terror racing through her.

She could feel, sense some knowledge rising inside her. There was something she needed to tell him, but as quickly as the thought flashed across her mind, it was gone again.

Where was that internal distance that had been so easy to find earlier?

Where was that ability to retreat? To hide from the sudden, bone-chilling fear and the flash of a face?

But it wasn't a mature male with a Bengal's slash across his face. It wasn't demonic yellow eyes glistening with rage as in the pictures Jonas Wyatt had shown her.

No. It was a young man. In such pain, so fierce and so determined to help them—

Liza stumbled from the bed, suddenly sick to her stomach, capping her hand over her mouth, terrified she would lose her pride and the lunch she had eaten earlier right there on the floor.

She wanted to hide.

She wanted to go away.

Oh God.

Oh God, she had to go away.

She had to escape and there was only one way to do it. There was only one place to hide. There was only that place so deep within herself that there was no chance of danger—

"Liza, stop. You're safe. Listen to me, baby, you're safe."

Stygian had her. His hands were wrapped around her upper arms, holding her to her feet, his voice was calm, firm, insistent, holding her to the present when all she wanted to do was sink as deep inside herself as possible.

"You're safe," he said again. "You have time for a quick shower. Dog and his team are moving in and they'll escort us to the hotel, along with Flint and Rule, where Claire and the team sent to collect her will meet us. Everything's fine."

She nodded slowly.

Everything was fine.

Everything but Liza. Because, in a few short minutes she had managed to lose her sense of her training, her independence and her certainty that not just Stygian but also Cullen and the team would be there to support her. For one horrifyingly dark moment, she was alone and facing almost certain death.

She couldn't let this happen to her. She couldn't lose herself this way every time something happened. She couldn't let those dark, hidden memories that weren't exactly memories, that she knew couldn't belong to her, erode her control.

And she wouldn't allow it to, she promised herself, not ever again.

Never would she be weak again.

CHAPTER 14

Claire was waiting with her parents, as well as Liza's, in the Presidential Suite, sitting still and silent, her hands folded in her lap as she stared down at them.

Entering the room, Liza stared at the assembled Breeds and parents, their expressions quiet, savage or just emotionless.

"Good, we're all here." Jonas Wyatt moved to the center of the room as Liza sat slowly in the wingback loveseat next to the matching chair her friend had taken.

Glancing at her father, she was taken aback by the anger that glittered in his eyes, and the barely hidden fear in her mother's.

"What's going on?" she questioned the director.

She'd rather hear any bad news from someone she wasn't certain she liked than to hear it from anyone else.

"Gideon Cross, the fourth member of the Brandenmore Omega experiments, has arrived in Window Rock, and he's asking specifically about the two of you. What, Ms. Johnson, do you and Ms. Martinez have to do with all this?"

He wasn't questioning her, he was interrogating her.

Liza shook her head. "Nothing. I don't know why he's asking about us, or what he wants, any more than we know why the Genetics Council has targeted us."

But a part of her did know—

"Are you aware that the county health department was broken into several weeks ago and only your and Claire's childhood files are missing?" Jonas asked then.

No, she hadn't known that.

"Dad?" She turned to her father questioningly. "Did you know?"

The health department would surely have informed him of the situation if they had been unable to reach her.

Of course, there was no reason why they couldn't have reached her other than the fact that Ray Martinez's cousin was the director there. If he had asked that she make him aware of any problems before Liza and his daughter were told, then that was exactly what would happen.

"There was no sense in worrying you," her father stated as though it were of no importance at all.

She could only blink back at him.

She wasn't going to berate her father in front of strangers, but there was a sense of disbelief and even a sense of betrayal that he had withheld something so important.

"We can discuss it later, Liza," he promised her, as though he had sensed her feeling of betrayal. "I wasn't intentionally keeping it from you."

Yes, he had been, but once again, she wasn't going to confront him here and now. Not when so many interested eyes were watching, suspicious, analyzing every move, every look, every word spoken.

Not when Stygian was keeping her from retreating, from hiding within herself by the invisible bonds of a mating she still didn't understand.

She turned back to Jonas, determined to hold on to the anger building inside her.

"I want to know why the Genetics Council and Gideon Cross have targeted us just as much as you do," she informed Jonas. "We're nobodies, Mr. Wyatt. An assistant and a receptionist?" She all but laughed at the absurdity of it. "Why target us because of two girls no one has seen in over twelve years?"

"Evidently, for some reason they believe the two of you

are those girls, or can lead them to the girls, as I've already explained."

"Then explain it again, Mr. Wyatt." With her gaze locked on the eerie silver eyes of the director, she stared back at him confrontationally. "I'm sick of hearing about these two girls and all the reasons why all these assholes think we can lead them to them. We don't know them. We haven't met them. And we sure as hell can't help anyone find them. So tell me why the hell they keep coming after us?"

She'd had enough.

"If none of the above applies, Ms. Johnson, then I have no idea."

"And you're a liar," she accused him roughly as she came to her feet, her gaze slipping to Wyatt's wife, Rachel.

She noticed the other woman was not jumping instantly to her husband's defense.

Let another woman call Stygian a liar and see how fast Liza could get up in their face.

Instead, Rachel Broen-Wyatt glanced at her husband with somber concern.

Wyatt's brows arched with curious mockery. "And how would you know if I were lying?" he asked. "Unless you know something that you're not revealing."

Liza stared back at him, holding on to the sense of mist and memories that seemed determined to overtake her.

Not now. Not even a hint of self-doubt could be allowed to escape or every Breed here would be on her like a pack of wild animals.

"Stop with the games, Jonas." It was Stygian, rather than her father, or Claire's, who stepped from the side of the room.

Except Stygian.

He would stand between her and hell, she suddenly realized. A part of her could actually feel—feel him as though he were an integral part of her being—determined to protect her.

Liza felt his hand settle at the small of her back, a warm weight that pulled her back from the slight distance she'd managed to achieve without realizing it.

A distance she desperately needed right now. She had been deliberately receding from reality, hiding from the world or from whatever truths or knowledge she didn't want to see until Stygian had come into her life. Now, she realized not just what a relief those retreats had been, but also how easy it would be to hide from any truth she might not want to accept. As well as the nightmares. Those hazy, terrifying dreams that had haunted her for so many years. The ones she never remembered, and hadn't wanted to remember.

Had she always done this? Was it because she didn't want it to be real? That she didn't want to face what she was beginning to suspect was the truth?

"I don't think I'm the one playing games." Jonas sighed as the mockery eased from his expression, leaving a sort of weary acceptance. "And I don't think your mate is either, Stygian. Whatever she knew has obviously either been stolen, or it's a knowledge she's unaware she even has."

The look the director shot her father and Ray was telling. He believed they knew the truth, and Liza was certain they did.

"You don't know what the hell you're talking about." Her father stepped forward, anger echoing in his tone even as Liza glimpsed a flash of guilt. "Do you think I wouldn't know my own daughter? That I wouldn't know if she had been replaced by another?" Heavy mockery filled his tone and marked his expression.

"Enough, Audi," her mother protested as she laid a hand on his arm, her fingers trembling as she caught Liza's gaze. "This is only upsetting Liza. Let's see what we can do to help her, rather than upsetting her."

The love she had always seen in her mother's face was there. There was also all the love and acceptance she had always known. Her life, until now, had been charmed. Loving parents, an uneventful past, a good job.

She had everything but the husband, kids and white picket fence.

"Mr. Wyatt," she said softly, never taking her gaze from her mother's. "If I were who you and the Genetics Council wanted me to be, wouldn't I know it?" She turned to the director, shaking her head at the solemn look on his face. "I wish I were Honor Roberts or Fawn Corrigan, and if I thought for a minute I could help your child, then I would. But I've grown tired of assuring you I'm not either of those girls, nor do I know them, know where they are, who they are, or what happened to them."

Breathing in roughly, she turned to Stygian. "Could we go to whatever little box of a room he's assigned us this time? It's nearly midnight, I'm tired and I have to be at work in the morning." She turned to Claire. "Claire, if you're staying here at the hotel, then I'd like to talk to you at breakfast."

"Claire won't be staying," Ray Martinez spoke up, his voice low and for the first time since they were teenagers, lacking any emotion when it came to her and Claire.

Liza turned to her friend slowly.

Claire's head was down, her gaze hidden. Liza knew that look. She'd almost forgotten it. Seeing Claire so silent and still, her attention focused entirely on her hands, was a sight she hadn't seen since before the accident.

For the briefest second, it wasn't Claire she saw sitting there. The girl she saw was much younger, her hair several shades darker, her body just a bit stockier.

Blinking, the image receded, disappearing as quickly as the memories that tormented her.

"Mr. Martinez, your daughter will be safer here." Command naturally hardened Jonas's tone.

"She's going with me." Ray was at the point of belligerence.

Liza had to agree with Jonas for a change. If Gideon Cross was indeed in Window Rock and asking about her and Claire, then at least for the moment, the hotel was the safest place.

Liza turned to her father.

Her parents were silent, her father's gaze apologetic while Ray and Maria Martinez stood stiff, unemotional.

"You could let her stay tonight," she whispered to the Nation's president. "Give the Breeds a chance to catch this Gideon Cross rather than giving him a chance to strike out at her."

A heavy frown filled Ray's expression then. "I didn't ask for your advice."

Liza knew that tone well. Ray was furious at the situation, and she feared that he would blame Claire, just as he did when she and Claire were children.

She turned back to her friend.

Claire was shaking her head, silently pleading with Liza not to begin a confrontation that would only result in additional trouble for her.

"I've had enough." Liza sighed wearily as she turned to Stygian, refusing to glance again at her father or Claire's. "I'm tired. I want to go to bed."

"We have two suites reserved here for you," Jonas informed her as he stepped forward once again. "Claire will be across the hall from you with Ashley and Emma Truing, if she decides to stay. Rule, Mordecai and Dog's team will have the rooms on each side of the two of you. You'll be protected."

"From what?" Liza snorted, shaking her head. "You know, Director Wyatt, you have to figure out why we're in danger before you can eliminate the danger. Good luck with that one, by the way. Because I'll be damned if I can figure it out."

She moved for the door, aware, surprisingly, of Claire moving behind her, silent, too damned silent, refusing to bid her parents farewell.

"Liza." It was her father who stepped forward before she could leave the room.

As he'd done when she was a child, he stood before her, staring down at her, his expression filled with guilt. "I'll fix it, baby girl," he promised.

How many times had he promised her that? He would fix it. And he always had before.

She was terribly afraid there was no fixing this one.

"I know you'll try, Dad." She nodded, her chest tight with the knowledge that he couldn't fix the danger she was in, no matter how much he wanted to.

"I won't let them hurt you," he promised her, and in his eyes she saw his determination to ensure her safety.

"Tell me," she demanded hoarsely. "Did you see Amber?"

From her peripheral vision she saw Rachel's gaze jerk to her as Jonas's eyes narrowed on her.

Regret and guilt flickered in his expression as he looked away from her.

"I bet Jonas swore he would never let anyone or anything hurt Amber again after he got her away from Brandenmore." Tears burned her eyes as one slipped her control and eased down her cheek. "And now, she's still suffering because of something he can't control. Something he's being given no help, or even the slightest honesty to combat."

Audi's jaw clenched spasmodically as his gaze swung back to her. "I don't have what he's here for," he bit out angrily.

"Then it won't hurt you to see the child none of us can help, will it? To understand, Dad, rather than meeting him in antagonism. The Navajo made the Breeds a vow. That vow was to extend to them all that was needed to aid their battle for freedom, safety and welfare that they could provide. There was no addendum that excluded anything, at any time. It was all they could do, when they could do it. And perhaps that's something both you and Ray are forgetting."

When her father said nothing more, Liza could only shake her head. Turning and walking to the door, she paused as Stygian opened it and stepped out ahead of her. She turned back to Claire's parents slowly. "I used to think you were so funny and so kind, Ray. Claire used to laugh all the time, and she knew how to have fun. And you knew how to be a father, but now, you just want to push her and the danger she's in aside. I guess politics really doesn't know any other loyalty or love besides itself."

Ray only glared back at her.

"Liza, that's not true," Maria Martinez protested softly. "It's not politics."

"Then perhaps you should explain to Claire one of these days exactly what it is, Mari. Because right now, I can't think of any other reason for the two of you to turn your backs on her," Liza suggested bitterly. "And that's exactly how it feels to her I bet. As though the two people who should be willing to fight for her, to protect her, act as though they don't even know her."

"Enough, Liza." Claire's voice was firm, unaffected, despite the glitter of pain in her eyes as Liza turned to glance at her. "I'm tired, and I'm certain you are as well. I'm leaving now."

"You're leaving with us," Ray stepped forward, only to stop as Cavalier moved to block his path. "You'll leave with us or you and Liza can both forget about coming back to work until this situation is entirely resolved. I won't allow you to risk yourself so easily nor do I believe we should place the Nation in such jeopardy as well."

He was lying.

Neither the Nation headquarters nor the Nation itself was in any danger, Liza and Claire were. Taking their jobs seemed more to be his way of punishing them for refusing to obey him.

"I've already e-mailed my resignation," Claire surprised her with her answer. "And I'm sorry, Father, for all the trouble you've been caused."

There were no tears, her voice wasn't husky, but Liza swore she could feel the pain tearing at her friend. That she could feel the gut-wrenching pain as well as the sense of complete abandonment that filled her as she left the room, Dog ahead of her, as Mutt and Mongrel followed behind.

"Why do I have a feeling neither of us will be returning when this is over?" Liza asked of the two men.

Audi was staring at his friend as though he didn't know him, while Maria had stepped away from him, turned her back on him and was obviously drying her eyes. Ray himself watched her, dry eyed, but his expression pulled in lines of doubt and uncertainty. Unlike the others watching him, Liza could see the torment raging through him.

What was driving these two men? What fears and emotions had caused each of them to come here, one to attempt to protect his daughter, the other who appeared intent on driving her away?

"When it's over, the jobs will be there if you want them." Ray shrugged as though it didn't matter, but his dark eyes glittered with torment.

"No wonder Jonas questions the honesty to be found

between the two of you where this situation is concerned," Liza whispered painfully. "I question it myself."

Casting the Martinezes one last glare, Liza turned and moved to the door as well.

"Stygian, after getting Ms. Johnson and Ms. Martinez settled, I'd like a moment of your time to discuss a few things," Jonas requested.

Stygian nodded shortly before opening the door and stepping from the suite. After a quick look along the hall, he turned back and nodded to her and Claire before he and Dog's team escorted them from Jonas's suite.

There was something surreal about the trip to the luxurious suite they had been given this time. As hard as Liza tried, once again her attempts to hide within herself were foiled, and with each step her confusion grew.

See, she told herself, this was why she had panicked earlier. Why the fear had taken such a hold of her once she learned Gideon was in town and asking about her and Claire. At any other time she would have allowed herself to pull back, to step behind a veil of emotionlessness, fearlessness. It made it easier to fight when there was no fear of the consequences. No fear of dying.

"Are you okay?" Stygian asked after the room had been thoroughly checked and Claire escorted to her room by Dog and his team.

She didn't like the look on Claire's face or the bitter knowledge in her friend's gaze. It was as though she had been looking at a stranger.

She turned back to Stygian, the man who assured her he was her mate, taking in the jeans, dark T-shirt and sober expression as he stood silently and watched her. His expression was uncompromising, his gaze flickering with blue demand. There was no give in him, but he wasn't taking either.

He was demanding a partner. He was demanding a woman that she wasn't certain existed.

The long, soft strands of black hair were tied back at the nape of his neck, revealing the powerful, savage features of his face that only amplified the glitter of blue in his gaze. He looked like a warrior. Her warrior.

"Answer me, Liza," he demanded. "Are you okay?"

"I'm fine." What more could she say? What more could she feel?

"Don't lie to me." Before she could turn away, he had her chin in his hand, forcing her head back, catching her gaze and holding it with his. "Something's wrong, I can feel it. Something more than Gideon, your parents, Claire's or Jonas's suspicions."

"You can smell it?" She snorted. "And don't you think that would be enough to ruin any girl's day?"

"No, I can feel it," he repeated, ignoring the latter. "I don't have to smell your emotions. You're my mate, I'll always sense them."

This was impossible to believe, yet she knew he wasn't lying. She could see the truth of the statement in his gaze.

"I needed this, didn't I? This mating stuff?" she asked, resigned, almost amused at the lack of anger she felt. She should have been furious with him. "What have you done to me, Stygian? Why did you do it?"

She couldn't escape. There was no way to retreat any longer. And as much as she had hated that distance as a child, as a teenager, she'd found she'd learned to rely on it as an adult. She wished, at this moment, that she could still access it. Because it would have made this Gideon situation a hell of a lot easier to deal with.

"What have I done to you?" There was that primal growl in his voice as his head dipped, his gaze becoming intent as he stalked around her in a tight circle. "Have I harmed you, mate? Have I stolen from you or somehow marred you?"

Pausing, his chest at her back, his hand at her hip, Stygian brushed her hair back from the nape of her neck as a shiver raced over her flesh. The heated warmth of his breath stroked her nape a second before she felt the rasp of his incisors against the sensitized skin.

A shudder of near-exquisite pleasure sizzled down her spine. Her nipples hardened to painful tenderness, her clitoris swelled and throbbed with rising demand while her vagina clenched at the aching emptiness between her thighs.

There was nothing benign or sedate about Stygian, just
as her response to him wasn't in the least muted. It was hot,
demanding, explosive. All those things she'd never allowed
herself to feel with anyone else.

"I mated you, Liza," he whispered at her ear. "You were
meant to be my mate, my woman. Of all the women in the
world, only you could ever be mine, now. Just as I'll now
always belong to you. Nature ensured you can't run, you
can't hide and you can't deny what we have."

"I didn't ask to run, or to hide," she informed him as her
lashes drifted closed, the feel of his lips barely a breath from
her neck, sending chills racing through her.

"But you would deny me if you could," he stated.

Would she deny him? If she could walk away from him,
would she do it?

She wouldn't.

Locked within the suddenly sensually charged atmo-
sphere, Liza knew she had no desire to leave.

"I wouldn't deny you, Stygian, even if I were able to."
She wasn't going to lie to him at this point. She wasn't going
to lie to herself.

She couldn't, even if she wanted to, because he would
know the lie for what it was. And there was no way to deny
the fact that if she could have chosen an adventure to destroy
her life, this would have been the one she would have chosen, and the man she would have chosen to have it with.

As though to reward her for not denying it, his lips settled
against her nape, taking small, leisurely kisses along the
column of her neck.

The velvet-rough texture of his lips, the heated lap of his
tongue against her flesh was incredibly sensual. It added
fuel to the latent flames simmering between her thighs and
heating her clitoris.

What he did to her should be illegal. What he made her
body feel, made her heart race for, should have been outlawed long ago by the United Nations and entered into the
Geneva Convention. Or something.

As his hands smoothed from her hips, running up, his

large hands cupping her swollen breasts, Liza knew he was destroying the woman she had fought to be for so many years.

He was destroying the security she had built for herself and the safety she had fought so hard to attain.

She rested her head against his shoulder, feeling her hair trailing down her bare arm, the skin revealed by the sleeveless summer blouse she'd hurriedly dressed in earlier.

"Let me hide," she whispered as he began pulling the light shirt up, over her breasts, then taking her wrists in a gentle grip, lifted her arms to allow him to remove it altogether.

"Why hide?" His teeth grazed her earlobe, sending erotic shudders racing down her back then back up again. "Come out and play, Liza," he dared her. "Live for me." He nipped at her earlobe before blazing a path of pleasure down her neck as his hands returned to her breasts.

Her arms curved back, holding on to his neck as his fingers plucked at her nipples, the tender buds so swollen, so responsive to his touch that the pleasure was excruciating.

Live for him?

She was living just fine for herself. She was doing fine hiding. She just needed to hide a little while longer.

But hiding wasn't going to happen when he touched her.

When she could feel the strength of his erection at her back. When she could feel his fingers plumping and caressing her nipples as his teeth raked her neck and his tongue licked a fiery path of pleasure along it.

"You're destroying me, Stygian," she whispered as the fingers of one hand released the small catch of the skirt he'd already removed from her body once.

"You complete me, Liza," he swore as the material pooled at her feet, leaving her clad only in the thong panties she wore and a matching white lace bra.

How could she complete him when she wasn't even certain she herself was whole?

One broad, calloused palm slid from her breast to travel down her midriff, over her stomach to the low, elastic band of her panties.

Sliding beneath the band, his hold tightened as her breath

caught, her thighs parting as his fingers found the saturated folds of her sex.

"Again?" Shock and bemusement filled her voice. "It's only been a few hours."

She hadn't expected him to want her now, not after Jonas had all but ordered his quick return to the suite. "Always," he groaned as the pad of his finger found the tight, clenched entrance to her pussy. "I would want you on my deathbed."

"Jonas will be pissed you didn't come right back to his suite," she reminded him as she tilted her head to the side to give him greater access to the back of her neck.

"Jonas will just have to deal." His hands clenched on her hips, drawing her tighter against his hips and the hardened erection beneath his jeans. "I have more important matters to see to first."

Her lashes drifted closed as she caught her breath at the feel of his fingers pressing between her thighs and finding the saturated slit of her pussy. They raked over her swollen clit, slid further between the swollen flesh then found the clenched entrance of her pussy.

The rasp of his fingertips against the sensitive opening to her inner core had her hips tilting out as her head fell back against his shoulder.

"It's a mating thing, right?" Breathless, she parted her thighs further, desperate to feel those wicked, knowing fingers pressing inside the slick, heated depths of her pussy.

"I doubt it." He breathed out roughly. "God, Liza, I wanted you twenty-four-seven before the mating heat even began."

"You didn't know me twenty-four-seven," she protested, barely able to speak or to think as she felt him rubbing inside her with each shallow stroke of his finger.

"I watched you from the moment your friend Isabelle walked across the bar to claim Malachi," he told her, his voice rough, filled with lust. "I watched and followed you to work and back home every evening. I watched you as the sun worshipped your body out by the pool and as you slipped out at night to swim naked."

She would have blushed if the thought of him watching her from the darkness hadn't been so damned arousing. Because it had been him she had thought about as the water caressed her naked body.

Moaning in rising pleasure as another finger joined the first to stretch her inner muscles with delicious heat, Liza tightened her grip on his neck, barely recognizing the strain in her arms from the position. All she knew was the incredibly sensual feel of his fingers stroking inside her, the pad of his palm rubbing against her clit and sending a thousand heated sensations rushing through her system.

"So good," she whispered, unable to hold back the words as the pleasure became so rich, so intense it nearly stole her breath. "Oh God, Stygian, it's so good."

His fingers thrust deeper inside her, sending her senses racing with the steady climb to ecstasy as the words tore past her lips.

Pushing past the delicate, tender tissue, his fingers scissored inside her, stretching the taut muscles and sending flares of exquisite heat wrapping around her clit, tightening the little bud with tormenting need.

"I need you, Liza." He groaned at her ear, the roughened rasp of his voice sending a surge of pleasure racing to her womb and clenching it with furious heat.

Her panties were pushed the rest of the way past her hips with his free hand as her pussy clenched and tightened on the fingers filling it.

"Oh yes." The words slipped past her lips as eroticism wrapped around her senses, his hunger amplifying hers.

As her panties cleared her thighs, a cry vibrated from her chest as his fingers slid free of the sensual grip she had on them.

She found herself bent over the couch.

Lifting her leg at the knee, Stygian bent it against the cushions as he pressed her shoulders to the thick pillows.

Liza gripped the heavy couch back beneath the pillows, fighting for breath, feeling her senses reeling as she wondered if she would ever have control of herself again.

She could have, she assured herself, given another minute.

Perhaps a few years.

As that thought drifted through her mind, it was quickly erased by the heat and iron-hot width of the head of his cock tucking against the slick entrance to her sex.

She was so wet her thighs were damp. The slick warmth spread over the swollen folds and the sensitive bud of her clit. Pulses of intense sensation swept through the little bud, echoed in her pussy and sent more of the slick response spilling from her vagina.

"So pretty." He groaned, his hands bracketing her hips as he held her in place. "Sweet, sweet baby. I can't think of anything but this." His hips shifted, pressing the thick head into the clenched entrance of her pussy as the heated spurt of pre-cum ejaculated inside her.

She was figuring that part out. The heated fluid enabled the tense, clenched muscles inside to adapt to the overly thick width of the erection beginning to fill her.

With each spurt, it eased her further, heated her inner tissue further, and intensified the need for his cock surging deep and hard.

She rolled her hips against the penetration, allowing the hard, heated flesh to begin pushing inside her.

Each shallow thrust opened her further, made her burn brighter, hotter than before.

Hoarse cries tore from her lips, falling into the pillows as he continued to push inside her, in and out, working each inch inside her with a patience that was killing her.

She wanted him pushing inside her, thrusting with hard, long strokes, fucking her with the hunger she could feel raging inside him.

With each spurt of the heated fluid inside her, the desperation for it grew. The need to have him pounding inside her built with a vengeance.

"More." The smothered moan was involuntary, a cry tearing from her lust-ridden senses as he pushed fully inside her, burying his cock to the hilt in the tight depths of her pussy. "Please, Stygian, please."

The heavy flesh throbbed inside her, the blood pounding through the heavy veins and vibrating against the inner walls tightening around it.

"Please what, baby?" He groaned, coming over her, his knee braced beside hers as he gripped her thigh and ground his hips against her rear.

"Yes. Oh God, yes," The shattered cry felt torn from her as bursts of ecstasy raced through her body.

His cock stretched her until she was certain she couldn't take more. Until she knew that without the addition of the mating knot becoming erect along the shaft there was no way she could accept the additional width.

Another heated spurt of pre-cum filled her, the Breed hormonal fluid sinking into the sensitive flesh, tightening it even as it enhanced the ability of the tender tissue to accept the width it was taking.

However it did it, each spurt made her hotter, made the need to experience the hard, driving strokes inside her more brutal.

"Damn. Ah hell, baby. Keep doing that." Stygian groaned at her ear. "Keep stroking my dick with that sweet, tight little pussy."

Her pussy tightened further. The involuntary clench of the muscles surrounding his flesh dragged a harsh cry from both of them.

"So fucking good," he whispered, his lips moving to her neck, his tongue taking small tastes of her flesh as his teeth raked it. "Ah, baby, you're so fucking hot, so sweet and good, I could stay like this forever."

But his hips were moving, grinding against her, his cock flexing inside her, the pre-cum shooting harder, hotter against her inner walls as the hunger rose with each second he lingered inside her.

"Please." Her ragged moan was almost impossible to utter as pleasure sent jagged forks of sensation tearing through her womb and across her clit. "Please, Stygian."

"Tell me, mate." He nipped her neck erotically. "Tell me what you want. How do you want me to please you?"

The long, midnight dark strands of his hair fell around his face to caress her arms, the tops of her breasts. The soft warmth, so at odds with the hard flesh and powerful muscle of the man taking her was a stimulus that nearly pitched her into complete rapture.

The need for orgasm was overriding. It was in every throb of her heart and every rapid pulse of blood through her veins. It was in every moan, every cry, and every breath she drew.

"Fuck me," she cried, the desperate, ragged sob tearing from her chest as hunger reached a fever pitch. "Please, Stygian, please fuck me, hard—Oh God . . ."

Moving, pulling back then lunging forward, Stygian set a hard, fast rhythm that had her crying, begging, pushing back into him with each forceful, shocking thrust inside her pussy.

Each hard, heated stroke inside the overheated depths of her cunt had her back arching, her hips lifting and incoherent pleas falling from her lips.

Yet he was in no hurry to find his release. He was in no hurry to push her into orgasm.

As the wide shaft delved repeatedly into the saturated depths of her sex, his large hands roved from her hips, up her stomach and to her breasts.

Cupping the swollen globes as he pushed inside the aching depths of her pussy, he growled at her ear, his thumbs tweaking her nipples, sending rioting fingers of electric sensation pulsing through her body.

When she swore she could take no more, that the pleasure would destroy her, his hands moved from her breasts, making the return path to her hips. There, one hand gripped the quivering flesh as the other slid caressingly over the curve of her rear.

Pulling back, forcing her to release the sensual clamp on his cock, his fingers slid between the cheeks of her rear. Returning in a hard, bold thrust, a calloused fingertip pressed against the forbidden entrance he found there.

Instinct had her stilling. Pleasure had her shuddering as she waited.

Stygian never paused. Moving against her, filling her, retreating, shafting inside her with increasingly hard strokes as the pleasure built with brutal intensity. At the same time, the hand at her hip moved lower and with the other, spread the curves, sending a prickling sensation pulling at the hidden entrance.

With each hard thrust inside her, the sensations at her rear increased. The parting of her flesh, the tip of his finger rubbing against the puckered entrance, sliding lower to gather her juices and ease them back, rubbing, pressing, sliding. Pleasure built to a golden haze that obliterated everything but the driving, uncontrolled race to release. To that moment when ecstasy slammed through her body and, somehow, Stygian pierced her soul.

Liza dug her nails into the cushions of the couch, panting for air as the overwhelming pleasure suffused every particle of her being.

The feel of Stygian against her back, surrounding her, holding her, taking her with a desperation and hunger that wrapped around her with such heat she felt seared by it, wrapped around her senses.

Heavily lubricated with her juices, the tip of his finger slid inside the snug entrance of her rear, adding to the fury of sensations spiraling through her body.

Her hips arched, driving the thick width of his cock deeper, lodging his fingertip further inside her as she relished each flash of pleasure/pain, each ecstatic stroke of blinding ecstasy. The sensations wrapped around her, burned over and through her nerve endings with each inward thrust, each pulse of the pre-cum that filled her and each touch of Stygian's caressing hands.

With his cock burrowing inside her pussy, his fingers, timing each stroke in rhythm with the other, the pleasure began to ride her with hard, electric pulses as a rising tension spiraled through her body.

With each hard stroke, she was pushed higher, thrown closer to the burning center of release.

It was building in her clit, in the depths of her pussy. It was tightening in her muscles, sending chills and waves of heat racing across her flesh.

His teeth raked the bend of her shoulder, scraping over sensitive flesh as her nails unlocked from the back of the couch and reached back, latching onto his hair and holding tight.

She needed him closer. So close their flesh felt connected. So close that she knew she would never be without him, no matter the distance that separated them.

"Yes," she panted. "Oh God, Stygian, yes. Right there. Don't stop—Don't stop—"

He didn't stop.

The thrusts increased in power.

The expert penetration of her rear went deeper, stroking, caressing naked nerve endings and finally sending her hurtling into the cataclysm of release.

The first white-hot flare of sensation erupted around her clit before striking the depths of her pussy. A long, shattered wail of pleasure left her lips, smothered with breathlessness, trapped against the cushions she buried her head in.

Stygian's incisors clamped on the bend of her shoulder, piercing the wound already there as his cock sank inside her again.

The first spurt of semen was followed by the intense swelling of his erection inside the heavy muscles clamped on it.

Spreading her flesh apart, pushing into it and locking his erection inside her, the force of the mating knot ensured there was no escaping his release as it filled her.

There was no escaping the man.

There was no escaping the emotions suddenly racing through her with the same force of his semen spilling into her.

Fear.

Hope.

Love.

She didn't want to feel any of the emotions she couldn't seem to hold back any longer.

Shuddering beneath him, her arm bent to maintain the hold she had on his hair as he covered her from behind, the feel of his teeth locked in her shoulder, the certainty that more than mating held them together, overwhelmed her. The well of emotion burning inside her now held her to him, opened a part of her she hadn't known she possessed, and she felt him move right in.

He was locked to her body.
He was locked to her heart.
He had invaded her soul.
And Liza knew she would never be free of him.

• **CHAPTER 15** •

Stygian's arms surrounded her, holding her close to his chest, the even beat of his heart a comforting sound beneath her ear after he'd carried her to the bed and tucked her in against him.

With her hand resting against the hard, corded strength of his abdomen, Liza tried to force her emotions, her need to be a part of him, at bay.

It had started the moment she had met him, she realized. This need to share every part of herself, to be with him what she had never been with anyone else.

No one knew her, not even Claire or Chelsea or Isabelle— not fully. She'd never wanted anyone to know her either, until now.

Until Stygian.

Oh, she had friends. Friends who knew parts of her, who cared for her, those who trusted her with their lives. The person they saw was a far cry from the person she was inside. The person she was, inside, seemed to come together in ways it never had, right here, in Stygian's arms.

"Sometimes, I feel as though I've never been real," she whispered, unable to still the need to share what she had never shared with anyone else. "It wasn't so bad before the wreck Claire and I were in. When it began, I thought it was involuntary, because I couldn't make it stop. But, in the past week, I've realized that maybe it wasn't involuntary, that maybe it was me all along." And the knowledge of that weighed on her heart like a massive stone, threatening to crush it.

"You're very real, Liza. Warm, living, breathing. How could you not feel real?" he asked her, his fingers caressing her bare shoulder, brushing against the mating mark and reminding her in a way nothing else could that she finally belonged somewhere.

She belonged to somebody.

"Am I? Was I?" Tilting her head back, she stared up at him, feeling the misery welling inside her. "Sometimes, it's like there's this other person that's just waiting inside me, biding her time, knowing she'll be free." Her eyes filled with tears as she admitted to him what she knew she could never admit to anyone else. And there was so much more. So many secrets she felt waiting to be free, and a knowledge that she could be—

"Trust me, baby," he whispered, the blue of his eyes holding her gaze, binding her to him as she swore she could feel him even into her soul. "I wouldn't betray you. Not for anyone. Not for anything. You understand that, don't you?"

Did he suspect what she suspected herself? What she was beginning to believe? That somehow the impossible had happened.

"I remember when I was five," she cried out, misery echoing in the low tone of her voice "I remember Dad teaching me to ride my bike. I remember my first day of third grade. I remember always being friends with Isabelle, Chelsea and Claire. I remember it, Stygian."

Those memories were so much a part of her that she knew those events had occurred.

Stygian tensed beneath her, his fingers pausing in their caressing motions for just a moment as Liza silently prayed for an answer. Any answer other than the one she knew they had to begin discussing.

A subject that had her chest tightening in such panic that she felt as though she had to struggle to breathe, to live, because the dark terror rising in her mind was something she feared more than she feared the truth.

"I'll protect you," he swore quietly, his tone rumbling with sincerity and his belief that he could do so.

"At what cost?" A bitter laugh escaped her. "What if there is no protection, Stygian? What if I'm really not who you and Jonas hope I am, but I'm just crazy instead? That's always a possibility. That's more a possibility than some miracle that I suddenly acquired a dead girl's memories and her life. Don't you see that?"

"I see a lot of possibilities, sweetheart." He sighed. "But your insanity, or any possibility of it, is not an option. If that were true, the animal instincts I possess would already have warned me of the possibility."

Liza stared up at the ceiling miserably, uncertain what to feel or how to deal with the suspicions rising within her mind.

She couldn't ignore them, nor could she avoid the truth any longer.

"What were the experiments Honor Roberts was a part of?" Her throat was so tight with fear she could barely swallow.

"The Omega Projects were research into using the unique development of age reduction and disease resistance and a cure that's been found in those couples who had mated."

Age reduction? Disease resistance and a cure?

Fear, panic, a certainty that this information would destroy her, began to invade her.

"And mating heat does that?" she whispered painfully.

His arms tightened around her. "Callan and Merinus Lyons have aged physically by one full year since their mating more than fourteen years prior. Her father, John Tyler, was dying of heart disease until he mated one of our female enforcers last year. His body has actually begun repairing itself. In the space of the time he's been mated, his organs have returned to prime condition, and his skin has lost ten percent of the aging damage."

Chills were racing over her flesh. The implications of what others would consider miracles began racing through her mind. Because what some would consider miracles, others would consider a sign of evil instead.

"That's what will happen to me?" she whispered.

"It already has if, somehow, you're Honor Roberts. The research notes we found suggest that aging retards at twenty-five without mating in subjects that were given the serum as children suffering from fatal diseases. Unfortunately, Brandenmore had those subjects terminated before we could find them. Only Honor and Fawn were thought to have survived."

Her fingers ached from being clenched on the comforter that covered them.

"Blood tests—" she began.

"Blood tests wouldn't work," Stygian injected. "The nature of the project changes not just blood type, but also genetics. Acts kind of like mating heat, which appears like a genetic virus to the body. The only way to prove inconclusively that you're not Honor Roberts is a deep-level core genetic test on both you and your father for a match."

"Why not just a DNA swab?" She couldn't lie any longer. She felt as though she couldn't breathe.

Sitting up, Liza clenched the blankets at her breasts and stared down at him.

"Because, with medical advances, even ten years ago, surface DNA could have been changed. All you would need is a scientist familiar with Clean Slate DNA, which is what Honor Roberts would have had at the time."

"Clean Slate," she murmured. "The Omega Project changed her genetic makeup to the point that it could have been so easily reprogrammed?"

Clean Slate DNA was a complicated process. It literally changed a person's genetic typing from one type to another and allowed for scientists and doctors to identify key components of the genetic strands that could be altered. It required another subject, a Beta, whose blood or genetic makeup didn't allow for certain diseases or health complications. So far, it had only actually been done on animals, as far as the world knew.

"The Omega Project simplified Clean Slate DNA," he told her heavily. "But once the project phase ended, Brandenmore decided it was time to terminate Faith, Judd and Gideon. Honor's father was part of the Genetics Council, which kept her out of the termination selection. Instead, once the other three disappeared and they learned there was more to the serum as the children matured, they decided to begin researching once again. Only Honor was left, and her father's influence wasn't great enough to save her from it. It was then her parents elected to aid her in disappearing."

"Elected to aid her?" she asked as she imagined what it would have been like for the parents.

Honor's father was military, he wouldn't have cried, she thought. He would have kept his head held high, but his gaze would have been damp. His expression would have been laced with misery.

"Her father gambled to save her life when she was less than two years old, fighting against it until only weeks before she would have died. He joined the Genetics Council, contributed to it. Lied for them, cheated for them and watched the slaughter of innocent Breeds so she would live," he stated, his voice filled with regret, but still the words sliced deep, their cruel imagery causing her to flinch. "It was nearly too late, but the scientists pulled it off. Ten years later she was home with her parents, happy, free of the leukemia and bargaining to get rid of the nanny she'd had in the labs.

"Her father thought the nanny was under his control only, but later learned that it was the Council that commanded her loyalty. She reported the signs of anomalies Honor was showing, that the girl was unable to hide, and the scientists were desperate to reacquire her."

Liza stilled, her gaze on her hands as she picked at the comforter as it lay over her legs. "What sort of anomalies?"

Because she had anomalies as well, ones she and Claire both had been taught to keep hidden, to never reveal lest they endanger them. This explained why their families felt it would cause their lives to be so irrevocably damaged in an age when unique abilities were prized.

"Honor had a photographic memory, but the nanny noticed the girl could watch movements, in either dance or fight, and within days she could execute them perfectly. She didn't just remember it perfectly, but how to apply it and when. Rather as Shiloh stated you were able to do the night Claire was attacked."

Liza didn't lift her gaze, but kept it on her hands, her nails, the quilt. Anything but Stygian, anywhere but on the fact that she was dying inside.

"And Fawn?" she asked.

"They weren't certain about Fawn." Reaching out, he pushed back the nearly hip-long wave of hair that had fallen over her face. "She showed signs of advanced code deciphering, even before the termination order went out. We need that ability to crack the code on the files Brandenmore had hidden. So far, even our best code breakers have only managed to decode a very minute amount of the files we found."

"Then you think there's something in the files there that will help Amber?" she asked quietly.

"At this point, we're willing to try anything," he admitted. "The few codes we've managed to break lead us to believe it's possible. It's very possible."

Liza had a photographic memory. She could watch certain moves, not so much dancing, which had interested her as a young girl, but in fighting, it was as though her brain could telegraph the moves from her sight to her actions.

And Claire, oh God help them, Claire could figure out a puzzle in seconds. Jigsaw puzzles, even the most difficult, were child's play for her.

She could feel herself trembling, shaking from the inside out.

Shaking her head, she looked up at him, uncertain, forcing back the fear. She had to force it back to be able to think, to make sense of everything.

"I can't be either of them," she whispered. "How could I be, Stygian? It's not possible."

But it was possible. It was possible enough that dreams, nightmares and memories that weren't exactly memories, that weren't exactly clear, came together in her mind.

Lifting his hand again, he brushed the backs of his fin-

gers over her cheek as he watched her with a quiet confidence she would do anything to be able to attain.

"I read an article before the rescues," he said then.
"Rumors of Breed creation had begun leaking, and some
enterprising young reporter had written of the possibility.
He stated unequivocally that the manipulation of human
and animal genetics could never result in a living, breathing,
intelligent being. Some things he stated seemed highly possible, but when in practical application, highly impossible.
And I had to smile, because it was that very creature he had
deemed impossible who was reading the article."

"A deep-level core genetic test could reveal the truth,"
she whispered. "The Clean Slate DNA manipulation can't
get past that."

"Proving the truth won't reveal the secrets," he stated
then. "And it's the secrets Jonas needs to save Amber."

It was the secrets they needed.

She stared back at him, seeing the long, ribbon-straight,
soft strands of midnight black hair as they trailed around his
strong face, the muscular column of his neck, the broad,
broad shoulders and powerful chest. He was savagely handsome, and staring back at her with an intensity that made her
feel as though she were the only woman in the world.

To him, she was the only woman in the world, she
thought, astounded. Yet, she wondered how she could be so
surprised.

She had waited for him.

She had waited for him to touch her, to bring her to life,
to awaken her.

"We'll go to the desert at daylight," he told her then. "Just
you and I, with Dog's team watching over us. We'll go to the
crash site before going to the area where the sweat lodge
was erected. Let's go back, Liza. Let's see if we can find
anything you may have lost."

"What if I don't come back, Stygian?" Her lips trembled
as tears darkened her soft gray eyes. Did she fear she would
get sucked back into some never-ending reality where she
could only watch the world go by, rather than experiencing it?

"I won't let you go." Tightening his fingers in her hair, he
pulled her head back, staring through the darkness to the
glitter of her gaze. "Never, Liza. You will never again be on
the outside looking in. You'll always be a part of me, and I'll
never let you go."

She didn't speak. As he loosened his grip on her hair, she
laid her head on his chest again and, he knew, stared into the
darkness.

"I couldn't feel anything when I was there," she said
softly. "No remorse, no love or hate. No fear."

"And now?" God, she was killing him. The emotions
building inside her were like a blow to his heart.

If only he had been here to save her, to pull her from the
darkness she'd been held in for so long.

"Now, I feel too much," she said faintly. "I don't know
what I'm feeling, and I don't know how to handle what I am
feeling. I just wish, when I was younger, that I had known
how to hold on to myself rather than allowing myself to
fade."

He would have held her to him, just as he was holding her
now, until she was old enough to be his reality.

Or, would he have held the wrong girl, and eventually,
the wrong woman?

The question raged in his mind as she fell silent and
eventually fell asleep against his chest.

That wreck; everything had changed the night Claire
Martinez had taken her father's sports car, Liza with her,
flying over a canyon and somehow missing the other side.

The two girls hadn't been found for hours, and when they
had been located, their fathers hadn't called the EMS immediately. Instead, they had called together the chiefs of the
Six Tribes, the medicine men of the Nation. Only after they
had treated the girls had an ambulance been called and they
had been taken to the hospital.

The accident report had been accessed by Diane Broen
before she had arrived in Window Rock. Her suspicious
nature had read something into those events that even the
Breeds had been unable to decipher. Something even Stygian had been unable to figure out.

According to the blood tests and surface-level genetic testing, Liza wasn't Honor Roberts. Her DNA was different, but the DNA used for those tests had been collected before the experiments conducted in the Brandenmore labs. The blood and tissue samples were those collected when she was a young girl, hospitalized for the wasting disease that had slowly been killing her.

Had a full-level DNA analysis been done? One that went to the very center of the genome, such as those done to detect recessive Breed genetics? After all, the serum used on the two girls had been derived from Breed hormones, while that used on the Breeds had been derived from both Breed and human hormones.

Barring that, had their DNA been compared to their parents'?

As he felt her slip into sleep, Stygian found his mind racing. There were too many questions, and far too many mysteries surrounding his mate and her friend Claire Martinez.

The fact, though, was that there was no evidence to even raise suspicion that Liza and Claire weren't exactly who they claimed to be. Nothing but the fact that since they were children, no blood, tissue or saliva samples had been taken from either girl, even during their stay in the hospital after the wreck.

From the moment they left the hospital, their personalities had been different. Their looks had been altered from the plastic surgeries needed, supposedly because of damage caused from the vehicle crashing into the canyon.

The fact that no blood and tissue samples had been taken then was highly suspicious and riding the cusp of being illegal.

There were Diane Broen's suspicions, there were Jonas's suspicions and his own, but that wasn't proof. There was no proof at all that she was anyone other than who she was supposed to be.

As he glared at the ceiling, he heard the faint hum of his sat-phone, which he'd set on the bedside table. Glancing over, the text message had him closing his eyes briefly.

Five minutes. Connecting suite.

The message was from Jonas.

Fuck, he didn't need this.

Dealing with Jonas wasn't something he wanted to do tonight, not while his own emotions were in such turmoil. Not while he was still trying to process the fact that his mate likely had no idea who she really was.

Not while he was still trying to get a grip on the suspicion that, somehow, the real Liza Johnson had ceased to exist somewhere around the time of that car accident.

In her place was Honor Roberts—but without Honor's memories, or the knowledge of who she was or who she had been. And if Liza Johnson was actually Honor Roberts, then that meant Claire Martinez would most likely be Fawn Corrigan, the target Gideon Cross was rumored to be determined to kill.

With a tight grimace, he eased himself from the bed.

Liza was sleeping. Stygian tucked the blankets about her shoulders to ensure she didn't get chilled.

Gathering his clothes, Stygian made his way to the connecting sitting room to dress quickly.

Once he pulled the low boots on and jerked the hem of his jeans over them, Stygian made his way to the door across the room, activated the digital keypad then punched in the code to disengage the locks.

Closing the door carefully behind him, he moved across the room to the entrance and opened the door to admit Jonas, Rule, Lawe and Mordecai.

Lawe Justice's rumored recent refusal of the position of assistant director of the Bureau of Breed Affairs hadn't changed the fact that he was still one of Jonas's most trusted advisors. The fact that he was there for the meeting Jonas had demanded proved it.

"What do you want, Wyatt?" Stygian breathed out wearily as he closed the door quietly. "Liza's asleep, but she may not be for long. So whatever you have to say that you don't want her to hear, now's the time to do it."

He had no idea what the director wanted, but he could sense the fact that whatever it was, Liza would be offended by it. The fact that the director insisted on meeting after she would most likely have been asleep was the first indication.

The look on Jonas's face wasn't comforting either.

Looking around the room, the director turned back to him slowly. "You're a lousy host, Stygian. There's not a damned thing here to drink."

"Yeah, well, I guess you taught me well then." He snorted. "There hasn't been a time I've come to the office that you've shared with me any of that whisky you're so proud of."

Jonas's lips kicked up at one corner as he inclined his head in acknowledgment. "Perhaps I made a mistake there," he stated, his voice remaining low. "I can get a drink when I return to my suite. What I can't get is the information you were paired with Ms. Johnson to acquire. Are you any closer?"

Stygian crossed his arms over his chest and glared back at Jonas. "What do you think?"

Jonas's nostrils flared as he obviously fought back his anger. "We don't have much time left, Stygian. Not just because of Amber. The Council has begun transferring key scientists in both genetics as well as Breed physiology and mating heat to highly secured, secretive labs, while known high-ranking members of their elite guard have been making their way into the desert several miles from here."

The Genetics Council's Elite Guard had, through the decades, been tasked with the kidnapping of the higher-profile women whose genetics were deemed essential for various creation projects. They were the best. The most highly trained, elusive and competent abduction specialists in the world.

"There's more going on here, and more players, than I can keep up with at one time." Cavalier's growl was rough, his voice almost ruined as he faced Stygian, his expression bland. "I've been tracking transmissions from the soldiers in the desert as well as between President Martinez and his head of security, Audi Johnson. Johnson and Martinez both are discussing the canyon where Liza and Claire went over. They're talking about whether or not they 'cleaned' enough."

Whether or not they cleaned enough.

Stygian grimaced as anger began to burn inside him. The Johnsons and the Martinezes knew exactly what had been done. They knew how their daughters had been brought back from the dead, and now Stygian wanted to know.

"Their fathers are lying to us," Jonas gritted out, the silver eyes flashing with merciless fury. "You know it and I know it. With half-truths and carefully worded denials, they're lying through their teeth. The only way we're going to get the truth out of them is by forcing it out."

Stygian gritted his teeth at the knowledge that regarding Liza and Claire's fathers, Jonas was entirely right. "Where does that leave us?"

"With Liza," Jonas stated softly, though his expression was determined. "I want to bring Ely and Cassie in, Stygian. Ely can run the samples just as she always does for mating heat, and Cassie can do whatever the hell it is she does. We could get the answers we need. And if we're lucky, maybe Ely can come up with something using the new mating tests she's developed."

Dr. Elyiana Morrey, the Breeds' head scientist and doctor, worked tirelessly on finding the answers on the why and the how of mating heat. She was certain the answers were in the deepest layers of the genetics strands, and had actually found a way to begin comparing DNA before and after mating heat. Now, she just needed the new mates to work with.

Because mating heat, like all things in nature, like all viruses that developed, never remained the same.

"I'll discuss it with her . . ."

"Discussing it would defeat the purpose," Jonas protested then. "If, as I suspect, a ritual took those memories and replaced them with someone else's, then warning her warns the safeguards placed on it. Risking that is out of the question. Besides, if she's aware of Cassie's identity when she meets her, then she'll be on guard. That will also steal any advantage we have."

And it was entirely possible Liza had heard of Cassie. She was friends with Ashley, Emma and Shiloh, and Cassie wasn't a taboo subject as mating heat was. She could well know Cassie's abilities to look inside a person and see the secrets that haunted them. Whether they knew they were haunted by them or not.

"You're asking me to do something no Breed has yet done," he growled. "You want me to betray my mate by lying to her."

"I want you to save her." Jonas breathed out wearily as he pushed his fingers through his hair and grimaced with bitter anger. "Her and my child. If we don't learn the truth, for certain, one way or the other, then the Genetics Council will take her and learn it for themselves. And if they take her, then you may never find her again."

That was Stygian's greatest fear. That somehow, the Coyote soldiers sent for her might actually manage to take her. If they took her, they could disappear with her in ways that Stygian could never find her.

Raking his fingers through his hair, he turned and paced away from the director, refusing to glance at the other Breeds there.

"Amber's becoming more ill by the week, Stygian." It was Rule who spoke as Stygian moved to the wide windows on the other side of the room. "The fevers are coming more often and they're taxing her strength further each time."

"Liza's my mate," he said bitterly.

She was his heart, his soul. They were asking him to betray every part of himself.

"And Amber is a child," Jonas said softly. "Liza is a grown woman with the ability to make choices to determine her own fate. She suspects, Stygian, we both know she does. She's doing nothing to learn the truth."

Crossing his arms over his chest, Stygian stared at the desert beyond the hotel, wishing to hell he'd find a way to keep this from happening.

"We're going to the crash site at dawn," he told them. "She wants to know."

"She'll fight it. She's probably fighting it now," Mordecai said behind him. "But I have a suggestion."

Stygian turned back slowly. "And that would be?"

"She keeps a personal journal on her laptop. I've tried to access it, but she's not powered it up since she's been here."

"And you know she has a journal how?" Stygian growled back at him.

"I was almost in when she shut it down the last time she had the computer online," Mordecai admitted. "I managed to pull some key words, though, which I used to be certain she may have information there. 'Dreams,' 'nightmares,' 'labs' and 'pain.'"

Stygian tensed further.

"All you have to do is plug it in, power it up and attach a flash drive, I'll take care of the rest. You don't have to steal a password or hack in yourself," Jonas assured him.

Stygian threw the other Breed a hard look. "And you think that will excuse the fact that I betrayed her? In her eyes or any others'? I'll always be the only Breed to deliberately break the trust his mate has given him."

"A mate who refuses to trust you?" Rule growled back at him. "She suspects she's Honor Roberts, Stygian, just as you do."

Stygian turned back to them again, the look he shot each of them filled with the mockery rising inside him. "It doesn't matter if she trusts me or not. That doesn't excuse betraying her."

"Distrust excuses many things, my friend," Rule said, as though reminding him of something he didn't already know. "But if there's no trust, there's no love. What loyalty should any of us have to a mate that refuses to love?"

"What loyalty should any of us have to a mate that refuses to love?"

At that point, Liza rose jerkily from the bed, pulled her gown over her head, collected her robe from the floor and put it on with a furious shrug of her shoulders.

She couldn't believe what she had heard.

Belting the robe with a furious jerk, she swept from the bedroom and headed for the connecting room.

Where had they lost their minds?

Just to begin with, had they forgotten that the connecting

suite was tied into the intercom on the room phone? Stygian had set it up himself, just in case someone, anyone, attempted to invade their suite.

They were listed as staying in the connecting suite, not the one they were actually in. The precaution had been taken to ensure he and Liza had a head start in escaping.

Instead, it had given Liza a heads-up.

A heads-up into the plans Jonas Wyatt had, and why.

Gripping the door to the connecting suite, she pushed it open hard enough that the sound of it slamming into the wall behind it had Jonas, Rule Breaker and Mordecai Savant swinging to the side, their weapons drawing and leveling on Stygian as he jumped in front of her.

Stepping around him, she faced the other three furiously before pinning Jonas Wyatt with her gaze.

"Have you once come to me and asked me to take a single blood test, or to allow you permission to access the database when you told me you needed it? You have lied to me continually, Jonas. To me and to the Navajo Council. But not once did you ever ask for help." she said, her voice shaking with her anger as he and the others slowly holstered their weapons.

"Would it have done any good?" Jonas asked.

"If I thought for one minute it would be used for Amber only, then yes, it would have," she snapped back at him, her fingers curling into fists, fury burning through her. "But as Stygian said, there wouldn't be a chance, would there?"

"War isn't pretty," Rule growled.

"This isn't war." She hated this. She hated him. She hated the bleak fury tearing through her. "You would use anyone, anything, to get what you wanted, wouldn't you, Wyatt? You want to know who I might be, but you still want that database. You still believe it will lead you to Gideon Cross, don't you?

And the information was in her journal. The chiefs of the Six had actually suggested she keep the information written down somewhere safe, despite her protests. She'd never understood why, nor had she given it much thought in the past months either.

"I'd use anything or anyone to save my child," he snarled back, the dangerous incisors at the side of his teeth flashing warningly. "Don't doubt that for a second."

"And pretending I'm Honor Roberts will do that for you? Ordering Stygian to betray the one person it would destroy him to betray would do that?"

"Is that why you rushed in here so quickly, rather than waiting to hear his answer?" Jonas asked her then, suddenly mocking rather than angry. "Afraid he'd agree to do as I asked, Ms. Roberts?"

"He wouldn't have done it," she sneered back at him. "If he were going to do it, he would have done it by now. He's had weeks to help you betray me and he's still refused. What more would it take to convince you? What more would it take to get you the hell out of Window Rock?"

"What would it take?" He took a step forward, only to pause at the sudden, fearsome snarl that sounded in Stygian's chest at the inherent threat in Jonas's move. "It would take you, Fawn Corrigan and that damned Breed you called Judd. The three of you, and I could draw Gideon in. Then, I would have what I needed to save my daughter."

"And what do you need to save your daughter?" Liza crossed her arms over her breasts and stared back at him curiously. "Tell me, Mr. Wyatt, what do they have that she needs if you can't access their memories?"

"Whatever's left in their bodies of the serum Brandenmore used. The changes that took place in their bodies would be apparent in both you and Fawn, while Gideon and Judd would show the changes to the Breed physiology. That's what I want."

As he spoke, terror chased through her.

It was all she could do to keep her expression closed, to contain her emotions and her rage. To contain her fear.

Because as he spoke, she saw herself, but she wasn't herself. Watching doctors, seeing the printouts lying beside them, reading the information. It made sense.

For only seconds, it was there. A formula, a child's pain-filled cries and the knowledge that, once again, the tests were going to hurt. Once again, they were going to experience hell.

She hadn't realized she was holding her breath.

She hadn't realized that for the briefest second, the pain that radiated through her could be felt by every Breed in the room.

And each of them flinched.

"Enough!" Stygian's arms were suddenly around her, pulling her against his chest a second before she was able to slip back into that distant, remote place she'd been unable to access since he'd taken her.

"I'm sorry." She was almost wheezing again.

God, she hadn't wheezed in so long.

"They can have the damned code," she whispered hoarsely. "I'll give them the damned thing. Just get them out of here."

"The code isn't what they needed," he told her, his own voice thick with fury now. "It wasn't the code. It was this, Liza. It was your pain he wanted to access, and you're giving him exactly what he wanted."

But was that it?

Staring back at Jonas, she saw a man tormented. His eyes flashed with enraged mercury, his expression becoming taut as he fought to wipe it free of emotion.

No, her pain wasn't what Jonas wanted any more than he wanted to see his own daughter's pain. He just wanted answers—answers and the key to save the child he loved as though she were created from his genetics rather than another man's.

"Don't you know I would help you if I could," she suddenly cried out to Jonas, desperate, terrified of what she suddenly felt rising within herself. "Do you think I would deny her for the hell of it?"

"No," he said, his voice stark. "Not for the hell of it," he finally breathed out wearily. "But to avoid hell? Yes, I believe to avoid whatever hell may be awaiting you on the other side, you would gladly walk through the flames barefoot and with a smile." He shook his dark head, turned to the two men watching them and jerked his head to the door before turning back to her. "I just pray you realize that whatever you're fighting to escape could well be my daughter's only hope of life."

"If that's true, if she's dying because Brandenmore gave her whatever he gave the girls he had before, then how did they survive? If it's killing Amber, Jonas, why didn't it kill them?"

Her fingers were digging into Stygian's arm as she demanded the answer, demanded to know the one thing no one seemed to be discussing.

To that, Jonas breathed out with weary helplessness, "I don't know, Liza. All I know is that from day to day I watch her struggle to live. To breathe through the pain. And every day I see the same question in her eyes. 'Why won't you help me, Daddy?' And it's killing me as nothing those fucking scientists who created me could have. I promise you that. There's no hell greater than seeing that in her eyes, hearing her cries, and knowing how helpless I am to save her if death is truly what she's facing. And if it is." His eyes suddenly flashed with an icy promise. "If I lose her because of your refusal to face whatever it is you're trying to escape, then I swear to you, I'll make damned sure you pay for it."

Before the sudden, fierce growl that vibrated in Stygian's chest could finish, Jonas was out the door and stalking back to his own suite.

As the door slammed behind him, it was Liza who flinched. Not from the sound of steel meeting steel, but the realization that there was the very real chance that he was right. If she was Honor Roberts, wouldn't she be desperate, horribly desperate, to keep from returning to the memories of a hell that had pushed her to reach out for a dead girl's identity?

Lifting her gaze to Stygian, she watched him, knowing the sacrifices he was making for her. He saw her as his mate. As the woman created for him and for him alone, and for her, he was willing to betray the vows he had made when he went into the Bureau of Breed Affairs as an enforcer. The vow to place all Breeds, their security and their safety, above his own.

Breaking a vow wouldn't be easy for a man like Stygian.

"I want to go to the desert now," she told him as she faced him. "I want to go to the crash site. And I want to see where the sweat lodge sat. Now."

"Liza—" he began.

"No, I want to go now," she demanded. "I want to know who I am, Stygian. I have to know who I am."

She had a feeling, though, she already knew.

CHAPTER 16

It didn't take long for Stygian to arrange the outing to the area where Liza and Claire had taken Ray Martinez's sports car over a canyon cliff.

After twelve years, evidence of the crash should have been completely wiped away; instead, there were still several signs of the wreck as well as the hastily erected sweat lodge that had been placed a short distance from where the vehicle had slammed into the opposite canyon wall.

As Liza stepped from the Desert Dragoon and surveyed the damage to the rock wall, she didn't attempt to fight any memories or sensations that swept through her.

One of the reasons why she was beginning to suspect she was Honor Roberts was the distant fuzziness of the memories of her life before the crash as well as the memories that seemed determined to torment her since Stygian had come into her life.

She remembered parts of her childhood well, especially those things her parents often reminded her of. Picnics at the lake, birthday celebrations, certain amusing or even embarrassing moments in her life. And though the memories were there, they had that hazy, uncertain quality as well. A lack of detail, or even periods of time when she couldn't recall certain memories at all.

Now, standing to the side of the Dragoon's multiple lights directed on the stone wall, it wasn't being in the wreck that flashed through her mind.

It was seeing the wreck.

Staring at the unnatural crack in the stone from the force of the vehicle slamming into it, she felt a flash of light tear through her memories, the ground rocking with the explosion as flames overcame the vehicle, and remembered looking down to see the two bodies that had been thrown clear.

Her father had told her that that memory was the result of having "died" more than once that night.

Three times.

She had died three times. The last time had been in the ambulance as she was being transported to the hospital.

Moving to the canyon wall, her breathing heavy and ragged, she reached out, touched the cool stone, then laid her forehead against it.

What could she feel moving in her brain? In her memories? What in God's name had really happened that night?

"Where did the sweat lodge sit?" Turning to Stygian, she acknowledged the fact that she had forced herself to ask the question.

"Dog and his team have been trying to rebuild it with the materials that were originally used," he told her as he led her from the headlights brightening the area to the curve of the stone wall as it continued to slice through the land.

It was just out of sight.

As she followed that curve, the lights of Dog's Dragoon flared on, spilling over the roughly made wooden structure.

There were a lot of pieces missing, she realized. They were all blackened from the fire that had been used to attempt to destroy them, charred, some more rotted than not. She imagined the missing were mostly ash.

"We found the burned wood in the back of a cave farther down the canyon," Stygian stated as he stood behind her. "The attempt to hide it was obvious."

"How do you know it was part of a sweat lodge?" Wrapping her arms across her breasts, she gave herself a chance to acclimate to the building tension invading her.

"The scent of the herbs used were still on the wood, but more so on the stones used for the ritual fire inside. Several of the Breeds in the area work with the chiefs of the Six Tribes and recognized the scent of the herbs immediately when we brought the stones to them."

The moment her eyes locked on the structure, memories began to slam through her brain.

She remembered walking to the entrance. She hadn't been alone.

Turning her head slowly, she looked at the bend of her shoulder where a hand had laid. Broad, strong, yet the flesh had been aged. It hadn't been a young man who had walked with her that night.

How could she have walked to the lodge if she had been thrown from that vehicle? And she knew Liza had been thrown from it. Her father had explained the wreck to her many times over the years. How the chiefs of the Six had been in the canyon that night, meeting in the lodge, so she knew it had been there. How they had run to the site and attempted to give medical aid until the EMTs could arrive.

Not once had it been mentioned that they had been taken, or had been conscious enough to walk, into the sweat lodge.

"The chiefs of the Six were here that night in a sweat lodge," she said, trying to find an explanation for the contradictions. "They were meeting as they sometimes do to discuss Navajo Nation matters."

"The herbs used in such instances are different, according to the Breeds we talked to," he told her softly. "The herbs used in that fire that night were ones that the Breeds had never known the chiefs to mix in a sweat lodge. One of them was a ritualistic herb, used only when their strongest medicine is required."

She nodded and forced herself to take a step closer to the entrance.

"It's safe?"

"Would I allow you to enter it without first warning you if it wasn't safe?" he asked.

She wanted to smile but couldn't find the lightness of spirit to allow her lips to make the move to do so.

"Do you know, I remember getting in the car with Claire, and I remember driving out here. I remember being so determined to be a rebel. To do all the things our friends were doing so we wouldn't be considered weak."

"You could never have been weak." The confidence that rang in his voice wrapped around her and gave her strength.

"Before the wreck, Claire and I were in our first months of becoming a pain in the ass for our parents. After we awoke in the hospital, it was as though our entire personalities had changed. Even our friends remarked that we were so radically different that it was as though they didn't even know us."

She and Claire had also been concerned because it was as though they didn't really know those who had been their closest friends.

"And it could be explained away the same as the reason for the plastic surgeries and the differences in your features," he pointed out.

"Because of the wreck." Inhaling deeply she stepped forward, lowered her head and moved inside the remnants of the sweat lodge.

Reality was like a mirrored mirage that began to shimmer around her. The past and the present were slamming together, attempting to merge and to separate as hazy images flashed before her and then escaped just as quickly.

She and Claire were laid out on the ground, bloodied, broken. There was a sense of urgency in the men who filled the small lodge and stroked the fire hotter, brighter, as the sizzle of water and the scent of herbs filled her senses.

But she wasn't lying out on the floor. She was watching—herself?

The murmur of voices whispered past her ear, and shadowed images moved about the lodge. Breathing roughly, she felt her senses being bombarded by memories that weren't memories, but rather misty threads of information that made such little sense. Clenching her fists, she fought to keep her mind open, to hold her fear back.

There was something there, information she needed. Liza could feel it drifting through her mind, just out of reach.

"What the hell happened? Ah God, Liza!" She swung around, expecting to see her father.

His voice was so angry, so agonized and filled with horror.

But he wasn't there.

Stygian stood watching her silently, his gaze intent, his expression somber.

"I don't understand," she whispered, turning back, the wispy images of a past that made no sense rushing over her again.

The two girls, she and Claire, were laid out on one side of the fire. On the other side—she could feel herself trembling as the memory rushed over her—were two other girls.

Claire turned to look at her—the Claire that wasn't broken and bloody—*"I'll never see him again,"* she whispered as a tear fell down her cheek. Linking her fingers with her, Liza tried to give her friend comfort where only confusion and fear existed. *"Perhaps it's for the best,"* Liza whispered. *"Perhaps it's the only thing that will keep us alive."*

The memories, hazy and fragile as they were, drifted away. But she wasn't left with nothing to fill the place of where the memory had been. It remained there, a part of her now, pulled from the deepest reaches of her subconscious and now a part of her conscious memories.

She wasn't Liza Johnson. Liza Johnson had died that night and Honor Roberts had taken her place.

She didn't have the memories, yet. She had no idea how to help Jonas Wyatt, but what she did have was Orrin Martinez's promise.

"One day, named for that which few men know— Honor—One day, you will realize, child, you have lived up to all the dreams your father had when he gave you a name of such distinction. Know now, your heart and your soul resonate with it, and into this new life you will take with you the knowledge that will ease the burden of loss for the parents who had such hope, and one day, you will fill the heart and the soul of one who never truly believed he had such."

Stygian.

She filled his heart and soul, just as he filled hers. But

there were so many other dreams, and so many others who were a part of her. And admitting to who, to what she was—

What she was—

Oh God, oh God—

"Liza!" Stygian caught her before her knees could collapse, before the shock could steal not just her strength but also her control. "Liza, are you okay?"

"Get me out of here." She was going to be sick. "Get me out of here, Stygian."

And he did just that. No questions, no demands. Lifting her into his arms and carrying her from the remnants of the sweat lodge, he took her away from the past and back into the present.

Nothing could steal the memory of those dark, terrifying days just before the ritual that had taken from her and Fawn the nightmares of their lies and had instead given them the peace and sheltered existence that Liza Johnson and Claire Martinez had been so determined to forsake.

And now, nothing could steal from her the realization of why they had been forced to make such a horrifying decision.

She could never again hide from what she was.

CHAPTER 17

But, it wasn't as easy as Stygian had hoped it would be, and Liza wasn't cooperating when it came to explaining exactly what had happened in that damned desert.

She shut down on him.

It wasn't the distance he had experienced from her before. That complete emotional and spiritual distance, which assured his animal instincts that she was nothing more than a perfect, breathing shell.

This was different, but no less disconcerting. It was as though a part of her was so focused on something else to the point that there was no room for anything or anyone else.

That focus had completely eradicated the mating heat, and it was infuriating him.

The animal that lived under his skin was enraged by it.

His cock was just tortured. He was so damned hard, so fucking hungry for the taste of her, the touch of her, that it was about to drive him insane.

Two days later, Stygian could feel his frustration level moving into overload and threatening his control to the point that it was becoming dangerous.

Where was the mating heat and how had she managed to dampen it when no other mate had managed to do so?

Heat, like in sex on a near-constant level?

Heat, like his mate dying for his touch twenty-four-seven.

Heat in the fact that they were supposed to fuck like minks and be unable to stay the hell away from each other?

Fucking.

Fighting.

Talking.

Bonding.

That was mating heat.

Where the hell was the mating every other Breed experiencing it got to have, yet it seemed was being denied him?

It wasn't that *he* wasn't experiencing it, because God knew he was.

His tongue was so damned swollen it felt like a fucking golf ball was wedged beneath his tongue on each side. The heavy throb of the fluid contained within it was almost painful, and each small droplet of the moisture that pushed free of it to infuse his system was torturous in its effect on his body.

His cock was so swollen and hard it was damned near unbearable. The heavy veins pulsed with blood and lust, tightening to the point that he knew there would be no ease without the touch of his mate. And that touch didn't seem forthcoming. The lust that should have been burning to tortured hunger inside her wasn't happening.

At least, it hadn't been happening for the past two days or nights.

Confusion, fear and a latent pain filled his mate's mind to the point that it seemed there was no room for lust. That inner focus, confusion and fear that swirled through her senses was so intense that he couldn't break through it.

And she refused to discuss it.

She wouldn't consider discussing her past, the doubts he had sensed inside her concerning who she was, or what she felt or remembered now.

And he blamed Jonas for that. Blamed him for it to the point that he could barely converse with the man civilly. If Jonas had kept his damned plan for betraying Liza to himself, then perhaps, Stygian thought, he would have had a chance to bind his mate to his heart and a chance to help her through the emotionally complex situation she was now facing.

Stygian wanted nothing more than to touch his mate, to kiss her. To love her.

To ease the fear and uncertainty tearing her apart, which was keeping her out of his arms.

The bonding that came with the mating heat was something he had looked forward to in the years since he'd learned of the phenomenon. That chance to so be a part of a woman; her heart, her soul, her life; that he knew he was no longer a singular person, but rather one part of a whole. Fused so tightly to his mate that their souls were one entity.

Yet, that wasn't there with himself and Liza.

As though the mating heat itself had suddenly stalled halfway through the process.

He could smell her need; it was there, buried beneath her confusion. He could smell her arousal, and just a hint of the mating heat, but it was the same as it had been when he'd felt her retreat so far inside herself that he wasn't certain how to find her.

The spiritual distance was no longer there, as it had been before. Instead, it seemed all the emotions, the fear, the pain and confusion that she had kept at bay over the years were tearing through her instead. And he had no idea how to help her. No idea how to bring her back to him.

Nothing he'd tried had worked in the past two days.

She didn't rise to any verbal sparring he attempted.

She evaded his touch and asked for time with such deepening pain that pulling back to give her that time was killing him.

She was holding herself in such lockdown that he knew that finding the key to release whatever she was fighting to hide within herself might be impossible.

And he knew, the animal instincts that governed him knew, if he didn't do something soon, he might well lose her forever.

Those animal instincts were raging. As though the animal he could have been was pacing furiously inside him, the tension from the situation building to the point that release, in some form, was becoming a necessity.

Pacing the sitting room restlessly, he turned to her at the sound of the bedroom door opening, his gaze narrowing on the dove gray cotton lounge pants and matching camisole.

The tank top smoothed over her pert breasts, hugging the lush curves just enough to cause his mouth to water. And fuck him, but her nipples were hard. Peaked and swollen beneath her bra, pointing against the lace beneath and refusing to hide from his gaze.

The need to lick those hard little points and burn the tender nerve endings with the hormone swelling his tongue was nearly irresistible.

A growl rumbled in his throat, drawing her surprised gaze.

His patience was nearing its end.

His mate. She was created to belong to him, and by damned, she would not hold herself and his rightful bonds to her heart for much longer.

Damn, it would be easy to pull the material from her body.

Not to mention sexy as hell.

He was only a breath from refusing to warn her of the kiss coming that would put her in the frame of mind for the wild, uncontrolled sex the animal inside him was demanding he initiate.

His kiss would ensure the heat then. It would do as it was meant to and make her as crazy for him as he was for her.

He took a step and stopped.

No. He wouldn't do it. If there was to be any peace in his heart that she had come to him of her own free will, then he had to force himself to have the patience she had asked him for two days before.

Since he couldn't fuck his mate, that left sparring with his partners. One or the other was going to have to happen.

Sparring it was.

"We're going to the gym downstairs," he told her as she moved for the coffeepot.

And God only knew he'd give anything to allow her that cup of coffee. Normally, caffeine was like a kick-in-the-ass shot of high energy to mating heat. But his patience was at an end. He didn't think he'd survive waiting to see if it would actually work.

Because right now, she looked good enough to eat from head to toe.

Her hair was still damp from her shower, lying in long dark blond curls that fell nearly to her waist. One long curl waved over her breast and tempted him to move it aside. To brush it over her shoulder as he pushed aside the strap of the top and began tasting soft, satiny flesh.

The soft cotton pants she wore skimmed over her soft curves.

"You can go to the gym downstairs," she stated with a shrug as she poured the coffee. "I have work to do."

She turned and moved to the laptop as though to power it up and do just that. Just as she had done the past two evenings. She stared at the screen, her expression still, her emotions ragged as she pretended to work.

Setting the coffee cup on the table beside the couch, she moved to open the screen on the device.

"Then bring the laptop with you," he growled. "I fucking don't care. I'm going to the gym, and whether you like it or not, you're going with me."

Nothing flashed in her normally expressive gray eyes. Not anger, fear or uncertainty. She stared back at him with such a blank look that his teeth clenched.

"Pack it up and get moving, Liza. Now."

She must have seen something in his gaze that warned her against crossing that line.

Glancing at the laptop, she sighed wearily before closing the top and securing it. "I'd like to get back in time to actually sleep tonight," she informed him.

"Why?" He had to force himself to throttle the anger building inside him. "It's Friday night, not Sunday, and it's not as though you have a job to return to."

"No, I don't, but I do have other things I can be doing

besides sitting on my ass and filing my nails." Her voice never raised, never changed inflection. "There is more to my life than a job, Stygian, or what's happened since you came into it."

"Such as?" Watching as she moved toward him, it was all he could do to keep from pushing her to the floor and mounting her.

His dick throbbed with a hunger that was becoming painful, imperative as the swollen glands beneath his tongue pulsed in heated demand.

"Such as the Navajo Scholars Fund I chair, the museum fund-raisers I help with, and the scheduling I do for the chiefs of the Six to visit the Nation's schools. Did you even care to check into anything I do besides what may or may not aid the Breeds in their little agenda here?" she questioned without inflection.

"I don't know, Liza, I rather liked the university's cheerleading squad and the fund-raising projects you were doing there," he drawled. "Don't you have a meeting coming up soon?"

"Not one you can attend."

Oh, that unbothered, unemotional attitude of hers was going to get her ass in trouble.

Better yet, it was going to get her ass fucked.

The need to take her down, to heat her arousal to boiling point and find that point of feminine submission was becoming a hunger Stygian knew neither of them was going to escape. Especially if she kept this attitude up.

"If you have to do this, let's get it over with. I'll be ready for bed early tonight," she stated as she headed for the door.

Stygian clenched his teeth, forcing back his growl as he followed her.

She would be ready for bed early tonight?

Oh, she didn't want to mention that bed right now. She really wanted to do her best to keep his mind off that bed.

"This is stupid, dragging me around like this," she informed as she stopped at the door and turned back to face him. "I do have things to do, Stygian."

There was no anger in her face. None in her eyes.

Son of a bitch, he wasn't mated to a fucking mannequin, and her impression of one was starting to piss him the hell off.

He was not going to get into a confrontation with her, he told himself—told the animal snarling inside him.

He'd be damned if he'd force the lust he knew was inside her to rise, even though he knew if he pissed her off enough, she'd relieve the ache torturing his balls.

She'd have no choice.

If he pushed hard enough, it would burn inside her as well. It was that push he had the problem with. He wanted a willing mate, one who came to him without a push or coercion.

One that came to him because she needed and ached for him as desperately as he did for her.

Opening the door and allowing her to precede him, he was suddenly struck by the faintest hint of the mating scent. Just a hint, nothing overt or heavy.

What the hell was up with that?

Every mate he had ever come in contact with had held a heavy mating scent. It was always unmistakable, and always heavy enough to ensure all other Breed males were warned away.

"Why do you need to go to the gym?" she asked as they moved into the hall to join Flint, Mutt and Dog. The fact that the mating scent was so subtle had his animal instincts pacing restlessly.

Glancing at the three men, the only thing that eased the dangerous rising possessiveness was the fact that each of them seemed completely unaware of Liza as anything other than his mate, despite the less than normal strength of the mating scent.

Strangely, Mutt, being his normal glowering self, was in the best mood of the three.

"Wow, we're having a party today," Liza observed mockingly as she too, obviously, noticed the lack of a genial mood.

"No kidding," Mutt grumbled. "It's sure as hell not been

the Fourth of fucking July for the past twenty-four hours. I swear they're"—he jerked his head toward Flint and Dog—"gonna start depressin' me soon." His deliberate country drawl had just the right amount of twang at the exact slow, deliberate speed needed to pull off the backwoods accent.

No one would ever have guessed that the Coyote the Genetics Council had called Mutt was actually so well spoken that detecting any sort of accent was usually impossible.

"What gives?" Stygian asked as they all entered the elevator, automatically placing Liza protectively between the four of them in the center of the cubicle.

"What gives is being stuck in this damned town babysitting," Dog growled irritably, crossing his arms over his wide chest. "I'd rather be out hunting."

"Hunting what?" Flint growled. "Even the natural prey is staying hidden. As if they would be in any fucking danger anyway. These three just enjoy the chase. Give them the chance to kill and they lose all interest."

"Yeah, at least our chase is actually the hunting kind. Not many of us are into outrunning them," Mutt grunted. "You're strange, Flint."

"Give me a break," Liza muttered. "You're all strange."

"Lady, you're a pain in the ass—both you and your friend," Dog growled, obviously talking about Claire. "That little hellion is going to drive me crazy."

The lack of any animosity toward Liza had Stygian rolling his eyes rather than threatening to tear Dog's head off. It was damned rare to see Dog reacting to anything in any manner other than mocking or sarcastic. The fact that Dog was so irate over a woman had him wondering if the Coyote—

"I'd kill myself before mating with that little harridan," Dog snarled as Stygian inhaled deeply. "So stop looking for the damned scent. It's flat-out not happening."

Flint snickered while Stygian shook his head. Claire would be happy to know that so far, the mating scent wasn't detectable. That didn't mean it would stay that way, though.

"I think this sparring session is just what we all need," Mutt growled as the elevator doors swung open, depositing them in the private gym Jonas had arranged in one of the conference rooms on the ground floor. "I could handle kicking your asses to hell and back. Might make all this enforced indoor boredom actually worth it."

"You're going to spar?" Complete disbelief filled her voice as she moved to face Stygian. "You brought me down here so I could watch the four of you spar?"

Staring into the narrowed gaze of his mate, Stygian suddenly felt more defensive than he liked. And he found he sure as hell didn't like being defensive in front of Liza.

"No, I brought you down here so you could do that work you were bitching about while I spar," he growled, hiding his confusion at the scent of—envy?

She was envious?

This proved true the rumor that intense training went into every member of the Navajo Breed Underground Network and explained why Liza and Claire were able to deny being a part of it, despite the reports they received that both women were. They wouldn't be officially inducted until their training was complete.

"And obviously, to fight off the hornies." Dog's mocking smile was back. "What happened to mating heat, Stygian? You should be sparring with your mate in the bed, not your buddies in the gym." He chuckled at what he considered a joke.

"Shut the fuck up, Dog," Stygian ordered, glaring back at him.

The son of a bitch was right too, and that just pissed Stygian off even more.

"What he should be doing is leaving me alone in our suite to work instead of dragging me down here to watch a bunch of overgrown little boys wrestle," Liza snapped, the sudden scent of her anger spilling from her like honeysuckle in the spring.

What the hell had finally managed to piss her off anyway?

If only it were her lust scenting the room so sweetly. If it were, he wouldn't have to spar with these yahoos.

"Stygian, why don't you just help your little honey find herself a place to work," Dog suggested with a hard smile.

"Preferably a place where she can watch us kick your ass," Mutt agreed with his best smile, which was actually a hell of a scowl.

Mutt would have made a hell of a poster boy for the Coyote bogeyman. Stygian had no doubt mothers frightened their children into good behavior with a similar visage of what could get them in the dark if they didn't behave.

"Yeah, why don't you just do that, Stygian," Liza agreed with a mocking smile. "So I can watch the four of you pound on each other like idiots."

Turning back to her, brow arched suggestively, Stygian let her know exactly why they were there.

Silently.

His gaze locked with hers.

He was going to pound on these three like an idiot, or he was going to end up fucking them both blind in that suite upstairs.

It was her choice.

Liza didn't have to be a Breed, she didn't have to have an incredible sense of smell to detect the lust fueling his gaze. It was there, burning like a neon blue flame in his black eyes.

She'd known he was aroused, known he'd wanted her in the past two days, but she hadn't known it was burning as bright or as hot as it was. As bright or as hot as she had each time she allowed herself to pull back from the job she was determined to finish first.

Turning on her heel, she stalked across the gym as she attempted to push back her own responding hunger.

She couldn't go there right now. She couldn't deal with the need that existed between them, with the hunger that tormented her whenever she allowed herself to forget the fact that she wasn't who she had believed she was for so many years.

She was accepting it, but it wasn't easy. She should have been suspicious before the Breeds ever arrived, and she probably would have been if it hadn't been for the dreams that had pulled her back from those realizations.

Dreams she had allowed . . . no, dreams she had forced

herself to push to the back of her mind when she awoke. Dreams she refused to allow herself to dwell on. Dreams that existed to fill her with fear and dread and caused her to follow the path to that other place, just outside reality, where no emotion, no dread and no fear and certainly no truth, could touch her.

A path she had found in a dream.

A dream where she had shown herself a way to escape.

I go here, she had told herself in the dream. *I hide here, because I don't like the world. Because it's frightening and harsh and I just want to get away from it. You can go there too. You can hide in my place, because I don't need it any longer.*

Why had it taken her so long to remember?

Moving into the small partitioned area set up evidently for those not interested in partaking of the men's antics, Liza sat down slowly on the surprisingly comfortable sofa that faced the gym.

Placing the laptop on the coffee table, she wiped her hands over her face before pushing her fingers through her hair and breathing out roughly.

That path to that non-real place was closed to her now. It had been closed to her since the night Stygian had made love to her.

Or mated her.

But the dreams were still there, and this time, the dreams weren't evading her memory once she awoke.

"God, this is so crazy."

Lifting her head, she stared out at the gym, watching with a sense of envy as the four men were indeed pounding each other into the mats.

Hell, she hadn't even known this room was here. If she had, she would have called Claire and asked her to join her. They could have invited Ashley and Emma—.

Her lips twisted mockingly. Perhaps she wouldn't have. They obviously knew the room existed and hadn't suggested it the few times she had talked to them.

But, if she had, maybe she wouldn't have had the chance to watch the spectacle she was watching now.

Flint came at Stygian with a hard flying kick, catching his powerful shoulder and doing no more than kicking him back. Gripping Flint's ankle, Stygian twisted it, hard. The other man flipped midair, following the direction that could have twisted his ankle from his leg before jerking free.

Coming to a crouch, Flint barely managed to jump out of the way as Stygian threw a hard side kick his way. Without giving the other Breed a chance to recover, Stygian was at him again.

A hard jab to the jaw jerked Flint's head back even as he delivered another into the younger Breed's hard, muscle-packed abdomen.

Flint went back. Barely catching himself, he managed to recover and send a hard jab to the side of Stygian's face.

The sound of fist meeting flesh and bone caused Liza to wince despite the fascination she was feeling.

The fascination as well as the arousal beginning to build between her thighs. Her clit was so swollen she was suddenly, heatedly, all too aware of the fact that it had been more than forty-eight hours since he had last touched her.

Since he had last kissed her.

And his kiss was simply . . . delicious.

It tasted just a little bit like cinnamon candy, coffee and chocolate. She loved cinnamon candy, coffee and chocolate, especially when she tasted it in his kiss.

Pressing her thighs together, she reminded herself she really didn't have time to consider his kiss right now. Or his touch. Or the way the tip of his tongue did that little swirly thing around her clit.

She couldn't consider the pleasure right now, or how much she had missed it. She definitely didn't want to consider how good it would feel to have him moving over her, moving inside her.

The feel of her vagina clenching, the moisture spilling to the folds beyond was so sensual, so incredibly erotic when combined with the memory of his kiss that she swore the hunger clenching her womb would make her crazy.

She wanted him now.

Ached for him now.

And he was too busy sparring with his buddies to even care.

She was ready to roll her eyes at herself at this point.

Jerking the laptop open and pulling up the Navajo Remote Database, Liza reminded herself that she was the one that couldn't handle her own life at the moment. Stygian hadn't asked her to allow the confusion and fear building inside her to come between them.

She had done that herself.

Opening the Community Center file, she tried to concentrate on the plans to renovate and add the nursery wing to the new center that had been built on the western edge of town a few years before. She'd been in charge of raising the money, and they'd completed raising the funds several months before for the expansion as well as additional computers for the after-school tutoring program.

She was halfway through the file when the odd flick of the screen she'd been experiencing for the past several weeks happened again. Frowning, she scrolled lower, wondering why her father hadn't been able to fix it while he'd had the laptop the week before. As it flickered again, she made the ultimate mistake of lifting her gaze and allowing the sparring session in the gym to catch her attention again.

For the past two days she'd fought with herself, forced herself to piece together fragments of memories, to find a resolution inside herself. To accept what she knew, who she knew she was. The need for him had been beneath the surface, the hunger for him had always been there, at the edge of her thoughts and her need. But the need to know who she was, and why she believed she was Liza Johnson, had taken so much of her that she'd had no choice but to step back and piece together the bits she knew, the fragments of dreams, the memories that hadn't really seemed like memories.

She wasn't who she thought she was, but there was no way to prove it to herself. There wasn't a single memory, a single dream or instance that she could use to pinpoint that she was Honor Roberts or Fawn Corrigan. There were no memories of either that she could pull free.

As she watched the Breeds sparring, she suddenly stiffened as Flint's fist went for her mate's face.

Stygian jumped back from the jab to his face but not before it connected.

His lip was split, the reddened hint of blood marring the perfect male curve.

Ah hell, Flint had split Stygian's lip?

Wouldn't that make kissing her later painful?

She could kiss the little boo-boo.

Licking her lips at the thought, her breasts swelled further at the surge of hunger racing through her body while her clit pulsed in renewed need.

Renewed? No, not renewed, it hadn't stopped pulsing since she'd first watched them sparring.

She wanted to spar with him. She wanted to have him take her down, strip her pants from her body, lift her to her knees and fuck her into a screaming orgasm.

Was that seriously too much to ask?

It wasn't like she wouldn't be willing to give as well.

Her tongue ran over her lips again, almost involuntarily this time. She could remember the taste of him, the strength and power of the broad head of his shaft.

So broad.

She'd heard Wolf and Coyote Breeds were thicker than normal, their cocks broad enough to stretch a woman until she was certain it was impossible to take him.

Their experience, she had heard, ensured their lovers took them, perhaps not with ease, but definitely with pleasure.

Exquisite, heated, torturous pleasure.

Moisture rushed from her vagina, slickening, preparing—

Clenching her thighs, she forced back a moan and fought to return her attention to the file she was working on. And the occasional flicker of the screen that was more irritating than an actual problem.

Or, it would have been if her mind was actually on the file she was supposed to be working on.

Returning her gaze to the gym and the combatants still

going at one another, the urge to be on the mat with her mate was only growing stronger.

She wanted to be the one sparring with him.

She was his mate for a reason.

She wasn't the hothouse flower he so obviously believed she was.

This hothouse flower was one week from final testing before her induction into one of the most professional, most secretive rescue forces in the world.

She could spar with him.

She highly doubted she could take him, but she knew he would take her.

Sensually.

Erotically.

Creaming her panties was an understatement for the slick moisture now gathered on her pussy.

Hunger didn't come close to describing the need rushing through her body.

Her nipples were so hard the lace of her bra was such an abrasion it was painful.

Liza wanted nothing more than to pull her clothes— No, she wanted Stygian to tear the clothes from her body. To want her with such strength, with such uncontrolled lust that nothing mattered but fucking her. But pushing the broad length of his cock inside her, driving her mad with each thrust until the wicked additional erection filled her, locking him inside her as his release spurted to the very depths of her vagina.

She wanted him until she felt on fire for his touch. Until the soft cotton of the dove gray lounge pants and matching camisole top were so irritating, so impossible to bear she wanted nothing more than to strip.

She needed to be naked.

She needed her mate naked.

Now!

CHAPTER 18

As sparring sessions went, it was one of the rougher ones.

Stygian knew he would have bruises in places he hadn't had bruises in years. Coyotes were mean gutter fighters, and that was just a fact of life.

That meant bruises in places a man normally didn't have to worry about bruises when sparring with them. He seriously couldn't remember a time when sparring with a Lion or Wolf that he'd ever had his arm dislocated by a kick *beneath his arm*.

How the hell Dog had managed that one, he wasn't certain yet. All he knew was the dirty bastard had caught him unaware at the same time Flint had been coming at him with a mean right hook.

Moving quickly to the side to avoid a hard jab at his nose—no one could accuse Flint of playing nice—Stygian came back with a powerful blow to the other Breed's stomach, quickly followed by a mean left hook that Stygian only barely softened before connecting with Flint's jaw.

Even pulling the punch, Flint was sent flying back against the padded wall. His dark hair dripping with sweat as he shook his head, Flint came back at him.

Blocking a hard kick aimed for his abdomen, Stygian

was in the process of sweeping the other man's leg out from under him when the scent caught him.

Like a sledgehammer, the scent of feminine lust tore through his senses.

He froze, his head lifting, drawing in the sweetest, most addictive scent he could have imagined.

In the same breath Flint delivered a powerful blow to his midsection with a kick that nearly knocked him from his feet.

A rush of air exhaled from his lungs as Stygian found himself crashing into the padded wall.

Done in by the scent of his mate's lust.

God help him, he had to get the others out of here. There wasn't a chance he was going to make it to their suite before he buried his dick inside the lush, honeysuckle sweet depths of her pussy.

Catching Flint coming in for another hard kick, Stygian gripped his ankle, twisted then jumped back as the other Breed did a midair flip that would have ended with his foot in Stygian's jaw if he'd been a breath faster.

Landing in a crouch, Flint grinned back at him.

"You're getting old, Stygian," he claimed. "You damn near knocked me out last week when you countered that same kick. But then"—his brows lifted suggestively—"the scent of your mate's hunger wasn't there to tempt you either. Was it?"

"You were faster this time," Stygian argued as he ignored the comment regarding his distraction.

"And you're a hell of a lot slower." Flint laughed as Dog and Mutt both paused in their sparring. "You're off your game, my friend."

Hell if that wasn't the truth, but even Flint was easing back, the unspoken agreement that the sparring session was over, understood by them all.

The scent of a mate's need sent a message to any other Breed in the area to keep away, to move beyond the scent if possible and at every opportunity to allow the mated couple a chance to be alone.

Inhaling sharply, he caught her scent again.

Arousal and an addition of something more had his gaze narrowing on her.

The arousal was uppermost, a subtle scent because of the distance, but there all the same. But it was also combined with the scent of envy and a natural aggression that had his animal instincts howling and his lips turning up in a grin of relish.

"Time to shower," Flint announced, though Stygian's attention never wavered from Liza. "We'll secure the room on our way out."

His attention was focused completely on Liza as she rose from the sofa and moved closer to the main mats. He was only distantly aware of the soft *ping*s indicating full security had been activated on the entrance to the gym.

There would be Breed enforcers stationed at the elevator and then farther along the hall as long as he and Liza were in the room.

Stygian anticipated they would be there for a while.

"Spar with *me* now." Her demand should have surprised him.

It didn't.

He already suspected the part she intended to play in the Navajo Breed Underground Network. He should have suspected it long before he had.

She was a mass of contradictions, deceptions and confusion. One could never take anything about her at face value, until he learned the answers to the questions she presented.

Moving once again, Liza toed off the sandals she'd slipped on before leaving the room. Leaving her feet bare, the pretty painted toenails a subtle candy pink, she stepped onto the mat.

Her arousal was no longer mixed with envy. It was now infused with a hint of feminine, sexual aggression and independence.

The intriguing scent had his dick swelling impossibly harder, throbbing with a demand he had no intention of holding back.

A growl sounded in his throat as his lips curled into a slow, dominant snarl.

"A challenge, mate?" he asked as he knelt and removed the baby-soft leather boots worn by enforcers.

Loosening the ties, his gaze holding hers, Stygian removed them without haste, refusing to allow himself to fumble so much as a string while she watched.

Male pride.

He all but grinned at the thought.

Of course, he couldn't allow himself to appear less than completely dominant and assured in her presence. God forbid this independent, striking young woman should ever have a moment to doubt his ability to love her.

To protect her.

He'd prove to her he was her fitting mate.

Removing his close-fitting black socks, Stygian straightened and stared down at her silently for long moments.

"You're my mate," he finally stated, hearing the primal growl that filled his voice. "I am well able to protect not just your safety, Liza, but your secrets. You've only to give them to me for safekeeping."

Reaching back and gathering her hair, she wound the long strands into a loose braid before securing it with the elastic band around her wrist.

"What if I don't know the secrets I'm keeping?" She surprised him with the answer.

"Then I'd say you're hiding from them," he answered, ignoring the flash of disagreement in her gaze, the hint of anger that darkened the soft gray color.

She didn't argue; instead, she moved.

The small, delicate-looking fist suddenly delivered a blow, not to the muscle-packed abdomen, but instead to the vulnerable area below, between his navel and the band of his jeans, only a breath from the engorged head of his cock.

The blow stole his breath an instant before he moved for her. Swinging away, he nearly had her before she suddenly dropped, rolled and came up behind him.

Before he could assimilate the surprise, her little foot landed in the back of his knee, stealing his balance and nearly taking him to the mat before he caught himself in a crouch.

The crouch and roll she executed before coming up behind him wasn't a typical response to the threat of being held from behind, even for their female enforcers. For her height and lack of physical strength, it worked perfectly. It also gave her the opening to come at him again before he could respond with a countermove.

Within two breaths, he was placed on the defensive by the very fact that, with nimble grace, she managed to elude his grasp and stay just out of reach.

And he wasn't playing with her.

Stygian had every intention of getting his hands on her and stripping her, first of that little top she wore. The one that tightened around her breasts and clearly showed the hard, pointed nipples beneath what appeared to be the lace of her bra.

The moves she was using weren't those she would have been trained for by the Coyote females. They were Breed male moves with the addition of a graceful feminine twist, an unexpected arch, kick or jab. And if she absolutely had to, a low, swift crouch and roll that placed her just out of reach.

He was impressed.

He was even more impressed, not to say highly suspicious of the fact that she used them so well. So well that he was beginning to suspect that it wasn't Ashley and Emma who had been training her. A male Breed had somehow been training her so secretly that he hadn't heard about it.

And he wouldn't have thought that were possible.

Remaining alert, keeping his eyes on her, Stygian arched his brow mockingly as she circled him, looking for an opening to bury that pretty little fist in some vulnerable area, no doubt.

When he saw his opening, he moved.

Ducking nearly to a crouch as she moved for him, Stygian managed to twist and come up behind her, both arms wrapping around her, trapping hers and shackling them to her side.

She didn't attempt to move her arms. Her first, natural reaction would have been to struggle with her upper body. At least, that was what it should have been.

Instead, in another surprising move, she lifted both legs. The heel of one slammed into his knee, taking him to the mat.

Most men, warriors, soldiers, would have lost their hold. Stygian was really rather proud of the fact that he kept hold of her.

Intense satisfaction then filled him as he managed to wrestle her to the mat beneath him, his body holding hers trapped securely between him and the mat.

"Who's been training you?" he snarled as he gave her ear an erotic little nip. "Tell me, mate, who have you been playing with?"

Not that it really mattered, Stygian thought as he rolled his hips against the gentle curve of her rear and allowed her to feel the hardened erection beneath his jeans. It didn't matter, because from now on, she would only be playing with him. He would be her only sparring partner. Only he would be training her to do any damned thing.

Liza could feel her juices spilling from her pussy, dampening the folds beyond as well as her panties as Stygian forced a hard thigh between her legs, forcing them open, then spreading them further to allow his hips to wedge into the cradle he created.

"Answer me, mate," he rasped as his incisors raked along the nape of her neck. "What Breed male has dared to train you so effectively?"

She forced a laugh past her lips—she had to force it, because all she wanted to do was moan and beg him to fuck her.

"What, us puny little humans aren't allowed to use any of your Breed moves?" She knew better, but pushing him was the agenda.

Pushing him to lose control.

Pushing him to fuck her.

Pushing him to force her control from her and to allow her just a few moments of peace from the thoughts and fears that kept swirling through her mind.

"No Breed males have trained me for anything." She kept the mockery thick in her voice.

He could detect a lie in her voice, and she had to be careful here.

No Breed males had been training her; instead, the Coyote females Ashley, Emma and Shiloh, and occasionally the Jaguar Breeds Chimera and Shiloh, and several Wolf Breed females. The other training she had was from the men that were part of the team she'd been assigned to with the underground network.

Did the big tough male Breeds think their smaller counterparts didn't have the ability to train anyone?

"Who has been training you then?" he growled in amusement as she felt his cock pressing into the vee of her thighs, pushing against the entrance of her sex through their layers of clothes.

She wanted the clothes from between them.

She wanted him.

Wanted him hard and deep and—oh God—taking her with the force and hunger that sent her careening into maddening release.

"Who said anyone was training me?" Closing her eyes, her nails curling into the mat where he held her wrists secure, Liza let the sensations, the excitement and intense sensuality wash over her.

"From now on, you want to learn to fight, you can come to me." His head lowered, his teeth raking the side of her neck.

"Come to you to learn to fight?" She fought to breathe, to fight back her tears as emotion threatened to flood her senses as well. "Really, Stygian, I've seen Breeds with their women. They're not allowed to fight." She smiled with a sensual, tempting curve of her lips. "They only get to fuck."

"Really?" he murmured at her ear, his dick jerking in excitement at the carnality in her voice. "Coyote females fight. Ashley and Emma are two of our best warriors."

"Breed females," she argued breathlessly. "Human mates aren't given the same options."

"Says who?" His tongue swiped over a particularly nerveridden area where he'd bitten her two nights before.

Pleasure sang through her body with a suddenness that

left her gasping and had more of her slickening juices spilling from her pussy.

"Diane Broen and every argument she and Lawe are rumored to have had." She was barely whispering as one of his hands pushed beneath her camisole.

"But Lion Breeds are assholes," he growled, his voice thick with sexual hunger.

"What?" Liza could barely make out what he was saying as his fingers released the front catch of her bra and cupped the swollen weight of one breast.

"I said, Lion Breeds are assholes," he repeated, the dark, lust-sharpened sound of his voice stroking her senses as his thumb stroked over the exquisitely hard peak of her nipple.

"Breeds are assholes." Her fingers dug into the mat again as his other hand—fingers long and powerful—began pushing beneath the low-riding band of her cotton pants.

It was all she could do to breathe.

Hell, she didn't give a damn if she was breathing or not, as long as he kept touching her.

His touch was like living lust. Hot and mesmerizing, it stole reason, leaving her helpless beneath him.

The air around them was thick and heavy with erotic heat.

His hard body above her was such a stimulant, so powerful and aroused she felt lost in the sensation of his weight against her.

"Wolf Breeds aren't assholes, though," he promised as the tips of his fingers brushed against the curls at the top of her pussy.

Liza felt the involuntary clench of her thighs, her vagina, the lush slide of her juices spilling from her body.

His fingers fluffed the curls that sheltered the top of her mound. Only there had she left that soft covering. Below it, the swollen folds were carefully waxed, overly sensitive, and heated, aching for his touch, for more than the firm pressure of his cock and their clothing between it and her.

His teeth raked against her neck once again, the pleasure singeing through every cell of her body.

The feel of his incisors rasping over her sent a rush of electrified sensation tearing across her nerve endings, heating her, burning through her mind.

A hard shudder of pleasure raced through her as arousal jumped to a hard, lust-driven punch of hunger to her womb.

Liza fought to ride the wave of muscle-shuddering sensual tension suddenly flooding her senses.

To make it last.

To make it crest to the orgasm that seemed so close, yet remained just out of reach.

The eroticism of having him cover her from behind, the heated length of his body holding her to the mat, his hands shackling her wrists, had her arching her rear, pressing the ridge of his cock tighter against her pussy as her thighs spread further.

She swore she was going to come from pure excitement. The extreme dominance and sexual awareness was a flood of knowledge so intense it was almost a physical caress.

Ecstatic pleasure flooded her body.

It tore through her.

It raced across her nerve endings, tightening her clit and her pussy to painful awareness.

She shouldn't feel like this.

No matter the rumors she'd heard of mating heat. No matter what her own instincts were telling her.

She shouldn't be feeling this.

This wasn't just sexual. It wasn't just pleasure. It wasn't just a need to be fucked into pure exhaustion, and God knew, that need was uppermost in her mind. It was quickly reaching a critical point and wiping her mind of any other instinct.

It was so much more than an intense need for release.

More than a need to be filled.

It exceeded the need to feel flesh against flesh, his cock buried inside her, or the detonation of an orgasm she knew would leave her flying into pure rapture.

It was more than she had ever imagined she could have because mixed with the extreme sensations and wave upon wave of pleasure was the instinctive knowledge that it was also a need born of emotion.

Burning in the very depths of her soul was the knowledge that the heart she'd managed to keep locked against all pain had been breached.

Stygian had somehow found a way to sneak in and take it over.

He filled it, possessed it. He controlled it effortlessly and she had no idea how he had managed to do it.

Fighting to make sense of it, to pull herself back from the never-ending rush of sensations to repair the breach, she was shocked at the sudden feel and sound of rending cloth.

Her top was torn from her, the light, ultrasoft cotton pulled easily from her body, only to be tossed carelessly aside. The feel of his broad, naked chest and stomach coming over her now bare back dragged a hoarse cry from her throat.

"Please," she cried out again, shuddering from the sensations spinning out of control inside her.

"Oh, mate, I have every intention of pleasing you," he rasped, his lips at her ear, caressing the sensitive shell. "Over and over again. Until neither of us can move. Until even the need for air is forgotten."

The hand wrapped around the curve of her breast slid free. Panting for much-needed air, she was more than aware of him working loose his jeans and pushing at the material as he lifted her just enough to push the denim down his thighs.

It took only seconds—breathless, destructive seconds—to remove the pants he wore.

Still, he didn't return to her. He didn't cover her and begin pushing inside her as she needed.

"Why did you do this to me?" She couldn't hold back the cry any more than she could hold back the rush of emotionally destructive feelings rising inside her.

"What did I do to you, baby?" Naked now, covering her, the engorged crest of his cock barely pressing against the slick folds of her pussy, he whispered the question as his lips stroked over her shoulder.

With his chin, he brushed back her hair as it fell over her shoulder, his lips returning to the overly sensitive flesh as one hand pushed beneath her hips, found the curls at the top of her pussy, then pushed beyond.

Liza jerked, shuddering at the waves of pleasure washing through her as his fingers found the swollen heat of her clit.

"There is nothing I want more than to sink into the snug heat of your pussy," he groaned as he let his lips find the mark he made at the bend of her shoulder. "To feel that sweet, wet heat snug around my dick. Sucking it with all the pleasure you gave when you took it into your mouth."

Her hips rolled, grinding against his fingers, fighting to get closer to the broad head of his cock as it tucked against the folds of her cunt.

"When you come, triggering my own release, the feel of your pussy clenching on the mating knot would take me to my knees if I did as I've fantasized and fucked you against a wall."

"Please." The cry was torn from her.

"Ah God, how I fantasize about you," he whispered, nipping at her shoulder. "I dream of watching you suck my dick, Liza. Watching as it parts your lips, feeling your hot little mouth working over it."

A rush of slick, heated warmth flooded her pussy as electric flares of intense sensation whipped across every cell of her body.

"You're ready to come for me, just at the thought of it," he growled, his lips moving to the mark at her shoulder again, brushing over it, sending another, sharper burst of wild pleasure tearing through her. "While my teeth were locked at your pretty shoulder and my dick was locked in your tight little pussy, I thought I would die from the pleasure."

Shudders raced through her body as she turned her head to the side, intent on begging for his kiss, pleading for the taste of it as the overwhelming addiction kicked in with a force that had her whimpering.

She couldn't bear it. What had been merely a desire for his kiss earlier was suddenly an agonizing, imperative need. A hunger she couldn't fight and didn't want to deny herself.

He was waiting for her.

As her head turned, the fingers of his free hand locked in

her hair, pulling her head closer as his bent to her, his lips catching hers, his tongue surging between them.

Instantly her lips clamped on it, her tongue pressing against his, stroking, drawing the lush, spicy taste to her mouth as the mating hormone spilled from the tightly swollen glands beneath.

The wild, sensual elixir sank into her system immediately. Suddenly, every touch was more intense, each sensation so vividly erotic that she was nearly driven over the peak of ecstasy with each new touch.

This was rapture.

His lips covering hers, his tongue fucking past them, pumping the heated hormone into her, infusing her with such a powerful, unending hunger that she knew she would never be free of it.

She would never be free of him.

As he kissed her, the light, teasing strokes against her clit were suddenly gone. His hands gripped her hips as he braced his weight on his knees and elbows and drew her rear sharply upward.

He used his knees to press her thighs farther apart, stretching them open then guiding the throbbing head of his cock to the flexing entrance to her pussy.

With each harsh beat of blood through her veins her pussy clenched, spasmed with incredible need.

The first, searing spurt of the pre-seminal fluid inside the desperately sensitive opening tore a cry from her as his lips smothered it.

She was screaming into their kiss as sharp, shocking forks of painful pleasure began attacking her vagina, her clit. It radiated through the intimate flesh and tormented, tortured her with a hunger she lost control of in one heart-stopping second.

Her hips slammed up and back, taking the head of his cock fully in such a sharp, blinding thrust of stretching pleasure that she had to tear her lips from his to release her cry—to breathe.

The intensity of the hunger, the need, the flood of pleasure and rushing demand for more were flying through her like comets spiraling out of control.

Each pulse of the fluid spurting from his cock had her pussy rippling, clenching, desperate for more.

Her fingers desperately gripped the edge of the mat, locking into the heavy material as she held on tight, the rioting ecstasy clashing, raging through her body as he pulled back, then buried the throbbing crest inside her once again.

It pulsed, flooded her pussy with searing heat as the hormone-rich fluid filled her once again.

Nerve endings were suddenly more sensitive, coming alive, pushing closer to the surface of her flesh as though desperate to feel each throb of his cock inside her.

Working his hard width inside her, stretching her, burning her tender flesh with ecstasy, Stygian rocked against her, possessing more and more of her soul even as he possessed each inch of her inner flesh.

The stiff length of his cock parted her entrance, pushed inside, filled her ever more with each thrust, until one hard stroke buried him to the hilt inside her.

A cry tore from her lips, meeting the harsh, primal growl that left his throat as his chest covered her back once again. Holding her hips elevated, his thighs bunching and tightening against hers, he began working the broad length of his cock inside her, thrusting, stroking, pushing in over and over again. Each driving invasion sent her inner muscles spasming around it as nerve endings screamed out at the ecstatic sensations digging into her senses.

Stygian's fingers tightened at her hips as he held her in place for each impaling of the fierce width of his cock. Working inside the snug heat of her pussy, the broad shaft caressed violently sensitive tissue and pushed her closer, harder, toward the burning center of ecstasy.

"Stygian, please," she begged, the sensations agonizing, so filled with such sharp, brutal pleasure that she feared she'd lose her mind from his possession. "Oh God, please. Fuck me. Fuck me harder."

Out of her mind with the sheer erotic rapture, she lost

herself to it. Control was gone. It couldn't exist alongside such exquisite sensations.

The shields protecting her heart and soul evaporated, turned to dust beneath the certainty that this man, this Breed, was the one anchor that would protect her through any storm.

Releasing her hold on those emotions seemed to open her further to the pleasure, allowing it to build with sharper, more heated intensity.

She couldn't bear it.

She couldn't live through it.

As her inner flesh sucked at his shuttling erection, she couldn't help releasing the mat with one hand, her arm curving back to bury her fingers in the long silken strands of his hair as it fell over her shoulder and face.

He licked at the mark on her shoulder.

His incisors raked over the little wound, and she knew—

Liza shuddered at the knowledge.

Her thighs clenched, her pussy gripped his cock tighter, spasmed and with a desperate, agonized cry, she felt herself suddenly hurtling through the blazing, blinding center of pure ecstasy—a rapture that imploded, crashed inside her and began setting off an explosive series of fireworks that radiated through her body.

Behind her, Stygian was still fucking her. The hard, driving strokes powered inside her with a force that triggered one ecstatic explosion after the next.

Throbbing violently, the blood pounding through heavy veins, each impalement was another sharp, brutally explosion burst of release until he buried inside her with one last desperate thrust. A snarl sounded behind her a breath before the sharp incisors sank into the mating mark once more.

She was jerking beneath him.

She was melting around him.

The feel of his release spurting inside her, the mating knot suddenly extending a portion of the already broad length of his cock, locking her in the desperately flexing muscle that milked at it, sent her rushing headlong into an explosion of pure violent ecstasy.

An agony of rapture held her suspended, exploding over

and over again inside the quaking depths of her pussy. Spurt after spurt of heated semen gushed inside her, filling the depths of her pussy as tears of agony and ecstasy spilled from her eyes.

It seemed never ending. The waves upon waves of such overwhelmingly intense sensation tore reality from her mind and kept her hips jerking against his, her body shuddering until she feared there was no way to survive it.

But as each pulse of ecstasy became shorter, less dramatic, until finally, with one last wave of electrified sensation, Liza found herself collapsed against the mat, soaked with perspiration and weak with exhaustion.

Behind her, his cock still locked in the heavy muscles of her pussy, his tongue lapping at the mating mark, easing the bite, Stygian's breathing was harsh, growls emanating from his throat at irregular intervals.

As the pleasure eased and a shadow of reality returned, she could feel the change within herself. Some feeling, some knowledge she wasn't yet certain of, that she knew would change her forever.

The knowledge of it had a wave of fear just waiting to tear through her.

"What have you done to me?" She was too exhausted, too drained to feel anything other than repletion at the moment.

Repletion, and a certainty that there was no preparing herself for what was to come.

"The same thing you've done to me." His voice was heavy, dark and indolent with the pleasure and release that had swept through him as well.

"And what is that?" She had to force each word past her lips.

Exhaustion was making her voice slurred, heavy. Making herself worry was impossible. Fear didn't have a chance.

Yet.

As she waited for him to speak, she felt him shudder above her, the knot that had locked him inside her slowly receding and losing possession of her inner flesh.

"What is it?" He sighed. "Possession. You own me, Liza. That's what mating ensures. Heart. Body. God, my very soul. You own it all. We belong to each other in ways we've never belonged before. In ways I never imagined I could belong to anyone." His lips pressed against her shoulder, warm, lazy with satisfaction. "I love you, Liza. With every part of my body, my heart and my soul. I love you."

Trepidation was rising inside her now. She'd already begun to suspect the truth, and the certainty of it now filled her with dread.

"I wasn't in the market to be owned," she whispered as panic tried and failed to rise inside her. "I liked myself nice and free and single, thank you."

"I think you're very nice," he drawled as he eased his cock slowly from the grip of her pussy and collapsed beside her before pulling her against the warmth of his chest. "You're free. You're single," he said gently as he brushed his cheek against her hair. "But, you have to admit, Liza, it's nice to belong, isn't it? To know you were the dream that kept me fighting for my freedom, for all the Breeds' survival. For this moment in time, for the heart of a woman I knew awaited me. Surely it's not so terrifying?"

Terrifying? No, it wasn't terrifying.

Levering herself up enough to stare into the drowsy depths of his now dark blue eyes, Liza glimpsed the wild, dark, primal core of the man now.

He was like the earth itself: safe, strong and as unpredictable as the wildest storm.

And he wanted to belong to her?

He believed he did belong to her?

"What makes you think I deserve you?" she whispered then, her lips trembling with a sudden surge of impending panic.

"What could ever make you believe that you don't?" He brushed her hair back, the gesture so tender, so gentle that her heart clenched in such emotion that it sent a shaft of agony radiating through her senses.

"Ah, Liza." His expression softened, though still, the arrogance and dominant male power was still there. "You deserve better than I could be. But I'm such a selfish bastard. Completely and irrevocably unredeemable where my need for you is concerned. I'd die without your heart to warm me now. I'd cease to exist if I thought I'd never have your love. I told you, no matter the fear, no matter the secrets you have, nothing can change what I feel for you. Nothing can ever touch my determination to protect and hold you. You and your secrets, should you ever trust me with them. I'm yours, sweetheart. But I'm not the only one who belongs. You belong now as well. To me."

She belonged, and she could feel it, whether she believed it was safe or not. Whether she believed, before him, she had even wanted it.

She belonged to him.

And she knew, somehow, someway, she knew—

"You'll destroy me."

CHAPTER 19

By the time Monday rolled around, Liza was more than ready for a break from the spiraling emotions converging on her.

The only thing that saved her was the ever-present sexual arousal that seemed to flame between them with just a look.

That didn't help when she slept though.

When dreams invaded and further confused her.

Who was she?

As she dressed for work the question plagued her, just as it had plagued her since she had gone to the crash site five nights before.

"Do you know, young children, the choice you have made this night?" Joseph Redwolf, grandfather to the mate of Braden Arness, Megan Fields Arness, whispered through her mind.

Holding the mascara brush carefully and applying her makeup, Liza fought to ignore the memory that wasn't really a memory.

It really was like a dream.

Just as her memories of her childhood were—until the day after that wreck, Liza really had no clear, concise memories.

Finishing the mascara, she picked up the lip gloss she

normally wore before her gaze landed on the tube of color Stygian had packed.

He'd collected most of her additional clothes and accessories, including the makeup in her bathroom the day before. For the most part, he'd chosen things she preferred to use, with the exception of several tubes of colored lipstick.

She'd bought them to use at Halloween with the Goth costume she'd intended to wear on Trick or Treat night. Instead, she, Claire, Chelsea and Isabelle had been called out by the Navajo warriors who fought for the Breed Underground.

The job hadn't been dangerous. It had been more a training mission; they provided distraction while the warriors spirited a young Breed they had helped escape years before, from beneath the noses of the Genetics Council agents sent to find her.

The Breeds and humans targeted by the Genetics Council needing rescue or aid were much fewer now than they had been in past decades. Those the warriors had hidden over the years though, sometimes needed additional help if the Bureau of Breed Affairs or the Genetics Council managed to track them down.

The young female they had moved in the fall had been such a Breed—one the Navajo warriors had hidden, along with her mother, when she was just a babe.

Where the girl had been taken, neither she, her friends nor the warriors who moved her would ever know. She was passed to another team and, Liza knew, would be passed several more times before she was relocated to ensure the secrecy of her final location.

Picking up the tube of lipstick and uncapping it, she stared at the berry-colored hue, like a fully ripe dark raspberry. Turning her gaze to the mirror, she applied the color, rubbed her lips together then stared back at herself.

The color made her eyes seem brighter, her complexion creamier. It brought a luster to the naturalizing effect of the makeup she wore and made her lips appear just a bit lusher, with a hint of sensual poutiness.

Taking a deep breath, she smoothed her hands over the

snug fit of the apple green skirt and eyed it as well as the white silk shell she wore with it.

That was as good as it got, she told herself before turning and striding out of the bathroom.

Her briefcase sat next to the bed, her laptop securely zipped inside.

Grabbing it, she made a mental note to turn it over to her father when she arrived at the office. That flicker in the screen was about to drive her crazy. Not to mention what it was doing to her eyes. While she was there, she intended to get to the truth of her past as well.

Ray had all but fired her and Claire the last time she had seen him, but hell, he'd fired them before. At least once a year he disagreed with something they said or did, then after a day or so, he'd get over it. He'd never really fired them. He loved Claire. Her father loved her. They wouldn't take their livelihood from them.

Walking from the bedroom, she met Stygian and Flint in the sitting room as they waited to escort her to the office.

"I'm going to be late," she told them as she walked toward the door.

"You always think you're going to be late," Stygian growled, opening the door and escorting her into the hall as Flint followed.

The edge of tension that had existed between them over the weekend hadn't abated, just as the edge of panic attempting to overtake her hadn't abated.

She fought off the panic with the same single-minded determination with which she fought back the emotions that threatened to overtake her. And there lay the crux of the problem.

Stygian wanted the emotion. He wanted every part of her, because as he stated, she had every part of him.

And that was what mates did. They gave each other every part of themselves.

And Liza was terrified of it.

Because she had no idea who, or what, was every part of herself.

Flanked by the two Breeds as she left the hotel, Liza wondered what life would be like if the danger was ever over? Would it ever be possible to return to the life she had once had?

Did she want to?

Stepping into the back of the SUV while Flint took the driver's seat and Stygian the front passenger, Liza sat back and closed her eyes.

She should have been on the sat-phone checking e-mail and messages. Her job didn't begin when she clocked in. It often ran over well into the night as well as her weekends.

This weekend, Stygian had commanded her attention though.

Each time he touched her, each time he kissed her, she had burned for him. Even after the Breed doctor's exam and the hormonal treatment she had given Liza, the arousal had still been there.

It was just deniable at times with the help of the hormone, while without the hormone, denying it was impossible.

Thankfully, the office wasn't far from the hotel. It was only a matter of minutes in light traffic before Flint pulled up to the front entrance of the Navajo Nation headquarters. The Navajo Nation Chamber and headquarters held the main offices of all the branches of government as well as the presidential and vice president's offices.

Gripping her briefcase, she allowed Stygian to help her from the SUV, the four-inch heels she wore making the height of the vehicle harder to navigate than her smaller car.

"President Martinez has several meetings throughout the building today," she told Stygian as they entered the reception area. "This afternoon he has lunch in Window Rock and several meetings with casino owners regarding new legislation concerning the casinos. Try not to scare anyone off."

"I'll do my best," he murmured as they reached the security desk.

Placing her palm on the biometric scanner, she moved to push through the security bars that enforced security to the rest of the building.

The flash of red and the low, strident buzz of denial had her stopping in shock and staring down at the display. ACCESS DENIED.

She felt Stygian move in closer in response to the two security guards who closed ranks in front of her. Liza stared around the spacious entrance as she fought to make sense of the denial.

As she looked up, Ronnie Shiloby, the Navajo president's chief of staff was moving rapidly from the elevators to the security desk.

"Liza." His smile was tight, his gaze concerned as he stepped past the security guards and waved them away. "Didn't you get your father's message, dear? I know he called first thing this morning."

Only a few inches taller than Liza, Ronnie's expressive blue eyes were concerned, his expression tense as he tugged at the blue silk of his jacket.

"What message?" She felt dazed as she wondered what message could possibly have explained the electronic refusal to allow her past the security desk.

"Come with me." Indicating the front entrance she'd just entered, Ronnie led the way, holding the door open as she and Stygian stepped outside once again.

"Over here." Indicating the deep curve of the building that then branched into a set of offices, Ronnie led the way to a small, shrub-enclosed patio off the cafeteria where several umbrella-shaded tables and matching chairs were arranged.

"I want to see my father," Liza demanded as he stopped just inside the patio entrance. "I want to know what's going on."

"I don't know what's going on, dear," he breathed out roughly before raking his fingers through graying black hair.

Frown lines deepened in his forehead as he watched her intently. "I know he called and left a message for you, Claire, Chelsea and Isabelle. Since you and Claire were at the hotel, he asked the others to meet there as well." He checked his watch. "He should be there any minute."

Liza turned on her heel and strode quickly back to the SUV.

"Liza, you know there has to be a reasonable explanation," Ronnie stated as she strode away from him, his tone worried now as Stygian opened the door to the SUV for the second time that morning.

Turning, she faced the chief of staff furiously. "No, Ronnie, there is no explanation for canceling my access before discussing it with me," she answered, her voice shaking as she let Stygian help her into the backseat before swinging her head around to face Ronnie once again. "I guess I can assume I've been fired?"

Her throat was tightening with tears and anger at the knowledge that everything she had worked for was being taken away with no explanation whatsoever.

Ronnie shook his head, raking his fingers through his hair once more as he stared back at her in abject apology. "I'm really sorry, Liza."

They knew each other well. This was Ray's second term, and though Liza had only just moved into the position of personal assistant from her former job as the president's scheduler when his former assistant, Isabelle, had taken a position in the office of the chiefs of the Six Tribes, she knew Ronnie well.

Besides the fact that they had worked together for over six years, they'd also known each other for years before that. Her father had worked with Ray for over twelve years, since his early retirement from the military where he and Ray and met.

Before Ray had become president, he had been a delegate for more than eight years. He had hired Audi Johnson right out of the military as head of security for the Navajo Nation Chambers, but Liza and her mother had already moved to the Nation when Liza was barely ten.

As the SUV pulled into the hotel parking lot once again, Liza dug into her purse, searching for her sat-phone.

She was on the verge of emptying the bag when she remembered leaving the device on her bedside table before showering.

No calls had come through before she left the hotel, though, not quite an hour before. If he had called, he had done so right before leaving for the hotel.

He could have called her before he canceled her clearance. That would have been the fatherly thing to do, wouldn't it?

The minute the SUV door opened and Stygian reached in for her, Liza was out of the vehicle and striding into the hotel. She didn't stop at the registration desk to see if her father had arrived.

Flint had been on the phone with Jonas as he pulled into the hotel, and no doubt he would let her know soon.

"Why would your father cancel your security?" Stygian asked as they entered the elevator alone and pressed the fifth floor button.

"Security risk, layoff, termination." She shrugged. "Either of the three means I'm out of a job."

"Has he called?"

"I left my phone in the suite." She grimaced as she gripped the straps of her purse and briefcase in a tight grip. "I never do that. But we've not been gone long, right? If he had called before I left, I would have heard the phone ring."

"Your father's waiting in the adjoining suite next to our room," he told her before murmuring an affirmative to Flint that he had given her the message.

Those damned earbud communicators. Jonas wouldn't let her have one.

"Should I tell him you'll be a while?" he asked her, his voice gentle as the elevator came to a smooth stop.

"No. Facing him now is just as good as later. Preferable, even."

His hand settled at the small of her back. The touch was surprisingly comforting, and far too pleasurable. For a second, a moment out of time, she could feel his cock pushing inside her, his lips on hers. She could taste his kiss, feel his touch.

"Now you're just making me horny," he drawled as they reached the suite next to theirs.

Liza remained silent.

Stygian's hard knock was answered quickly by Dog.

A scowl covered his face while his light gray eyes were the color of hard, cold steel.

"Join the party," he invited, his voice low. "We're just all getting ready to have fun."

Liza stepped inside and looked around the room.

Her father stood with Ray Martinez on the far side of the room. Ray leaned against the desk behind him, his arms crossed over his chest, a heavy frown pulling at his brow as his dark eyes flashed in anger.

Audi Johnson stood to the side of the desk, hands braced on hips, lips thin with obvious impatience. To the other side of the Nation president, his legal advisor and Isabelle and Chelsea's father, Terran Martinez, stood, leaning against the wall rather than the desk.

"Did you show up at work too before you realized you'd been fired?" Chelsea sat on the couch next to Claire, who had her head down, concentrating on her fingers.

"Pretty much," Liza agreed, moving to the couch to join her friends, always aware of Stygian close to her. On the love seat across from Claire and Chelsea, Isabelle and Malachi sat silently as well. Isabelle was obviously upset; Malachi appeared furious.

She turned to her father. "You didn't call, Dad. You let security deny me access."

Her father's lips thinned. "I did call, Liza, the call didn't go through. I've tried to contact you since three in the morning. I learned at about six that your sat-phone signal had somehow been hijacked and your phone was connected to another source and uploading data to it."

She blinked back at him. "I wasn't uploading anything."

"No, you weren't," he agreed. "Any more than you were uploading from your laptop, but both were in the process of a large upload. I managed to sever the upload and the connection, but your phone and laptop Wi-Fi chips have been permanently disabled."

"The laptop screen was flickering again this weekend," she stated, moving to set the briefcase on the floor as though it would somehow incriminate her. "Just like it did last month."

Her father nodded. "There's a serious security breach with each of your electronics," he told them. "The Breeds obviously are not included in that statement." There was a vein of animosity in his tone now.

"Is there any way the Breeds can help, Mr. Johnson?" Malachi offered cordially.

"Oh, there sure is—"

"Dad, don't—" Liza knew that tone of voice, the look in his eyes.

"You and your buddies can pack the hell up and get off Navajo land. And take those God be-damned Genetics Council agents with you."

Isabelle's expression flared with fury as she made it half-way out of her seat in defense of her lover.

Malachi caught her instantly, pulling her back to his side as he leaned close, his head over hers as he whispered something intently at her ear.

"That's enough!" Liza stepped forward, overwhelmed by the sheer disbelief that her father had said such a thing. "That's unfair, Dad, and you know it."

No matter any of their personal feelings, her father still considered Isabelle a favored niece. To say such a thing to the man she loved was horrendous.

"This is none of your business, Liza." He used that cool, firm tone that assured her he still considered her a child and just as easy to control.

"Oh, well now, I just have to beg to disagree." He'd taught her to stand her ground and to fight for what she believed in.

She'd never imagined it would one day be her father she was having to defend a friend to, though.

"Trust me, Liza, it has nothing to do with you," he repeated, his gaze brooding and filled with anger.

"When my lover is one of the Breeds you're trying to run off Navajo land, then yes, I do believe it is my business."

Her father's shock was surprising. "There's no way I heard you correctly." His gaze was colder, harder now than before, shocking her.

Surely he had already guessed?

"Why are you so surprised?" Her arms crossed over her breasts once again. "You knew we were sharing a suite. You knew he had been at the house when we were attacked. As for Malachi, you seem to be forgetting what Holden Mayhew would have done to Isabelle if Malachi hadn't been there."

"What he did wouldn't have happened if it wasn't for him." Audi's finger jabbed in Malachi's direction. The Breed followed his mate as she jumped from the love seat again.

"Because rather than trying to give her to the Genetics Council, he would have just raped her himself." Claire surprised them all as she stood, fury flushing her face.

"Claire, what is wrong with you?" her father snapped, his gaze suspicious. "Son of a bitch, are you on something?"

The accusation had silence suddenly filling the room as all eyes turned on the Nation's president.

Liza couldn't believe the words had left his lips. That he had dared to say something so horrible to Claire, especially in front of so many people.

The look on Claire's face was so rife with tortured pain, Liza could only stare back at her miserably before turning to her own father again.

"So if we stand up to either of you then we obviously have to be on something? We can't possibly be adults who are simply sick and damned tired of being treated like children, could we?" Liza asked them as her chest tightened with pain.

Ray had always aggressively fought Claire's independence with every weapon he could come up with. This was one of them. Accusing her of doing drugs as past friends did, or not caring about her family, whatever it took to get her to back down and obey his demands rather than living as she longed to do.

Behind her, Stygian let his hand grip her hip as he moved closer.

She was certain no one heard it, even she didn't, but she felt the growl rumbling in his chest.

"I didn't say that," Ray snapped back at her.

"Neither of us did." Her father stared back at her as though he didn't know her, though.

"No, it's the same accusation he used when she tried to leave and go to college in California, and the same one he used when she tried to take a job at the casino rather than the receptionist at the Navajo Nation headquarters. For

God's sake, she's his daughter and didn't even get the assistant's job. She was pushed down to a damned receptionist as though she were some lowly distant cousin he felt responsible for," she accused Ray. "And he used the same tone of derision and disgust when she announced she was moving into the house with me too."

"What other reason would she have to treat me so disrespectfully?" Ray charged.

"There was no disrespect, Father." Claire straightened her shoulders as she battled her tears. The sight of it broke Liza's heart. "You can't bear the truth now, any more than you could bear it when I was younger. I'm starting to wonder if you wouldn't have preferred to see Isabelle raped or murdered than to see her with a Breed. Just as I wonder if you wouldn't have preferred I died in that crash."

"Enough of this." Terran stepped forward, his dark eyes blazing with anger as he glanced at Ray and Audi. "I'll be damned if I'll stand here and listen to you insult my child as well as your own. We're not here to discuss who our adult children have taken as lovers. We're here to discuss their safety and the fact that the security they placed on their phones and laptops has been broken." He turned to Liza. "That, my dear, is the reason your, Chelsea's, Claire's and Isabelle's security clearance was denied so quickly. The signal we tracked moved from your phone to your laptop, slid past the encryption and began sending files to a location we've yet to track."

Liza stalked from Stygian into the next room. She moved across the sitting room to the bedroom and grabbed her phone off the bedside table.

Returning, she slapped it on the desk beside her father before moving to the couch, collecting her laptop and dropping it at his feet. "There you go. If you had listened to me last month, when I told you it was acting strange, perhaps you would have found the problem before now."

Her father watched her with a hard scowl as she moved back to Stygian.

His arm slid around her, pulling her to his side as she stared back at her father challengingly. "Are we still fired?"

"Until we determine what's going on, yes, you are." It was Ray Martinez who stated the obvious. No doubt, he was the one who gave the order to rescind their security as well.

Liza nodded slowly, her gaze never leaving her father's.

"Liza, I know you're hurt and angry," he said. "But, rather than blaming us, you and Isabelle should look to your new friends." His gaze moved to Malachi and Stygian. "We couldn't track it, but we know damned good and well that signal didn't leave this hotel."

Stygian felt his mate tense, felt to the bottom of his soul the sudden suspicion and anger that invaded her delicate body, and he knew she was remembering the night she had overheard Jonas attempting to convince him to betray her—to bug her phone and laptop for the access code into the Navajo database.

"I think it's time you leave, Dad," Liza stated then, the scent of her pain slicing through his soul. "We need to get ready and go job hunting, it seems. Since we no longer have jobs."

She couldn't describe the hurt flowing through her or the sense of betrayal she felt.

"Liza, we couldn't risk the possibility that whoever was using the phones and laptops to hack into the database could actually manage to slip through the final layers of security," her father argued as frustration tightened his expression. "Surely you understand that."

"I understand that you live less than twenty minutes from this hotel," she burst out furiously. "Twenty minutes, Dad. And rather than driving over here to tell me what was going on, you let me walk into the offices only to be stopped by security as though I were some criminal myself."

Grimacing, he turned his head away for a second. He folded his arms over his chest, braced his feet apart and just stared back at her silently.

"So now I just get your military face," she accused him, her voice thick. "As far as you're concerned, the subject's closed, right?"

"I apologized, Liza," he stated firmly. "Once I had my information together, I came here, but you had already left."

"You called my phone, knowing it was compromised and

a call wouldn't go through. You couldn't call Stygian or Jonas, but you obviously got hold of the others."

"Dad called me," Claire stated with a hard, cold anger Liza considered uncharacteristic of her as she let Liza know that her father hadn't tried to stop the humiliation she had suffered earlier.

"Claire, that's enough," her father warned her, his tone harsh, harsher than Liza had heard him speak to her since they had awakened from the wreck they were in as teenagers.

"God, this is incredible," Isabelle stared at the two men, confusion creasing her face. "Claire and Liza have always behaved above reproach. They have never done anything to shame either of you, and this is the only way you can treat them now that they aren't following your orders?"

"Isabelle, that isn't true," Audi argued. Liza noticed his voice was even sincere. "This has nothing to do with the mistakes you girls are making in your current lovers—"

"Oh, excuse me!" Isabelle demanded then. "Our mistakes in our lovers? You can go to hell! As for you, Uncle Ray, you can jump and accuse Claire of doing drugs because she had the nerve to argue with you? And you can't go out of your way to warn your daughter not to arrive at the office after you've canceled her clearance? I'm sorry, Audi, but that's exactly what it sounds like."

"Isabelle." It was Terran who stepped in at that point. "There are things you don't understand, sweetheart."

"They why not explain it, Dad?" Chelsea rose slowly from her seat as well. "Because it's obvious the two of them"—she nodded toward Liza's and Claire's fathers—"aren't going to explain a damned thing."

Terran grimaced, his hand lifting to rub at the back of his neck as he glanced at the other two men, his expression uncertain. Finally, he gave a brief shake of his head as his expression turned resigned.

"I'm out of here," Chelsea bit out, the fact that she was at the end of her patience more than obvious. "I've had it to my back teeth with the half-truths and manipulations going on here." She turned to Liza. "When our parents decide to be honest with us and tell us what the hell is going on, I hope someone lets me know." She stalked from the room, the door slamming closed behind her.

"Is she safe?" Liza asked Stygian softly as her friend slammed out of the room.

"She's safe." The growl in his voice sent a chill racing up her spine.

She didn't dare glance back at his expression, not while she was watching the trepidation in her father's eyes as he glanced behind her.

"Gentlemen." Stygian stepped forward then. "Leave."

The order was given in such a primal, furious tone of voice that Liza flinched.

Liza's father glowered back at him. "This meeting isn't over."

"It's over." As he spoke, the door opened and Flint entered with Dog, Mutt, Mongrel and Loki. Behind them walked in Jonas Wyatt.

"What's going on here?" Liza asked Stygian, her voice low.

"This room is tied into Breed security." Lowering his head, he answered her in a tone that she doubted anyone but she could hear. "Jonas has been watching."

"Did you bug my laptop, Stygian?" While she had his attention, had him close enough to ask where no one else could hear, she took the opportunity.

"I would never betray my mate." The forbidding tone of his voice was almost enough to make her nervous.

It was a warning—she didn't dare question him further, and she didn't dare disbelieve him.

The animal he was so related to was clear in his voice, the dominance and arrogant strength shadowing it.

No, he hadn't betrayed her, she could bet her life on it.

CHAPTER 20

Liza watched with a frown as Jonas and her father stood, staring each other down.

Both men were incredibly strong-willed, each with an innate arrogance that no doubt grated on the other.

They were two men who would never get along. They would rarely see eye to eye.

And one was about as stubborn as the other.

Jonas wouldn't leave Window Rock until he had answers, one way or the other.

If her father knew those answers involved his daughter, then hell would freeze over before he'd tell Jonas a damned thing.

Unfortunately, in the meantime, a little girl was suffering and she and Claire were on a roller-coaster ride they couldn't seem to stop.

"I believe, Mr. Johnson, you were asked to leave." Stygian stepped around her, placing his body in a protective position in front of her.

"This is ridiculous, Stygian," she muttered.

Turning his head and pinning her with his gaze, his lips formed the words, "Trust me."

She sighed. She trusted him fine, it would just be nice to

know what the hell was going on, and to make sense of her father's and Ray Martinez's attitudes.

"Liza, you know I would never hurt you," her father stated as she watched him silently.

No, he would never hurt her physically, but emotionally, she was learning, was another thing.

"Dad, that's exactly what you've done." Tears thickened her voice, humiliating her, making her feel like the child he obviously believed she was.

"Your feelings are hurt, but I'd much prefer your feelings or your pride singed versus the alternative," he stated cryptically.

"And that alternative would be?" It was Jonas who spoke up as her father, Ray and Terran moved to leave the room.

Audi stopped, his expression tightening, gray eyes flashing in anger. "The situation you've provoked, Director Wyatt. You're placing her life in danger," he bit out, unable to hide the anger in his voice. "You and your refusal to allow the past to die."

"Audi, stop," Ray snapped, his voice low.

"My refusal to allow my child to die?" Jonas snapped back, the liquid mercury of his gaze shifting dangerously. "We asked for your help when we arrived, yours and President Martinez's. You refused. I will not leave here until I have the answers I came to find."

"We don't have what you want," her father snarled, surprising her with the frustrated fury in his voice.

"And you think your training can actually dissipate the lie you fucking stink of every time you're questioned on this." Jonas was suddenly on him, his voice raised, all but nose to nose, fiery anger and a dangerous warning echoing in his tone. "Let me tell you who you are dealing with, Mr. Johnson. You are dealing with a Breed whose senses are far superior to those that obviously trained you to lie to a Breed."

Panic tightened through her.

Why?

Liza could feel the fear rising in the depths of her soul, a sense of such horrible panic that the premonition seemed apocalyptic.

"Tell me, Mr. Johnson, exactly what are you hiding?"

She wanted to scream.

Liza had to fight to hold back a cry of denial, a furious demand that Jonas stop, that he leave, that her father hold his secrets as he had always done.

Her heart was racing in her chest, the blood thundering through her veins with such force that she would be amazed if everyone in the room couldn't hear it.

"Easy." Stygian's voice was so soft, so low, she wondered for a moment if she heard it. "Your secrets are safe."

She heard him. Everyone's attention was on Jonas and her father, so no one saw him lower his head or heard the words he whispered at her ear.

"Audi has kept your secrets this long, Jonas won't draw them from him. I give you my word." Once again, so low, so quiet, it reached her ears only.

Her heart rate eased.

Stygian wouldn't lie to her. He wouldn't give her his word unless he was certain.

"I'm keeping many secrets from you, Director Wyatt," her father stated sarcastically. "Many. But I assure you, if I could give you any information, any clue in your efforts to save your daughter, then I would do so."

The look of pain that flashed across Jonas's face was so overwhelming, so deep, that Liza would have given any- thing in that moment to help him.

"I have a daughter," Audi said as Jonas moved back slowly. "And I know the pain you're going through. If I could help your child, you wouldn't even have to ask."

"You've been asked to leave," Jonas's voice was grating now. "Please do so."

Stepping back, he watched the three men. His expression was stone cold, but his eyes raged with agony.

Watching as her father, Claire's and Isabelle's left the room, Liza then turned her attention to Jonas.

His head lowered as he slowly shook it and said softly, "He said if he could give me what I needed, not that he

didn't have it." He turned his gaze to her. "He would willingly burn in the fires of hell for you, wouldn't he?"

Her father would never sacrifice her for Jonas's daughter.
That knowledge swirled around them, struck at her heart
and caused a single tear to slip free of her eyes.

"Dad forgot to take my laptop," she said, unable to bear
the pain in his eyes or the fear she couldn't fight any longer.
"If you can bypass the new security Dad set up on the database with it, then you're welcome to it. Perhaps it will be
easier with the laptop itself rather than just tapping into it."
The last she said with painful mockery as she picked up the
briefcase and handed it to him. "While you're in there, if
you could ignore the journal file, I'd appreciate it. I tend to
collect passwords, though no one is really aware of the
habit." She stopped and then stared at Jonas as the panic
rose inside her again. "No one is aware of it but one of the
chiefs of the Six who suggested I do so."

"Passwords?" His voice was thicker, the harsh sound brutal in its intensity as he accepted the laptop.

"Yeah. Passwords." She refused to feel guilt. She was terrified of the choices she was making, but she wasn't going to
be frightened.

This had gone too far. If there was nothing to hide, then
what she was doing would hurt no one. "Like my father's
security key to access the database. I want your word it will
be used for nothing else, Jonas, and you'll destroy the file
once you're finished."

"I swear to you that no matter what is found, the only
information I'll use is any that will help my daughter, or
those who were involved in the Brandenmore experiments."

There was a warning in his eyes. If she was one of those
girls, he wouldn't walk away from it.

She consoled herself with the fact that the only access
codes she had ever "collected" were those that weren't
harmful: the Genetic Database codes. Her parents' personal
Internet codes and those into their home computers.

Ray's home Internet access code was there, but only
because Liza and Claire often worked at his house when
Claire spent the weekend there. Even the code to her father's

laptop, the one he used to keep information needed for the security of the Nation, was in there. She prayed Jonas was as true to his word as she had always heard he was.

If she was who she hoped she was, then there was no harm to be done.

No information regarding the Navajo Breed Underground Network could be on the networks or computers that would be compromised. If it was, then perhaps she should have never been told that such information was forbidden to be written down, or placed on a computer.

Relinquishing the laptop to him, she pushed aside the panic and the fear of what would be found. She couldn't live with herself if she ever learned she could have saved Amber Wyatt's life.

"Jonas, whatever his faults, whatever his secrets, my father loves me."

"Would you submit to a Core Level DNA test?" Jonas asked then.

Core Level. The deepest genetic testing available and the only level that a recessed Breed could be identified at. It was also the only level at which proof of genetic tampering could be proven.

"You believe my father had my genetics tampered with?" she asked him. "That technology is only now a thing of science fiction, Director Wyatt."

"And Breeds were only a part of science fiction one hundred years after the first one was created," he said gently.

Liza clasped her hands together, her fingers holding to each other in a fierce grip as she fought to control fears that had no name and panic that had no reason.

"No DNA tests, Jonas." It was Stygian who rejected the idea.

As Liza fought to hold control over the shadowed screams that had her lips trembling, Stygian gripped her hip as he stood behind her and faced his director.

A spasm of what Liza could only describe as agony crossed Jonas's face before he glanced away from them for a moment. Turning back, he nodded slowly before focusing those strange eyes on her.

"Thank you for the help, Ms. Johnson."

"Jonas, I need to discuss a few of your new security measures before you leave," Stygian stated as he slowly released her.

"Talk on the way back to my suite," Jonas breathed out roughly. "Amber had a difficult night and I'd like to get back so Rachel can rest."

That hard knot of searing guilt gripped Liza's chest as Stygian moved past her and followed Jonas out the door.

Left alone, Liza drew in a hard, deep breath before covering her face with her hands and fighting back the sobs rising in her chest. As she did, the memory of what she had told Stygian three nights before raced through her mind.

"You will destroy me—"

She had just given Jonas Wyatt the means to do just that, she feared, and she had done it for the man she had given her heart to.

As strong, as fearless and filled with honor as he was, she couldn't allow him to see her as weak as she knew she was.

She was terrified.

"Why?" Jonas asked as they stepped into the hall and started moving toward the presidential suite.

"Contact Dash," Stygian urged him as he caught the director's arm to draw him to a stop. "I need Cassie here."

He didn't know why, he had no idea why his instincts were certain the DNA tests were the wrong answer, yet Cassie, the eerie little waif who saw ghosts, was the right one.

"Dash refuses to bring her out." Jonas's lips pulled back in a frustrated snarl. "Do you think I haven't already tried that?"

"Try one more time, Jonas," Stygian urged him. "You know how Dash and Cassie work. Dash will refuse at her request because she's waiting on something. Tell him to tell her it's time. Tell her I need her here, Jonas. My mate needs her."

Once, when Cassie had been a little girl, she had stopped him as he moved across the backyard of the Ruling Pride's home. She'd looked up at him, solemn and eerie, and told him the day would come when he would need her to help his mate—his mate would make a choice that would require her help. Cassie'd promised she would be there for him.

That time had come.

Staring back at him, Jonas sighed wearily as he nodded his assent. "I'll contact Dash." His expression turned questioning then. "Are you sure this is what you want, Stygian? If she sees Liza as anyone other than who she is, she won't hold back, you know that."

He knew it. He hated it, but he knew it was the only answer.

"A Core Level DNA test isn't going to convince Liza of anything, and if her genetics were wiped and replaced, there will be no way to know for certain who she was before the wipe," Stygian warned him. "Cassie will see more than DNA. She'll see her fears, a memory, a nightmare or whatever the hell it is that Cassie sees that will pull those memories free if she is Honor or Fawn."

"She's Honor Roberts, Stygian," Jonas said then, his gaze heavy. "I can sense it. I feel it. That woman is Honor Roberts, and I know beyond a shadow of a doubt she can help us save Amber."

Jonas stared back at Stygian, hating what he knew he was putting his enforcer through, hating what he knew that young woman he claimed as his mate would soon go through.

"I'll protect her, Stygian," he swore with a desperation that burned inside his soul. "I swear to you, if need be, I'll give my own life to protect her if I'm right. I'll do whatever it takes because I know together, she and Fawn Corrigan are all that can save Amber."

"How?" Stygian snarled in frustration now, unaware until this moment that the question raged inside him. "How can they help her, Jonas? They were children. They would have no idea the makeup of that drug."

"Honor Roberts had a photographic memory before she entered that lab," Jonas hissed, hope suddenly burning in his eyes. "The reason the Genetics Council wanted her back after they released her to her father was because of the anomalies her Council-controlled nanny noticed. She'd

developed a photographic memory and was often left with
the coded notes and diagrams the scientists used while
developing the serums they tested there. Judd and Gideon
developed the photographic memories after the tests began.
Each of the three would make certain, day by day, that they
saw the notes and files on the tests and the serum used.
Fawn Corrigan never saw the codes that we know of, but
that nurse told us what she never told the scientists: Honor,
Judd and Gideon would write out or draw what they saw,
and Fawn would translate it. She could crack a code without
a key, Stygian. She could decipher all the files we have, all
the notes, everything we haven't been able to crack where
those experiments are concerned. With Honor's memories
of their particular serums and experiments, her memory of
the codes used, combined with what little we know where
the serum Brandenmore gave Amber is concerned, and all
our questions would be answered."

Together, they would have the ability to save Jonas's
daughter's life and to help decipher all the encrypted files
scientists had left over the decades of Breed research and
the mating phenomena.

One without the other wouldn't work.

"We also have Gideon to worry about." Jonas sighed as
he looked up the hall to the suite he and his family occupied.
"He knows by now where Liza and Claire are. He's probably
already one step ahead of us." He turned back to Stygian.
"And he couldn't care less about Amber or what it would do
to her parents to lose her. All he cares about is killing Honor
Roberts, Faith Corrigan and the Bengal Breed who was a
part of those experiments with him."

"He won't get her," Stygian growled, praying to God he
was strong enough to keep Liza out of Gideon's reach.

Jonas nodded, clasped his shoulder then turned and continued up the hall.

Stygian watched him go. Jonas's shoulders were as
straight as always, his head as arrogantly lifted as it had ever
been. But Stygian could feel the weariness dragging at the
director, as well as the fear.

If they lost Amber, then Jonas's mate, Rachel, would

never be the same. Hell, no one who had ever met that child would ever be the same.

Two years old, bright as hell, loving, generous. The heart Stygian sensed within the toddler was one that shined with such compassion that seeing her pain, feeling her fear, could humble him as nothing else he had ever known.

This particular spell caused by the serum she had been injected with had lasted longer than any other. At the most, until recent weeks, the spell would last a few days to a week and then the child would pull out of the weakness and pain and once again she would be her bright, childlike self.

This time, she was growing weaker, the pain at times so strong that Stygian could sense it even across the distance between Jonas's suite and his own.

There were times he swore he could feel the toddler's tears.

And there was nothing he could do to help her. He held Honor Roberts in his arms every night and listened to the nightmares that plagued her.

Her pleas that the pain stop, the terror that filled her as she begged that "they" not harm her again was killing him. All he could do was hold her through the dreams that he sensed filled her with horror and pray she would remember them when she awakened.

And she never did.

She never remembered them and he never mentioned them, because his animal instincts reined in the words each time he began to mention them to his mate.

Returning to the suite, Stygian followed the scent of his mate to the suite they shared and stood in the connecting doorway, just watching her as she stood in front of the heavy curtains that blocked the small balcony outside.

"How could they do it?" she asked softly, though she never turned from the view of the curtains. "How could anyone change something so basic as a teenager's memories, her hopes and her dreams?" Her voice became softer, her pain became deeper. "How could they steal that part of a person and give them someone else's?" She turned to him then and the tears that glistened in her eyes, the dampness on her cheeks, broke his heart.

"Tell me." Liza sobbed then, her breathing hitching as she wrapped her arms across her breasts and fought to hold back the rage that would have had her screaming. "Tell me how they could do it, Stygian? How could science have reached that peak?"

She couldn't fight the truth any longer. She couldn't fight the knowledge that even if she wasn't Liza Johnson, then she still had no idea who she was.

Or what she was.

If she had been one of Phillip Brandenmore's experiments, then only God knew what he had done to something as basic as her very DNA.

"Science hasn't reached that peak." He finally sighed. "Your DNA can be altered but never completely changed. A Core Level DNA test, as we discussed before, isn't the answer either. Because those core genetics can, in certain instances, be changed but nothing can change it back. As for the memories, I can't explain those, Liza."

Miserable, so frightened of what was coming, it was all she could do to hold back the shudders that would have worked through her. Terror waited on the fringes of her control, just waiting to strike, to take over her mind with all the shadowed, barely remembered nightmares that haunted her sleep.

"It happened the weekend of that wreck." She had pinpointed that much at least. "I remember waking up in the hospital, and there were bandages on my face. Dad said the wreck had damaged it, but I remember thinking then, sensing, that he wasn't being honest—not completely. And when they removed the bandages, there was a second that I didn't know the person staring back at me from the mirror they gave me."

She remembered that.

As Stygian took her in his arms, Liza remembered that moment as clearly as she would always remember that first kiss she had shared with Stygian.

Staring in the small mirror, she had seen her eyes, her hair, her face.

Her nose was too rounded, the arch of her brow hadn't been right. There had been something odd about the shape of her lips and the sharp, high cheekbones. But there had also been the knowledge that there were several scars marring her body that were too old to have been caused by that wreck.

"Stygian." Her lips trembled as more tears escaped her control and slid from her eyes. "I'm scared. I'm so scared."

She was suddenly terrified of what was coming, of what memories could spill free when Liza Johnson accepted, to the very depths of her soul, that she no longer existed, and released whoever was trapped inside.

"No." That growl, it was pure, wild Wolf—a low rasp of danger as primal and fierce as any animal that walked on four legs. "No fear, Liza. Trust me. Trust me to guide you through this. To hold you when it hurts, to protect you if there's danger."

In a few short steps he was before her, hands gripping her shoulders, holding her firm, capturing her gaze as flares of brilliant blue gleamed in the black background of his gaze.

"Trust me, Liza, I'll protect you."

Lips trembling, her chest tight with the need to cry, Liza laid her head against his chest.

She needed to hear, to feel the beat of his heart.

She needed the warmth of him wrapping around her, holding her, providing a haven in a storm of spiraling emotions and fears.

"No fear, baby," he whispered again, his arms wrapping around her, his head lowering until his lips were against her ear, his strength holding her on her feet. "No matter what comes, no matter what happens, no matter who you are, I'll be here, and I'll hold you."

Curling her fingers into the material of his shirt, she closed her eyes tight.

"Hold me now," she cried out, the pain burrowing so deep inside her that she felt the raking talons of it digging into her heart.

A surprised gasp left her lips as he curved his arm beneath her knees and lifted her until he was cradling her in his arms.

A feeling of intense feminine weakness swept over her as

she looped her arms around his neck and let her head fall to his shoulder.

"I'll hold you, baby," he promised as he moved into the bedroom, but rather than laying her on the bed, he sat in the heavy, wide chair that sat in the corner of the room. "I'll always hold you."

Cupping the back of her head as she gazed up at him, he held her in place, his head lowering, his lips settling against hers.

In less time than it took for her heart to beat, Liza was ready for him.

CHAPTER 21

Her breasts were swollen and sensitive, her clit throbbing, her pussy becoming moist and aching. Her skin was sensitive, the mating mark at the bend of her shoulder and neck tingled, became heated. She wanted him to touch the mark, wanted his lips on it, wanted to feel his tongue licking over it.

Her lips ached for his kiss, her body burned for his touch. Her fingers tingled with the need to feel his body beneath them. To stroke his powerful body, feel his muscles flexing beneath the dark bronze flesh.

Staring up at him, drowsy sensuality thundering through her body, a small, uncontrolled whimper left her lips as his tongue pressed against the seam of her lips. The spice and cinnamon taste of his kiss infused her senses, heated her blood, and had her arching closer, desperate for more of him—for that deeper, harder kiss. For all his hunger, driving and uncontrolled as they both lost their senses in the pleasure.

Closing her lips on his tongue, Liza drew more of the sensual taste to her sense, reveling in the exquisite sensations beginning to spin through her senses.

Only here could she find peace. Only in Stygian's arms in his kiss—his touch.

Turning, shifting in his arms until she could straddle his powerful thighs, Liza gave in completely to the pleasure rising inside her. Dragging her skirt up to allow her thighs to spread further over his, Liza ground her aching pussy against the hard ridge of his cock as it rose beneath his jeans.

Quickly undoing the three small buttons below her neck, Stygian then gripped the hem, pulled his lips from hers and as Liza slowly raised her arms, he stripped the top from her.

The shell was tossed aside carelessly, forgotten as he found the front clasp of her bra and flicked it open.

"Stygian." Arching in pleasure as his hands cupped her breasts, Liza felt the pinpoints of heated pleasure beginning to flare through her.

The rasp of his sensually rough palms cupping and stroking the under curve of her sensitive flesh sent a surge of heat flaring in her nipples. The tender peaks tightened further, becoming so engorged and sensitive that the need for touch was nearly painful.

Already tight, the hardened tips throbbed, pulsing in need as his fingers avoided the nerve-ridden buds to stroke and caress the flesh around it. And he was killing her. She needed his touch there—no, not just his touch—

"Please." She couldn't fight the need or hold back the demand.

Her fingers burrowed into his hair, clenching in the long, cool strands to direct his lips to the tight, aching buds of her nipples.

The wet heat of his mouth surrounded one tender tip. Wet heat closed over it and began drawing on the sensitive flesh with hungry pulls of his mouth. His tongue joined in the play. The building heat that surrounded her nipple rose with each lash of his tongue. Each time he licked over it, around it, rubbed his tongue against it, Liza whimpered with the rising sensations.

Her fingers tightened in his hair, holding him closer, demanding more.

"It's so good," she whispered hoarsely, the sound of her own voice shocking her, but not enough to pull her back

from the spiraling chaos of pleasure beginning to overtake her.

And it did feel good. It was so much better than good.

Fighting to breathe, Liza arched in his arms as he kissed
a slow, fiery path to her other breast and the tender peak
begging for attention as well. His lips surrounded it, his
mouth suckling at the pebble-hard bud as Liza's thighs
tensed. Her hips moved against him, rubbing her pussy
against the denim-covered cock beneath it.

Sensation shot from her nipple to her clit as his teeth
raked against the tight tip. Gripping it between his teeth and
bearing down on it, Stygian used his tongue to torment it
with fiery pleasure.

Licking, stroking, rubbing against the tight peak, Stygian
pushed her closer to an abyss of pleasure that she had no
idea how to ease back from.

"Oh God, yes." The liquid heat of his mouth working the
tight bud of her nipple was destroying her self-control.

Each draw of his mouth, each lash of his tongue against
the throbbing peak sent flares of incredible heat lashing at it
before jagged bolts of sensation shot from her nipple to her
clit.

Fiery pleasure wrapped around her, blazing across the
rest of her body as she felt his hands tugging her skirt the
remaining distance from the top of her thighs to her hips.

His fingers smoothed down the elastic straps of her garter
belt then back to the loose material of the tap pants she wore.
Slipping his hand beneath the leg opening of the material, it
took only seconds for his fingers to find the swollen, throbbing bud of her clitoris.

"Stygian. Oh please, please, yes." Lifting to him, her lips
parting as his came down on hers once again, Liza couldn't
hold in her mewls of pleasure.

The sensations were so good.

The pleasure was lashing at her.

It was striking at her nipples where the fingers of one
hand plucked at the sensitive peaks.

It tightened around her clit as he rasped at it with the fingers of his other hand, rubbing against it, exciting it as she moaned at his touch.

From her clit, his stroking touch slid through her heavy juices to the clenched entrance of her aching cunt. Rimming the slick, heated flesh, his fingers stroked, caressing, pushing her to the verge of begging him for more.

She needed his touch there. She wanted him filling her, thrusting inside her, fucking her.

His lips lifted from hers, moved along the line of her jaw before finding the outline of her ear. His fingers rubbed against the entrance of her vagina before he eased the tip of one broad finger inside.

Desperate pleasure flooded her. Lush, slick, her juices spilled to his fingers, easing his way as he penetrated her further.

"So sweet and hot," he growled at her ear as she bore down on the impalement, desperate to feel his touch deeper, harder.

"Do you know I love fucking you, Liza? Pushing my cock inside you and feeling how hot and slick your pussy gets for me?"

This fingertip retreated only to return, the impalement burning through her senses with the addition of a second.

Calloused, firm, he worked them deeper inside her, rubbing against the sensitive tissue with wicked expertise.

Easing inside her, Stygian parted his fingers, sending electric pulses of pure sensation racing through the intimate flesh. Fiery arcs of pleasure raced through the delicate muscles he was impaling, drawing a ragged moan from her as her vagina clenched desperately around his fingers.

"Feel how tight you are around my fingers? So sweet and tight. When you clench around my dick like that, it's all I can do to keep from coming the second I get inside you."

A moan of rising pleasure broke free of her lips as his fingers retreated only to return with a deeper, harder impalement.

Sensation burned through her. Fingers of erotic, blinding pleasure tore across every nerve ending in her body. Each stroke of his fingers through the clenching, snug tissue sent waves of pleasure rushing to her clit and clenching her womb.

"So pretty." His voice was a ragged, primal growl at her ear. "I love seeing your face as you take me, Liza." His fingers worked harder inside her, fucking her with just enough force to build the rising hunger sharper inside her.

His lips stroked down her neck, his tongue licking over the sensitive mating mark before blazing a trail of pleasure to her pebble-hard nipples awaiting the touch of his lips once again.

When it came, the moist heat surrounded the tight peak, sucking it with firm deep draws of his mouth as his tongue licked and tasted the tormented bud.

His fingers pushed inside her, sliding free of the clenched grip of her pussy, returning to stroke her ever closer to the edge of release.

Hips writhing against the penetration of his fingers, her lips parted, panting for air, Liza forced her eyes open to stare into Stygian's.

"Not yet," she whispered desperately as the pleasure began to reach a critical peak. "Please, Stygian. Not yet."

The strokes eased, stilled, until he was filling her, keeping her poised on the edge of release.

"Ah baby, you're so close," he murmured. "I could throw you right over the edge. Feel you as you come around my fingers."

"I want to feel you." Sliding her hands to his chest, she pulled at the first button of his shirt, then the second.

Her vagina involuntarily clenched around his fingers, the spill of moisture slickening her further as she fought to find more than solitary pleasure.

"God, Liza." His free hand slid to her hip, gripping it firmly as she slid her hand to the bare warmth of his chest.

"I want to feel all of you." She moved to the next button, fighting to breathe, fighting not to come as he stroked ultra-sensitive tissue with just the tips of two fingers. "Please, Stygian."

Slowly, so very slowly his fingers slid free of the clenched depths of her sex. With both hands, he gripped the edges of his shirt and jerked.

Buttons popped from the fabric and flew in all directions. The rending of the material before he tossed it carelessly to the floor had a thoroughly feminine smile of sensual smugness curling her lips.

Hers.

He was just hers.

Lifting her body from his, her fingers went to his belt and quickly loosened it. Pulling at the metal tabs that secured the denim, she had his jeans open as his hands joined the battle to push them below his hips.

The heavy length of his cock rose between them, the broad head flushed dark, the heavily veined stalk throbbing imperatively as Liza stroked her hand from tip to base and back again.

Lips parted, her gaze still locked with his, Liza lifted against him. With one hand steadying the broad length of his cock, she rested her head against the side of his, her lips at his ear as she lowered herself against him.

The head of his erection pressed against the snug entrance. Within seconds, the pulse of pre-cum ejaculated from the tip and sent a rush of sensual warmth to heat her pussy.

His arms wrapped around her, holding closer as her hands slid to his shoulders, her fingers curling against his powerful shoulders as his hips began to move, to lift to her. Hard hands held her hips steady, moving her, helping her to take him in small, stretching increments as mewls of pleasure rasped in her throat.

"Yes," the low, desperate cry slipped from her lips. "Hold me, Stygian. Oh God, don't let me go."

"Never," he growled as his hips jerked in a hard, shallow thrust, forcing his cock deeper.

Slick, wet, her pussy clasped the iron-hard intruder as Liza began to move with him, riding him slow, easy, taking him inch by inch until the thick shaft was lodged fully inside her, stretching her with erotic strength.

Striking impulses of ecstatic pleasure raced through her.

Moving above him, rising and falling as sensation after sensation began to suffuse her senses, Liza gave herself to the spiraling flight to ecstasy and the mate moving beneath her with fierce upward strokes of his hips.

Primal and intense. Erotic and raging with a sensuality impossible to overcome, each upward thrust of his cock stroked, caressed, rasped against tender flesh and sent sparks of pleasure so heated, so filled with sharp, burning bursts of rapture that there was no resisting it.

No resisting the rapid, spiraling flight to the center of raging, exquisite bliss.

Exploding around her, inside her, the pleasure detonated with a force that stole her breath.

Her nails dug into his shoulders as Liza lowered her head, her lips parting, teeth locking in the hard muscle at the bend of his neck as his incisors bit into the mating mark left on hers.

A growl sounded at her ear, fierce and filled with primal dominance, as Liza felt herself sinking into the waves of sensation that electrified, exploded over and over, and sent a rush of fiery ecstasy tearing through her again and again, until she was left shuddering in his arms. The feel of the additional swelling in his cock locking him inside her as he spilled his release was another sensual rush of violent sensation that sent another, lesser explosion tearing through her.

It was like being surrounded by pleasure—plugged into pure sensation and feeling it racing beneath her flesh, through her veins, sizzling around her clit and streaking through her pussy.

Locked in his arms, she whispered his name, so intent on the sensations that she forgot to hold back the emotion.

"I love you." She sighed breathlessly as the final pulse of pleasure shuddered through her. "Oh God, Stygian, I love you."

And she did.

She loved him breathlessly, completely.

While she hadn't been looking, he had stolen her heart, and she knew there was no chance of ever getting it back and being the same again.

Now, she only hoped she could survive it.

"I love you." He kissed her temple gently before moving.

A sharp breath of reaction parted her lips at the rush of pleasure when he pulled from her. Still partially erect, his cock caressed across violently sensitive nerve endings, sending a rush of pleasure sizzling through her before it abated once again, sated for the moment.

"Lie here a second, babe." He laid her on the bed before shedding his jeans completely and moving to the bathroom.

Returning moments later, he cleaned the slick, wet proof of their arousal from her thighs and the folds of her pussy with a damp cloth. Then drying her gently, he pulled the blankets over her before moving back to the bathroom.

The sound of water running brought a smile to her face.

When he returned to the bed and slid beneath the blankets with her, Liza curled against his chest, needing his warmth, needing him holding her. Feeling his hand sift through her hair, his fingertips rubbing against her scalp, Liza let herself sink into the comfort he was offering.

"Don't let me get lost, Stygian," she whispered as the exhaustion of the past days began to catch up with her.

Emotions, nightmares, fear and anger had plagued her, making her sleep restless, her dreams dark and impossible to remember when she awakened.

"I won't let you get lost, baby," he promised as he soothed her.

For once, there was no distance, no emotional storm, no desperation to hold herself aloof, and no arousal. There was just the comfort he was offering her and an overwhelming sense of safety.

"Sleep, Liza," he crooned, his voice gentle, his hands incredibly tender as he soothed her. "Right here, rest against me, we'll figure out our next move later. I promise."

And he always kept his word.

Her eyes drifted closed, her breathing evened out and she allowed sleep to settle over her.

Maybe, was her last thought, maybe, in Stygian's arms the nightmares would stay away. Maybe she could sleep, just for a little while. Just long enough to find the strength to face what she feared was coming—

The destruction of everything she had believed she was—of everything her life had been.

Because life as she knew it was over.

CHAPTER 22

Stygian stared out over the desert landscape from the top of the spherical column of stone that rose above the valley floor, just behind the hotel, his gaze narrowed, his animal instincts humming in danger.

Something was out there—

"What are you hearing from your contacts?" he asked Dog quietly.

"I know they're here, I just haven't been able to find them. Since word went out that Cassie Sinclair was arriving in the area, more teams have been sent out, but like the others, they haven't been glimpsed."

The Genetics Council was sending out their best teams now, evidently. With the creation of the scent reduction drug, it was becoming harder and harder to track the bastards down too.

"They have to buy supplies at some point," he stated. "Are there men in town watching for that?"

"We have several teams watching." An edge of irritation colored Dog's tone. "But what the fuck are we watching for and how do we cover every damned business that could possibly provide their supplies? And if they follow directive command and work with humans to supply their needs, then we're fucked there."

Wasn't that the truth. Window Rock had dozens of businesses supplying outdoorsmen, hunters, weekend vacationers and the list went on.

"Why this area?" Stygian asked as he surveyed the land again, paying particular attention to the small canyon that ran alongside the road. "What are they looking for? There has to be more than just Honor, Fawn, Judd and Gideon. They have to be after something more."

"Not sure, but there were signs of movement in the canyon night before last and several times last week. Loki has been flying over the desert, twenty miles in each direction, to track them. He's been able to track and explain all movements but this one and another about four miles to the east of the hotel."

Stygian rubbed at his jaw thoughtfully. "Any chatter?"

"Strangely, nada." Dog shook his head. "If it hadn't been for Loki, we wouldn't know about this." He nodded toward the canyon.

"This the same canyon Liza and Claire crashed into when they were fifteen. The one we took her to?"

"The same canyon we also found evidence of a sweat lodge in," Dog told him. "You know, Navajo medicine is shrouded in history. There are a lot of things they're rumored to be able to do though."

"Such as?" Stygian asked absently as he stared through the binoculars into the canyon.

"I've had Chimera working with Joseph Redwolf for a while now, Megan Arness's grandfather. From what she's uncovered, there's a legend that the memories of a dying warrior can be passed to a warrior who needs the skill or the information that could be gone forever. There's no information whether it's ever been done before, but the legend is there. She's also learned that they've been shredding and burning records from more than a decade back, which were contained in a secured, secret location where the tribal chiefs are said to store the written history of their secrets and the recipes used for certain rituals, handed down since long before their lands were ever invaded by the white man."

Stygian lowered the binoculars, his arms propped on the edge of the boulder he'd been resting against.

"The Navajo medicine men are rumored to still know many of the ancient rituals," he said thoughtfully. "How close is that supposed secured, secret location to the canyon where the girls wrecked?"

"We don't have a clue. Even Chimera doesn't know where it's at. But she's smelled the ash on Joseph's clothes when he returned from the desert. And he didn't lie when she asked what he had been burning. He told her he was burning another's past."

Fuck.

Fuck.

He could feel it.

In his gut, Stygian could feel the vibrations of an interference that had likely saved Liza's life as child, but could cost her that life now.

Liza?

To her friends, to her family, she was Liza Johnson. It was Liza Johnson's memories she carried, but it wasn't Liza Johnson's personality. Just as it hadn't been Liza Johnson's destiny to be in this place, at this time. It was Honor Roberts's. And now, Honor no longer had the very information that could save her life.

"At the same time the wreck occurred, two men supposedly from a unit Audi Johnson had trained while in the military showed up as well. Cullen Maverick and Klah Hunter. We suspect Klah is Judd." Dog leaned against the boulder they were using as shelter, his gaze narrowing, the lines fanning out from his eyes, the marks of squinting into the sun, or his gaze narrowing on distant targets, stood out in stark relief as they narrowed once again.

Between his teeth he clenched a cold, thin cigar that he had yet to light. Crossing his arms over the desert-tan shirt that covered his chest, the Coyote watched Stygian assessingly.

"Stranger things have happened," Stygian murmured.

Hell, he knew better than that.

Judd wouldn't have left the girls without his protection. Even in the labs, both Judd and Gideon had risked their lives more than once to protect both girls. "There was a reported attack on two teenagers and a young man, matching Honor's, Fawn's, and Judd's description, as well as two Native Americans accompanying them, six hours from Window Rock, less than twenty-four hours before the wreck," Dog continued. "Several soldiers identified as working for Brandenmore Research were found dead as well, their bodies obviously having been dumped there rather than left where they were killed."

"The underground network that has always helped the Breeds in escaping and relocation are rumored to be on Claire and Liza's asses every time they leave the hotel. The Breeds that were here, before Liza and Claire came on our radar, say the members of that network are rumored to never leave a kill where it was made, if killing is necessary," Stygian murmured.

"True," Dog agreed. "We also have the fact that there's a team shadowing Liza and Claire, a report that the two girls have always had shadows. Shadows our Breeds could never identify or track. They're damned good, Stygian, if they can evade us."

"I've glimpsed them," Stygian admitted. "Each time I've sent Flint or one of my own team out to track them, they simply disappear."

"What's your gut telling you?" Dog asked when Stygian said nothing more. "What are your animal instincts telling you?"

The bastard knew exactly what his instincts were telling him, Stygian thought as he glared out at the desert once again.

"When it happens, no matter how much she suspects it, it's going to destroy her," he snapped, enraged at the thought. "She believed she was one person. Her parents, her friends, everyone treated her as though she were Liza Johnson. To definitively learn the truth will destroy her."

"Not if Honor's memories are still there," Dog stated. "If she's having nightmares, then no doubt they are. Someone has simply overlaid Honor's memories with Liza's. They've done just enough to keep her safe and to keep her alive."

"And now the Breeds will destroy that security," Stygian retorted. "What a fine gift to give my mate."

Dog breathed out roughly at the thought. "Too bad Liza's medical records from the lab were destroyed. We know her DNA was changed by the treatments she received there, but we have no idea what it changed to. Have you asked her to have a Core Level DNA test done?"

"That's not the answer," Stygian argued. "As you said, we have no idea how Honor's DNA was changed. It wouldn't prove anything."

"It would prove she's not related to Audi Johnson," Dog reminded him. "Just because she carries his familial scent doesn't mean anything other than the fact that she lived as his daughter, in his home, for so many years. A Core Level test could reveal the truth."

"It would." Stygian agreed. "Unless a genetic wipe was done, which we suspect it was."

"You think her natural father would ever have allowed her genetics to go unprogrammed, Stygian?" Mockery filled the Coyote's voice now. "Who are you fooling, my friend, and why?"

Thank God Liza hadn't asked that question, or seemed to have suspected the truth of Honor's father's love for her. No, her natural father would never have allowed such a thing. Any more than Stygian would allow the Core Level testing for the simple fact that telling her she was Honor Roberts wasn't going to help her. It would only endanger her.

"You bastards and your mating bullshit," Dog retorted irritably. "You'd keep your mates from getting a scratch even if it meant risking stitches in the long run."

"You'll understand when you find your mate," Stygian informed him as the memory of ecstasy clashed with every fear he had for her.

Nothing mattered but taking away all chances of pain, of risk, of anything but that which would bring a smile to her eyes, laughter to her heart.

"I like to think I wouldn't ignore reality," Dog growled.

"My mate will always have to fight. If she's not prepared for that, then she'll have to become prepared. She'll have to face the knowledge that hell awaits her every minute of the day, and I hope I'm man enough—Breed enough—not to forget that just because she's my mate."

"Just because she's your mate, nothing will matter but protecting her from that hell. Nothing will matter but giving the gentleness in her, the compassion in her, a chance to grow. Seeing her fight will destroy you. Knowing she may have to fight will remind you of every weakness and limitation you have. She'll change every rule you live by and every belief you've been certain could never be altered."

"God, just shoot me first." Dog grunted.

To that Stygian had to laugh. "She'll fill your soul with such light, Dog, with such humble certainty that you simply don't deserve the pleasure she brings to you, that suddenly, your creation, the hell of training, all of it, suddenly becomes worth it, because it brought you to this one woman that only death can steal from you. And though her death would mean yours as well, still, it's worth every moment you have to spend with her."

Mating Liza had been the most humbling experience of his life, and given him the most pleasure and happiness he had ever known.

Even amidst the danger and the fight to ensure her safety, Stygian knew there was no other woman, no other life he would face if it meant facing it without her in his bed and in his life.

"Like I said, save me from mating if it's all that," Dog grunted. "I'd rather just go ahead and eat one of my own bullets, I believe."

Stygian was saved from a reply as the communication devices they wore in their ears suddenly activated.

"Be advised. Arrival in progress."

The lack of identities assured him and Dog that it was the Sinclair family that was landing on the helicopter pad on the roof of the hotel.

The Sinclairs were arriving a day earlier than expected.

Stygian's head jerked around to stare at Dog, certain the Breed had drawn him out here to allow Jonas to complete some manipulative little drama he might have in mind. Dog was just as surprised. His eyes widened as well as he slowly straightened from the boulder.

They both shot from their positions at the same time, jumped over the ledge that led to the position they had taken to survey the desert.

Hitting the soft incline with the flat of his boots, arms extended, Stygian went into a sliding crouch as he raced to reach the bottom of the towering stone pillars that jutted up from the desert floor.

They were approximately thirty miles from the hotel once they reached the Dragoon parked at the bottom of the tower.

He was screwed. There wasn't a chance in hell he would reach the hotel before Cassie got to Liza.

"Arrival completed. Justice, Breaker, confirm positions and secured access to base two."

"Confirmed, in position and access to base two secured. Arrival completed and en route."

"Be advised, Team Three, movement along area seven detected."

"Team Three moving out," Loki answered the call.

"Team three confirmed, advise base two when in position and movement sighted."

"I guess Dash still has a ban on Coyotes in the princess's presence," Dog growled in irritation as they hit the base of the rock column they'd taken as a lookout and went at a full run across the short distance to the hidden Dragoon.

Dash Sinclair rarely allowed Coyotes in his daughter's presence because of the distress it placed her in with the visions that bombarded her.

"Control, be advised, Enforcer Black and C dash one en route." He gave Dog's call sign rather than naming him. "I request my mate remain secure until my arrival," Stygian activated the link at his ear as they jumped into the Dragoon. "ETA in twenty."

There was no way the Dragoon was going to gather enough

speed with its weight and weapons array across the rough terrain between their location and the hotel.

"Request noted," Control responded blandly.

"Control, be advised, I request solitary security for my mate until my arrival," he gritted out as the Dragoon shot from the hidden shadows of the shallow cave he'd found to park it within.

The request was a demand. As Liza's mate, he was well within his rights to make it, and to have it heeded.

"Repeat, Enforcer Black," Control came back. "Your signal is deteriorating."

"The fuck it is," he yelled out as the Dragoon jumped a shallow, dry bed, and Dog cursed beside him as he held on to the safety grips hanging from the roll bars above them. "Control, advise the director—"

"Repeat, Enforcer Black," Control cut in over the demand. "Please repeat, your comm-link is fading."

"Jonas, I'll make your mate a fucking widow," Stygian yelled into the link. "You conniving bastard, don't you do it."

He stomped the gas, knowing there was no more speed to be found as the vehicle bounced over the rough terrain, stirring up clouds of dust that nearly obliterated the vision outside.

"You're wasting your fucking breath, Wolf," Dog snarled from beside him. "You know Wyatt and you know that freaky little witch of Sinclair's. Stop wasting your time threatening Wyatt and figure out how you're going to deal with the fallout instead."

"By killing Jonas," Stygian snapped back.

"Yeah, you and the rest of the world," Dog sneered. "Good luck there."

Stygian snarled in fury, tore across a shallow creek bed and fought to right the vehicle as he all but forced it up the sharp, uneven incline.

The Dragoon wasn't meant for the speed or the terrain he was using it against, but he had little choice. He had to get to Liza. He had to get to her before Cassie did, and he knew there wasn't a chance in hell . . .

• ◆ •

Cassie tilted her head to the side and regarded the older woman that stepped into the sitting area of the suite she and her father, Dash, had been shown to, from the connecting bedroom.

Immediately, her gaze went beyond Liza Johnson to the hazy form of a young woman, of approximately the same age, that moved behind her. The form had long blond hair, gray eyes, higher cheekbones and her lips were more lush, but with a slight resemblance to the woman known as Liza Johnson.

The flow of natural, sun-kissed hair was like a halo around the spirit's head, while her gray eyes watched Liza with a mixture of sadness and fear. This was the real Liza Johnson, Cassie sensed. The woman the young girl would have become had she not died in a fiery crash at the bottom of a canyon.

"Liza Johnson," Rule Breaker—God love his heart but she did love his name—stepped forward for the introductions. "Dash Sinclair and his daughter, Cassie."

Liza stopped in the middle of the room, watching them warily, her darker gray eyes moving between the three of them before they settled on her. Cassie sensed the flash of trepidation.

"I see you've already heard about me." Cassie sighed as her gaze moved to the misty form of the young girl now standing close beside Liza.

"It's nice to meet you both." Liza extended her hand to accept the handshake Cassie extended, before taking Dash's proffered hand as well.

Her father was still as handsome as he had been the day he had rescued her and her mother, Cassie thought, but this was one of the rare times that a woman hadn't sighed in appreciation of her father's rough, dangerous good looks.

"A very nice avoidance of my statement." Cassie laughed.

"Don't taunt her, Seer," the spirit chastised her. *"She's facing more than you could understand."*

Spirits chastised her often these days.

"Yes, Ms. Sinclair, I've heard of you." Liza nodded, her gaze darkening, not with fear, but with a flash of resignation instead. "If you're looking for Stygian—"

"No, I'm here to meet you," Cassie assured her before turning to her father. "Dad, I'm sure I'll be fine now," she promised him. "Could Ms. Johnson and I chat for a minute, privately?"

Her father scowled at her.

"You shouldn't be here. You're going to ruin everything. Go away. I'll find you later."

Yes, the spirits had learned to do just that. This one had been calling out to her, though. Cassie had sensed it even before Stygian had requested her presence. She'd sensed this spirit since the moment she had met him, knowing they were somehow tied together.

"I'll be right outside," her father promised her.

The spirit turned to Liza then. *"Tell her to leave. You're tired. You know Stygian will want you to wait for him before talking to this woman."*

A frown creased Liza's brow. "We should wait for Stygian," she said, though her jaw tightened and her gaze flashed in irritation at herself as she heeded the subconscious demand of the spirit at her side.

Cassie tucked her hands into the back of her jeans and watched the woman and the spirit with a heavy heart. "I'm here to help you, Liza." She glanced at the spirit as she spoke before meeting the other woman's gaze once again.

As she spoke, Cassie wasn't surprised to see the dark-haired being that slowly wavered into view on the other woman's left.

It was all she could do to hold back her shocked surprise as the spirit of Honor Roberts appeared, looking as she would have without the plastic surgery that made her look more like Liza Johnson. The alterations to her face weren't drastic. An added fullness to her lips, a rounding of her aristocratic nose, her cheekbones had been sharpened, and her eye color darkened from blue to gray.

The two girls hadn't looked much alike before the alterations, but just enough had been done to bring her closer to

Liza Johnson's facial features, while the differences between Honor and Liza had been explained away as damages that had to be corrected from the wreck.

It was obvious the spirit of the true Liza Johnson was weary. She was tired of lingering in the half state, not alive and yet not dead. While Honor Roberts appeared to be patient, if concerned, with Cassie's presence.

"It isn't time." Honor Roberts shook her head as she watched Cassie worriedly. *"You can't do this right now."*

Oh, how she wanted to question these two, to learn the secrets they hid. To know their thoughts, their fears in that state; one held to the earth through ancient magic, the other kept silent, unable to take her rightful place within the body she was still held to, yet could not share.

"Liza, don't you think it's time we talked?" Cassie asked, holding the other woman's gaze, wishing she could read her as easily as she could hear the two spirits standing to each side of her.

"Ms. Sinclair, I'm certain you're here to help," she said tensely. "But you're not someone I can deal with right now. If I wanted to talk to any ghosts that followed me, then I have six tribal chiefs that would be more than willing to talk to me."

"Oh yeah, right, like they're going to give her any answers." The young blonde beside her rolled her eyes sarcastically. *"Those old geezers won't even take her phone calls when she gets up the nerve to call them."*

"Are you certain they're that willing to help?" Cassie asked as she withdrew her hands from her back pockets and moved to a nearby chair. "Have they been answering the calls you've made to them?"

Liza smiled faintly. "Jonas probably told you he compromised my phone the second he had the chance. He's known all along I was trying to reach the chiefs."

Cassie nodded at that as Liza sat slowly on the couch across from her.

"He didn't mention it actually," she said, her smile commiserating. "But knowing Jonas, I have no doubt he did just that. He's very worried about Amber."

"You could draw that damned Breed a road map and

he'd still ignore the obvious," the dark-haired vision cursed Jonas, as most fully living creatures did as well. *"He wouldn't listen if he could see and hear us, as well. He's like one of those junkyard dogs that just refuse to let something go."*

"Amber's his little girl." The other vision sighed as she berated the darker one. *"He can't let this go, and you know it."*

"Just as you know that he's refusing to see the truth," Honor's spirit stated irritably.

It was all Cassie could do to keep her expression from revealing her complete amazement at these two. It was no wonder the woman they knew as Liza Johnson couldn't navigate her way through the drifting nightmares and fragmented memories to find the place she needed to be.

To remember.

"There is a time and a place, Cassie." Honor's spirit suddenly turned to her, the wavy, hazy figure all but glaring at her as though she had read her thoughts. *"The time has not yet arrived."*

But the place was here? Was that what she meant?

"Ms. Sinclair, did you hear me?" the woman known as Liza questioned her, a hint of her irritation showing in her tone.

Cassie blinked and turned back to her quickly, only now realizing that her attention had been focused on the two spirits tied to the other woman.

"I'm sorry." Shaking her head, she smiled, a bit abashed. "My attention drifted."

"What do you see?" The immediate question was almost a whisper, and one filled with trepidation. "Tell me who you see, Cassie."

"Not yet, Cassie," the true spirit belonging to the woman, Honor, turned to her quickly once more, beseeching, her voice pleading though her expression was filled with demand. *"Chaos hasn't arrived yet. You have to wait."*

"It's not so much what I see, as what I sense." Cassie focused on the other woman with a sigh.

She had learned long ago not to disobey the spirits that came to her when they made such demands. She had no idea the fate that awaited this woman, nor did she know the part the two spirits were to play.

"Then what do you sense?" There was an edge of fear, but her voice was filled with the need to know, to understand what was happening to the life she had once thought she'd known.

Cassie glanced at the wavering figures, their somber faces, the aching fear and uncertainty that shadowed them.

"Cassie, those who did this, those who hid me and gave her the life Liza was unable to live, knew what they were doing, just as they knew what was coming," Honor whispered as the two forms began wavering, dissipating slowly. *"Let me be safe, Cassie. Please, please let me and Stygian be safe."*

If anything happened to the woman known as Liza Johnson, if she died, then Stygian would follow her, Cassie knew. He was an intense Breed, known as a lone wolf, and he had mated this woman. He had given himself to her body and soul. If he lost her, then the Breeds would lose him.

The two slowly eased away, disappearing slowly as the woman known as Liza watched her with curious uncertainty.

"What do you see?" Liza asked again softly, almost too softly to hear, as though she were frightened of what was coming.

Cassie sighed wearily. "I didn't come here to see anything, Liza. Stygian is one of my dearest friends, as are Jonas and Rachel. I've been worried about all of you and wanted to make certain there was nothing I could do to help."

Why was she here?

Cassie wanted to rage, to scream. The spirits she had seen today were not the ones that needed her the most. Yet, the moment she had met Stygian, she had felt these two tied to him.

Was there another?

She looked around the room, opening her senses, calling out to any other that could be lurking, frightened to reveal themselves.

But there was nothing there.

There was no other spirit lurking in the room, no areas in the small sitting room that seemed blurred, or wavering. There was no hint of paranormal presence, and yet Cassie could still feel that cry, the one that resonated within her senses the moment Jonas had called with Stygian's request. "If there was anything you could do to help, then only Stygian is aware of it." Liza sighed as she pulled her long hair over a bared shoulder and sat back against the couch.

The sleeveless cotton top and jeans the other woman wore looked cool and comfortable, but Liza was anything but comfortable at the moment. She was off balance, and she felt that way because of Cassie's presence.

"If there's nothing I can do, then I'll go see Rachel and Jonas." Standing to her feet, Cassie looked around the room once more, searching, wondering where the presence that had called out to her was hidden.

Liza rose as well, her expression drawn, the tension that was tearing her apart inside evident in the set of her face and the shadows in her eyes.

"If you need me, Liza, I am really good at keeping secrets," Cassie promised her sincerely. "I can be a very good friend."

"I've heard that about you as well." The small smile Liza gave her was one that assured Cassie that the other woman at least believed her, even if she wasn't willing to take her up on the offer.

"Ask Stygian to call me later then?" Cassie asked as she headed for the door.

"Are you going to tell him something you didn't tell me?" Liza stopped her with the question.

Turning back, Cassie couldn't help but smile. "If I did, Liza, he's your mate, and I know Stygian well enough to know that he would tell you anything I might tell him."

Relief scented the air as Liza nodded, some of the tension easing out of her as Cassie left the room.

Now what? she thought as her father met her outside the door. Why the hell did it seem so important that she be here?

❖   ❖   ❖

As the elevator stopped on the fifth floor and the doors slid open smoothly, Stygian was immediately aware of the additional security forces along the floor.

Dash had been slowly amassing his own pack to ensure the protection of his family. Cassie was one of the most valuable members of the Breed community, simply because of their love for her.

As a child, she had managed to pull Sanctuary as well as Haven together and created bonds that had become unbreakable as she matured.

She had been the only hybrid Wolf Breed child for many years, and was accepted as the Feline Prides' adopted child due to the months Dash and Elizabeth Sinclair had been forced to leave her in their care.

As a young adult and the only Breed who seemed to have the ability to effectively argue Breed law without revealing the secrets it hid and protected, she had become even more important.

Nodding to the additional Wolf Breeds who lined the hall leading to Jonas's suite, Stygian made his way to the entrance, stepping inside as the probationary enforcer opened the door for him.

"Stygian!" The happy cry sang from Cassie's voice as she jumped from her chair, her long black hair flying around her too delicate form as she raced across the room.

Dressed in jeans, white sneakers, and a white T-shirt claiming BREEDS RULE, in black, she looked more like a kid than a young woman rapidly approaching her twenty-first birthday.

She stopped inches from him, her blue eyes twinkling teasingly as she stared up him.

"You dog," she accused him with a grin. "You went and mated and now I can't even give you a hug. Tell me you're totally happy and I'll forgive you."

Stygian couldn't help but laugh. Cassie had a way about her that simply invited laughter.

"Come here, imp." Despite the vague irritation that came with holding a woman other than his mate after mating, he still gathered Cassie's slight form into his arms as she threw hers around his neck. "Trust me, I'm totally happy in my mate. Now, how have you been, sweetheart?"

No one who knew the fragile young woman could dislike her. She was filled with charm and compassion, and despite the ever-present shadows in her eyes, she spread happiness wherever she went.

"I've been completely bored now that Styx has mated," she told him as she stepped back with a little pout. "Who am I supposed to cause trouble with now?"

Stygian grinned back at her. Styx Mackenzie, the red-haired Scot Breed, had been her partner in crime for all her hijinks until he had mated the year before.

"I'm sure Breeds are standing in line to help you cause trouble." He chuckled before turning to her father and clasping the hand held out to him. "Dash, good to see you."

The man was black-haired, blue-eyed, standing over six feet tall and still in his prime despite the fact that he was now in his forties.

Mating, as with all Breeds, seemed to have frozen him into the age he had been when he mated the human Elizabeth Colder.

Just as it had delayed her aging as well.

"Elizabeth, you're as beautiful as ever," Stygian swore as he passed the back of his hand over the silk of her hair where it flowed to her right shoulder.

The greeting seemed to come about naturally over the years. Female mates were incredibly sensitive to any male's touch other than their mate's. The mere act of shaking hands was mildly painful if a female was in mating heat, and something no Breed would inflict on any other's mate.

After the first phase of mating, the heat came in cycles rather like a female's menstrual cycle. There were times, though, that the heat itself wasn't detectable after mates had been together six months or longer.

But friends and family had developed a habit of, rather

than touching, the males passing the backs of their fingers along the right side of the female's head in a gesture of affection, just in case mating heat had flared again.

"You're as handsome as ever, Stygian." She grinned before stepping back to her mate's side. "It's good to see you again."

"And I've already met your mate," Cassie told him as he turned his attention back to her. "I'm surprised you asked me to come, though. I think even you sense that there are no answers to be found right now. And once they are revealed, I don't think it's something you—or Liza—are ready to know."

That knowledge was out there now.

Stygian stared back at her, silent, wondering why she had made the statement and why she would put that between himself and Jonas.

"I wanted her to have the chance to come to that knowledge herself," he told her, reminding himself that he should have remembered that Cassie rarely practiced tact when she was around those she loved. And she did dearly love Jonas Wyatt—poor kid. "Those memories won't be easy for her to accept. But I'm smart enough to know the danger she's facing, Cassie. I won't risk her because I might not be ready to know whatever the truth may be."

Cassie didn't say anything; she just stared beyond him, her blue eyes glowing neon now.

How she did what she did, no one knew for certain. What she actually saw, heard or felt, no one could detect. Unlike most Breeds and humans, there wasn't a Breed yet that could sense anything Cassie was feeling.

Cassie saw the form that wavered into her view. She almost flinched. Every part of her soul filled with pain, filled with an agony she couldn't understand.

Chills raced over her flesh—hot and then cold, as Cassie felt herself weakened at the sight of the spirit that slowly materialized beside Stygian.

This wasn't Honor. It wasn't Liza.

Who was she? What did she want and who did she belong to?

The spirit was slowly shaking her head, her hands clasped in front of her, her caramel-colored hair flowing over her face as her brown eyes stared back at Cassie pleadingly.

Who was she?

"Please. He'll hear, no matter where you are, no matter where you speak, he'll know. Please don't betray me, Cassie. Please don't let him kill me."

Oh God, who was she?

Why was this woman's pain driving inside her skull like steel spikes? Why was her fear like a blanket, heavy and hot, making it hard to breathe, to focus on the information she could have sensed from the spirit facing her.

"Cassie?" She was silent for so long, the tension in the room growing so heavy, he couldn't resist the need to remind her they all needed answers.

Her lips quirked with an edge of bitter amusement. "I don't always have the answers," she stated softly, turning to him as if focusing her attention had become a task.

He barely restrained his surprise, knowing from the quiet near whisper of her voice that the message was meant for him alone.

What the hell was going on? What was the message in her neon eyes, the plea he could sense there? Raking her fingers through her hair restlessly, she turned away from him, the shadows in her eyes seemed to darken.

"I think I need to rest for a while," she stated then, her voice quiet as she turned to her parents. "I'd like to go to my room now."

"You can walk down with your mother and me," Dash stated before turning to Jonas. "We'll talk later."

"Just let me know when," Jonas agreed as the Wolf Breeds accompanying them led the way from the suite.

Stygian watched Cassie with narrowed eyes, knowing— just as he was certain the rest of them did—that she was escaping. Whatever she had sensed, or even seen, she wasn't ready to reveal yet.

"There are days I have a tendency to forget how exasperating that child can be," Jonas stated as the door closed behind Cassie and her parents.

They all had that tendency, though Stygian had rarely sensed her pain, or that feeling of a silent message, as he did now.

Stygian knew who Liza was. At least, he was pretty certain she was Honor Roberts rather than Fawn Corrigan. He knew for a fact she had not been born Liza Johnson. Honor Roberts for all intents and purposes was dead. She had died in the desert twelve years before, the night Liza Johnson and Claire Martinez had gone over that canyon in a sports car that didn't belong to them.

Honor Roberts had died in Liza's place. Or at least, her spirit had. Because there wasn't a doubt in Stygian's mind that Liza had always believed to the bottom of her soul that she was Audi and Jane Johnson's daughter.

And, Stygian knew, her father knew the truth.

Audi Johnson knew Liza wasn't his daughter, though Stygian couldn't be certain what Ray Martinez believed.

If Ray Martinez knew or suspected, then Stygian intended to pay the man a visit and advise him on how to treat his daughter with respect rather than resentment.

"Before you head back to your room, we need to go over a few security revisions I want to make." Jonas raked his fingers wearily through his hair as he moved to the conference table that had been set up and spread out with not just hand-drawn maps and notes but also several electronic data pads.

"Have you heard from Dog on the movement he's tracking in the desert?" Stygian asked as they headed to the table. "He headed back out to meet up with his men."

"Control advised he was in place and tracking it, but he hasn't sighted anything yet." Handing Stygian a data pad, he picked up his own. "Here are the changes I'm considering—"

Stygian listened, but he watched the director as much as he did the plans that had been drawn up.

Jonas rarely showed the physical signs of weariness or worry, and he hadn't aged a day since his mating, but worry creased his forehead now and there were shadows in those mercury eyes that hadn't been there before.

Amber was getting worse.

And the knowledge of that was taking all choice from Stygian's hands.

Something would have to be done soon.

◆   ◆   ◆

Dog moved into place, watching the four Coyote Breeds waiting in the overhang of the canyon's cliff.

Moving confidently, Mongrel and Mutt flanking him, he moved along the canyon wall before stepping into the cave-like overhang.

The four Breeds looked up, their hard faces sharply hewn, their eyes cold, hard.

"Satellites tracked your asses," he growled at the men, irritation lacing his voice. "I told you to watch your fucking asses.

The commander snorted at the information. "Yeah, we knew that. Let them go on guard for a while, it will make them more vulnerable when we move in."

Thane could be a bastard, and he was one of the few Breeds that Dog would hate to go up against. He was also one of the few Breeds he would trust his life with. The three Coyotes that followed Thane were of the same ilk, though their personalities varied. All four were hard, cold, almost dead inside though. And nothing or no one mattered more than preserving the Breed communities.

No matter the cost to themselves.

Dog eyed the other Breed for long moments as Loki, Mutt and Mongrel shifted behind him.

Thane was as tall as he was, at six four, powerfully muscular and without fear, he was a deadly enemy. His coloring was different from most Breeds. Rather than the blond to light brown hair, his was pitch black, his eyes blue, the Irish heritage from his mother clearly apparent.

"You still carrying a grudge?" Dog asked, knowing Thane hadn't been happy at the loss of one of his men in an operation against a hidden start-up lab in the Middle East that had been holding abducted Breeds.

"The bastard was a death wish walking," Thane admitted. "There's no grudge to hold."

Nodding, Dog moved to the gas fire ring and poured a cup of coffee into one of the extra metal mugs sitting next to it.

"We need to move soon," Dog told them. "The Sinclair girl's arrived, and only God knows what she might sense or reveal. Stay out of sight of those fucking satellites so we can at least blame it on the bastards in the North. That way Jonas won't send a team your way when you make your move."

"We know what we're doing," Thane stated.

"Maybe I'm just reminding you," Dog mocked. "You have a problem with that?"

He wasn't about to treat the Breed commander any differently than he would any other, even if he did often respect him more.

Thane quirked his lips in hard amusement.

"Don't have a problem with that, Dog," he drawled. "I was just reminding you as well."

Like he needed reminders of any sort.

"Move into position tomorrow," he told them, his gaze moving over each man. "Wait for my signal."

"You think you can maneuver them that easy?" Thane asked as the others watched curiously.

"I can maneuver anything or anyone," Dog informed him confidently.

He knew his limits, but his abilities to be just as calculating and merciless as Jonas Wyatt were in doubt. "The four of you just make sure you're in place. I don't want to risk our agenda and I sure as hell don't want to risk our plans here. There's too much riding on it."

"What do you have riding on it? Maybe it's time you let us know what the hell is going on here, Dog," one of the younger Coyotes in Thane's group sneered mockingly. Dog didn't have time to challenge him, but he couldn't let it go either. In a dominant, powerful move, Thane was suddenly on his feet and throwing the younger Breed against the rock wall of the cave as the knife he carried at his thigh was pressing into the other Breed's jugular. "Need to know," Thane rasped, his scarred lips pulling back into a demonic snarl as a growl rumbled in his chest. "If you needed to know, then I would have told you." There was no fear in the other Breed's eyes, only the knowledge that he had pushed too far.

"There are boundaries, boy," Thane told him, his voice brutal as he glared into the younger Breed's eyes. "Step over the line again, and you won't have another chance."

"Understood." The other Breed didn't lower his gaze, he didn't look away. He didn't show submission; what he showed, though, was agreement. That was all Thane needed.

Stepping back, he released the other Breed and moved back to the position he had taken before the low fire and lifted his coffee cup to sip at it as though nothing had happened.

"Then we're all on the same page here?" Dog looked around at each man, their nods assuring him everything and everyone was in place and knew their places.

Finishing his coffee, he set the cup back in place before sauntering to the opening of the overhang.

"Be in place on time or you lose half of your commission," he informed them all without turning back. "And stay out of sight of those fucking satellites."

"Dog."

It was Thane who had him pausing and glancing back.

"What are you going to do when Jonas learns the game you're playing here?"

Dog's brow arched. "He's never going to know."

CHAPTER 23

"I want out of this suite, and tonight."

Liza was waiting in the sitting room when Stygian walked into the suite.

Dressed in jeans, low-heeled western boots and a white cotton camisole top, she looked like a wet dream come to life.

Denim encased her legs and ass like a lover's hand, making him simply jealous as hell at the thought of another man thinking all the nasty thoughts that were rolling through his mind.

The long, heavy strands of dark blond hair were pulled up from the sides of her face and secured at the top of her head then left to tumble down her back.

The camisole smoothed over her breasts before disappearing into the band of the extremely low-rise jeans, which were secured with a wide belt. That belt and the cotton of the camisole tucked into her jeans, he swore, were the only things covering the upper curves of her pussy.

"It's not safe—"

"What isn't safe is keeping me locked in this room one more night," she warned him, the scent of not just her irritation, but also the edge of panic she was barely holding on to, reaching his senses.

Why panic? What had happened to leave her feeling the desperate fear she was fighting to keep such a hold on?

"We have signs of two different teams in the desert watching this hotel. Tell me you're certain they're not watching for you and Claire and I'll take you wherever you want to go."

He crossed his arms over his chest and stared back at her, wondering if he could dare take her where other men could see her, watch her, perhaps attempt to touch her without the animal inside him going completely berserk.

As it was now at just the thought of such a thing happening.

"Fine, I'm certain they're not watching for us," she said with a shrug of bravado and an air of superiority. "Now, I want out of this room."

He would have been amused if it weren't for the fact that he could feel his primal instincts pacing furiously at just the thought of any other male touching her, coming on to her, or in any way threatening his tenuous hold on her emotions.

And he was very well aware of the fact that his hold on those emotions was tenuous.

Fuck!

Was he refusing to allow her out because of the danger, or because of his jealousy and fear of losing her?

There wasn't a single female Breed mate that wasn't constantly in danger, yet they weren't locked in their respective communities on a permanent basis. Hell, some of them didn't even live within the Breed communities, and so far, their protection even during times of danger had been effective.

There were ways of ensuring their freedom as well as their security, and Stygian knew it.

"Why? You haven't been here long enough to have contracted cabin fever, so why is it so imperative that you get out tonight?"

"Because I've finally had enough." Her chin lifted, eyes narrowed. "Enough, Stygian. Now get me the hell out of here."

Yeah, she'd had enough. The scent of her determination

to get out of the hotel was so heavy in the room that Stygian could sense nothing else coming from her.

He nodded slowly. "It will take a few hours to arrange everything."

"Claire and Chelsea are going as well," she informed him. "So while you're picking out bodyguards, pick out theirs."

He would have grinned if it weren't for the fact that his dick was driving a spike of agonizing hunger raging through him.

She was hot as hell when she got all stubborn like that. She made him want to cover her and show all the ways he could definitely control all that feminine aggression roiling through her.

Liza watched the flare of arousal, brighter, hotter than she'd seen it before as it flared in his gaze. Giving in to him was a desire that wasn't easy to push back. It tugged at her with regret and pricked at the determination racing through her.

She couldn't stay in this room any longer.

She couldn't stare in that mirror another second and see the girl she had been, the fear she had known, the desperation that had been so much a part of her that summer.

Remembering was a bitch, and the memories weren't comforting ones.

They were filled with fear and the stark reality of everything that had been taken away from so many.

Each time she stared into that mirror, she saw the results of the plastic surgery that had been done. A bit here, a bit there, a tilt of the eyes, a difference in her cheekbones. Just enough to make her look enough like Liza Johnson—

Just enough to make Fawn resemble Claire.

And she remembered that ritual, the words spoken, the scent of the herbs, the cadence of the chants and the feel of the dew from the sweat lodge as it rained down upon her.

And that moment—that heartrending second—when Honor Roberts had slept, and who Liza Johnson had been had slipped inside her.

It had begun slowly, moments after Cassie Sinclair had

left the room. A fragment here. A fragment there. Nothing solid or concrete yet, but enough—

The loss of who she had been had saved her.

The death of two young women, buried with the utmost ceremony, and in the utmost secrecy, had allowed her and Fawn to live in peace—for a while at least.

Tonight, she wanted to dance them out of her mind, drink them from her consciousness and deal with them tomorrow.

Not tonight.

Besides, she also needed to discuss a few things with Claire.

Did the other woman remember as well?

Was that the reason for the fear each time Liza had nearly given herself away?

"Liza?" She nearly flinched as he moved to her, his tone deep, rasping as the backs of his fingers grazed her cheek. "Where did you go, baby?"

Swiping her tongue over her lips nervously, she gave a quick shake of her head. "I'm right here, Stygian. I'm just hoping you'll take me somewhere. I have yet to leave this damned room and I can't handle it any longer."

Thoughtful, with a gleam of disbelief and skepticism, he stared down at her before nodding slowly.

"Let's see if we can get you out of here for a few hours then," he said, sending a flare of anticipation racing through her.

"Thank you." Relief raced through her.

"I'll go arrange things with security so the others can go as well," he told her as he moved away from her, taking the sense of warmth that wrapped around her whenever he was near.

Turning, she moved to the windows and gazed at the darkness surrounding the hotel.

Rubbing at her upper arms to dispel the chill racing up them, she eased back from the window, suddenly wishing Stygian were still there.

The windows were bullet and laser resistant, the room itself highly secured.

Yet Gideon Cross had managed to bug Jonas Wyatt's room, which she was certain was even more secure.

There was something not quite right, though, something out of place, out of sync.

Tilting her head, she stared out into the darkness, wondering what was missing, or what was added.

Something wasn't right—

As the thought raced through her mind, a blinding flare of light suddenly flashed through the room. The resulting explosion seemed to rock the entire hotel.

Liza went to the floor, rolling, instinct and her photographic memory of the location of each piece of furniture flashing through her mind as she scrambled behind the sofa.

Shards of glass scattered around her as though World War III had erupted in the Navajo Suites. Flashing a brilliant red and yellow, the emergency lights sent a kaleidoscope of color racing through the room as Liza came to a crouch and quickly peeked around the couch.

Three dark-clad, masked figures were moving through the room. Two to the bedroom, while one began tossing furniture aside, throwing it out of his way. The electronic black shield covering his face gave him an automaton look, while the scrolling red ribbon of the auto-detection technology glinted at the top of the shield.

Shit!

Flipping behind the furniture before his head turned her way, Liza drew in a hard breath. She had only seconds to find a place to hide, or to reach the door.

The inner security lock had engaged when Stygian went out. It would take precious time to slide it aside—time she didn't have.

Hurriedly moving to the opposite side of the couch, Liza dived behind the heavy chair that had already been thrown aside within a heartbeat of the couch bouncing against it.

The opened door to the connecting suite was just ahead of her, two figures racing from the room.

"She's not there," one rasped.

"She's here. We tracked her before the window went in.

Find her, damn it. There wasn't enough time to get through the door."

"Bright fucking idea blowing the lights," another snapped.

The other didn't speak.

Where was he?

Liza stared around her, heart racing, terrified to make the move to sprint for the connecting door and the exit leading into the hallway.

With her hands planted against the floor, her body ready to vault across the distance, she considered her chances—

The chair went flying.

Screaming out Stygian's name, Liza sprinted for the connecting door as hard hands gripped her arm and a growl echoed through her senses.

Turning in the grip and kicking her leg out to connect with her assailant's knee, she was gripped with rage. The heavy padding over the vulnerable area minimized the force of the blow, bringing no more than a guttural grunt as his grip tightened.

As he brought his other arm up to grab her neck, his fingers only brushed her flesh before she knocked them away, twisted again and dropped, screaming at the wrench in her arm a second before he released her.

Her foot slammed into his shin.

Padded.

Throttled rage escaped her at the triumphant laugh that echoed around her as another suddenly grabbed her other arm and within seconds she found her arms twisted behind her.

"Hurry, damn it, we don't have all day." The order was harsh, a sudden, ear-splitting automated shriek began blaring through the halls outside.

Throwing all her weight against the grip the two men had on her, Liza kicked both her feet out, connecting with the third's chest and sending him stumbling back as the other two lost their grip on her.

Crashing to the floor, she ignored the bite of pain that drove into her flesh through the denim of her jeans and her undefended hands as she hit the shards of glass below.

Kicking out again, she tripped another while grabbing the heavy base of a lamp that had fallen from the table next to her. Swinging out, she let a satisfied snarl leave her lips as it connected with the face shield of the assailant who had been giving the orders. The crack of the sensitive shield sent a thrill of pleasure racing through her mind as she ducked from the other before twisting around, gripping the shield and tearing it from his face.

Let them join her in the fucking dark.

"Fuck. Get that little hellion. She just tore off my shield!"

"We have Breeds in the hall! We have Breeds in the hall!" another yelled.

"Move out!"

Liza twisted around in time to see three dark figures jump from the shattered window, arms outspread. A breath later, three shadows seemed to streak through the air as flares of light erupted outside.

The door to the suite exploded inward and in a blinding, horrified flash, Liza watched as a dozen Breeds rushed the room.

It had happened before . . .

◆   ◆   ◆

Soldiers had rushed the room, forcing Honor, Fawn and Judd to begin firing. They couldn't use caution not to kill.

They had to kill or be killed.

Rushing into the night, a vehicle screaming to a stop as the door was thrown open and Judd rushed them into it.

The rest was a flicker of a memory. The race through the desert, the Navajo warriors who were trying to explain their plan.

Two girls were dying an hour away from a crash into a canyon. The daughters of two highly trusted members of the Navajo Nation. No one would ever question their identity. No one would know who they were, or what had happened if the ritual worked.

A ritual that would cause Honor and Fawn's spirits to sleep while the knowledge, partial memories, and the identity of the other girls became theirs instead.

Not their spirits. There was no magic that could hold their spirits, and those who loved them would never countenance it. But memories, knowledge—that was different.

But they had to hurry.

Time slowed.

Candles flickered as she and Fawn were drawn inside the rough sweat lodge. Six Navajo medicine men were seated in a semi-circle around the glowing fire.

On one side of the burning embers, lying on two beds of folded blankets, were two young girls, so broken, so close to death that she felt agony tearing through her.

These were the girls whose places they would take.

The explanations had been made hastily an hour before as they raced through the desert with Terran Martinez, the son of one of the spiritual elders now sitting across from her.

The two girls had crashed into a canyon hours before. Their spirits had been taken, they'd been told, having already moved beyond life, but a part of them remained. Enough that an ancient ritual could be performed before the bodies took their last breath.

That ritual would give Honor and Fawn the lives that had been taken in a remote canyon when the girls' car had exploded and thrown them free.

Too much speed, the confidence of youth and inexperience behind the wheel had resulted in the crash.

Fate, Terran had whispered, his niece and her best friend had met fate, and provided Honor and Fawn the means of escape.

Orrin Martinez waved his hand to the two makeshift beds that lay beside each girl. "Take your place," his voice rasped through the hastily erected sweat lodge. "The sand is falling through the glass of life, and time is running low."

Honor lay down, her heart racing, her throat tightened, as the blond man she'd been told was Audi Johnson and his wife, Jane, took their seats on the other side of the fire.

One of the medicine men whispered something; a second later, Audi and Jane reached out and dropped what appeared to be a handful of dried plants on the burning embers and rocks in the center of the shelter.

Sparks flew up, showering the air with pinpoints of red as the acrid then sweet smell that suddenly filled the air swept through her senses.

"Do you know, young children, the decision you have made this night?"

It was a scene from the oldest western movie they had ever watched. Not that they had ever been allowed to watch much television where they had spent most of their lives.

But she knew, as her eyes met Fawn's, that this was the only decision they could make.

The steam that rose from the center pit, the hiss of water trickling upon the red-hot stones and the acrid scent of the pungent dried herbs that wafted thick and heavy in the air, all added to the sense of disbelief that swirled through her head.

"I know the decision I've made," she answered, though her voice cracked with fear, and with tears.

Wizened, his lined face and deep, dark gaze reflecting his sympathy, the chief of the Six Tribes nodded slowly.

She turned her head to watch her friend. As always, stoicism defined her. Staring at the ceiling above, her gaze resigned, her expression still. It was more than courage that filled her. There was no fear, no panic—nothing but that resignation that tore at her heart.

Fawn had known no peace, no lack of pain, both physical or emotional, for nearly the whole of her life.

Even here, amidst these whose only concern was that of her safety and her comfort, she knew no peace.

But then, neither of them ever had, not really. The reasons for it had merely been different, the years of being so ill, of knowing such pain, were now too much a part of them.

"Know you, that when it is over, strength will be yours. There will be no fears, no nightmares to combat. You will be the child you have whispered to the Almighty that you wish to be," he whispered to Fawn, his expression so gentle, so filled with tenderness that even she felt a part of her calm at the sound of it.

Watching Fawn, she saw the shame that filled her friend.

The fear she always felt shamed her, made her feel weak. She wouldn't listen when they tried to tell her it only made her stronger.

"Ah child, such heart and compassion you hold within your small body," the chief seemed to understand each of those fears, to the point that as Fawn finally turned her head and stared into his dark gaze, her lips had trembled and Honor had watched her eyes fill with such hope.

The sense of pure peace and certainty that filled her expression left Honor suddenly thankful that Judd had convinced them to take this only path they could find to safety.

"Child." He turned to her then, holding out his other hand to her.

She wasn't afraid.

She had faced her fears and knew the monsters that lurked in the dark. The unknown wasn't nearly as terrifying as all the terrors her past held.

"See you these four?" She followed as Orrin reached out a hand and gestured to the warriors, their faces streaked with war paint, their dark eyes flinty in the light of the burning embers of the fire. "They will guide you on your journey. You know not their faces, but their strength will ease your way and help you keep the secrets you have hidden for so very long."

She nodded. It wasn't the pain she would ever fear. She had known pain. Pain that seared her insides and wrapped around her mind until she prayed to God to die.

No, pain was the least of her fears, because she had learned how to conquer it.

"There will be no fear, there will be no pain," he promised Fawn then, grief tearing at his voice. Fawn was trembling and a single tear slid from the corner of her eyes. "It will be just peace."

A trembling smile, one of hope, quivered about her lips.

"It is time then." Orrin sat back, his head lifting, his palms turned up as a low chant began to fill the lodge.

Honor eased her hand to Fawn's and gripped it, knowing how alone her friend often felt since they had lost Gideon.

How frightened she felt now, knowing that even though they wouldn't remember him, they were also losing Judd as well.

"I won't see him again," Fawn whispered. "I won't know him."

She knew who Fawn spoke of and breathed out softly.

From what Judd had said, Gideon would kill them all now if he could.

"It's for the best. It will keep you safe. He'll kill you if he can."

The younger girl's breathing hitched as she fought to hold back a sob. "He wouldn't kill me, Honor. I know he wouldn't."

"Child." Orrin Martinez gripped her hand, drawing her from Fawn's tear-filled gaze. "Neither destiny, fate, nor the battle you are to fight on this earth can be avoided. It can only be delayed. To each of you—" He drew back as the chanting began once again. "To each of you, a protector will be sent. When it is time, when the memories must surface to guide the battle you must fight, your protector shall appear. One in the form of chaos, and one—" He looked to Fawn with gentle eyes. "One, my dear, in the form of death."

A brilliant arc of light filled the room at Fawn's throttled cry of fear, and another herb was tossed on the burning fire, the wicked red stones that the water hissed upon sending a rush of steam to fill the sweat lodge as the chanting increased.

Light flared. The winds roared outside. There were cries, both startled and filled with anger, from outside the lodge. She swore she heard gunfire—

Honor turned her gaze from Fawn's and stared up at the crisscross of wood that made up the low ceiling and watched as the droplets of steam seemed to come to the point of the ceiling before feathering down, landing on her face, her arms, her legs.

Whatever upheaval gathered outside, inside she was safe.

She would have thought it would be hot in the lodge, but it was cool. Moisture washed over her overheated flesh and soothed it, then seemed to fill her lungs with a slightly sweet, slightly bitter taste.

With each swallow, the taste of the moisture comforted her, sent lethargy stealing through her and for the first time in as long as she could remember, she didn't wonder what tomorrow would bring.

She knew what it would bring.

They had explained it to her.

They had told her how the nothingness would be a comfort. How the years of pain and sorrow would slowly ease and who and what she had been would be but memories for others.

Who and what she had been would be no more until chaos filled the night.

Tonight, Honor Roberts and Fawn Corrigan would die.

The six chiefs of the People, the old men who came together from more than one tribe of Native Americans, to help them, to save them, filled Fawn with awe.

It wasn't awe Honor felt, though. It was gratitude.

Finally, the fight to live, to survive, was a fight others could struggle through. Perhaps now, she and Fawn would have the chance to just live.

At least, for a little while.

♦   ♦   ♦

What had taken hours to actually happen flashed through her senses in a matter of minutes. It was there, like a cascade of frightening images clicking into place, pulling in those odd, half-formed memories that had tormented her over the years and rebuilding her from the soul out.

But as it did, a sense of overwhelming pain shuddered through her.

She was Honor Roberts—without family, without a past, a heritage or a true place in the world.

"Chaos," she whispered as she stared back at Stygian where he crouched in front of her. "A night of chaos, Stygian."

Concern and a hint of gathering strength flashed in his eyes.

She knew what he was doing—he knew what had happened in those few flashing moments that she had only stared up at them, neither hearing nor seeing whatever was happening around her.

"Stygian—"

His fingers pressed against her lips to shush her. "Let's get you out of here, get those cuts bandaged." Lifting her into his arms, Stygian had every intention of getting her the hell out of there before Jonas arrived and caught the scent Stygian had the moment he approached Liza.

The scent of knowledge.

It was the scent of resignation, truth and the awareness that Liza's scent had drastically changed. Changed more than mating heat could ever be responsible for.

As though a stopper had been pulled free, allowing some physical part of her loose, as well as the subconscious, her entire scent had suddenly changed, and Stygian knew why.

She wasn't hiding any longer.

Whatever had happened, however she had managed to avoid the three forms that had been seen flying into the room, it had done more than cause a few scratches on her knees, palms and cheek.

It had done far more.

"Stygian," Jonas was moving into the room, his tone dark and demanding

Too fucking late.

Staring down at his mate, he saw the knowledge in her gaze that the reckoning was here.

"Later, Jonas!" Striding into their bedroom, he placed her on their bed, turning and meeting Jonas before he could push his way into the room.

"Later," he repeated, stepping past the threshold and holding the door open only inches to ensure he heard if Liza were in danger again.

God, he wouldn't be able to leave her alone for a second for years—for a lifetime.

Terror was still tearing through him, cramping his guts and burning through his mind.

The knowledge that the attack on the hotel was designed

to take his mate had come the moment the signal to his security had vibrated in the watch he wore.

The explosion of the windows had set off the alarm and given him the precious seconds he needed to turn from the elevator and race back to her.

If he had actually been faster and caught the doors before they closed on the cubicle, then he would have been too far away from her.

If the Breeds heading down to the bar had been seconds slower and hadn't been in such a hurry, then it would have been all over and his mate would have been gone.

"I need to know what happened, Stygian," Jonas growled, his gaze narrowed, his nostrils flaring as though to pick up her scent. "And she'll need to be debriefed."

"I fucking said later." The animal snarl slurred his words, the primal, predatory sound jerking the attention of every Breed that had converged in the room to them.

Stygian could feel their eyes on him, their hackles raising and their animals preparing for battle.

Eerie silver eyes flashed in a suddenly stony face.

"You take me for a fool," Jonas growled, though his tone was pitched so low Stygian had to strain to hear him.

"I take you for a Breed that has no idea when to step back and keep your machinations to yourself," Stygian snapped back. "You will back off. This is my mate they nearly disappeared with, and I'll be damned if you'll take her from me before I know she's unharmed."

Stepping back, Stygian didn't give the other man a chance to comment or to argue before closing the heavily reinforced door in his face and locking it.

The sound of the metal bars inside the steel door snapping into place could be heard even in the other room. The implications of what he had done weren't lost on him.

He could have made Jonas an enemy for life.

His mate's safety, both physical and emotional, was far more important.

"Liza." Moving to where she had sat up on the bed, her gaze on the floor, Stygian knelt before her, one hand tucking beneath her chin to lift her gaze to his. "Are you okay, baby?"

She shook her head slowly, the tears contained in her eyes slowly falling.

"What's wrong, baby?" Cupping her cheek, he felt fear tear through him. "Tell me where it hurts."

She swallowed tightly, a whimper leaving her lips as more tears fell.

"Come on, Liza, tell me what's wrong." Keeping his voice low, he had to fight back a howl of pure rage at the pain he felt radiating through her.

It wasn't physical pain.

There were no broken bones, no internal injuries, he would know if there were—the scent of them would have hit him within the first second of rushing back into their room.

Her lips trembled more as she parted them.

"Liza's dead."

His heart seemed to still in his chest as a sob tore from her.

As she clapped her hand over her lips, he watched as she fought for control, won it, then swallowed again against the pain building in her soul.

"No, sweetheart." He shook his head.

"She's dead," she whispered again, wrapping her arms across her stomach and bending over, her head touching his shoulder as instinct had him wrapping his arms around her. "Oh God, Stygian. She's dead. She died twelve years ago and now—" A shudder raced through her. "And now, they'll find me, and she'll die again."

Resignation filled her pain-threaded voice, trembled with it and sliced against the emotions he realized she alone was responsible for awakening.

"Look at me. Look at me, mate." Hardening his voice, he forced her to lift her head and stare back at him once again. "You brought me to life. You showed me all I have to live for, do you imagine for a second, for even a heartbeat that I would allow anyone to take you from me now?"

"You know who I am," she whispered, her voice so low

he was reading her lips more than hearing her. "You know. They knew—" Her eyes flashed with terror. "I can't hide anymore. If I can't hide, they'll find me."

"Who will find you? Tell me who will find you?" What enemies did she fear that she could ever imagine he wouldn't destroy?

Her hand reached out, fragile fingers shaking as she laid them against his cheek. "The Genetics Council," she whispered. "You know who, and you know why."

"Why?"

"I have a photographic memory, Stygian. I have had it since birth, and the serum I was given only increased its power. That's why I had to die. That's why when Liza Johnson died, I was given her life. I know their weaknesses and they'll never allow me to live now."

The animal inside him rose, stretched and smiled in anticipation.

"Oh, baby, I promise you, they won't touch you. Not now, not ever."

She shook her head. "You can't stop them."

"I can't, but sweetheart, trust me, you can." He knew she could and he knew exactly how she would do it.

"How? How, Stygian, can I stop them? I couldn't even escape them." She was shaking in his arms and he hated it.

He hated her pain.

He hated the bottled rage.

And God help him, he hated the part he had played in it.

CHAPTER 24

The terror chasing inside her was killing him, it was killing her, and he wouldn't allow it.

"The same way Callan stopped them," he promised her, his hands cupping her face, drawing her lips to his for a precious, though far too short kiss. "The same way, Honor. But instead of telling the world, you'll tell the Breed Cabinet. Who you are. The experiments and the secrets the Council is so desperate to hide. You'll tell them all of it. And you'll weaken them as they've never been weakened before."

She shook her head again, slowly, the terror only growing in her eyes. "It's not that easy."

"It will be—"

"You don't understand," she cried out, her agony searing his senses. "It's not just me. I don't have all the information. We were a team, Stygian. Me, Fawn, Judd and Gideon. We were a team and you only have me. Fawn won't remember until she dies," she sobbed as Stygian felt his soul freeze, felt fury tear through him. "And I won't tell you where she is. I won't, Stygian. I won't trade her life for my own—or God help me, even for Amber's. I won't do it."

"You can't know this." Gripping her shoulders, he gave her a little shake, desperate to make her listen, to make her understand. "Sweetheart, listen to me. If we know who she is, where she is, we can and we will protect her. I swear to you—"

"And Judd, can you find him? What about Gideon?" Anger was building in her now even as the pain kept her tears falling. "He'll kill her, just as he swore he would kill me and Judd. He'll see us all dead, Stygian, and trust me, Gideon is strong enough to do it. And he's crazy enough. He won't stop until he steals our last breath."

"Why?" Stygian raged, fury tearing at him and enraging the animal inside him into a feral frenzy. "Why, Honor? Why would he want to see any of you dead?"

"Because Judd and Fawn forced him to live," she rasped desperately. "They wouldn't let him escape into death and, without me, they didn't have the key to take his pain away when they transfused him with Fawn's blood that night. We're a team. We made certain of it, believing the Genetics Council couldn't kill us if they needed all of us. We destroyed ourselves and didn't even know it." She stared up at him, tortured, the scent of her pain tearing at his soul. "We never imagined, Stygian, that one of us would ever want to kill another of us. Let alone, all of us."

Fighting back her tears, Liza fought to hold on to enough control not to collapse into complete, heartrending sobs.

She'd spent twelve years—she'd believed she'd spent her life—with a loving family, far away from the Genetics Council and the danger they represented.

She'd left a loving family, though. A father who risked his and his wife's life to help her find Orrin Martinez. A mother who had risked forever losing the child she had dreamed of for so many years and the husband she loved with all her heart.

Her parents had been dedicated to each other and to her.

"I was two when I was diagnosed with leukemia." She couldn't sit still. "It was a particularly resistant, fatal leukemia."

Moving quickly to her feet, she pushed her finger through her hair, wanting to rip the carefully highlighted medicinally colored strands from her scalp.

Behind her, Stygian moved to his feet, watching her intently.

She could feel his gaze—feel the worry and concern directed toward her, wrapping around her.

Just as his arms would be around her if she allowed it.

She wanted it.

She needed him to hold her with an intensity akin to pure desperation—and she couldn't allow it.

"You're still here," he said behind her.

Yes, she was still here.

"My parents loved me." Her breathing hitched painfully as she turned back to him. "They loved me so much that when my father was offered a place within the Genetics Council Experimental Genetics Division, he accepted eagerly. You see, he knew about Brandenmore. And he'd heard the rumors of the project he was working on." She could feel the rage, the pain, streaking through her, threatening to send her screaming into pure madness.

"He knew about the Omega Project?" His voice was carefully level.

Liza could feel the effort it took for him to hold back. A distant part of her realized she was sensing it, and realized why.

The why was tearing her apart.

"I was placed in Brandenmore's labs two weeks before the doctors predicted my body would be consumed by the leukemia." She turned back to him, fighting and failing to hold back her tears. "I was there for ten years. Ten years so hellish I prayed to die nearly every night that I existed in that hell. I begged my parents to let me die and I begged every scientist, tech and soldier I could speak to."

Crossing her arms desperately over her stomach, she bent over with the remembered horror of the hell she'd existed within and fought to remain on her feet.

She didn't have to fight for long. Within a heartbeat his arms were around her, his broad chest catching her tears as he held her to him.

"They tortured them," she sobbed, grief tearing through her as their screams echoed through her memories. "I would beg them to stop. I would scream and threaten and still I had to listen to their screams."

Fawn wouldn't be able to talk for days after the treatments.

Gideon would growl like a feral cat while his eyes would glow that eerie, predatory amber.

Judd would stare up at the ceiling, refusing or unable to sleep until his body could function once again.

"What did they do to you?" His broad, warm hand cupped the back of her head, holding her to him as she held on to his shoulders, her nails digging into the material of his shirt as she fought to just hold on to her sanity.

Her memory was so incredibly accurate that any moment she could pull the most minute detail from even the darkest, most agonizing second of those years there.

Shaking her head, her fingers clenching in his shirt, Honor felt as though she was sinking into a pool of pure emotional acid. There was nothing but pain in the past, and she had realized why each day of her life after she became Liza Johnson.

"Tell me."

The primal creature that helped create him echoed in his voice. Man and animal existed in such harmony inside him that there were times she could actually forget he was a Breed. If she wanted to. But, Honor realized, she wanted always to know exactly who and what he was.

"I would pray to die."

The growl that vibrated in his throat was so similar to those Gideon and Judd would emit whenever they were forced to care for her and Fawn after the treatments.

"I was the only one they showed any kindness to. Father couldn't even force them to show Fawn mercy, and he tried. He tried so hard." She stared back at him, shaking her head as she fought and failed to hold back her sobs. "He did everything he could. He bribed them, he begged them, and still, they didn't care when she screamed and screamed in pain."

Her father had raged at the scientists, he had even gone above their heads and petitioned the Council itself for mercy.

And they had refused.

"She was so tiny, Stygian." Her voice broke as she felt her heart breaking for the child Fawn had been. "She was so delicate that sometimes I wondered how she held her head on her shoulders. Yet she always did. She would turn her back on us and I could see her shoulders shaking as she sobbed silently. As she wrapped her tiny arms across her stomach and rocked, silently begging for comfort. And it was only Gideon that could force the scientists to let him go to her. It was always Gideon that held her, that rocked her, and sometimes, he even sang to her."

And how envious she had been as she had watched the young man rock her friend. As she watched him lift his head and stare at the bars above the cages they were forced to exist within as the scientists watched the bonds growing between the four of them.

"Once the experiments drew to a close, I thought we were all being released. My parents came for me, took me home, and I tried so hard to acclimate to being free, even though a part of me knew I would never be free. Two years later, someone from the Council arrived, though, and they demanded Father return me to the labs. I was the only one left, they told him. Judd, Gideon and Fawn had died in an escape attempt."

Honor remembered the agony that had knifed through her when she'd heard her friends were gone, and with them the information that had been amassed over the years.

"But you knew better," he encouraged her to continue.

Honor shook her head. "Not at first. The Council's messenger was telling Father how they knew about our photographic memories, and how they needed whatever I had seen to begin the project once again because Gideon and Judd had destroyed the files and data in the escape attempt. That was when I knew that they were alive. Gideon would never have allowed Fawn to die. Just as Fawn wouldn't have allowed Gideon to die. That night, Father put in place the escape plan he'd already mapped out for me. He managed to find someone he knew could hide me. This man contacted me within hours of Father telling the messenger he needed a few days to arrange everything. My father then made certain I was in a place where his contact could slip me away. A few weeks later I was reunited with Fawn and Judd. We ran continually." She tried to dry the tears that continued to fall. "We never had any peace. Then, one night, they found us before we could run. They crashed into the room just like they did tonight. And before we could think, Fawn, Judd and I were shooting. We were shooting to kill rather than wound, fighting for our lives because we knew they would kill us with the tests if we had to suffer them again. We managed to get away just as the man that helped me escape arrived with another and drove us to where two girls were dying in the desert."

"And then you became Liza Johnson," he whispered.

He was dying inside with her. The pain searing her soul was ripping his to shreds as well. The agony of the blood she had been forced to shed that night, the lives she had been forced to take, no matter the reason, would always haunt her now. It would torment her, just as the knowledge that it had been another girl's death that had been her only escape from certain hell.

Laying her head against his chest, concentrating on the steady beat of his heart, she nodded wearily. "And then I became Liza Johnson."

"Claire Martinez is Fawn, isn't she?" he asked her then. "Liza and Fawn both died in that wreck, didn't they, Honor?"

She shook her head. "They took Fawn away."

And they had.

She had to be careful. So very, very careful to keep him from sensing the lie she knew she had to tell.

"I'm your mate," he said then, his lips at her ear, his voice so soft she had to strain to make out the words. "My first loyalty is to you, and let me tell you, you reek of that lie, sweetheart. If you want to hide her, protect her until those memories return, then you're going to have to let me help you. Without your trust, mate, I can do nothing. I am nothing."

She pulled back to stare into eyes the color of the darkest blue.

Could she trust him?

Did she dare?

God help her, did she really have a choice?

"It was a ritual," she whispered. "The medicine chiefs did it. They gave us Liza and Claire's lives and completely took the memories from us of who and what we were until the time came to remember. One would have their memories returned in a night filled with chaos, the other . . ." She swallowed tightly. "The other with her death."

"And you don't know which is which?"

A strained, mirthless laugh escaped her lips. "I'd pretty much say tonight was chaos. And I know none of the bastards died." A sob escaped as more tears fell. "That leaves Fawn's death." Shaking her head, she tightened her grip on his shoulders, fear and desperation building inside her again. "That leaves her death, Stygian. I swore I'd protect her. I swore—oh God." Her fingers fisted in his shirt as she shook with the pain and fear tearing through her. "Oh God, Stygian, even as Claire Martinez she's not known any peace. She's not had a moment to be happy because Ray can't forgive her," she sobbed. "He won't forgive her because Claire died and she lived, and there's no way she could make up for it. And I broke all my promises to her, because I promised to protect her."

He could do nothing but hold her. Hold her. Rock her. All he could do was try to comfort her, because the pain inside her was killing him. To feel her shaking so violently, to feel the pain racking her slender body and to feel her sense of failure as though it were his own, was more a hell than the twenty years he'd spent in those fucking labs.

And he'd be damned if he'd allow her to fail in this, because losing the young woman she'd always fought to help protect would kill her.

"*We'll* protect her, Liza—"

The door between the rooms swung open.

Jerking around, Liza stared back at Jonas in terror.

He knew.

She could see it in those liquid silver eyes.

He knew.

Somehow, he'd heard it all.

Stygian snarled in raging fury, his muscles bunching as he moved to tear away from her, to jump for Jonas as the other man lifted the small electronic device she knew had somehow allowed him to hear everything that was said.

"We'll all protect her." An animalistic, primal rasp so rough and terrifying it seemed to scrape across her nerve endings came from his throat.

"No." She tried to jerk from Stygian's grip, suddenly terrified of what Wyatt would do to gain the answers he needed to protect his daughter.

She couldn't stop sobbing.

Fighting to be free of Stygian, she only wanted to escape, to get to Fawn, to hide her—

"For God's sake, the melodramatics are driving me insane." The door slammed behind him with a crack of steel against steel that reverberated through the room. Rage glittered in his liquid mercury gaze, as did disgust and irritation.

"You'll destroy her," she cried.

"Get serious." Exasperation filled his voice as well as his expression. "No matter the stories mothers tell their children about the bogeyman of the Breeds, I am not a cruel person, Ms.—" He paused, his head tilting to the side before his expression tightened and a savage determination filled his gaze. "Ms. Johnson. And I am well aware of the ritual that overlaid your memories with those of the two girls who died twelve years ago. Forcing those memories was never my goal. I merely hoped mating would instead allow the memories free. I have always known your secrets."

"You couldn't have known." There was no way. No one present that night would ever have spoken of it.

Crossing his arms over his chest, he stared back at her confidently. "My dear, sometimes one has to learn how to maneuver those he cares for into completing their destinies rather than meeting death," he sighed. "I knew Honor and Fawn were in Window Rock. I knew somehow your father and the president of the Nation were involved. That led me to suspect that, perhaps, the accident their daughters were in at the time of Honor's and Fawn's disappearance may have been fatal. That would have allowed the two young girls the ultimate escape if Liza Johnson's and Claire Martinez's deaths were never revealed. What was a mere suspicion when this began has, over the weeks, been confirmed. That is beside the fact, as wondrous as such a miracle is, as adept as the earth is at obeying the requests of men such as Orrin Martinez and Joseph Redwolf, still, the scent of the genetics left inside you after those experiments is still there if a Breed knew what he was looking for. And I knew what I was looking for, my dear."

She was barely aware of the fact that her nails were now biting into Stygian's arm.

"If you figured it out," she whispered, "then Gideon will as well."

Jonas snorted skeptically. "My dear, do not imagine Gideon Cross has yet to figure any of this out. And if he has"—the smile that tugged at his lips was definitely amused this time—"if he does, then trust me, the last thing he'll do, once I'm finished with him, is want to kill."

The tears had stopped.

Stygian could almost, almost forgive Jonas his games for the simple fact that Liza—hell, Honor—was no longer crying.

His mate. He couldn't bear her tears or her pain.

It didn't matter her name, it didn't matter who she thought she was or who she had been. She was the other half of his soul.

"What do you mean?"

For a second, gentleness flashed in his gaze before it shifted to calculating amusement. "Gideon is a man driven mad by his inability to do as the animal inside him demanded. To protect. To ensure the safety of those he was bound to. The animal is tearing him apart, clawing at the man's subconscious and creating a madness that only one thing will cure."

Honor shook her head. "There's a cure?"

"Of course there is," he assured her, his lips quirking

briefly as he crossed his arms over his chest, tilted his head to the side and watched her with eyes the color of living silver. "All he has to do is listen to the animal inside him. All he has to do is find his mate, and protect her."

She blinked back at him. "Who is his mate?"

"Fawn," Stygian said softly behind her. "Son of a bitch, that's why he's so enraged. She's his mate. The bastard isn't feral, he's in mating heat."

"Fawn was a young woman when she forced that transfusion on him without the knowledge or the medication the scientists had been using to control what they believed was the feral fever that came from it. But the animal inside Gideon also knew she was still too young to mate without consequences," Jonas explained. "That's why the animal inside him went crazy when it happened. The opposing parts of his psyche were suddenly coming together, doing whatever it would take to force back the mating heat until she was old enough, strong enough to endure mating a Breed. Now, I just have to maneuver him into the right place at the right time, to ensure he realizes it. Once he does, then the animal tearing him apart inside, now that the woman is old enough to handle the mating, will settle and the mate will emerge."

"Do you know where he's hiding?" she whispered, feeling Stygian's arms tightening around her, holding her closer, sheltering her.

"Gideon never hides," he sighed then. "He's here, right beneath our noses, somehow. Watching, waiting, hoping to pounce when we lead him to you and Fawn. Just as the Council soldiers are. Which is why we're not going to let anyone know that you've remembered anything. As far as everyone involved is concerned, you're still Liza Johnson and Claire Martinez is exactly who she seems to be."

"How?" she whispered. "Any Breed that comes close to me will smell the deception. Every time anyone calls me Liza. Anytime I pretend to be her, that scent will be there."

He stared back at her for long, thoughtful seconds. Long enough that Stygian finally growled in warning.

"Where's Judd? Who is he?" he asked with a faint glimmer of amusement in his gaze as he glanced over her shoulder at her mate.

She shook her head. "I don't know, Jonas, and that's the truth. I haven't seen him since the night of the ritual, and not because I forgot who he was either. Judd never came around me again."

But she knew he was close.

"Don't hold information from me, Liza." Jonas sighed as he prowled closer, his gaze intent. "Tell me, as I stare at you now I can smell the truth of what you're saying, but I can also smell your lie."

"Then any Breed can," she whispered, fighting back the tears gathering again.

"Not in this lifetime," he growled, turning to Stygian. "Do you smell her lie?"

Liza stared up at her mate, watching as confusion flashed across his face.

He inhaled slowly then narrowed his gaze on her and inhaled again. "All I smell is her truth. She's never seen him."

"But her subconscious knows she has," Jonas all but whispered. "That's my gift, Stygian. You and your mate now know what no one but my own mate has been given the secret of. Even the scientists who knew died by my hand. I don't give a damn what you believe. I can sense, and even smell, what only your subconscious knows."

Liza shook her head. "I have a photographic memory stronger than you can even realize," she informed him, her voice scratchy, so hoarse from her tears she didn't sound human herself. "I would know if I had seen him."

"Only if your subconscious wants you to know," he stated deliberately. "And the added complication of your Breed genetics makes that part of you much stronger. Stronger even than that extraordinary memory of yours."

Shock had Stygian tightening his arms around her when Liza would have jerked away from him.

"He's crazy," she cried out. "I'm no Breed."

Stygian shook his head, staring down at her as though he were only just realizing it. "That's why the mating heat was so different. It's the reason why your ability to fight is so extraordinary. And why your scent took me aback as I rushed into the room. Breed genetics."

She was shaking her head as he spoke. "It's not possible," she whispered numbly.

"It's not only possible, it's a fact," Jonas assured her. "Now, we just have to figure out how to use it to keep Honor Roberts hidden until we can find the others." His gaze flashed dangerously then. "I know who Fawn is, Liza. I know Claire Martinez is the girl that escaped those labs with you, but I must know any weakness she has, as well as her strengths. If we're going to save her and Gideon, then I have to know who and what I'm facing. And I have to know where I can find Judd."

Liza felt numb inside. Everything she had believed weeks before was a lie. The life she had lived, the parents she cherished, the friends she thought she had grown up with. It was all a farce. A farce that had kept her alive for the past twelve years and one she now had to uphold to save the only sister she had ever known.

She shook her head as she stared back at Jonas.

"Fawn was always so tiny. Judd and Gideon used to call her the little fairy. Every year on Claire's birthday, a fairy is left where she can find it. And they're always very, very expensive. She keeps them in a secured storage center in town where she can go look at them whenever she wants to."

Jonas nodded. "That would suit Fawn." Then his gaze sharpened on her. "And what about you?"

"I must amuse him somehow, he's always leaving me knives. And I've learned how to use every one he's sent." Her breathing hitched painfully. "But I don't know who leaves them or how they do it."

He didn't leave girly little knives either. They were always lethal and always intended for one thing and one thing only: spilling blood.

"Where do we go from here, Jonas?" Stygian asked from behind her. "Don't play games with me where she's concerned. The time for your manipulations where Liza and I are concerned is over."

Liza. She had to stay Liza, not Honor. At least for a little while longer.

"Now, we're tracking her assailants." His expression tightened once again. "Once we have them in custody and we learn how much the Genetics Council knows concerning them, I'll handle that end. Until then, what you do remember of those years and the serum you were given, I must know." Agony flashed in his gaze. "If I lose my daughter, Ms. Johnson, then it won't matter the battle we're fighting or the need to move with caution. I promise you, there won't be a scientist or an individual associated with that organization that I will allow to continue breathing. That, I promise you."

That promise Liza felt to the bottom of her soul.

"I still don't remember everything." She was holding on to Stygian as though he were a lifeline, terrified she was going to sink into the fears tearing through her now. "But—" She lifted her hands from Stygian to rub at the ache in her temples. "Jonas." She stared back at him miserably. "There were so many injections, and only Gideon knew what each one was. I was assigned to the scientists that worked with the blood transfusions and who analyzed the data on the blood tests and the different hormones that showed in them. Fawn worked with the techs that coded the information, and Judd was with the group that created and administered the medications for the different side effects. Gideon was with Brandenmore and his scientists as they created the serums for the different groups and administered them."

"There was more than your group?" Jonas growled.

"Unfortunately." She had to bite back the sobs that still ached in her chest as more tears fell. "I don't know how many, or what they were focused on. Only Gideon knew."

Jonas's jaw clenched tight as his gaze flashed with a brutal fury.

"Then we'll just have to ensure we draw Judd and Gideon in. Until then," he continued. "No one outside a very select group, chosen by me, will know that you are now aware of your identity or that we're aware you're anyone other than Liza Johnson. Not even your parents will know. Claire Martinez, especially, will be kept in the dark."

"What are you going to do?" she asked as Stygian's arms wrapped around her once again.

He'd remained quiet, but it was as though she could feel him, sense the careful calculation and the plans he was working on himself as she and Jonas spoke.

Dropping his arms from his chest, he slid them instead into the pockets of his slacks as his lips quirked mockingly once again. "Why, Ms. Johnson, I'm going to do exactly what I've been doing for the past months. I'm going to pull in the final two pieces. Once I have the four of you together, then I pray to God, I'll have the key to saving my child."

With that, he moved to the door, calmly, carefully opened it and stepped into the sitting area of the suite. The door closed behind him almost silently as chills raced up Liza's spine.

"Will he keep her safe?" she whispered.

"As a mate in her lover's arms," he sighed as his arms wrapped around her and pulled her against the warmth of his chest. "She just might not enjoy the experience."

Turning to him, exhausted, still torn and filled with doubts, she allowed his arms to surround her, to wrap her in the comfort and the warmth she'd always ached for.

"I wouldn't have missed it," she told him, feeling his lips at her temple, the beat of his heart beneath her ear.

"Missed what, baby?" he asked gently, as though he didn't know.

He had to know.

Tilting her head back, she stared up at him, her eyes filling with tears, but this time, tears of thankfulness, of joy.

"You." Her voice was thick with that emotion. "I wouldn't have missed what we have, Stygian. Not for anything."

His hand lifted, brushed back the hair at her temple then cupped the side of her head as his lowered to hers. "Neither would I, mate. Not for the world, or the safety of anyone in it, would I have missed a single moment we've had, or all the moments to come.

She wouldn't have missed it for anything; now she just prayed the past she had managed to escape for twelve years didn't find a way to turn around and destroy them. Then she didn't think, regret or fear. As his lips slid over hers, his tongue stroking against them, parting them and sending brilliant forks of sizzling pleasure to race through her body, Liza knew there was nothing on the face of the earth that could have convinced her to miss this moment, this life and this man.

The taste of the mating heat filled her senses, washing through her, sensitizing her nerve endings and leaving her wet, needy, wanting his touch, his hold as she had never needed anything before.

Wrapping her arms around his neck, she held on to him, feeling the heat and incredible hardness of his body as he lifted her closer. As he gripped her hips, lifting her and bearing her back on the bed as he came over her, Liza felt a sensual, feminine weakness sweeping over her.

This was the most incredible pleasure. Watching him come over her as he leaned close, the fingers of one hand moving for the buttons of the light cotton blouse she wore and slowly loosening them.

Her heart rate jumped as the backs of his fingers brushed against the mounds of her breasts. A moan whispered past her lips as he flicked open the front clasp of her bra and eased the cups from the swollen breasts.

"Stygian, yes." Her hands moved from his shoulders to his hair, reaching for the thin strip of leather that held the silken strands back from his face.

"Not yet." Catching her wrists, he pulled them back over her head, anchoring them to the mattress with one hand as his lips lowered to the hard tips of her nipples.

Arching, straining against his hold, she whimpered as the heat of his tongue licked over the pebble-hard tip and his free hand slid along her hip before moving to the small metal tabs of her jeans.

Her legs shifting, thighs tightening as heat began building in her vagina, her moisture easing along the swollen folds, she toed her sneakers off, desperate to do whatever it took to get as naked as possible, as fast as possible.

As her shoes hit the floor, the last tab slipped free at the same moment, and Stygian's lips parted and covered the desperately swollen bud of her nipple.

"Oh God." Liza arched as he sucked the tip into his mouth, his tongue lashing at it as he began pushing at the denim and her silk panties. Working them over her hips as she lifted for him, pushing the jeans to her thighs, then to her knees until Liza could work them free of her legs, he rumbled a growl of approval in his chest at her anticipation.

His hand stroked from her knee, moving slowly upward, the calloused pads caressing up her inner thigh as her legs parted for the intimate touch. His fingers moved to the slick, bare folds of her pussy, easing between the swollen flesh to stroke against the clenched, snug entrance as pleasure bombarded her and searing flashes of heated sensation raced over her nerve endings.

Her juices eased from her inner flesh, meeting his fingertips to heat and slicken them as she arched against him, feeling the electric arc of pleasure/pain that struck her womb as his mouth tightened on her nipple, his tongue burning it as he lashed at it.

Lifting his head from the tight, throbbing peak of one nipple, he moved his lips to the other, sucked it inside and licked it, tormenting it. His teeth gripped the tender bundle of nerves, drawing a startled cry of pleasure from her as she tried to lift her hands, tried to touch him.

His head lifted.

The blue in his eyes obliterated the dark irises, gleaming between his thick lashes as he stared down at her, watching her face as his fingers stroked from the tight opening of her vagina to the swollen, throbbing bud of her clit.

"Stygian," she moaned, arching to him, her hips lifting as she became desperate for a deeper, harder touch. "Please, don't tease me."

"Tease you?" The rasp of his voice stroked against her senses, adding to the sensations. "Oh, mate, teasing isn't what I had in mind."

His fingers circled her clitoris, easing along the slick, hot cleft and following the wet heat that spilled from her pussy and eased lower to heat the forbidden entrance to her rear.

Her entire body was heating. Sensations were tearing through her, blazing through her senses and tearing at her control as Stygian's head lowered and his lips covered hers. As he released her wrists, Liza lifted her arms, wrapping them around his neck, holding on to him as his tongue stroked against hers, teased it, flickered against her lips until they closed on it and suckled at it hungrily as the taste and heat of the mating hormone began to speed through her system.

The arousal built, tearing at her, making her desperate for more, for his cock fucking inside her, stroking into the clenched depths of her vagina.

Their moans began to fill the room, desperate and filled with torment as the hunger began to burn through their system and lash at Liza's senses.

She pulled at his shirt, jerking it up his muscular back before flattening her hands and running them to his midriff to push beneath the material.

"Take it off," she cried out as his lips moved from hers to spread hungry kisses to her jaw, her neck. "Take it off now."

Levering to his knees, he jerked at the hem, intent on doing just that as she lifted herself as well and began tugging at his belt. Loosening the leather, she pushed it out of her way to jerk at the tabs of his jeans, pulling at the closures to part the material and release the heavy width of his cock.

She didn't bother to glance up at him. The thick, heavily veined shaft throbbed, pulsing with the need to fill her with his release. To thicken inside her and lock him so intimately inside her that there was no escaping for either of them.

Neither physically or emotionally.

"I want to taste you," she whispered as a bead of pre-cum eased from the slit at the wide crest.

Bending her head, lifting her gaze to stare up at him, she let her tongue lick over the flared cock head, her inner muscles tightening as need burned through her clit, swelling it further.

"Ah hell, baby." One hand buried in her hair, tearing it loose from the clip that held it back from her face as her lips parted and slid over the engorged crest. "Ah fuck yes. Wrap your pretty mouth around it."

She was drunk on excitement now, flying into a supernova of sensation as Stygian's fingers clenched her hair, tugging at the strands and creating a pleasure/pain sensation that rocked her to her core. As her lips surrounded his cock head, she stretched them with the same erotic sting as his cock pushing into her pussy. The hunger for him began to overwhelm her.

The thick crest filled her mouth, throbbing in it as she used her tongue to lick and rub at the underside as she tasted the salt and male essence of him and moaned with her need for more.

It was so erotic, so sexually charged that electric fingers of sensation pricked over her flesh, driving her higher into the wicked heat of a hunger she had no will to resist.

Who she was wasn't who she was. Her friend was someone other than who Liza had believed her to be.

It didn't matter that they had made the choice to take this destiny. All that mattered was finding herself here and now. With her mate's dick pushing between her lips, stretching them as a growl rumbled in his chest from the pleasure—that was all that mattered.

The world outside the heavy steel door could go to hell for all she was aware of at the moment.

As her lips sucked, her tongue stroked, Liza pushed at the denim until it was below his thighs, giving her unlimited access to the tight, hairless sac of his balls.

Oh God, she needed more of him.

Stroking the tightly drawn flesh beneath his cock as she worked over the engorged cock head, licking it, sucking at it, she teased the flesh below with her fingers as she stroked and teased it with merciless hunger.

She needed to drive him to that brink of control where nothing mattered but her. Where his only thought was burying himself so deep inside her pussy that they were no longer two entities, but merged into one. That place where pleasure both physical and emotional, joined and burned them from the inside out, melding them together.

"Sweet Liza." He groaned above her. "That's it, baby, suck my dick. Work that pretty mouth over it."

Her pussy clenched, spilling more of her juices as her clit throbbed desperately and her vagina ached to feel the heavy width burrowing between her thighs.

"Ah, baby, I'm going to die right here if you don't stop."

His cock seemed to thicken in her mouth, the head pulsing, pounding at the roof of her mouth as she moaned in excitement, arousal tearing through her at the knowledge that he was close, so close to coming for her.

As that thought flashed through her brain, a heavy spurt of the pre-cum that always filled her as his cock began penetrating her pussy filled her mouth.

She had only a second to recognize the taste of the mating hormone his kiss held. That, and the heated sensation of a taste resembling cinnamon and coffee before he was jerking back from her, his erection pulling from her lips. A second later she found herself flipped to her stomach as his hands gripped her hips and dragged her to him, pushing her knees under her until she was kneeling at the edge of the bed.

The head of his cock slid through the cleft of her ass, paused at the tiny opening there, and as her lips parted on a cry, the heated ejaculation spurted against her rear entrance, penetrating it, and suddenly sending a blinding, fiery flare of sensation tearing through her forbidden flesh.

"Mine," he groaned above her as one hand shaped the curve of her hip and the other held his cock flush against the clenched entrance to her anus.

Seconds later another hard spurt shot against the opening, penetrating further, relaxing the tight opening and sending a surge of need racing up her spine.

Oh God, she hadn't expected this, not like this, not this soon. She may have ached for it when his finger pierced her there, but she hadn't imagined—

"My mate," he snarled above her again, leaning over her, the naked flesh of his chest against her back as the iron-hard crest pressed, parting the ultratight entrance and stretching it to accommodate the unusually thick width attempting to penetrate it.

Pleasure tore through her nerve endings as a cry rasped her throat, her fingers digging into the blankets beneath her as behind her, Stygian began working the width inside her. Each time her muscles clenched at the hard cock head burrowing inside the previously unexplored tissue.

Agonizing ecstasy—there shouldn't be such a thing, she thought hazily—pierced her anus along with his cock, shooting through the exposed nerve endings until she was screaming into the blankets and backing into the impalement.

"No more hiding from me," he growled at her ear, his teeth nipping the lobe as his hips pressed against her again, pushing further inside her rear as another spurt of the natural lubricant eased and relaxed her flesh, making way for each shallow thrust that pushed him further inside her.

Liza was lost in a haze of sensations that made no sense. The need for more. Deeper. Harder.

Pain and pleasure combined as ejaculation of the pre-cum inside her heated the inner tissue of her rear, relaxed it, yet sensitized it further and burned her with an agony of pure sensation as his cock eased deeper. Penetrating the tight ring of muscles just inside the entrance, he was suddenly lodged fully inside her, sliding in to the hilt as she screamed out at the piercing heat and near rapture suffusing her.

She couldn't hold herself up. She was trying, but her arms were shaking as the sensations began to demand her full attention, her full strength. Clenching on the thick penetration, the inner muscles of her rear spasmed around his cock, flexing and shuddering in reaction to the possession as she felt the pillows suddenly being shoved beneath her.

She collapsed against them, her head turning to the side as Stygian's teeth clenched lightly at the mark he had left on her shoulder and his hips began to move.

Each shallow thrust inside her tender flesh sent a furious surge of heat striking at her senses. Feminine weakness surged through her, a wave of sexual submission opening parts of her mind, her woman's heart and soul that she never knew existed.

No, she would never hide from him again.

"Mine," he snarled again before his tongue licked against the mark, sending another bolt of sensation to attack her nerve endings, to push her higher, deeper into the spiraling vortex of pleasure, pain, ecstasy and the dominating force of Stygian's possession.

Her hips moved into each thrust, pushing back as he entered while cries fell from her lips each time he retreated. Feeling the fucking inside the ultratender depths, stretching the muscles there, burning her alive with a pleasure that built to a critical height, Liza was certain she would never survive it.

As the pleasure began to burn through her nerve endings, the feel of his hand pushing between her thighs, his fingers parting the folds of her pussy, had her stilling in shock. A second later two fingers penetrated the depths of her vagina, stroking inside as he retreated partially from her rear, only to ease back as his hips pushed forward again.

As he synchronized the thrusts of his fingers with the engorged length of his cock, his thrusts became harder, deeper, faster.

Liza was screaming his name, or breathing it, trying to scream out at the agonizing pleasure building inside her, burning through her mind and tearing through her senses. Each thrust into the sensitive entrances only pushed her higher as the electric shock of each stroking thrust began to set fire to her nerve endings.

She was flying out of control. Gasping for air, her chest tight, her body tensing until she was certain she would break, certain she couldn't bear more—

She exploded with a scream.

Her clitoris raked against the pad of his palm as it pressed against it, her pussy flexed and tightened around his thrusting fingers as she felt the explosive contractions that began attacking her inner flesh. His cock jerked back, leaving only half of the steely shaft buried inside her as she felt the widening of the shaft just outside the entrance.

His release began erupting inside her in hard, fiery spurts, filling her rear as his teeth locked in her neck and Liza began shuddering, jerking beneath him in an ecstasy, a blazing possession of her feminine spirit that she had no hope, no desire to ever retain.

She wanted nothing more than this pleasure. Nothing more than being held by her Breed, her mate. Being held by him, protected by him—

"Oh God, Stygian," she cried out, unable to hold the ragged words inside any longer. "Oh God, I love you. I love you." She was sobbing the words, the vows, the promise to always hold to him, to follow him, even if it meant following him into death.

Stygian growled at her shoulder, his hips jerking, pushing the swollen mating knot against her rear cheeks as another fiery blast of release filled her as her pussy tightened on his fingers in yet another clenching shudder of rapture.

She was lost in the pleasure, in the possession, and in the Breed she knew would never leave her aching and lost.

She no longer had to hide, at least not from this man. Here, in his arms, she was who she was, whoever she wanted to be, however she needed to be.

Right here, held to him, she was safe, protected and loved.

She'd suffered hell and then lost herself. Now, in his arms, in his love, she'd found paradise and herself. And she knew he'd protect them both with the same fierce determination and strength of will he'd used to find her.

Forever.

Stygian would hold her forever.